'(*The*) *Armageddon Trade* is a disturbing book that makes the credit crunch sound like a breakfast cereal.'
Roy Close CBE, WWII SAS veteran

'With uncanny accuracy, Chambers takes you into the mind of the young gun bank traders. He's been there and done that himself. But disturbingly, he also takes you into the mind of the fanatical terrorist. Whoa!'
Paul Wilmott, Quant and founder of Wilmott.com

CLEM CHAMBERS

THE ARMAGEDDON TRADE

NO EXIT PRESS

First published in 2009 by No Exit Press,
P.O.Box 394, Harpenden, Herts, AL5 1XJ
www.noexit.co.uk

A CIP catalogue record for this book is available from the British
Library.

This is a work of fiction. Names, characters, places, and incidents either are the product of the author's imagination or are used fictitiously, and any resemblance to actual persons, living or dead, businesses, companies, events
or locales is entirely coincidental.

ISBN 978-1-84243-297-6 (Hardcover)
ISBN 978-1-84243-298-3 (Trade Paperback)

2 4 6 8 10 9 7 5 3 1

Typeset by Avocet Typeset, Chilton, Aylesbury, Bucks,
Printed and bound in Great Britain by JH Haynes Ltd, Yeovil, Somerset

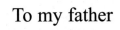

To my father

THE
ARMAGEDDON
TRADE

Chapter 1

'Enough, enough already,' he muttered, clicking the button marked 'flat'. The numbers on his pulsating screen flashed a variety of colours and there was a series of *pling* noises. He stood up and looked around, rubbing his eyes. Eight fifty. He had traded for five more minutes than usual.

'You off, Gordon?' asked Nipper, the trader who sat to his right.

He popped an antacid into his mouth and nodded.

'You're weird.'

'I know,' Gordon replied, not bothering to look at the other man. He *was* weird, that was certain, weird on a number of metrics.

All the textbooks said that the job he did couldn't be done. The golden rule of markets stated you can't call the direction of prices, and to sit all day at a screen to try and trade a profit was a waste of time. There are ways to make money in the markets, as emphatically proven by the banks' crystal towers in London's Docklands, and a financial institution like the one he worked for had many trading edges, but none that could help predict the future.

So he sat there each weekday proving the theory wrong.

He understood his success in the light of the typing monkey legend, fated by sheer numbers to write Shakespeare accidentally. Everybody knew the story that if an infinite number of monkeys were sat down with an infinite number of typewriters and time on their paws one would ultimately write the Bard's complete works. Well, he was that one monkey and for now the pages were rolling out on cue.

Every time he sat down at his machine he typed another financial sonnet.

With seven billion people on the planet, someone had to be the seven billion to one trader and he just happened to be that man.

He liked the monkey story, because when he had started at the bank that had been approximately his job: clueless ape. He had left school at sixteen and been taken on as a runner. Thanks to a local community programme for teenagers leaving school early, he had landed inside the portcullis of a financial behemoth. He was just part of the bank's local PR budget, but he didn't care: by pure luck he had entered another world, one of black glass and white marble.

No one was called tea-boy any more, he was an 'associate', but tea-boy was exactly what he was, fetching and carrying all day. He didn't mind. For starters the money was unbelievably good, triple what his friends were earning in the grey world outside. The bank was clearly a seat of power and to be the tiniest part of it filled him with a kind of reverent awe.

He would happily have done any job there while he waited for the day when someone on a floor above decided to let him go. Out of the blue, though, he was transferred to one of the many dealing floors after an intern, very much a blue-blood marked for higher things, had come a cropper on the ski slopes and left a dry wadi where there had been a river of coffee, tea and caffeinated soda.

The overstressed dealers didn't want to look up from their screens, just needed their drinks ever present. As far as he was concerned, that was no problem. The traders were the soccer stars of the bank; stressed, brilliant guys who won and lost fortunes. They were paid like international strikers until the day they were fired or were rich enough to tell their bosses where to stick their jobs. Where before they'd had to wave and shout, 'Oi,' across the floor in the intern's general direction, *he* had constantly circled and made sure their favourite drink was there and at the right temperature.

Now he pulled out the sports bag from under his desk and headed to the lifts. The antacid tasted peppermint and fresh in his mouth as the cooling sensation hit his stomach. He liked his routine. It was the key to his success.

He went down to the gym, got changed and jumped on the running machine. Today was going to be a little different. At ten thirty he was up for a review with the boss. It was bonus season and that was an exciting prospect. He'd been doing great and expected a repeat of last year's good fortune.

He had grown to love the office gym. It was a temple of employee welfare, a high church of fitness. With thousands of people in the building, it had features and equipment beyond the dreams of the average health-club member. Ironically, outside lunch hours it was practically empty and it was clear from the generally corpulent state of most of the bankers that few had a taste for physical exertion. He jumped on the running machine and set the pace to fifteen kilometres per hour. The trainers in the gym didn't like him running so fast, but there wasn't much they could do about it. These days, where he was concerned, all people ever did was suggest and smile politely.

'Why don't you take it a bit easier, vary your routine?' the chief trainer had asked him one morning, halfway through his programme.

'Got to get high,' he'd said. 'If I don't get high I can't trade.'

The instructor simpered. 'There are other ways to get your serotonin up.'

He'd stared at the guy. All he wanted to hear was his feet thudding on the rubber. 'Sure, write me a programme.'

'Absolutely.'

It hadn't worked. Nothing burnt off the stress or cleared his head like running flat out for an hour. If he didn't run, he felt dirty, like a seabird caked with oil.

It took ten minutes on the treadmill for the brain chemicals to kick in. First, at some indeterminate point, his body burst into sweaty life and from being dry and stiff he was suddenly loose and wet. Then the images, disjointed and dreamlike, would start to run in his head. The pounding of his feet and the whirring of the machine mixed with the music blaring in his ears, a little narcotic to discharge another set of neurons.

He didn't understand how the other traders could sit there all day watching a handful of pixels crawl across the screen. They thought it was strange that he could just get up and leave the action, no matter how hot it was, and vanish for hours at a time. They understood why the bosses let him. He was making so much money he was free to do as he pleased. They thought it was perverse that someone who could pull in such a lot in so short a time shouldn't pile it on every trading second of the day.

He hadn't always traded like that. To begin with he had sat in front of his screens and traded every blip. Though he loved the game, it twisted him into an emotional wad, like the notepaper he scrawled on and binned. He'd made money when the market opened and after lunch, but after about an hour he'd hit losing streaks. He'd just about kept

12

up with the rest of the traders but he was getting more and more wrung out each day. He became irritable, started to see everything and everyone as an impending problem or a potential enemy. He'd found himself talking about his life in trading jargon: he would 'hit the offer' on some fish and chips, he would be 'short' of Arsenal for the cup. Weekends found him staring at walls, thinking about the markets, and at night he dreamt about them.

His trading buddies had the answer. Booze. They were keen to educate their junior brother in the art of getting utterly drunk after work – it was a tradition for traders to be fuelled by alcohol – and beer was a pretty good medicine … but by nature he wasn't a drinker.

Then one morning he'd realized something. He was going to get fired. As he walked through the vast revolving door into the main atrium of the bank, the thought had struck him as if someone had spoken it into his ear. 'I'm going to get fired,' he said. He looked at the expanse of polished marble, the huge abstract art on the wall above the dozen receptionists, the smart, handsome people filing through the turnstiles. 'I'm going to get fired because every normal person here does.'

For a trader, normal is not the same as it is to the man in the street: normal doesn't mean everyday. Normal is a description of what happens if you take a series of events and tally them up, then examine how many happen. If you track dice rolls, for example, the result of, say, a thousand is normal. The thousand rolls will make a thousand scores, and if you tally each score and plot it, you end up with a 'bell curve', which shows the probability of the way things tend to turn out. It's a chart of the gravity of chance, a bell-shaped image that affects everybody's life more than almost anything else.

This normal distribution was the foundation of the bank's method of doing business, and when it came to people, they simply threw out the part of the bell curve that represented low-scoring dice. This meant plenty of fresh recruits in and lots of old hires out.

So, to be normal or in any way average meant that one day, and probably soon, you would be fired. You didn't need to be worse than anyone else, just on the wrong side of the cut when the bell curve was in for trimming.

He had been trading for nine months but suddenly, as he observed the dark-suited security officers watching the staff come and go, he imagined himself being escorted out of the building.

After all, what was he doing there in the first place?

Now he looked at the timer. He'd been running for thirty minutes, and that made him smile; when time jumped forward he felt as if he was fast-forwarding the whole world around himself.

Gordon wasn't his real name. They had given it to him – but not before they'd called him Ken. Everyone seemed to get renamed on the floor and his original name had been Ken because that had been the name of the previous tea-boy – or, rather, the one he'd been awarded.

'Thanks, Ken,' said the head trader on the first day, not looking up from his screen.

'Ken?' he'd asked hesitantly.

'Yeah, Ken – short for Kenco.'

The silence made the trader look up to see the damage on the runner's face, but Ken was smiling. The trader liked that. He pointed at a screen. 'So, Ken, what's the Bund gonna do?'

Ken squinted at the screen. He knew nothing about any of it, but the graph appeared to be rising. 'It's going up, way up.'

The trader clicked his mouse. 'Right, we're ten million short.' That meant he was betting the market would go down. He gauged the runner's expression for the sort of emotion that might give him a kick: shock would be enjoyable but indignation would give him a reason to goad the kid, but the new boy wasn't having it.

'Can I get you anything else?' Ken said, as if he didn't get, or didn't care to get, the put-down.

'Apple.'

'Yes, sir.' He turned.

'Oi.'

Ken turned back.

'It's Frank,' said the trader. '"Yes, *Frank*."'

'Yes, Frank.'

Chapter 2

The pace of the machine slowed and he looked down, knowing he would see red LEDs telling him the run was over. He slowed too, and stepped off to the giddiness that always hit him when he was back on solid ground. He picked up his towel and wiped his face, neck and hair, then headed off to the locker room. It felt wrong not to go to the bench pressing machine but he had the meeting at ten thirty and by eleven he'd be back trading.

That morning a year ago he had decided to change his pattern. If he made his money when he was fresh in the morning and after lunch, then perhaps taking breaks was the answer to avoiding the losses. He consulted the net, and after reading a piece on learning curves, decided to see if restricting himself to the amount of time during which people could learn effectively, would save his trading. After all, learning must be the toughest job the brain could do so maybe rest was the key. According to the article, a person could learn for forty-five minutes after which the brain had filled and wouldn't retain any more information. It wasn't clear how long his brain would take to empty itself again, but as lunch seemed long enough to do the trick, an hour seemed a good period to try.

He experimented with trading and sitting about inertly, but found the constant ticking of the charts and the random outbursts of his brethren insufferable. He ended up staring at the screens again, riveted by every twitch of the charts.

Then he took to walking the halls, but that seemed a bit weird. He felt like a ghost with no place to call home. But getting away from the screen helped and soon enough, after he'd tried the coffee shop or the cafeteria, he ended up hiding in the gym.

UK equities opened at eight a.m., which gave him an optimal window to eight forty-five. Sometimes he might stretch the trading period to nine, but if he did he soon felt the fog of uncertainty falling over his decisions.

An hour of distraction would make him fit to trade again at ten, but he liked the hour from eleven to twelve, when the market was working up its appetite for lunch; the ten to eleven period was listless. He decided to lie low till just before eleven and work till eleven forty-five. That gave him a bridge to lunch and afterwards he could switch into e-mail mode.

The US opened at two thirty and, with lunch and e-mail, he could hide his absence from trading, then kick back into gear to trade until three. He would fill in the hour till four with a coffee break and a slow walk to the toilets, then trade till the close and get in some auction and after-market action before packing up to go home. The only questions were, would this system continue to work for him, and how long would it take them to spot him goofing off for most of the day?

Milling about the huge office complex wasn't the answer. Even though in the couple of days that he had absented himself his trading had been spectacular, he felt his purposeless presence was not going unnoticed. Wherever he showed up, people wanted to help him. If he was in the cafeteria he had to be eating, or drinking coffee in the coffee shop, or training, being coached or evaluated in the gym.

While he sat in a chill-out area reading a fitness maga-

17

zine, a couple of track-suited execs drifted past. He didn't recognize them but they were clearly very senior and, from their relaxed smiling faces, totally at one with the world. These guys must have serious pressure on them, he thought. He slapped the magazine closed. He was being a complete idiot. He could legitimately come down here for an hour and burn off his stress. As long as he brought in the results, he could spend as much time as he liked in the gym. No one would notice so long as he made his numbers.

That had been the real beginning of his successful trading. Until then he had been normal.

As the trainee trader he had been a fast learner, but as Ken he had been a god. After his first communication from Frank, the head dealer, the big man had asked him to call the direction of the Bund, the massive German government bond derivative, every time he had come near his desk. He was always happy to tell the boss whether it was going up, down or nowhere. He even elaborated and predicted when and where it would turn. Frank seemed fixated on Ken's predictions, and Ken was quite proud of the rough accuracy of what he suggested. Not that it seemed a difficult thing to do: the patterns were so obvious even a child would have seen them. As Ken, he could imagine how boring it was to trade: observing a slowly moving graph all day must be like watching grass grow.

Then had come the day, about three months later, when Frank had pulled up a chair and asked him to sit down next to him.

He'd done so nervously, wondering if he'd somehow got himself into trouble. Perhaps they were about to play a trick on him. The traders were a rough lot. Under tough, profane exteriors and thick calloused skins lay hearts of pure greed and perversity. It didn't seem to him that they cared about anything more than money and proving to each other who was bigger and better.

But that was OK with him. They didn't hide who they were, and they weren't paid their enormous salaries for anything but their ability to make huge amounts of money for his generous but rapacious employers. The reason he was paid so much to serve tea, coffee, sodas, doughnuts and fruit was that these fat, rude, uncouth, prematurely aged hooligans could pull vast sums out of thin air. It was a simple reality that kept his nice little East End life well on the rails.

But right then, he knew, something unpleasant was going to happen to him. It was their way. A practical joke was coming up, he was sure.

'You want me to teach you to be a trader?' asked Frank.

Ken laughed. 'Do monkeys eat bananas?'

Frank smiled. 'Great. Go up to HR. They'll sort you out.'

Ken flinched. He'd feel a right idiot going in there telling them Frank had said he should see them for a trainee trader position. They'd look at him pityingly and tell him they'd had no such instruction, and when he came down again they'd all be laughing at him.

'Wait a second,' Frank said absently, as Ken sat there rigidly trying to think how to react. He fished in his pocket and something flashed. Frank tossed it at him and he caught it. It was a heavy gold Rolex Cosmonaut. 'You've got to have a proper watch if you're gonna be my trainee. That's yours from me.'

Ken looked at it.

Frank looked at him looking at it and an evil grin came over his fat face.

'You're winding me up, right?' said Ken, gazing at the watch. He held it out to Frank.

'No, no,' said Frank, taking it. He unfastened the band and held it out to Ken.

'You're giving me this watch and a job as your trainee?'

'You bet.'

Suddenly Ken felt the eyes of the other traders drilling into him, and when he looked round they were all leaning out of their positions, grinning, almost hungrily. 'If I take the watch,' he said, a little bit too much emotion rising, 'and you're taking the piss, you'll not get it back.'

'Take the watch!'

Ken smiled, gritting his teeth. He leant forward, expecting it to be snatched away to a chorus of laughter. Frank would have to be fast. His fingers wrapped around the heavy bracelet and he felt it drop from Frank's grip. He felt the weight again. It was so heavy he knew it was gold. 'That's amazing,' he said, and slipped it on.

Suddenly the traders were on their feet, clapping. They surrounded him, shaking his hand and jostling him.

'That's amazing,' he repeated, 'amazing.'

The grey-haired smoothie from the yen trading desk took his hand in a formal practised clasp. 'Not as amazing as the profit Frank makes from your daily tips. You sit next to me on his days off.'

Ken was overwhelmed.

The next six months were probably the best of his life. Suddenly he was no longer Ken but Gordon. Eventually he gave up wondering why and asked.

'You're Frank's Gordon boy, aren't you?' came the reply.

'Golden' and 'Gordon' weren't especially alike, but the pun seemed to make the dealers happy and he sat happily next to Frank and watched him trade. Every now and then Gordon asked a question and every now and then Frank wanted his call on the market he was trading. It seemed easy work, and while Frank stared at the screen Gordon spent a lot of his time studying trading courses on his own monitor or deciphering technical books full of impossible equations.

The bank had its own in-house university at which it rammed people with crash courses in financial theory, but Gordon was far from the educational standards of the graduate firsts who were his fellow students, so he found it impossible to follow. Instead he read and reread the course notes, trying to memorize the information in the hope that it would ferment into understanding. Frank arranged with the firm for him to be tutored in maths and, to his relief, he absorbed what he was taught like a sponge. How was it, he wondered, that learning had seemed so hard and stupid when he was at school yet now it was so vivid?

He would have worked there for nothing, but he hadn't left school at sixteen because he was lazy. He had left school to support his family, little though there was of it, and now he could put his pay slips on the mantelpiece with considerable pride. Close to four grand net a month and maybe a chance of a 25 per cent bonus at Christmas.

The Christmas bonus was legendary in the City, and up to now he hadn't operated in Bonus Land: the back office, where he had been a minion, was a backwater for payouts. He'd had the distinct feeling that for every supersonic Christmas pay packet there were a hundred disappointed faces and a thousand living the dream of one day hitting the big time.

Yet he dreamt: the watch on his wrist, he realized, was part payment on the dream from Frank. Like his job, he wasn't even sure it was his to keep, but if it was on his wrist he was sure at least that he was in the game.

At first it overawed him to see Frank push millions back and forth, sometimes in seconds. Take a million at the fractionally lower bid and sell it at the fractionally higher offer and you had a tidy profit in an instant. Keep doing it all day and fortunes accumulated.

Traders called the difference between the million bought cheap and the million sold a little dearer the 'spread'. Trading the spread was like picking up fifty-pound notes in front of an oncoming high-speed train. While the track was empty, the fifties mounted up, but if the market suddenly went against Frank, leaving him midway between buying and selling, he had only seconds to run before disaster struck. His stack of numerous small profits might be blown away in moments if things took off in the wrong direction. He might buy a million, ready to sell for a bit higher, only to have the market fall away, leaving him with a million pounds' worth of contract cheaper than he'd bought it. There were two ways to escape: hold, and pray for a return in the market, or a brutal cutting of losses.

This was often when he, Golden Gordon, was called into play.

'Where's it going, Gordon?'

'Back up a bit, then back down,' he might say.

Frank always took his advice, and if he was wrong twice he would bail out of the position in any event.

The system worked well and Gordon noticed that Frank was doing less in the way of buying cheap and selling high, or 'making the spread'. Instead he was increasingly taking big directional positions, where he would buy a pile of Bund contracts and let them ride in his chosen direction.

They would look at the long-range chart and discuss it. He would say whether he thought it was going up or down over the next month. On Monday they would look at the weekly chart and again they would agree the direction. Then they would divine each day, after which point Gordon would get back to the course and Frank would do his trading. Only events like statements from central banks or breaking news would change that rhythm, and when something happened Frank would make sure Gordon was right by him at the screen to call the short-term moves.

Frank didn't let the other traders near Gordon. Whenever they asked for Gordon's opinion, Frank would explode. At the mere sniff of interference he would leap to his feet and wave his hands around and swear. 'Fuck off, go on, fuck off.'

Gordon found this embarrassing and on occasion he had been cornered by worried traders from the floor with chart printouts. They collared him in the toilets, at lunch or in the hallway. He knew Frank would go nuts if he found out, but he'd comment off the cuff, then add that he didn't really know anything about that particular market. Nevertheless his input seemed appreciated.

He wasn't sure why they all wanted his advice; it seemed clear to him that a share, commodity, bond or currency was either going up or down. They had piles of clever strategies, a seemingly infinite knowledge of how everything fitted together, yet something simple like seeing the trend from a series of patterns seemed beyond them. Then again he had read lots of books on chart patterns and he couldn't understand what they were trying to say. Everyone seemed to want to draw straight lines on charts, when clearly nothing that went on had a straight nature. But he didn't let that worry him. He just read the books and courses, did what Frank asked him to do, and when Frank spoke about trading he listened.

Then one November day he had come into the office and

sat down at his desk to watch the market open. It was unlike Frank not to be there already; in fact, Gordon couldn't remember ever having been in first.

There were ten minutes to go before Frank needed to get his orders in and start trading, but Gordon noticed, as he looked at his screen, that there were no open positions. He recalled that the night before Frank had 'gone flat' – but he had thought nothing of it. Frank did what Frank did. 'Flat' was a state of grace, like floating in the calm heart of a hurricane. The markets didn't stop when they closed. They churned away in the minds of the players and moved in a ghostly dimension as the world economy ground on. For a trader to be flat, with no open positions, meant that the impact of a catastrophic overnight change was removed. He could go home and get on with his life without the spectre of disaster hanging over his head. Everyone wanted to be flat before the close, which was likely the reason it happened so rarely.

Gordon began to fret, a burning sensation in his stomach, which heightened his uncertainty. He found himself looking around the floor hoping to see Frank at some other desk, talking with another trader. Suddenly it was eight and still no Frank. The market opened and a fantastic rally raced by that they would have ridden for a thumping profit. Gordon slumped in his seat. Then he got up and walked over to the next trader, who looked at him shiftily.

'Got a stomach settler?' Gordon asked.

'Sure,' said the trader, pulling out a jumbo carton from a drawer. 'Doesn't everybody?'

Gordon broke out a couple of Rennies and crunched. He immediately felt better as if some venom had been neutralized. At the same time he caught what he thought was the shadow of Frank through the layers of plate glass between him, the trading floor and the atrium beyond. He sighed audibly.

'Got you bad, has it?' said the trader, knowingly.

'What?'

The trader tapped his bulging gut. 'The acid lifestyle.'

Gordon nodded. 'Yeah, I guess so.' He turned and went back to his seat as Frank strode up to their station.

'Come on,' he said, motioning him up. 'We've got a meeting.'

Gordon jumped up. 'Meeting?'

'Yeah, your yearly review.'

He gulped. 'Oh, right.'

'Just me and you and the head of trading.'

'Head of trading? You mean Wolfsberg?'

'The very same.'

'Oh, right.' A surge of acid. He ran back to the other trader and his Rennies. 'Don't mind, do you?' he said grabbing the carton.

'Sure, but you owe me big.'

'Sue me,' said Gordon, sounding a bit like Frank. He dashed back to Frank. 'OK, ready.'

Frank laughed with more than a hint of cruelty. 'Let's go, then.'

Chapter 3

Wolfsberg looked very stern, like a headmaster about to suspend him from school. 'Well, Jim,' he said, shaking Gordon's hand, 'I've been following your progress.' He smiled, not necessarily benign.

Gordon sat down, following Frank's lead. Only his nan called him Jim. In the outside world, his friends had called him Jimmy. Jim – or was it James, Ken or Gordon? – smiled weakly back at the big boss.

'Your performance has been exceptional.'

Exceptional. The word shuddered in his mind and melted like ice-cream. That meant good, didn't it? Then he panicked and tried to recall every possible meaning of the word 'exceptional' and any configuration that could lead up to, 'And we'll have to let you go.'

He noticed a silence in the room: he was supposed to say something. He kicked in, 'Thanks, that's really good to hear.'

Wolfsberg went on: 'You've got a bright future here. As you know, with Frank leaving, we're going to have to make changes but––'

His mouth fell open and his eyes bugged out.

'I hadn't said yet,' said Frank to Wolfsberg, shrugging nonchalantly.

Wolfsberg pursed his lips and scowled. 'Well, anyway, we're going to have to move a few things around and we think it's time for you to have your own trading place.'

'He's ready for it,' said Frank.

Wolfsberg nodded. 'Frank's profitability has been stellar since you've been working with him and we hope that, after taking some time out, he'll consider coming back.'

Gordon looked at him hopefully but Frank gave no indication that this was the plan.

Wolfsberg picked up an envelope. 'So,' he continued, 'after consideration of your performance we're proposing the following bonus.'

Gordon's attention snapped back to Wolfsberg, who was holding out the envelope to him. He opened it and took out a sheet of paper. 'Four hundred thousand,' he said flatly, as if it was only forty. His eyes counted the noughts again. 'Thank you,' he said, a little stiffly, then a big grin cracked his face and he started to laugh. 'That's a hell of a lot of money.'

Frank smiled into his lap.

'It's not bad, is it?' said Wolfsberg. 'Not a bad start.'

'Thank you,' he said to Wolfsberg, 'and thank you, Frank. You know… well …' He stopped, stumbling for words, and took a deep breath. 'Thank you, both.'

Four hundred thousand pounds, he thought, taking another look at the letter, four … hundred … thousand … pounds.

'Well, that's all,' said Wolfsberg. 'Here's to another successful year.'

Frank got up. 'It was good,' he said. Gordon followed his lead. They both shook hands with Wolfsberg and made their exit.

'You're leaving?' said Gordon, as soon as they were around the corner.

'Oh, yes,' said Frank.

'Oh, shit. Why?'

An empty lift opened in front of them and they stepped in.

'I promised myself that when I got to ten I'd quit. Well, now I've made it and I'm off.'

'Ten. Ten million?'

Frank nodded.

'Wow, that's a lot.'

'And, thanks to you, I'm there a couple of years early.' He smiled. 'I told them if they didn't look after you I'd take you off to a fund.'

'Really?'

'They obviously didn't disbelieve me.'

The doors opened and they got out. 'I'm going to be fucked on my own,' said Gordon, clutching his bonus letter.

'You'll be fine. Do what you taught me – buy when it's going up and sell when it's going down.' Frank laughed. 'What a fucking joke.'

'What is?'

'Taking positions like that. It's a fucking kurtosis.'

Gordon knew all the words like 'kurtosis', which meant the outer limits of what could happen when you rolled the dice. Fools were at one end of humanity's bell curve and kurtotic, just like the genius at the other end. It was the only thing they had in common: they were both a kurtosis but at either end of the bell curve. If the fool and the rocket scientist were dice rolls, they would be two and twelve.

Trading was like rolling a thousand dice at a time and the chance of scoring twelve thousand was the same as rolling two thousand. It was just as possible to become a trading genius as it was to perform like an utter imbecile. Yet the control of events by the player was exactly the same: none.

All the books said that trading the way Gordon and Frank did was against the rules. Every future moment was

28

unconnected to the last. The theory said there were no trends, just random fluctuations, but the chart told him whether it was going up or down so Gordon didn't believe what the professors had won their Nobel prizes discovering. No one else on the floor agreed with the theories either. Even though it would seem that the other traders weren't making a killing like him and Frank, they still believed they were smart enough to beat the market.

The idea that the markets were random was obviously rubbish: how else could Canary Wharf be full of banks with trading desks making money? Saying you couldn't make money trading was like saying the whole place didn't exist. The paper in his hand was proof that it was easy enough. People might win Nobel prizes proving it was some kind of statistical trick – but if even an East End kid could do it, how impossible could it be?

'Thanks for this,' he said, waving the envelope at Frank. 'That's enough to set me up for life.'

Frank pulled a face. 'A quarter of a bar won't get you far,' he said. 'You got to have five mil to be comfortable. Five mil at five per cent doesn't leave you much more than ten K a month to scrape by on once the taxman's had his piece. After tax, you'll end up with around two hundred and fifty, just about enough for a down payment on a decent flat.'

Gordon knew there was logic in that, but it wasn't one he'd had much practice with. He hadn't been planning his future, he'd been trading with Frank and being paid a fortune. It had been a wonderful ride that was bound to come to a quick end. And it just had.

'When are you going?' he asked Frank, as they entered the floor.

'Right now.'

A security guard was standing by their desks and a

dustbin bag lay on the floor. 'Morning, Mr Jones. I've packed all your personal effects and I'm to escort you out.'

Frank looked at the bag. 'You can carry it.' He turned to Gordon and wrapped his arms around him. 'Thanks, mate,' he said meekly, as if all the blood, bile and poison that sustained him had drained away. 'Thanks. You keep doing what you've been doing and soon you'll have your own ten bars.'

Gordon could feel the trading floor watching them, some riveted, some mildly curious, some gloating.

'Actually,' said Frank, to the security guard, 'give me my stuff.' He took the bag. 'Let's get going.'

He watched Frank lead the guard out, then sat down at the big man's desk. The market was going up, he was going to buy and go very long. He bought a load, a big fucking load. Pretty soon he was longer than a rhino on Viagra. When the market stopped rising he sold out of his positions and continued to sell, going short in the process, fucking short, until, when the market stopped falling, he covered his short positions by buying back until, like Frank the night before, he was flat. In an intense and incredibly risky hour he had made the company the value of his yearly bonus.

His stomach started to burn, and burnt as badly as it only ever had once before, that moment in the morning – an age ago, it seemed. Those trades had been way, way too big: he had used Frank's full credit line and gone in with both feet. That was really very stupid. Frank never did it, not unless he was staring at a solid-gold, dyed-in-the-wool, hundred-per-cent hand-delivered-by-Christ message that it was safe to do so.

He felt sick and gobbled a couple of tablets. Fuck it: he was going home.

*

In his six months on the floor he hadn't really talked to any of the other traders. Frank had kept them away and they knew he was off limits. At first he'd thought it was to protect him from the constant sparring they got up to. You might think of it as bullying but it was more the rough-and-tumble of schoolboys jostling for position. After a while, though, he'd started to wonder and had asked Frank about it.

'It's to keep you pure,' said Frank. 'I don't want you polluted by any trader-superstition crap. It's bad enough how many of those books you have to read, but those guys, they'll fill your head with so much shit you won't know which end your arse is.'

Some of them lived in the area, like he did, but their places weren't like his. He was a local, what they would consider a slum dweller. Not that there were any real slums anymore in that part of east London. Since Canary Wharf had arrived, all the houses had been done up and were expensive. But he lived in a council house, one of the few still maintained by the corporation. It was a brick tenement that old-fashioned slum dwellers had considered a step into paradise when it was erected before the Second World War.

The walk home took about fifteen minutes from the glass towers, just short enough to make it bearable even in the worst London weather. He normally enjoyed it: it was a buffer between his high life in the bank and his real life at home.

He walked up to the third floor of the low block and down to the end of the balcony that ran the length of the building, an aerial alley for the second row of flats. The windows were either frosted glass or blanked by net curtains, some with window boxes, neatly tended by the old people who lived there. Next door's ginger cat bowed at him as he passed – he made a clicking sound with his tongue and gave it a scratch on the head. There was something comfortable about the passageway, with its gritty, milky odour. It was a friendly path to the comfort of home.

He unlocked the latch and went in.

Nan was at the kitchen door, looking at him blankly. 'Bill?' she said.

'No, it's Jim.' Bill, his dad, had been killed when he was five. So had his mum. They'd gone together in an accident. 'I'm home early.' He was their only child.

'Is everything OK?'

'Yes, Nan, everything's just fine.' He collapsed into his chair in the parlour. 'I got a bonus today.'

'A bonus? What for?' she asked, almost accusingly.

'For good work.'

'You? Good work? That'll be the day. Two short planks like your dad.'

'You're full of beans today, Nan,' he said, perking up. Sometimes days would go by and she'd say nothing. She'd move around and cook and wash, but she'd seem to be on a kind of autopilot. He'd talk and she'd listen, or she'd just sit and watch the TV like a vegetable, doing nothing much beyond the small daily chores she had done her whole life.

He loved his nan; she was his whole life. She'd brought him up single-handed after his parents had died. He kind of remembered them, big smiling figures lodged in his mind like excerpts from some film he'd seen but forgotten. Nan had been the rock he'd clung to when his early world had vanished.

Then something had happened. He was nearly thirteen. One day, Nan went peculiar. The first time it happened, she became vague and forgetful. She seemed sleepy and distant, but still her usual self, only gentler. After a week he started to worry, wondered about finding out how to ring the doctor. Nan was acting strange, and then was her normal self again, bustling and bossy, energetic and active. The hiatus was instantly forgotten.

Time passed and occasionally the same slow, forgetful person returned until he became scared for her and for himself. It wasn't as if she was incapable, just under the weather, but what if she suddenly got really sick? What would happen to her and him then? Yet every time he thought about ringing for help she'd snap out of it, apparently oblivious to what had happened.

He was getting older and he started to take the load. He did the shopping, which now made her fretful and panicky. He paid the bills and managed the money, forging her increasingly scrawled handwriting on cheques and letters once he realized that they scared and depressed her as well.

It wasn't as if he hadn't worked it out: his nan was going senile. He knew old people did and that there was nothing he could do. Though in a way there was: he could look after her, like she had looked after him. He was fifteen and soon he could leave school and get a job. That would sort the situation. Otherwise they'd just slap her in a home, him in care and that would be that. She'd die and he'd live who knew where? A shitty orphan in a shitty world. There wasn't anything wrong with her really, just a fear of changing anything or going shopping, and she had a problem with names. Once he was sixteen he could get it all sorted out.

Then he was sixteen and he did leave school, and he tried to find out if anything could help her and nearly screwed everything up. He was still too young to look after her officially and there was nothing they could do for her except have a health visitor drop in. They were clearly in two minds about him, but his seventeenth birthday was only weeks away and by the time they could make any decisions he'd be out of their control anyway. They let it lie.

He realized that as long as he didn't make a fuss, things would return to normal and, sure enough, they did.

She would burst into tears and cry for hours over silly little things, go on about imagined noises, sit by the window and stare out of it for ages. But that was all right by him if that was what she wanted to do. She was his nan, and he wasn't going to let them take her to some piss-smelling ward with infection and drugs to see her off their books. He loved his nan, and while she lived he would make sure she was all right.

'Have a read,' he said, handing her the bonus letter. She went off for her glasses, fixed them on her nose and tried to decipher the note. 'Can't,' she said. 'Writing's all squashed up.'

Suddenly he realized something. He wanted her to know how much money he'd made and show her he'd done well, but he feared it might confuse her. He held out his hand for the letter and she gave it back. 'Anyway, Nan, no need to worry about money any more. I'm on a good earner.' He got up. 'I'm going to listen to some music in my room.'

'Want a cuppa?'

'Yes, please.'

His bedroom was tiny, barely big enough for a single bed, a table and a cupboard. It was papered with the same nineties *Toy Story* wallpaper that had served its decorative purpose since he'd moved in and which he had later plastered with pullout posters of cars and girls and what have-you.

He picked up his wireless headphones from the floor, started the music player on his computer and lay on his bed. The random mode flipped to a random music folder and picked out a random composer, a random symphony and a random movement. He sighed. Somehow the sound of strings always made him feel a little less stupid and a little more capable of coping with whatever happened next.

He looked at the Ferrari on the wall; he could buy it now, and the racing motorbike, only thirty grand. All these treasured dreams were only a small signature away. But it was still a dream, which would fade when he woke up.

Save the money, he thought. Keep it coming in till they ring the bell and turf you out.

He closed his eyes. He had already got as far as he could go and the rest was a free ride.

He wondered about the chalk tablets making their way along his gut and about the acidic lifestyle he was living. It was pretty near picture perfect as far as he could see – so of course it couldn't last.

Chapter 4

There was only one thing Ali Muhammad liked more than food and that was money. He was good with money and money was good with him. The world was a simple place: you took and you didn't give back. That was the secret. Yet his fellow men didn't get it: they'd give something and expect something in return. That always amused him because he never promised to give anything back, or if he did that was all he gave, but there was always an expectation of more. He didn't bother to ask why they expected some kind of fairness or equity: he didn't offer it and he didn't give it.

Taking and keeping had made him wealthy quite quickly. He hadn't made any friends in the process, but he hadn't set out to. He wanted money and he played that game and won at it. As in any game there could be only one winner and he made sure that as many of the odds as possible were stacked in his favour. That way he seldom lost, and even when the game was over he could carry it on until he got what he wanted out of it or was forced to give up.

His peers dreamt of a quiet life or a spectacular end in doing God's work. He understood the angry ones, but God hadn't made him so smart just to blow his head off in an attempt to punish some ignorant atheists: his life was far too valuable. Money made everything work. Money was the sweat of God. Without it, nothing was built, no kingdom raised. No starving cleric had conquered: it was the rich followers who spread the word. It was the clever merchants who had carried the faiths of the world from port to port. It was the wealthy who built the temples and mosques, or the hard-won pennies of the poor, extracted from them by the beggars who ran the religions and no more believed in their gods than he did, except when it served their purpose.

In that much he was a religious man. His business was money, just like the business of religion was about money. This was the business in which he was going to get rich and, these days, rich meant an amount of money few people could grasp. It was a long time since a millionaire had been wealthy. Ten million, a hundred million – these were figures that could leave you wanting. It wasn't till you could put your hand on a billion or two that you could consider yourself rich. Rich was having what you wanted, when you wanted, how you wanted. With a billion or two, everyone who mattered became your friend, and the great men you read about in the papers became your servant. A billion or two, that was his target. His measly hundred million was just a fraction of the treasure that the modern world was giving up to clever businessmen. His ten-million-pound jet had dented his wealth as a car strained the bank account of a poor man. That wasn't rich. Rich was when nothing material could bite into your wealth. Rich was having so much money only the unique was worth owning.

The Jeep he was riding in slewed and pulled off the dusty road beside another truck.

His skinny escort turned to him. 'Now, Dr Muhammad, I must ask you to tell me if you have any tracking devices on your person. It is OK if you have, but this is your only chance to tell me, and if you have, I will take them and we will go on. If you do not tell me now and it turns out later that you have, you will be killed. No hard feelings.'

'Of course I haven't.'

'Think hard. Be sure nobody gave you anything that might contain one.'

'No, no.'

'It could happen,' said the escort, happily.

'No, I'm sure.'

'OK, then, now we go to Karachi Main Hospital and put you in the scanner.'

He looked at the escort. 'Really?'

'Really.'

He shrugged. 'I guess that makes a lot of sense.'

'Let's get in the next truck.'

They got out and walked to it, and as they got there the driver hopped out and opened the back.

The escort took out a pouch. 'Sit on the edge, please.' He produced a syringe and held it up. 'We're going to knock you out for a bit. You understand.'

He wondered about hygiene. HIV was absolutely what he didn't want. He regarded the syringe with horror.

'Don't worry, it's a new one – wouldn't want to infect a brother with something nasty. Took it out of the packet myself. I'm actually a doctor, you know. Want me to take out your appendix while you sleep?' He smiled.

Ali undid the cuff-link on his left shirt sleeve, rolled it up and sat down. He didn't feel the prick, just the hand of the doctor holding his upper arm.

'It won't take immediate effect, but if you'd care to sit back on the mattress you'll soon drift away.'

'Thanks,' he said, lifting himself in awkwardly. He crawled the three feet back to the mattress and arranged himself as comfortably as possible on the dusty surface. He was scared now, which wasn't like him at all. He was safer than the US president: he was their banker, the man who kept their money hidden. Without him it would be lost. Killing him would be like throwing all their money into a furnace or pouring it into the deepest oceanic trench. Keeping him alive was probably more important than keeping the Sheikh himself hidden. But there he was, lying in the back of a truck in Pakistan, a drug coursing through his body and nothing he could do but...

He became aware of himself but he couldn't tell which way up he was or what was around him. There was no light, no sound. He realized he was in a bed and felt terrified until suddenly his eyes opened and he was lying on his side. He sat up and tried to focus as his mind began to work. He was alive, that was a good start, and he wasn't in the dusty, oily truck. As a matter of fact he was in a cool room. His disorientation was fast fading, only to be replaced by another kind. The light streaming through a gap in the curtains was not bright and bleached, but soft and gentle, suggesting cool weather. He must be high in the mountains. Yet the room hardly seemed like the kind of primitive area he'd expect at some basic remote location. For one thing there was cheap European wall-to-wall carpet on the floor. He got out of bed, went to the window and opened the curtains carefully.

'Jesus Christ,' he exclaimed, looking at the shrubs of a north European back garden. 'What the hell am I doing here?'

There was a knock at the door and he turned to see his nameless escort standing there. 'Good morning, Dr Muhammad, glad to see you awake. I'm afraid you've been sleeping much longer than planned.'

'I hope you don't mind but I've taken a look.'

'Sure,' said the doctor, 'no problem. It could be

anywhere, right? I mean in western Europe.'

'North-western Europe.'

'Exactly. Impressive place to hide, don't you agree?'

He smiled. 'Very.'

'Moving about and covering trails is really quite convoluted and difficult, these days. I'm getting quite tired of it myself, but that I shall have to endure. It's only once or twice a year now. Every time it's a big risk but, God willing, a great humiliation to our enemies.'

'Is he here?'

The doctor shook his head. 'No, but he will arrive at some point and will talk with you for a time. Can I get you anything? A drink, perhaps?'

His mouth tasted foul. 'Yes,' he said, 'or a coffee.'

The doctor fetched it, excused himself and left him alone. He felt pleased that he was not locked in although it would have been easy to climb out of the window and jump to the ground. But he wasn't there to play games: he was there because he was their key person, their banker, and whatever they needed to tell him, he had to be told in person by the Sheikh. That was the scary part: whatever the secret was, he had to be told by the man himself, a man who redefined the concept of 'most wanted'. The greatest hero and the greatest villain of all time was breaking cover to tell him something so important that he was prepared to risk everything to meet him personally. Would it not be worth a hundred times the fifty million dollars on his head?

That was his thought: for this meeting to be necessary the opportunity must be worth billions. If that wasn't a possibility he'd never have agreed to it. His anonymity was just as crucial to him as it was to the terrorists. It took just one tiny slip and all his carefully laid plans would come unpicked and he'd be turfed out of his rich, happy world into an inferno of thuggish law enforcement. They would take everything he had, they would torture him, they would throw him into the darkest, most disgusting cell in the vilest prison they had. He would suffer unspeakable things for the rest of his life. He only risked the prospect of such a hell for a shot at a billion-dollar cut.

He might be the perfect banker but he could have made it clear that that was all he was. With their money disintegrated they could hardly force him to do anything. But that wasn't how the system worked. If you did as you were asked, you got to do more. If you were uncertain, you were allowed to do it your way. The strength of the system was that this volunteer mindset called up incredible actions from its followers. While the heroes did amazing things, the others fell away to be admirers and passive followers. It was a beautiful system, and he had the perfect attitude to take advantage of it and ride its energy. He was their banker, the man who made their money flow around the world as if thousands of policemen didn't exist. He was so clever that no one, not even they, had any idea how much there was. He loved that, and made sure he capitalized on it in such a way that no one was put out.

There was a fair chance that God protected him – if there was a God, he would have to: while his children may have organized themselves into cells that operated independently of each other, they were still a single organism with a mind, heart and blood supply. He was the heart and he pumped the blood to wherever it was needed.

While this had made him wealthy, there was always the possibility that something tragic would befall the great leader and his organization would collapse. If it did, all the invisible money would be his and then he would be truly rich. Until that time he would do his job, take his cut and trust in Allah.

He glanced at the bedside table, then opened the cupboard and drawer for something to pass the time. He found the Koran and put it back. It was going to be a dull day.

As night fell, boredom gave way to expectation. He had only met the Sheikh once before and it was the meeting that had made him. With the Sheikh's blessing he had suddenly become a magnet for money. His puny little hedge fund was soon ballooning at an incredible pace. One thin million turned into hundreds, and his job became the art of receiving the money, dispersing it, bringing it back and dispensing it without attracting attention.

Thankfully, it was all beautifully organized downstream. There was one investor per continent and he imagined that each collected from a handful of sub-investors, who in turn collected from a handful of sub-sub-investors. How these relationships were firewalled he didn't know, but he did know that his money came from respected organizations, every one a blue-chip name. That was perfect: it meant that if the worst happened and he was compromised he had a completely plausible explanation. As far as he was concerned, his customers could only be legitimate financial institutions. They were, after all, regulated by the various massive bureaucratic financial bodies that fanned out across the world. The monies were already in the system and he was doing the usual business of a hedge fund, which was to take funds and invest them as he saw fit, in the nooks and crannies of the financial system. The fact that his transactions were complicated and money came and went to flow from and into all kinds of instruments was nothing if not expected. A hedge fund might trade commodities in Africa one minute, currency in Hong Kong the next, then buy an office block in Colombia before swapping it for a bond in Italy.

An extra night's overtime became some notional laundry bills, which became a charitable donation, which became an IT consultancy contract, which became an offshore outsourced project that fed back a dividend to the holding company. This was the process that broke the chain of causality of where the money had originated. He could lose money from one hand and make it in the other. He had the perfect front.

That first and only meeting had been a long time ago and nothing had happened for many years. It wasn't until the big money had started to roll in and an image of a palm tree against a smoky grey backdrop dropped into his email inbox that he had realized something was afoot. It hadn't taken him too long to work it all out. The palm tree had contained an encrypted message, and once the idea had dawned on him, it was a quick search to find the decoder on the internet. He had slowly read the instructions of what to do, which seemed simple enough, and magically there was a greeting and an order to buy a big block of stock in the emergency rights issue of an Indonesian palm-oil plantation on the brink of bankruptcy. Someone was clearly keen to rescue this obscure, far-away agricultural company and, like a good steward, he would execute the order. His long-forgotten plan had suddenly sparked into life: he had finally managed to tap into the vast subterranean river of money he had always imagined was flowing somewhere just beyond his senses.

Outside, he heard a car slowing down. A door seemed to be opening and he recognized that the vehicle was pulling into a garage. His heart beat faster as he heard the door close. This was it: the moment when he would learn what this dangerous and mysterious rendezvous was all about.

Chapter 5

Ali opened his eyes. What had happened? Bright yellow hot light flowed between the blinds and filled the room, which looked and felt like a hospital ward. What the hell had they done to him? The last thing he remembered was hearing a car pulling into a garage. That was most likely the Sheikh arriving.

When he woke again it was dark and he was very thirsty. Beside him, he found a switch bulb on the end of a piece of cord and pressed it.

A nurse came immediately and he muttered something about thirst, and soon she was back with some water.

What the blazes had they done to him? He felt as though they'd pretty much killed him. After he'd drunk he lay back and the pretty nurse raised the bed so he could sit up. He felt utterly weak. He wanted to ask how long he'd been there but his voice just hissed. He saw that his arm was attached to a drip. Saline? he wondered. Was he in Pakistan, fucked up by their stupid games?

The nurse was saying something, but he wasn't listening. They could have killed me, he kept thinking, and then where would they be? A wave of panic washed over him. He couldn't remember anything after the sound of the car driving into the garage, then the door shuddering closed.

He groaned. How utterly stupid was that? They'd dragged him all over the world and what had they achieved? Nothing. They'd fucked him up and he had no idea what had been said. He'd remember, he thought, of course he would. He was sick. It would all come back once he'd recovered.

The next morning he felt a lot better, terribly ill rather than on the edge of death. His mind was almost clear and he guessed he was still in Karachi. Neither the doctors nor the nurses seemed to want to talk to him. They just came and went, took notes, changed bed pans, brought food. The saline went in the afternoon and he lay wondering when he would get his memory back. He was far from his normal self. His thinking was still hazy, rather like it got when he'd had too much to drink. He felt as if he was shaking off some awful flu.

Night came, and when he woke the next morning he felt merely sick, the kind of sick that would have sent him to bed to rest it out. He ordered the nurse to bring his things, and when they arrived he called American Express on the last drips of his mobile's battery. He told them where he was and that he needed to get back to London on the next available flight. After he'd asked the nurse to recharge his phone, he went back to sleep. Two hours later, two American Express staff were at his door, and while he was getting dressed they closed out the paperwork with the hospital and made sure everything was in order for his ride to the airport.

As soon as he was ready, he stood up and went into the hall. He felt tottery but his spirits were up now that he was on his way home. An orderly rushed up to him with a wheelchair and he sat in it. He put on his jet black Ray-Bans and thanked his Amex helpers weakly but with a grateful smile.

'We've a limo and an ambulance waiting for you outside,' said the senior man, a serious Pakistani in his late thirties with a bushy moustache and a white streak through his raven black sculpted hair. 'Which would you prefer?'

'Limo,' he said quietly. 'I'm not too bad, really, just very weak.'

The Amex men sat with him in the limo and saw him through Customs and Immigration. At the door to the plane they wished him a safe flight, at which point the first-class purser and his steward took over. He would have been bloody impressed and grateful if he hadn't felt so poorly.

After take-off, he put his seat right back and a stewardess came with a blanket and laid it over him. He tried to recall what had happened but there was still nothing in his mind beyond the creaking of metal springs as the garage door closed. If they wanted to keep their plans secret, they had certainly achieved that.

Chapter 6

So, Christmas-bonus meeting number two, he thought, for the hundredth time, as he rose in the lift from the gym to Wolfsberg's floor. He popped a Rennie into his mouth as a preventive measure. Maybe he'd get the same again. He reminded himself there was no Frank to demand a bonus for him. He hadn't made any friends, cosied up to anyone or even interacted with the other dealers once his new trading regime had kicked in. He might say a few words now and again, but in reality the other members of the prop floor had a deeper relationship with the office photocopier than with him. Trading was a game of concentration, and interrupting a trader was an invitation to have your head bitten off. So it was natural that the others left Jim alone. It was as if Frank's ghost stood behind his chair, swinging an ecto-plasmic baseball bat. They knew what was good for them so they left the kid alone. He was friendlier with the girls in the canteen than he was with his co-workers.

His direct boss, Sebastian Fuch-Smith, or Fuck, as the dealers called him, would also be at the meeting. It was a stupid name but everyone had a silly nickname and there was something satisfying about calling the boss something rude. Swearing and abusing others was a standard relief mechanism among the traders. The wilder the market moved, the more profane they became. There was no longer any collection of words in or not in the dictionary that could shock him, and as often as not, when the market kicked off, he would find them streaming from his mouth too. In their split-second environment crudeness was an efficient release.

He had no problems with Fuch-Smith. The meeting would probably be the longest single period he had spent with him in the year since the man had taken over as head trader. Not that Fuch-Smith did much trading from what Jim saw: he was more of a manager than a dealer, more a spy for upstairs than a trader.

Wolfsberg's PA came out to him when he checked in at the floor's reception and he was ushered into the office. Wolfsberg had clearly gone even further up the hierarchy in the year since they had last met: his office had gone from normal glass cube to palatial corner suite.

Wolfsberg and Fuch-Smith greeted him and shook his hand rather grimly. Stomach acid would be spurting onto the alkali at that very moment, he thought, and maybe his face was going red. It didn't feel as though it was.

'This is for you,' said Wolfsberg, and pressed an envelope into his hand.

It's the sack, he thought. He smiled and sat back, not opening it.

Wolfsberg and Fuch-Smith stared at him.

'I think you should open it,' said Fuch-Smith, a hint of urgency intertwined within his beautiful diction.

Oh, shit, he thought. 'Sure,' he said. He flicked open the flap, took out the letter and unfolded the expensively stiff paper. Not the boot, he thought. The few words on the page couldn't amount to an explanation of harsh action. 'Brilliant, two hundred and fifty grand.' He realized then that something wasn't right. He knew he had just gone white. There was an extra zero.

Two and a half million.

He stared at Wolfsberg and Fuch-Smith in stunned silence.

Wolfsberg looked uncomfortable. 'We've had to temper it a bit. We just haven't got a handle on your risk profile yet. It doesn't look like it, but you might be taking a lot more risk than we think.'

Fuch-Smith gave a friendly nod. 'We'll make sure it washes out next year, all things being equal.'

Of course he had heard people got such bonus payouts, but to get one himself – it was like being hit on the head with a gold bar. 'Thank you very much,' he said stiffly, like someone receiving a parking ticket.

Wolfsberg looked at Fuch-Smith, who looked at Jim, who was folding his letter in an attempt to cover his shock.

Wolfsberg tried to break the awkward silence. 'I heard they're calling you Moby on the dealing floor.'

'Really?' he said. 'I didn't know that.'

Wolfsberg seemed even more uncomfortable.

Jim turned to Fuch-Smith as if he should have told him.

'As in Moby Dick, the great white whale.'

Jim gazed at him blankly.

'You know,' said Fuch-Smith. 'Big fish. Big swinging Moby Dick, the big fish.'

'Right,' said Jim, 'got you.' Nothing was making much sense to him, but it might later. He turned to Wolfsberg. 'Right.' He made a clicking sound with his tongue. 'Thank you, both, and a merry Christmas.' He got up and they did too. He wondered if the money was in his bank account yet; probably not. Could they change their minds and not pay him? He shook their hands and made a rapid exit.

Wolfsberg shrugged. 'What do we expect? Normality?'

'I'll give him some personal time.'

'Don't screw with the golden goose, Seb. Let him do what he wants to do. Let him sit how he wants to sit. If he likes green, change the carpets. If he wants to trade naked, make sure the place is nice and hot.'

Fuch-Smith nodded. 'You can rely on me.'

As he sat at his desk Jim thought about taking the rest of December off. He got four weeks' holiday a year but hadn't taken any. He was about to type the email to Fuch-Smith, when suddenly his boss was standing by his desk. 'Fancy coming round for a drink this evening and a spot of dinner *chez moi?*' he said, his majestic voice galloping around Jim's head.

'Can't,' he said, wondering where the Chez Moi was. 'Got to look after my nan.' He hadn't meant to say that – it had come out because he was so surprised to be asked anywhere by Fuch-Smith.

'OK.' Fuch-Smith smiled. 'Another time, perhaps?'

'Yes,' said Jim, going back to his screen. 'That'd be cool.'

He didn't put in the holiday request: home wasn't exactly Fun City.

Everything on TV was the same as ever, but he sat with her for a couple of hours because he knew she liked it. She held her knitting in her lap and fiddled with it. It was the same slab of work she'd sat with for a couple of years, but although she'd lost the knack of putting down the rows she seemed content to have it with her. She had been very calm these last few weeks, back to a more alert state in which she knew him from his father, and spoke and thought with a fragment of clarity that reminded him of her old self. Every now and then the old bustle and vim showed itself in a flurry of activity. She would start hoovering or dusting, talk about her early years in the Docklands warehouses; the stevedores and deal porters, the skulduggery and thieving, the faces and the life of a young woman in bombed London. These days of lucidity were the treasured days of his life: when Nan was well, everything was sweet. When she was sick, grey clouds of unhappiness hung low.

He got up from his chair. 'Night, Nan. Time for a spot of surfing, then bed.'

'I shall happily die in my sleep tonight,' she said.

'Don't say that, Nan,' he said, used to her sporadic doom-laden statements. He gave her a kiss.

'You're a good boy,' she said, ruffling his hair.

'Love you, Nan.'

He woke up with a start. What if she had been right? He listened, holding his breath. He exhaled in relief as faint snoring emanated from the room beyond. It was nearly Christmas, another year done. He'd soon be twenty-two and getting old.

Chapter 7

He hadn't felt his normal self at the open – the market looked plain weird and the lack of volume made the picture vague. He sat there for forty-five minutes and didn't trade. The charts were telling him something as clear as a bell but he didn't understand the message. Maybe his bonus had gone to his head and screwed him up.

'You're weird,' said Nipper, looking up from his screen.

Jim grimaced at his dwarfish, scrunched-up colleague. 'I know.'

'Whatcha reckon?'

'No clue.'

Nipper shrugged. 'It looks dead to me.'

When he got back from the gym, things were no clearer. 'You know,' he said finally, as a peculiar sensation welled inside him, 'these charts look sick. Fucking sick.' The nearest dealers looked up – they'd heard the strange yelp in his voice – and stared at him curiously. 'They look really, *really*, REALLY fucking *sick*!'

Out of the window there was a bright flare and they all looked around. At the Blackwall Tunnel refinery a huge fireball was rising into the air.

They stared at the explosion, then at Jim, and then at the black cloud again. There was a frozen moment when everything on the floor seemed to stop. Then, with an eruption of profanities, the traders hunched over their screens and got to work.

Jim told his software to go short as far as his significant credit limits would allow. He was selling stocks he didn't own, looking to buy them later for a lower price and making a fat profit. It sounded like something that should be a crime, but it wasn't: it was just another financial wheeze to gamble on the swings in the market.

There was pandemonium on the floor. Everyone seemed to be shouting and swearing at the top of their voices. Dealers were closing their longs and going short, hammering at their keyboards and crashing their mice about as they closed and opened their positions to get ready for a drop. He was there well ahead of the others. He had no complex positions to deal with. With four clicks of his mouse his software was sweeping through the FTSE 100 and selling everything until he had no credit in his account to sell more. His billion had moved the market down about a quarter of a percentage point.

Jim zoomed out of the chart and his jaw dropped. It was bloody obvious now: the FTSE was going to drop from 16,100 to 13,820 and do it in the next thirty minutes. He looked out of the window at the pall of smoke. Another cloud appeared to be rising, on the north side of the river this time. What the fuck had happened?

He looked at the FTSE future contract. A minute had passed and it hadn't moved by much. Most markets were populated by trading robots these days, managing the titanic but mundane order flow that drowned any prop trading that might go on. As such, unexpected news could take minutes to be factored in – unless, of course, your building had clear sight of the incident.

*

The duty officer watching the CCTV in the tunnel's control room shot out of his chair. A petrol tanker was heading down the ramp. He hit the red panic button. Tankers weren't allowed into the tunnel. Ten tons of petrol ignited would incinerate everyone in its mile stretch. He didn't see the motorbike riding behind it until it swung out into the other lane and pulled alongside the lorry.

'There's a bike with someone on pillion,' he was shouting into the phone. 'Oh, Christ!' He groaned. 'He's carrying something!'

'What can you see?'

The controller was staring intently at the screens and didn't reply.

'*What can you see?*'

'There – taking the corner. They're right in the middle of the tunnel.'

The pillion rider lifted something onto his shoulder and the lorry began to slow.

'It looks like an RPG! Oh, my God ...'

The screens in the control room flashed white. The watching men heard first a roar and then a rushing hiss as air was sucked into the tunnel. The controller spun round in time to see a fireball jetted from the entrance ten yards ahead. He bolted for the door, a wave of heat engulfing him. He threw it open as the windows behind him smashed, heat searing his back. His screams were drowned by the roar of the inferno as he tumbled down the stairwell to the exit. He flung open the door and was engulfed in a cloud of choking black smoke.

He dashed blindly forward, away from where he judged the blaze to be, coughing as his lungs filled with acrid smoke. His legs were buckling and he fell to his knees, begging God for mercy. He collapsed onto his back, and as he tried to breathe, the black cloud lifted off him and the wind blew it away.

From their distant tower the tunnel resembled a gigantic firework. If they could have looked west they might have seen another attack unfold.

The man carrying a bundle across Westminster Bridge looked as unremarkable as any of the throng that congregated to see Britain's most famous landmark: Big Ben. He pulled the old raincoat off his load and lifted the RPG to his shoulder as a packed bus passed him. He fired it at the vehicle as it was crossing to the south side of the Thames. There was a crash, as if a sledgehammer had slammed into a sheet of metal, but no explosion as the rocket punched through the thin shell of the vehicle and arced harmlessly into the river. The attacker stared at the bus incredulously. Now the driver stopped it in its tracks and opened the doors. Immediately the passengers flooded out into the road, unharmed.

The attacker raced across the street and round to the front of the Houses of Parliament. He ran into the road to avoid the meandering tourists and headed towards the main entrance. He vaulted the roadblocks that were designed to stop a truck bomb and dashed headlong at the checkpoint that protected the main door. He saw a middle-aged policeman and thought he saw him bring his machine-gun to bear. He pulled the cord of the detonator.

In Manchester and Birmingham two vast gasometers had exploded. Rather than go to heaven in the process someone had rigged bombs to them and set them off via SMS messages as soon as news of the London attacks had been broadcast on TV.

*

As the first confused information hit the wires, the automatic trading robots were ripped off-line and the market panic began.

Jim's phone rang. 'Support the market,' Wolfsberg said.

'Pardon?'

'Buy the market. Keep it from falling.'

'Impossible,' Jim said. 'I haven't got those kinds of limits.'

'Your limits are off.'

Fuch-Smith was now standing beside him. Jim looked at the chart: the market was down a thousand points. 'There's no point. It's falling another fifteen hundred and then it'll go back up. Supporting it now is just throwing money away.'

'Support it.'

'If I do that, we could lose a hundred, two hundred – maybe five hundred million.' He saw the chart clearly. 'Anyway, if we make it bounce now, it'll bounce maybe twenty points, then fall another three thousand, maybe five, straight down, and it won't rally for weeks.' He peered up at his direct boss, whose face was as red as a boiled lobster's shell, then at the chart again. 'Fuck me, that would be apocalypse! Christ knows what we'd lose if we went all in now.'

There was silence at the end of the line.

'If it bounces now you think it will fall another five thousand points?'

'Yes. Look, give it another ten minutes and then I'll go in. That's all it needs. If it hits thirteen thousand before that, I'll pile in anyway.'

'OK, you got it.' The line went dead.

'Ten minutes, thirteen eight twenty, we go long.'

The price was falling and the order books had stopped behaving like the stately voucher-dispensing system they normally were. Thousands of orders came and vaporized, like water on a hotplate. It was amazing to witness. The market was alive, twisting and turning like an injured animal. The clockwork toy that normally clicked and jerked was now a sinuous snake that hissed, thrashing back and forth with every millisecond, slithering down and down. The slamming dagger of the chart was approaching fourteen thousand. He closed his shorts.

'That's five hundred mil for the house,' he said. 'Let's buy.'

'Buy!' cried Fuch-Smith, at the top of his voice, 'Buy, buy, *buy*!'

The volume of trades was mind-blowingly high, higher than anything they'd seen before.

'The systems are going to crash now – you watch,' said Nipper. 'Overload's gonna take the computers out.'

Fuch-Smith looked at him with horror. 'Those IT boys better have enough fucking juice or we're screwed.'

Jim was clicking furiously.

Fuch-Smith looked at him; the price was 13,900. 'Moby?'

He clicked and shot back in his chair. 'Bombs away.'

The price hit 13,880. Suddenly the spread, the gap between the price you could buy and sell at, opened. Jim took a sharp breath as a huge chasm opened up between the price people were buying and selling at. The market was being torn apart. Normally the gap was half a point between the selling and buying prices, but suddenly it was ten points wide.

'I'm taking the market up twenty points,' called Jim. 'I'll take out all the sellers, buy all the stock they want to sell and take the price up twenty points.'

Fuch-Smith coughed and Nipper whistled, then went back to his screen. 'Moby's long – way long!' he screamed.

There was a collective wave across the floor and the pandemonium rolled on.

Dr Ali Muhammad sat up with a start. This was wrong! Synchronized attacks across London and already, after only *fifteen minutes*, the markets were rallying. How could that be? He had tried and tried to remember his meeting with the Sheikh and thought he'd got it straight in his head. Something was going to happen just before Christmas. Three hundred million to be readied for investment, and something massive to happen on 9/11/11. He'd got his positions lined up a week in advance for the first leg, moving into short positions in London like a stealthy ninja. Two hundred million in capital bought him two billion in short stock positions; the only real risk in the gambit was if a piece of insanely good news sent the market up before the following attack kicked it down.

Yet doubt lingered: everything was still so horribly frag-mented in his mind that there was always the possibility he had simply remembered what had never happened. Yet here was proof: an attack on London before Christmas.

The London part of the plan was important: previously, an attack on an unspecified location had turned out to be in the wrong time zone and in the wrong place to affect the markets. An outrage in Africa in the middle of the night was no use to him. His positions had been utterly neutral to the event and all he'd got out of it was a bill for the commis-sion and an agonizing few days of getting out of a massive position in such a way as not to push the market against him. He wished the trading strategy of shorting the market while setting off a big attack wasn't such a favourite with his clients. Life would be so much easier if he could just shuffle the money around for them and keep the interest for himself, rather than play at being the devil's trader.

Sadly, it was one of their holy inspirations: hit the beast and drain its blood at the same time, was one of their big ideas. It was certainly a sweet tactic when it came off – and when it did, it came off big.

But this wasn't looking good. He stared at the chart. The rally must surely be a technical bounce, merely a temporary halt in the ongoing descent. He was looking for a twenty to twenty-five per cent drop and it had barely dropped fifteen.

Suddenly he broke out in a sweat. He was sitting on a hundred million pounds' profit, but if this wasn't a fool's rally, it was the real thing: a rally back to par. His short positions were so large that closing them quickly would move the market yet further up. The price was now only two thousand points down and rising steadily. He looked away from the screen and tried to concentrate. If it went less than eighteen hundred points down, he would start to close.

The spread had closed now and the price had rallied sharply for two hundred points, then started on a milder trajectory up.

'I think we should stop,' said Jim. 'I think thirty billion long's enough.'

Fuch-Smith had long since sat down and looked coma-tose, rocking back in his chair sucking a cheap biro, fixated on the chart. 'Right,' he said finally.

Fifty minutes after the explosions everyone was sure that thousands had died, although in fact it was fewer than two hundred souls. They looked to the FTSE index to tell them how bad the situation really was, and as the market rallied they were reassured. Although many had perished, the market told them the overall picture wasn't so bad. As it recovered, it told the country and the world that the unfolding atrocity had been just a cruel flesh wound that would become another memorial scar.

'I'm going to lunch,' said Jim, searching his pocket for his last Rennie. He started to get up.

'Lunch!' exclaimed Fuch-Smith, reanimated. 'You must be joking.'

Jim shook his head. 'No point sitting here. We're long, it's going up and I want some lunch.'

'But you can't! It's madness to leave thirty billion out there and go to lunch.'

He glared at Fuch-Smith, frustrated, then picked up a black marker pen from his desk. 'Look,' he began, 'I'm fried. We can't get out now. This is what'll happen.' He drew a continuation of the chart line on his monitor, from its shaking end until the close at four thirty. He fattened the line, the marker's nylon tip squeaking, the black mark's passage particularly wide over the lunch break. 'If it goes outside this band I'll be in the canteen.' He dropped the pen. 'OK?'

Fuch-Smith looked at the ruined screen. Every tiny point tick was two million pounds. At the equivalent of a thousand points down there was a sharp incline on his line for four hundred points. 'Wait here for that,' he begged, pointing at the prediction a few minutes ahead when the markets headed sharply up.

'OK.' Jim sat down again. By now they were surrounded by traders, all of whom were long to their limits. They stood back and watched. Every few moments the real chart line would appear below Jim's ragged line. But when it did, it immediately disappeared behind the ink as if it was scared of the light. Suddenly the market was only a thousand points down and everyone appeared to be holding their breath. Jim sat back and stared out of the window at the black cloud spreading ever thicker on the horizon.

'Moby, Moby, Moby, Moby,' the traders chanted, as the price suddenly arched up and followed the steep line of the predicted rally.

He looked at the spoilt screen. 'Can I go now?'

Fuch-Smith nodded irritably. 'If you must.'

As he got up the traders slapped him on the back. It hurt, but he smiled: the pain somehow relieved his tension. 'Some fucking stupid game,' he heard himself say.

A data packet micro-second away, someone in a small Mayfair office was panicking. It was all going horribly wrong and if he didn't get out fast not only would his profits be gone but soon he'd be into losses. That absolutely wasn't the plan at all. As he bought, so the market kept rallying. He'd be lucky to get out even. His eyes were watering and he was shaking. This wasn't how it had been before.

Fuch-Smith was riveted to the screen. It was just totally impossible that this could be happening. There he was at someone else's trading station, thirty-two billion pounds on the line in the most incredibly volatile moment ever, watching the market follow a marker-pen trail scrawled across a screen by a trader who had stalked off to have lunch. How the blazes was he meant to unwind a thirty-two-billion-pound position? How was the market meant to follow an ink trail? What kind of bonus was he going to get if the market continued to follow the scrawl of the demented *wunderkind*? The floor would make nigh on four billion pounds. Two whole big ones by Moby alone.

Moby's phone rang and Fuch-Smith picked it up. It was Wolfsberg. 'Exceptional,' he said. 'Truly exceptional. What's the status?'

'All under control.'

'What's the plan?'

Fuch-Smith looked at the black marker trail. 'It's going to start flattening in about thirty minutes and we'll look to ease out.'

'We're still in support mode, so nothing in a hurry.'

'Gotcha.' A thought crossed Fuch-Smith's mind. He snapped his mobile open and punched in a few digits. He gave an account number to the spread betting clerk at the other end of the line, then went on, 'Give me five hundred pounds a point and close me at a five-hundred-point gain. Stop me out for a minus twenty.' He had bought nearly five million pounds of index future and told them to close the trade if it went up five hundred points. That would make him a quarter of a million pounds. After what had been happening it seemed like small beer but an extra quarter bar in the kitty couldn't do any harm.

Within moments his highly leveraged spread bet generated another few million pounds of upwards pressure. It was just a gnat bite, but as waves of traders piled into the rally, so the market became a one-way bet: upwards.

Jim didn't like going back to his desk so early: his eyes wouldn't be fresh enough. But Fuch-Smith seemed overjoyed to see him – and his chart prediction had held good while he'd been away, he thought proudly. The rally had gone exactly the way he had seen it, but even he was impressed with the result. 'So, you and me, we've made two and a half billion,' he said, sitting down. 'What next?'

'I think we should lighten the load.'

'Flat by close?'

'That would be perfect, but not at the cost of turning the tide back.'

'Those bastards,' said Jim.

'Right,' said Fuch-Smith, taking a moment to connect Jim's words with the bombers who had set the whole thing in train. 'Yes, complete bastards,' he added.

'We've shown them,' said Jim, clicking away.

'And all those yellow-livered chicken-shit cowards who ran to sell,' chimed in Nipper.

As Jim started to unwind the huge position, the chart's ascent trailed off. He looked at his black line and layered his selling to try to keep the market from falling under his own predicted line. In front of the market he hung hundreds of offers to sell at a variety of prices a little higher than the current price. Everyone knew the market was going back to par … maybe not today, but probably tomorrow or the day after. His offers to sell were an invitation to buy now for a slightly higher price and make a profit later. It was a 'buy now while stocks last' lure that offered traders across the City a chance to recoup some of their losses from the earlier panic.

Jim hung out his orders on every stock at every level, chunks of flesh for the hungry shoals of market barracudas to tear at. Slowly over the next four hours they bit and bit, ripping at his bait and chewing their way inexorably towards the price equilibrium of the start of the day.

Dr Ali Muhammad watched the market tick up and up. His fantastic profit had shrunk to nothing, and though he was out and safe, a few hundred thousand gained was all he had to show for his trouble. It was sick compensation in comparison to the fortune he'd been planning for. At least he couldn't be blamed for failing to turn this historic action into a fortune: the chart was there for anyone to see. They simply hadn't done enough damage to make the black-hearted callous heathens care. If they were going to use the markets against their enemies, they had to hit harder – much harder.

Fuch-Smith watched Moby work. He was clearly a fucking genius. That was how a genius must look: he sat calm and still, making the odd click, all the moves fitting together as if to some cosmic plan. He felt like a dunce. In about five minutes the books would be flat and they'd be up so much money they could pack up and go home and not come back for a year. The whole floor had cleared billions. The other traders had followed Moby's psychic line, maxing out their trading limits long and making their best days on record. Even his stupid spread bet had come in and closed out giving him a fat tax-free win.

It was a magical moment.

Bill Rock, the president of the company, had sent him an email on his BlackBerry: 'Outstanding.' If next year went OK his bonus would be so big he could buy back the family seat and go riding around it for the rest of his days.

'Flat,' said Moby, switching off his screens.

'Flat,' Fuch-Smith echoed, and sighed. 'Thank Christ that's over.'

Jim smiled at Fuch-Smith. He felt exactly the same as his blue-blood boss, with his perfect blond mop and his golden tanned face, with its sharp jaw and sea-blue eyes.

Jim ran his hand through his own blackish short-cropped hair. 'Yeah, I know exactly how you feel. Can't bear these long stints.' He waved at Nipper. 'Got any of the white stuff?'

Nipper threw him a box of Rennies.
He caught it. 'Thanks.'

The ginger tom miaowed at him as he scratched its head, then rubbed itself on his trouser leg. 'Bet I stink of sweat, don't I?' he said, and petted it some more.

He opened the door and Nan was standing there. No, she wasn't. He blinked and stepped over the threshold.

'What's happened?' she said, but she didn't. He dropped his kitbag, closed the door and turned on the hall light. Odd that she hadn't switched it on.

'Nan,' he called. He walked quickly to the sitting room. She was asleep in her chair. No, she wasn't. The room was quiet, still and empty. She was there but she wasn't. There was nothing in the air, no her. She was gone. He went over and touched her cold face. He wanted tears to well in his eyes, he wanted to want to cry, but he didn't. He had known this would come, it had had to one day, and he had wished for her sake that it would so she could be free of her broken mind and walking renewed in heaven's flower-filled pastures. While he wasn't religious, he did believe there was a life after the one he was in.

'Oh, Nan.' He knelt and kissed her cool face. 'Keep an eye on me from up there, won't you?' He held her hand. 'I'm going to miss you so much.'

Chapter 8

For the first time in his life he went to Trafalgar Square for the New Year celebration. Everyone seemed drunk and happy, dancing, shouting, jumping, singing. He felt empty. He hadn't had much of a life so far, he thought. He only knew his life with his nan, his days at school, and the rather abstract and remote life he lived at work. Other people had girlfriends and cars, houses and children. They had families and friends, went on holidays skiing or to fantastic desert islands. They had horses and boats and educations. They went to the movies, the opera, the theatre, Wimbledon, fashion shows, flash charity galas, Cheltenham, cricket at the Oval, lunch at the Houses of Parliament. What did he have? He had nothing but a mind-blowingly big bank account. What the hell was he meant to do with it? He didn't know how to spend it – what could he spend it on?

The police were out in force, the attacks of the previous days sending the Old Bill buzzing around London, lights flashing, every day since. He wondered how they'd got on at the desk; surely they'd made so much money they were just sitting back, waiting for the dust to settle. He knew how it had gone all the days he'd been away: whiplash, whiplash, whiplash, lots of sharp rallies and sudden falls, like the gyrations of a boat tied to the pier on a stormy day. The market had actually gone nowhere in aggregate, just thrashed up and down in violent jerks. The chaos would take a couple more weeks to go away.

The firm had sent a big wreath to the cremation, much larger than his small one. It had pissed him off that he hadn't bought a bigger one, but Nan wouldn't have seen the point.

The firm had asked to send a representative to the service, but he'd said he'd prefer it if they didn't. It was a quiet family affair, he told them. It certainly was: just him and the vicar, and outside the heavy, sickly smell of pork scratchings.

He stood at the edge of Northumberland Avenue and watched the revelling crowd, then held out a finger impulsively and traced the chart of his life. For the first five years it went straight across, then dipped sharply followed by a steep rally, just like the FTSE the other day. A flat period followed. Then, as he became a teenager, the bear market had started. It had jagged downs with little recoveries but the trend was always slipping and sliding away. Started work: the trend was flat, he was getting older and more secure as Nan had seemed to hit a bottom of sorts. Then the job kicked in, giving his invisible graph a slow, steady rise – until *whoosh*: a huge rally, more rally, a vertical bubble rise … and crash. He traced the pattern again in the air, like a child painting with a sparkler.

'We're going to get a double top,' he said to himself. 'Definitely.' Things were going to get better again, he knew. It couldn't be hard to feel better than he did that moment, but then what?

He couldn't see more than the double top.

He walked across the road to the packed square. 2011 was going to be a year of change for him. He had a lot of catching up to do. He had a whole world to acquaint himself with and tonight was as good as any to get started.

*

Fuch-Smith looked over the stern of the yacht into the water below. He was on the sort of high he hadn't enjoyed since he was made head boy at his public school. Four billion pounds' profit in a day was the stuff of legend and everyone at the bank had been looking at him as if he'd grown a couple of feet taller. They all knew about Moby, the brilliant East End trader who was the engine of it all but, as the boss of that floor, it was Fuch-Smith's scalp and his management that had pulled it off. Now here he was, standing on Bill Rock's yacht being fêted, with his fiancée, like a rock star. Nothing had ever tasted as sweet.

All he had to do was keep it together for the year and he was sure of the sort of bonus that would set him up for life. He had it all clear in his mind: keep the trading tight, keep everyone away from blowing themselves up and let Moby trade them all to a stellar return. Things would have been fat even without the huge coup, and as long as he could show a roadmap of returns, with the possibility of another coup in some future upset, then this time next year the skies would open and gold would rain down on him.

He clasped the rail. Perhaps he'd even be yacht rich.

His dream was the restoration of his family seat, which stood dilapidated in the rump of the grounds it once controlled. He had earmarked a large part of this year's bonus to put a new roof on and replace the lower-floor windows. The building's Grade I listing meant he might as well pile money on the long gravel drive and ask people to take a bagful for every piece of work they did. However, it was the historic family home, an estate that had risen in the eighteenth century only to fade in the nineteenth and slide headlong into oblivion in the twentieth. Now there was a prospect that the family fortune would rise again – because of him; or rather, as he knew full well, because of

Moby. It would be roof and windows this year, windows and floors the next. Then get the land, buy it piece by piece, rolling back the ravages of the centuries until he and his family could look out over the rolling countryside and know, as their ancestors had known, that it was all theirs.

If it hadn't gone tits up by the summer he would close the grounds to the public and perhaps, just perhaps, put out feelers for some of the old fields. He didn't want to make it too obvious that the family was back in the money or the bastard farmers would never let him have them back, not at any price. They'd cut down every tree in the park, grub up every hedge and plough it all together into one great ugly featureless field for the smallest farming subsidy. For an extra sack of grain they'd happily knock down the old house too.

With a little more luck and no disasters, he'd be able to put the whole dynastic jigsaw back together. That was his dream as he sipped his champagne.

But his plans hinged on the young cockney sparrow who had somehow mastered the impossible task of reading the markets. Moby was his saviour and his Achilles heel. No one seemed to know anything about him, except that he appeared to live in a dodgy pre-war council block and that his grandmother had just died.

He hoped to God that the old lady's death hadn't broken the spell. Things never went so well as when they were about to turn sour.

He felt a gentle tickling on the back of his neck and turned to find his fiancée, Jemima, standing behind him. 'Breathtaking sunset, darling,' she said, in the deep, sexy voice she saved for special occasions.

'Yes,' he said. 'Quite the wildest I've seen.' The skyline

was indeed on fire, a roiling of mauve, orange and red filaments.

'Are you worrying?' she asked.

'Planning,' he said. 'Always planning.'

Jim stared at the fish and chips laid out on the kitchen table. How exactly did you go from this to anything better? How did you change your life from nil to something? He broke off a bit of cod and ate it. He felt down. It wasn't a surprise. He knew he'd feel sad. He'd have felt bad if he hadn't. He ate some chips. Nan wasn't the only reason he was feeling low: it was the hopelessness of not knowing what he was supposed to do now. He had to open a new chapter, start a new story, build a fresh life – but how did anyone go about doing that? He had an amazing job and all the money he could ever need. Maybe he should just get on with things as they were and see what turned up. He ate more fish.

For a start he needed a girlfriend; if he didn't get one soon he'd probably die of frustration. So far, looking after his nan, getting home so she didn't go loopy with panic, had destroyed any chance of a relationship in the outside world. On reflection, that was the worst part of his old life – the monkish celibacy. That could change.

Then he needed to get himself educated and move out. That was it: go out and pull, get learning, move on. That was a plan: work, move, pull, learn. He was sure he could do three out of four and the pulling would come; after all, he wasn't ugly – or, at least, he thought he wasn't. He tugged at his short hair. Even if he was, ugly men had girlfriends – he saw as much at work. The traders were a bunch of truly ugly mugs and almost everyone had a babe in tow or an ex-babe at home, drumming away at them for more cash.

*

'So,' said Rock, gently waving his steak knife at Sebastian Fuch-Smith, 'I want to know about this whiz kid Moby Evans.'

Fuch-Smith smiled charmingly. So that's what I'm doing here, he thought. Nice one. He put down his knife and fork and took a sip of claret to clear his mouth. 'Yes, quite a mivvy.'

Rock looked at him, querying.

'A talent,' Fuch-Smith explained hastily. 'Blindingly fast. He's our secret weapon. There's no point in being right if you can't get the orders in fast enough and play the order flow as things develop. That's how we use him. The traders come up with the ideas and he executes them. How he keeps all the thousands of symbols in his head I don't know. It's a hell of a lot of team work but having faster execution helps a lot. We've got a brilliant group.' He raised his glass. 'As we've seen.'

'Currencies, bonds?'

'Well, we all flap around when there's nothing much on, but Moby's big plus is when we hit action. That's when he's a real value add.' He tried to look as relaxed as possible and a little bored. 'He's a key support person for the group. When the team has decided on a play he's the guy doing the order flow. His execution's astonishing. Quite brilliant.'

Wolfsberg looked past his bejewelled wife to Rock; he was following the younger man's tack. Rock was sniffing to find out how they'd made their killing, and if he spotted it was Moby, they'd transfer him to New York. Passing him off as some kind of superstar order entry clerk might just work.

*

'Having someone who can actually get the orders in the

book like a concert pianist is a rare skill. The traders love to hand off to him when the action gets fast.'

'Would you miss him much?' asked Rock, looking closely for Fuch-Smith's reaction.

He seemed irritable, but not massively so. 'Yes, we'd miss any of them. It's been hard work building the team and now it's knitted so tightly together it would be a pain to lose anyone. There are so many damn hedge funds out there trying to poach staff it's a constant battle. On top of that, in my experience, it doesn't take much to knock a floor off balance, and trading's going so well that anything popping up to threaten it would be a nightmare.' He shrugged. 'But no one's indispensable.' He stiffened. 'Except maybe the Bobble dealer – we'd definitely have trouble without him. He's the one who called the big move on the big day. He seems pretty thick but when it comes to the big calls we rely on him.'

Wolfsberg nodded earnestly.

Rock relaxed in his chair and smiled. Bobble guy to New York, he noted mentally. He imagined a fat man whose outline was a letter B. He imagined the cartoon Bobble trader singing 'New York, New York'. When a team did too well, Rock's responsibility was to fuck them up. No team could do too well: it screwed everyone else, undermining the hierarchy. Not that the hierarchy wasn't always in constant flux, but that was the dog-eat-dog game of board-room politics, a vicious power struggle that could be tipped out of balance if any group became too successful.

Chapter 9

Everyone on the trading floor was pleased to see Jim back. 'Happy New Year, Moby,' they said, one by one, as he passed.

'Happy new year,' he said to Joe, the enormously fat option specialist. Joe just ate and ate and ate as he traded. His calculations were full of the sort of maths that had got him a PhD. While he stuffed his face he punched numbers into his Excel spreadsheet, producing funny-looking curves that meant nothing to anyone but him. Jim wondered whether he made any money. He'd heard he didn't, merely moving his trading funds around in the vain hope that one of his equations might pay off one day.

'Happy New Year, Badger,' he said to the Bund Shatz trader.

Badger sat quietly all day, waiting for someone to sell him Shatz contracts, then closed their equivalent on another market. Because the Shatz was a seldom used contract it had a massive spread and Badger simply laid off the exposure. He hedged his bets and waited to close his illiquid position when someone eventually bought the contract off him. Thanks to a giant spread, the whole torturous process had a tidy profit attached. It was practically risk free but tedious. With a bit of luck he could make a million a year for the firm. Not bad, but not exactly great either. Whatever happened, Badger just sat tight and grabbed what contracts came his way. Some days nothing would happen and on others, like the day of the attack, the contract was alive and kicking and he could make the trades necessary to complete the profitable sequence over and over again all day long.

Then his tedious days of staring at a motionless screen were repaid. Instead of the usual mind-numbing dearth of activity there was a deluge of action. While his streak was nothing when compared to Moby's colossal bonanza he didn't care, he was no great white whale.

Jim saluted Flipper, who was camp and fat, not as fat as Joe, porcine rather than elephantine. He had a tendency to roll his eyes and lisp and he was the purveyor of a 360-degree mince that rotated around the small of his back. He could be moody, especially when he lost money. Flipper wasn't to be confused with Nipper. Flipper did something similar but different from Nipper. He decided which way the market was trending in whatever market he felt good about. He jumped on the trend he thought he saw and stayed aboard until he thought it had ended or was going against him. He was right more often than not.

Nipping was a different trick. If Nipper thought the market was going up he'd sit on the lower-priced bid with an order to buy. If he thought it was trending down he did the opposite. At some point, hopefully, someone would fill his order. When one of Nipper's orders got filled – say, a share that was trending higher – he immediately placed it back on the order book somewhere a bit higher up, waiting for the direction of the market to push the price up and take the shares back from him for a profit. While Flipper hung on to a share as long as he thought the trend would last, Nipper rotated stocks or contracts from one side of the book to the other, hoping the trend would give him some margin of error.

Muppets, as they were known on the floor, common traders and speculators, didn't understand the importance of the 'bid' and 'ask'.

This small difference between the price you can buy and sell at is the margin that the market makes to survive on. In the long run, every market move up is cancelled by a move down, but the spread between bid and ask is always there, chipping away. The profit from a plunge is cancelled by the loss from a rally so that the only real profit to be had is made by capturing the difference between the bid and ask as traders trade backwards and forwards. All other profits are illusory, a trick of statistical probabilities that ensures most traders lose while the odd lucky winner ends up thinking he's a genius.

As such, Flipper was playing a mug's game, the impossible task of making money from market direction, while Nipper was making it from the only winnable game: scalping the spread.

Everyone knew the market was random but no one believed it. They had to believe beating the market could be done, and while they worked on it they found ways of making a living, eking out profits from wrinkles like the spread. Then along came Jim. With a flash of his felt-tip pen he could give Flipper a trend to sit on all day. Flipper was no longer an institution muppet, he was a winning trader, riding his rock-solid trends for bumper profits. If only Fuch-Smith would give him more capital to risk he'd be making all the money in the world, but there was no convincing him to give Flipper more rope to find a way of hanging them all. A decade's profits were in the bag. Everything else was just to be looking busy.

Surely Jim was just a lucky winner. He'd read the theory. There were seven billion people in the world and one would trade randomly like a seven-billion-to-one winner. He might be that particular lucky fellow. Perhaps just being a billion-to-one trader would be enough or perhaps, in a world of chance, he might be the ten-to-one possibility that some guy could have ten times the luck of seven billion people and be a seventy-billion-to-one winner. Such a guy could put a dollar on the red and watch it come up red thirty-six or more times and leave the table with sixty billion dollars as a result.

What someone like that could do with the leverage of a major bank behind him was anyone's guess, but certainly every winning streak had finally to end, and if the lucky chap kept gambling he would eventually lose his shirt.

Jim, the trading Moby, was just a big egg-timer of luck, dripping it out a grain at a time until one day it would all be gone and his chart lines would be as irrelevant as everyone else's.

'Happy New Year, Dirk,' said Jim.

Dirk didn't look up from his screen and simply raised his hand. If asked he would have said that he 'fucking hated' Moby. He was a fundamental trader. As a good old hedge-fund manager-style dealer, he took macro-economic trades and tried to back them in such a way that he couldn't really lose. In theory this sounded great, but in practice Dirk was always exposed to something.

On the big day, market volatility blew up all his expensively laid positions, which were balanced by a vast convoluted structure to make money out of the fact that, as the future came and went, people overpaid for the insurance a future or option could offer them. The attack had created such massive volatility that his strategy was immediately fifty million pounds in the hole. What had been expensive insurance that he was selling short before the attack was now utterly cheap and rocketed up in value.

The moment the attack kicked off, Dirk was over; his arse was going to get fried. When they broke down his pyramid of dealing they would find that he was about as safely hedged as a nudist running down the street waving a bag of crack cocaine. He couldn't even start to calculate the size of the financial hole he had dug. Everything had gone to fuck.

He'd have to wave goodbye to his massively over-mortgaged flat in Docklands. His wife would leave him when he had to take the kids out of school and suggest that the only way to pay off the credit cards was for her to get a job. He was more fucked than a blonde on roofies at a Hell's Angels' jamboree. As he had looked at Moby's insane monitor scrawlings, he laughed. There was only one logical way out. He was dead meat anyway, so he immediately bought millions of pounds' worth of the most whacked-out long options he could get onto. He filled his boots with long-shot toxic crap derivatives; with the bank's no-limit capital, there was nothing to lose but more. By sunset he had made his position back and put another hundred million up on the scoreboard. It was like falling from twenty thousand feet and landing unharmed in a swimming-pool of naked supermodels. How could he not hate that fucking know-nothing Moby? What was the point of his life if it took some spotty kid to pull him out of the shit and not even know how he'd done it?

Jim sat down next to Nipper. 'Got any antacid, mate?'

'Green or red, Zantac or Tagamet?'

'Ooh, I'll take a red and a Tagamet, please.'

'Right you are.' Nipper handed them over on a sweaty palm.

'Sorry to hear about your grandmother,' said Flipper.

Jim smiled sadly. 'Thanks.' He brought up the chart of the last close. It was clearly going up, so he waited for the open, at which he would hit the offer for a couple of ticks, sit back and watch it rise.

He looked around the floor. There were about thirty traders down his end and he realized that only about a dozen were on his personal radar. He'd make it his painful duty to get to know them all a little better. If any group of people could introduce him to the real world, they were it. He scanned his email. Fuck had called a group meeting for seven a.m. tomorrow. That looked important.

Chapter 10

Sebastian Fuch-Smith stood at the front of the meeting room and waited for the appointed hour. Generally dealers were naturally early birds. If you couldn't rise at five and be at work, bright as a tack, by seven, you simply weren't going to last in the job. 'Early to bed, early to rise, makes a man healthy, wealthy and wise,' he had once quoted.

'Or a milkman,' Flipper had pointed out.

Fat Joe was the last to arrive, loaded up with doughnuts and a Venti *caffè latte* with enough animal fat to gum up the arteries of a grizzly bear. He was clearly happy to be the last in. He dumped his calories on the boardroom-style central table and dropped with a thump onto a leather swivel chair.

'Right, chaps,' said Fuch-Smith, with a flip of his floppy quiff. 'Good news and bad.'

They stared at him with the moroseness and confidence of kids about to leave school for good.

'First the good news. Last month we went right off the dials, blew off the roof, went into orbit, landed on the moon, set up camp there and put in a flaming Tikki bar.'

'Fuck! Something terrible's happened,' exclaimed Dirk.

Fuch-Smith held up a policeman's commanding palm. 'Hold on a moment there. Last month we made four billion pounds.'

The room broke into a chorus of whistles and cheering. They knew, of course, it was stratospheric, but to hear it said was too much for even their professional cool to stay intact.

'That's more than the whole of last year's total European divisional take,' grunted Joe, and shovelled a large percentage of a whole doughnut into his mouth.

'Now the bad news,' Fuch-Smith continued. 'The chance of us getting a five-hundred-million-pound bonus is approximately zero.'

There was an equally emotional groan.

'And this is why,' said Fuch-Smith. 'It's a one-off. The last couple of years have been damn good, but this performance was an order of magnitude better, and when you take into account that it's basically the result of a single day, it's infinitely out of whack. They are not going to pay out in the normal way on this result.' A lot of huffing came his way from the audience. 'But we can collar an enormous result next Christmas if we play our cards right.'

'What's the idea?' Jim asked.

'This is what we're going to do. We need to keep up last year's general performance and not fall back to 2009 levels – and, God forbid, we mustn't end up back at 2008 levels. If we have a 2008 you can forget any dreams of untold millions.' He smiled. 'But, chaps, our edge is that we ran support, and support could still do them a serious mischief next time around. In their minds they'll be seeing that profit as the right side of a billion-pound coin that could come up either way. To them it could just as easily have been the other way around. Remember, the customer might have choked on a billion-plus bill, and, chances are, the bank would have had to swallow a lot of such a loss.'

They nodded knowingly.

Jim smiled at Fuch-Smith. What the fuck was he talking about? What customer?

'So,' continued Fuch-Smith, 'the reason they're going to pay out big is because we're going to outperform again, and in their minds we'll be the only thing between them and a multi-billion-pound hole next time around. A good all-round performance will show we're better than just lucky, and that next time the balloon goes up we'll perform well, rather than drop them in the crapper. Then, come next December, your pay packets'll make your eyes pop out. But, remember, this is team play. The moment any of this looks like we got lucky, they'll write us off as a fluke and our bonuses too. So let's keep it tight, let's keep it team play.'

They were grinning like hungry weasels – and suddenly Jim realized they were all looking at him. 'What?' he demanded.

'Team play,' said Dirk. 'That means *you*. Everyone has to work together, but mainly that means us working with you.'

Jim mirrored Dirk's haughty pose. 'Well, if that's the way it's got to be, that's the way it is.'

Fuch-Smith sagged with relief and a massive boyish smile broke across his face. Jim was the main variable in his stratagem. All the profits were coming from the cockney wonder. Unless they spread them about a bit, it would be impossible to hide that a supernova inhabited the trading floor while a bunch of dense white dwarfs rotated point-lessly in its vicinity.

Now the main worry was that the magic would lose its power. In his mind that was the way it worked. The trend ended as soon as everyone had bought into it. Then the market turned – and screwed as many of them as it could.

'Well done, Moby,' said Fuch-Smith. 'If we work together closely we can all come out of this minted.' He imagined the new roof on the decrepit family mansion. It was paid for, so he had done at least the minimum required of him as its heir, and more than his father and grandfather had managed. If he could keep it together for another year, he could achieve the impossible: the restoration of the Fuch-Smith family's fortune.

'Remember, everybody, nothing flashy. The same as last year – just more team work.'

Jim smiled to himself. He'd certainly get a lot of face time with the crew now.

Chapter 11

Three hundred million was an awful lot of money to move around. If it had been legitimate cash it would have been a simple matter of making a standard request and having it go from one account to another. Making three hundred million move from one account to another was a lot trickier when you'd have difficulty in explaining why you had it and why you were sending it to who you were for no apparent good reason.

Money was the engine of all the goings-on in the world. For evil purposes money had to move differently. From corruption to crime and terrorism, at most stages someone had to be paid but in such a way that it was invisible and unaccountable. Money could be the ultimate smoking gun. It was as dangerous as it was powerful as it was inconvenient.

Authorities around the world had increasingly clubbed together to stop money sloshing untracked around the system. This came hard to many politicians and other such gatekeepers. Since the beginning of time they had relied on the same financial byways to parlay their influence into hidden affluence. Yet as the likelihood of being targeted by terrorism loomed larger than ever before, they had allowed financial sluice gates to be constructed across the vast rivers of illicit cash.

The last thing anyone wants to do is to pay for something illicit in a way that can be traced back to its source, and for dodgy dealings, cash is king. But cash is unwieldy and insecure, much better off in a bank. Cash may be king and safely anonymous, but it's also unwelcome in anything but the smallest chunks.

There is only so much that can be done with a sack of cash and only so much that can be carried about. You can buy a Lear Jet with the right kind of credit card but with a pocketful of cash you might even be refused an economy airline ticket. Cash is only welcome at the trivial end of life's expenditures.

To hurt even the best organized criminal undertaking you need only contain the flow of their assets. So, cash control is the obvious place to start.

However, where there's a will to get over barriers, someone will find a way. Where there's a need to launder money, someone will provide a launderette, be it a casino, an antiques shop, a fast-food joint or a charity for the overseas needy.

Dr Ali Muhammad was just such a top-level operator, overseeing a clandestine pyramid of independent and opaque money-processing operations, all working for a single cause. He dealt with money already neatly washed within the banking system. He was living proof that, however high the walls that went up against them, there was always a way under, around, over or through for those smart and motivated enough to engineer a route.

Even so, organizing three hundred million dollars to be picked up in a single drop by a complete stranger took the sort of planning and finesse that had earned him all the interest on the capital he administered.

Making interest was definitely against *their* rules and he wouldn't have dreamt of admitting to such a thing. They had their beliefs and he wouldn't violate them. But what a fantastic conceit it was – what money he had made on the back of that tacit understanding.

Very soon he would have three corporations set up. Each offshore, each perfectly pukka. They were venture-capital companies, poised to make investments, all funded by the rich and famously mysterious princes of Saudi Arabia. A couple of 'Arab' guys on an expensive holiday in Bermuda had done the trick on that front. They had smiled mysteriously and signed lots of papers in front of the functionary and his administrative staff. The Arabs had babbled incomprehensibly between themselves, brooding and handsome in their flowing white gowns. Their advisers had smiled subserviently and agreed that everything seemed in order.

It was more fees and minimal work for the professionals. It was all very equitable. By the time the funds were in the system, the blood and shit spent to create them had long since been washed away.

With a bit of brains, a little class and a charming manner, Ali eased great slabs of money around the world with no fuss. When the day came, he would simply sign over the shares in the corporations to new hands and change the bank mandates to new signatures.

What the recipients did next was up to them but he would be out of the picture and, like the millions of Ali Muhammads in this world, blur and merge into anonymity.

In fact, he was starting to think about more than blurring: he was considering vanishing himself entirely. The three hundred million dollars would buy one hell of a lot of something and he wondered what that would be. Maybe they were tired of trying to profit from the plunge. Maybe they wanted simply to wipe the financial system off the face of the planet. Had they said what would happen to him?

When he tried to recall details, a dark doom-laden cloud

filled his mind. All he could remember was the grinning shrunken face of the Sheikh glorying in some imagined event.

Could three hundred million dollars buy three nukes? Three nukes would equal New York, London and Tokyo, he thought. Might that be the plan? Put the nukes in three containers. Send each one, with a small crew hidden aboard, to its destination for the suicide bombings of all time.

No. That couldn't be it. Could it? If it was, they wouldn't have told him to go back to London.

Then he had a striking thought. They couldn't do that. They wouldn't do that. Everything they were was actually an offshoot of the West. The technology they used, the dollars they spent, the medicines that kept them well, the weapons they used – they were all invented, tested, manu-factured and sold by the Christian world. Their world was just about incapable of making even the simplest of the technologies they used. The phones they spoke on, the encryption they used to stay safe, their ideas on the struc-ture of their struggle, the net propaganda: all this fertile soil was down to the Christian manure their roots fed on. Away from it, everything would wither and perish. If they broke the back of the West, the first to perish would be their own children, swept away by a famine that would circle the globe. No, they would continue to use the technology and knowledge of the West to their advantage; they would continue to eat away at the inside with the aim of rebuilding an old world within the new.

'Eat away?' he exclaimed. 'That's never the story.' Hate and death were the story. They were stupid birds fighting more stupid birds for seeds lying on the ground. Fighting and fighting even though there was enough to go around.

Pecking and flapping, then threatening and chasing, puffing out chests, shrieking and hectoring. That was how life was: there was no thought of general wellbeing for all, just the pleasure of dominance, the excitement of thwarting, the satisfaction of hurting the weak who deserved it, crippling the fit who didn't deserve to have it so good, proving that you were right and everyone else was wrong. That was how the story went and three hundred million dollars bought an awful lot of trouble.

He imagined looking out of the window and seeing the flash of a nuclear detonation. He clicked his mouse and opened a browser. It was all nonsense, of course: there would be just another group of children ready to spill their guts over some landmark for a shot at a heaven full of virgins. There would be a few less cretins in the world and a few more millions for him.

Chapter 12

Jim was confused. The address on The Highway Sebastian Fuch-Smith had given him was not a restaurant called 'Chez Moi' at all. It looked like an everyday block of flash flats. He peered at the scrap of paper on which he had written the address and it made sense: 46, 125 The Highway. It hadn't looked right to him the first time round but now it did. It must be Flat 46. He'd thought it weird, Fuch-Smith calling his apartment a name like Chez Moi. A house got a name but not a flat. What did it mean anyway? He pressed the intercom of Flat 46. Maybe he'd fucked up and got the wrong address.

Jim waited what seemed like a long time. Then there was an electric clunking noise and a grating sound, followed by a muffled female voice: 'Eeeble squerble berble ick OK?' it seemed to say.

'It's Jim,' he said to the mouthpiece.

The intercom gave a garbled exclamation, followed quickly by a horrible honk. The door buzzed. He pushed it, pulled and pushed it again, and suddenly it obeyed him and opened.

There followed a clatter-clunk as the intercom was hung up.

He'd never been into one of the expensive Dockland blocks before and looked around inquisitively. They had once been derelict warehousing and before that the pulsating heart of maritime London, filled with goods from all over the world. Docklands had been a rough, tough part of town then, the original place where coppers had always gone round in pairs and sometimes threes. The area had been a nest of crime, violence and prostitution, all sorts drawn to the docks by easy pickings and the exaggerated behaviour of the sailors who fetched up there paid and desperate to live it up.

There was not a spot of dust, litter or damage inside the building: it was just like the bank – picture perfect. The lift was carpeted and mirrored. It spoke when the doors closed and again when they opened. He walked down the quiet decorated corridor to the door marked 46 and pressed the bell. There was a chime, the sort you never heard any more except at the next-door old lady's flat. 'Bing bong,' it went, just as if the vicar was going to appear, all teeth and smiles.

Instead there was a rattle, the door opened and a tall, beautiful, black-haired woman stood before him. She smiled. 'Jim,' she said, 'do come in. I've been dying to meet you. Sebby's not here but, by God, he's meant to be.' An enormous smile flashed across her face. 'Not to worry.'

He stepped over the threshold. The place didn't look furnished. There was no carpet and not much stuff around. He felt he must be leaving dirty footmarks on the wooden floors and heard the boards creaking as he followed her.

'Up here,' she said, climbing a flight of stairs.

He went up into an enormous living room, great plate-glass windows on one side looking out over a panorama of the river. The Thames was no stranger to him, but he immediately fell in love with the view. 'It's beautiful,' he said, watching the waters at full tide rush past from left to right.

'Isn't it?' she said. 'Isn't it just? Would you like a beer? Or a glass of champagne? A Kir maybe.'

Kir? If he took that she might think he knew what it was.

He hesitated. 'Tough choice.' He smiled. 'I'll have a beer, thanks.'

'Stella, Bud, Grolsch?'

'Bud.'

There was a clunk downstairs.

'Ah,' she said, 'that'll be Seb.'

Jim turned in time to see Fuch-Smith enter the room.

'Hello there,' he said, 'sorry, I was detained – Jem's fault, of course. Had to deal with her Merc at the garage. Why she can't tell them what's what I *do* not know.'

'You're so much better at it, darling. As a man you can bluff so much more convincingly.'

'Fat lot of good that did,' he said. 'They're still adamant that the engine needs a new head. All under warranty, of course, but even so, sounds like nonsense to me.'

'What do you drive?' she asked Jim.

'Don't have a car,' he said. 'I walk.'

'You can't possibly walk everywhere,' she said, laughing,

He shrugged. 'Everywhere I need to go.'

'Mix me a Campari and soda, will you, sweetie?' said Fuch-Smith, breaking the flow of the conversation. 'It's the least you can do, having inflicted those oily car people on me.' He slumped onto a white lounger as Jemima gave Jim his bottle of beer. He'd been kind of expecting a glass, but obviously this was the way it came in this world.

'No real need for a car in London,' Fuch-Smith said, bolstering Jim. 'More trouble than they're worth. If we didn't have to zip back and forth to the country we wouldn't bother either.'

'Got nowhere to put a car,' Jim said, going to a chair and sitting.

'Parking!' exclaimed his boss. 'What a complete nightmare.'

Jemima returned with drinks for herself and her fiancé and sat down next to Fuch-Smith. 'So,' she began, 'tell me all about yourself.'

Jim was trying not to admire the tanned legs poking out from beneath her black cocktail dress too obviously. 'Not much to say,' he said lamely.

'Do you shoot?' she asked.

'Shoot?'

'Pheasants? Clay pigeons?'

'I don't think Mob– er, Jim's a shotgun man, are you, Jim?'

'No,' he said, 'never.'

'Well, you need to take him, Seb, get his eye in.'

Fuch-Smith swallowed a mouthful of Campari. 'Not a bad idea. What do you think, Jim?'

'Why not?' said Jim. 'Though I'm not sure I'm keen on the idea of killing things.'

'We could all shoot clays,' said Jemima. 'That's much more fun. And much less fuss.'

'Fancy a spot of Indian in Brick Lane?' suggested Fuch-Smith.

'Always on for a curry.'

'Jolly good. That's a hole in one, then.'

Jemima stood up. 'I'd better go and dress down.'

So that was how it was for those kind of people, he thought. That was how they lived, with confidence, oozing charm. They floated through the world like they owned it. Well, they did own it in many ways – in fact, in every way. Their feet didn't touch the same earth his feet trudged. They were as much at home with the view of the Thames as they were with a pint of cheap lager in a dodgy curry house somewhere down a dark alley. He was handsome and smart; she was beautiful and fascinatingly sexy. He felt like a monkey on a stick, squeaking in front of royalty.

He had a wad of twenty-pound notes and a cash card in his pocket while Fuch-Smith flashed a black Amex that practically made the waiter drop his card machine. He felt cowed and freakish. He *was* a freak – by anyone's standards. He'd been a freak at school, he was a freak at work and a freak at home; his life was as freakish as any circus pinhead's. He had to change that. He had to break that trend.

There was absolutely no reason why he couldn't. He had all the money in the world, so there was nowhere he couldn't go, no one he couldn't impress with stories of trading at a big bank, almost nothing he couldn't buy. He stared at the fluorescent stars painted on his bedroom ceiling. First thing to do was to leave home, do what any normal man would do: pack his bags and ship out into the world.

He was Moby, the big white whale, the man who made billions in a day, the trader who had saved the stock exchange from imploding, the only person who could look into the charts and see the future. He was the guy who came and went as he liked in an organization so tight that anything within a hundred metres of its arsehole got sucked in, never to be seen again. He was grinding his teeth. If he couldn't climb the real ladder of life, he'd be the most pathetic monkey there ever was.

Dr Ali Muhammad had made a decision. 11 9 11 – or, as the Americans would call it, 9 11 11, would be his final move. One big plan, then he'd be gone. The family would be OK – they'd never know what had happened and they wouldn't want for money. He'd go to ground for a few quiet years, then ease his way back into a normal life. The idea of a normal life appealed to him now. How good would it feel not to sit on a time bomb of his own making?

He was the banker to a group of maniacs, and some of the cleverest people in the world were looking for the money he hid for them. It was only because he was so much smarter that he kept ahead of the game, but accidents could happen …

Now it was time to plan his exit, but first he'd make the money disintegrate, then crystallize out into his new life. This time, though, when 11 9 11 came he'd have to make certain there was no magical rally, ensure the market dumped like never before – and he'd come up with a cute plan. It meant risking himself a little with a couple of people, but they were very highly regarded and proven. Pretty soon the stratagem would fall into place. He felt a certain excited anticipation as the days passed, one slow moment at a time. 11 9 11 would quite possibly be the biggest crash of all time.

Chapter 13

Jim was irritated: every time he clicked his mouse or typed in an order there was a certain stickiness to the entry. He was sure it hadn't been there before and it wasn't on his other machine. It was like having a shred of meat caught between his teeth.

The traders were coming to him with their charts and he was scrawling a line on their printouts as he traded. Some thought he was a wizard while others clearly considered him an arrogant shit. He wasn't always right, but he was right enough for them to keep coming back for their five seconds of his attention.

'Fuck, fuck, fuck!' he shouted, throwing his keyboard across the desk. 'The fucking thing's not working properly.'

'I'll get IT down here,' said Nipper. 'They'll fix it when you're in the gym.'

'Thanks,' he said, feeling like a petulant kid. 'How are you meant to trade with all these interruptions and glitches?' He took Dirk's inflation chart and squinted at it. 'Jesus,' he said. 'Nothing much here.' He did a scribble on it representing the next three years' impact of European monetary policy.

'No,' said Dirk. 'Looks pretty dramatic to me. Bird flu strikes at last. A small comet hits Moscow. The euro gets swapped out for the lira. That might do it.'

Jim scowled. 'I never said I knew anything about economic shit.'

Dirk shrugged. 'Well, I'll get some tinned food in anyway and load up a few mil of those fucked-up options that seem to come in handy in this parallel reality.'

'You do that,' said Jim. 'Someone's got to buy them.'

Dirk turned away, muttering to himself.

'Right, I'm off,' said Jim.

'You're weird,' said Nipper.

'I know,' said Jim.

It was eleven and the market was about to shake its fat sluggish arse for about thirty minutes. Oil was going through $220 a barrel and equities looked like they were going to roll over, then rally.

'This fucking keyboard still isn't right.' He opened a notepad and hammered in some random characters. There seemed to be a tiny off-putting lag.

'Five three one two,' said Nipper, and flipped him an antacid.

Jim banged in the extension number. 'Moby here. My fucking computer's up Shit Creek and the markets are about to buck all over the place in an almighty clusterfuck and I'm going to miss a bar.'

'I'm sending someone right up.'

'Make sure they're senior.'

'The shift chief'll be on his way in thirty seconds.'

He slammed the phone down. Almost satisfactory, he thought.

The IT shift chief laboured over the machine, mumbling that it seemed perfectly all right to him. He had logged in as 'administrator' and was busily, apparently futilely, poking about at random within the software innards of the machine.

Jim was pacing up and down the aisle, grinding his teeth.

Dirk looked up from his screens and grinned. 'OK, Mr Hyper-Stagflation, want me to fix your computer?'

Jim stopped. 'Sure, absolutely.'

'I'll trade it for a proper time-slice of your famous whale-sized brain on my charts.'

'Deal.'

'Right. Pay attention. This is how it's done.' He rose from his chair. 'Follow me.' He walked to Jim's desk and tapped the IT wonk on the shoulder. 'Excuse me, my good man. I have the solution you need.'

The engineer swivelled in his chair. 'What is it?'

Dirk smiled politely. 'Take the fucking machine out and bring the good Moby a new one. No dicking around. Just take it out now and get a new machine. We've already lost more profit than could have bought two hundred of these things and a few years of your time, so get down on your knees, unplug the computer and take it away.'

'Oh, I can't do that,' said the engineer, insulted to his nerd core. 'It's not that simple. These machines are individually tied to the network. You can't simply unplug them.'

'Let me show you how.' Dirk got onto his knees and crawled under the desk.

The engineer looked at Moby, the trading legend, and was at a loss as to what to do.

Suddenly there was a sharp clunk on the desk and a curse from Dirk, who had banged his head. He was reversing out of the cavity, swearing. He stood up and grabbed the engineer by the arm, dragging him out of the chair. 'I want you off the floor right away,' he said, his face bright red.

'But,' said the engineer, mind clearly boggling at the unexpected display of aggression and insanity, 'what about the machine?'

'No,' said Dirk. 'Off the floor now. Right now! Go, go,

go!' He pointed down the aisle to the main door. 'Get going this second, before I decide to thump you.' He grabbed the engineer by the elbow. 'Let me show you the way.'

Everyone was staring.

The IT shift chief tore his arm away from Dirk. 'Fuck you! You're in trouble for this.' He stormed off.

'I don't think so,' said Dirk, darkly.

Jim was utterly confused.

'We've got to get Fuck,' Dirk announced.

He was already on his way over.

'Ah,' said Dirk. 'There he is. Follow me.' He marched towards Fuch-Smith, who was looking as perplexed as Jim felt.

'What the blazes?' he exclaimed, as they came within earshot.

'Meeting room,' said Dirk. He ploughed on, and Fuch-Smith followed.

Dirk burst into the room and as soon as Jim and Fuch-Smith entered he slammed the door behind them. 'There's a fucking key logger on Moby's machine.'

'What?' said Fuch-Smith.

'What?' said Jim.

'A fucking key logger.' He gazed into their confounded faces. 'A key logger. Something that logs the keystrokes of the person typing stuff into his computer.'

Fuch-Smith looked at Jim, then at Dirk. 'OK, give me more,' he said.

'Everything Moby's typing is being recorded. Normally key loggers are bits of software but this one's like a little plug that fits between his keyboard plug and his computer.'

'OK, go on.'

Dirk put his hands on his hips. 'So, since when isn't our stuff logged by the wankers in IT anyway? Everything's already logged, right? Half the software running on our kit is recording what we do, so why the fuck is this rinky-dinky key logger plugged into the back of Moby's machine?'

Jim had gone white. 'So that's why my input was lagging?'

'Probably.'

'But it only started today.'

Fuch-Smith was white too now. 'I'll get onto Security,' he said. 'Gracious! Great job, Dirk! This is really worrying.'

'I'm going off site,' said Jim. 'No point me staring at my screens if I can't trade.' He grimaced. 'Move me to another desk or something, but I can't trade on that lagging machine.'

'Right,' said Fuch-Smith. 'Didn't realize you were so sensitive.'

'Sensitive? Bollocks! I'll be back for the US open.'

Fuch-Smith nodded. 'Quite right – and meanwhile I'll get to the bottom of this.'

There were a hell of a lot of estate agents along the waterfront in Wapping. With housing prices depressed for the last two years they were pleased to see Jim and even more so when he told them he was looking for something at about a million.

There was something about the slick but aggressive salesmanship of the agents that gave him a queasy feeling of uncertainty about moving. It was clear to him that the market would sink a long way further, so his thoughts turned to renting.

Soon he was looking out on the Thames in the empty living room of a show flat. He turned to the pretty young estate agent. 'What sort of place do you get for ten grand a month rent around here?'

She seemed a little startled. 'Oh, a bloody palace,' she said. 'You're looking at a couple of mil plus kind of pad.'

'Really?' he said. 'Do you do that kind of thing?'

'Yah,' she said, 'if that's what you're after.'

'Not sure,' he said. 'I'm a trader by profession and it feels that things might go belly up in property, so maybe renting might be the way to go.'

'Trading at Canary Wharf?' she enquired.

He was warmed by her attention. 'Yes, prop trading.'

'Had a good year?'

'Blowout.'

'Wow,' she said. 'That's great.'

'Renting would be good because you never know, do you?'

She nodded.

'Might not be so great next year,' he continued, 'or I might get moved to Tokyo.'

'Quite,' she said, smiling at him. 'Where do you live now?'

'The Causeway.'

'Up on the river?'

'No,' he said. 'Back off from there.'

'Oh, right,' she said, trying to imagine where that might be and coming up blank.

Jim looked at his watch, which flashed as he pulled it out from under his cuff. 'Got to be heading back,' he said. 'I can come in tomorrow if you've got some stuff for me to look at.'

'Terrific,' said the agent, eagerly. 'What time?'

'Lunch time?'

'Wonderful.' She grinned. 'Fantastic. I'll put together rentals between ten and fifteen K a month. Furnished or unfurnished?'

'Furnished.'

'Right you are.'

Why was she staring at him funny? he wondered. Had he done or said something stupid?

When he got back to the office he found he'd been moved to another desk; now he was sitting to the right of Nipper, not to his left. They'd set up the desk just like before and his old station was untouched.

He traded the US open, then went to see Fuch-Smith.

'So, what's it all about, Seb?' he asked.

Fuch-Smith looked troubled. 'It's very strange,' he said. 'There's three of the bloody things around the floor and I'm not sure exactly what we plan to do about it. I mean, we log everything already. There's no way we'd let anyone make a single entry or message without having records in triplicate, backed up and off-sited. I wouldn't be surprised if they don't have a thermometer in the chairs just so they know what temperature our bums are at. So that means it's not us – or, rather, it's not an official thing.'

'Which means it's someone else.'

Fuch-Smith nodded. 'But none of us would give a tinker's cuss what another was doing. If we wanted to know we'd just ask. OK, so you might get passwords to trading accounts this way, but they're locked to machines and, anyway, I can't see any of us caring about it, can you?'

Jim shook his head. 'I could trade from anyone's account whenever I liked. Hardly anyone logs off when they take a break. And I must have half the floor's passwords in my head and the other half are on Post-it notes on monitors. It's not as if they're particularly secret.'

'You must have a good memory. I can hardly remember my own.'

'It's orangepeel7.'

Fuch-Smith coughed slightly.

Jim shrugged. 'That kind of thing just gets sucked up in my brain.'

'We've been told to leave the loggers attached until further notice. They'll put you back at your old desk tomorrow and hook it up so you have your old set-up but the bugged machine isn't actually on the network. It'll be a kind of deception. Frankly, I don't know what they're playing at. I'd rip the bloody things out if I was them. Some silly ploy by Security. It's their chance to play at being policemen again, I suppose.'

'I was wondering,' said Jim, 'whether this might be to do with "the big day".'

Fuch-Smith raised his eyebrows. 'Why?'

'Well, something's been bothering me that I don't understand and this kind of feels connected.'

'How so?'

'We supported the market on the day, and when I'd thought a bit, I couldn't see why we would. I mean we trade, right, we don't support anything. We buy, we sell, we don't care why, how or when. Then there was the time when you said about the customer choking. What customer? It's like I don't understand any of it.'

Fuch-Smith screwed up his face as if he was sucking a lemon. 'Well, what do you need?'

'I don't know,' said Jim. 'Nothing, really. But an explanation of any of it would be nice.'

'First,' said Fuch-Smith, 'I have no clue about this key-logging business. It's all very worrying. Something's wrong but we're onto it and we're going to straighten it out. As far as the support goes, you can have the short answer or the long answer.'

'Give me the short answer first.'

'Well, the short answer is, if there's a terrorist attack, we support the market for the British Treasury. We do that in the same way as other departments might buy sterling or sell euros when the Bank of England wants to support the pound or boost its Forex reserves.

'The customer's idea is that these attacks can only do real damage if they create a loss of integrity in our institutions, of which financial markets are a key component. While the shock of a terrorist attack is brutal, the real effect is minimal unless the outcome is allowed to get out of control. When something nasty happens it's our job to prop up the equity and derivatives market until normality returns.'

A massive grin spread over Jim's face. He'd been working for the government to save Britain from international terrorism. That was overwhelmingly cool. All of a sudden he felt like a hero. 'Is there more?'

Fuch-Smith slumped a little and looked uncomfortable. 'Well, not much really.'

'Go on, spill.'

Fuch-Smith took a deep breath. 'That's all this department is here to do. Well, that's what it was set up for. Prop desks went out of fashion years ago. You simply can't make money playing the markets anymore, not unless you cheat. It's a fifty-fifty game. The only way to make money is to front run orders or insider trade and, funnily enough, that's been illegal for ever. Any prop book that's making money has to be a fluke or a fraud. We are, in effect, the emergency market-support department, "the plunge team".

'I expect, though I don't know, that this is all done to keep cosy with HM Treasury, because of all the other work we do for them, with bonds, advice, privatizations, et cetera. As I understand it, we get our losses underwritten and we get to keep the profits if things go the other way, which isn't a bad deal as things turn out.

'However, we aren't meant to be doing as well as we are, day to day. We're meant to scrape a living and keep out of trouble. It's simply not meant to work the way it is. That's why my predecessor was happy to head for the beach. When prop desks make money there has to be a trick involved, which is bound to come back and bite you on the arse.'

'But we make a ton of money.'

'Yes, we do.'

'And we don't take big arse-biting risks.'

'No, we don't. We're making big money and we're utterly by the book. I know, I check and check. I'm not playing the ostrich, just hoping no one's cheating – I don't want to get fired because of some rogue trader.'

'So what does it all mean?'

Fuch-Smith smiled. 'It means nothing. It means we're doing a great job. In fact a mind-bogglingly great job, and we've got nothing more to do than keep doing what we've been doing.'

'And the logging? There must be a connection, right?'

'Who knows? For now it's just a mystery.'

'It could be anyone, right?'

'I haven't the foggiest idea. Just keep it under your hat – that's the only way we'll get to the bottom of it, if we ever do. And the stuff about support, keep that close to your chest as well. Let's play it cool.'

Jim nodded. 'No problems,' he said. 'I'm as keen on the next Christmas bonus as anyone.'

'Just keep trading away and scribbling on those charts and everything will turn out just fine. It's my job to make sure nothing goes pear-shaped. Well, that's the plan anyway. Trouble is, it's still a long way to 2012.'

'Almost twelve months,' said Jim.

'We'll get there,' said Fuch-Smith.

Chapter 14

Jim flicked through the market charts like a kid through a flip-book. He could see that the January equity markets were going straight up without the slightest pause. It was going to be an old-fashioned bull-market rally. It would be a simple matter just to buy all the big caps with strong charts, sit tight and watch the profits roll in. However, this would freak out the folks who watched risk. What they liked to see were lots of fast trades, not a large static position left to run. Hyperactivity looked safer to their mathematical models: it meant he was on his toes and watching, ready to flee the markets at the first sign of trouble.

The old trader maxim was that making money in the markets was like running in front of an oncoming steam roller to pick up a dollar bill. One stumble and you'd be crushed, yet as long as you were fast, focused and fit, you could scamper to safety. Standing in the middle of the street and waiting was a recipe for disaster, or so the thinking went. However, if you knew nothing would come down the road for days, you could just wait there and collect the money without any dashing about. The trouble is you couldn't know what was around the corner, so staying put was a lazy, greedy, high-risk bet, anathema to the trading management. It wasn't trading, after all, it was investing, the game for boring old fund managers with a slick line in patter.

Survival in the short term was more important than fat

medium-term profits, so when Jim looked at the charts for January, his only option was to trade the upcoming rally as a series of short-term swings rather than as a Napoleonic long-term strategy. That would keep everyone happy.

'Drop by my office at 10.45 tomorrow,' said the email from Fuch-Smith.

That sounds ominous, thought Jim.

Dr Ali Muhammad had sat in the place before. It was a hot, sun-blasted hilltop overlooking a brown land punctuated by patches of stressed green cultivation. Above, the sky was bright blue and the sun was blinding. He peered out onto the flat featureless valley below. To his left large stands of cedars flanked the slopes, and in the far, hazy distance another range of hills seemed ghostly and forbidding. The landscape echoed with a forlorn resonance as if soaked in untold pain and suffering. There was no beauty for miles, just exhausted, worn-out, blighted countryside, scarred and ground down by millennia of habitation. The very hill itself seemed composed of the rocky compost of aeons of human life. As untold generations had built and bred, smashed, broken and buried, so the remains had risen up from the valley to become a hill. Then the hill had grown in importance and was considered a mountain in the flat, featureless landscape below.

As he watched, he saw the human creatures crawl over the denuded land, every stone valued, every clod of exhausted earth delivering a little bread to sustain their tenuous lives. That mouthful might make the difference between life and death to one of their children. No one was a friend when such worthless things could be so precious. Every animal, every bird, every insect was a deadly enemy to be killed and, better still, eaten.

This was the real world, the world of old; the world only recently vanished in the flabby spoiled West. Flabby was good. The flabby ways of the West allowed him not to care about such things as food, clothing and shelter. While, obscenely, thousands died each day from a lack of nutrition, his acquaintances moaned about the difference in quality between farmed and wild salmon. They considered such issues suffering because they lived without kings and holy men.

The Sheikh sat down beside him, so much smaller than he was in real life.

'We must roll the world back to an earlier age. We cannot win it back if it is to spin further into the materialistic life of machines and computers.'

Ali turned to him. 'Why so?'

'Because modern life is against God. Embracing modernity is embracing Satan. There are no machines in any holy book. No electricity, no cell phone, no aeroplanes, no antibiotics, no kidney transplants, no iPod, camcorder, internet, tractor, nitrogen fertilizer. As these ungodly things have arisen, so has our empire fallen. Let me ask you this. Who is closer to God, a peasant starving in his field or a fat businessman like you in his two-thousand-dollar suit?'

Ali looked at his feet. 'But surely you're not suggesting the struggle is hopeless?'

'But of course not,' came the reply. 'We must roll back the world, and when we have, things will return to their natural balance. The world is ripe for it. The seas are rising, storms wreak devastation. The modern world is destroying the very earth it lives on. The system is ready to fall under its own weight, and when it does, it will come crashing down in a mighty avalanche that will sweep everything away. We need only strike a holy blow that sets the first boulder rolling towards the precipice.

'Did you know that a shout can start an avalanche? In certain places in Switzerland you are cautioned to be silent so that a mere cry does not make the mountain shed its load into the valley below.

'We live in the times of the holy avalanche, and we shall shout so loudly that the face of the mountain will crack, collapse, and all will be swept before it. Then, and only then, will we rise, when the earth has been cleansed of its ungodly filth.'

Ali looked out over the desolate plain. 'But surely we will all perish?'

'We shall all perish soon enough, but we will be welcomed in heaven, martyr or not. For after this apocalypse the world will be reborn fresh and it will be beautiful, renewed.' The dwarfish Sheikh stood up, and grew tall. He held out his arms. 'When Rome fell it made way for the true faith and we conquered the world. Yet the world corrupted, so we fell from grace and the ways of evil took hold. Science progressed, and the world swelled and bloated like a diseased body.

'But as with all diseases, be they from Rome or Athens or Washington, they cannot be sustained for ever by the body of the earth. They must kill the body they live on and perish alongside its corpse.

'And we will hasten that day and you, my faithful follower, have helped bring it forward. It is now at hand. For that I embrace you.'

Ali stood up and let the towering Sheikh enfold him in a giant bear-hug. He felt the giant's breath on the back of his neck, then a sudden rush of heat. He felt teeth bite into him and a great overpowering pain overcome him as his flesh tore, the huge brute bearing down on him crushing his body under its weight.

'No!' came his muffled scream. 'No!'

Now Ali knew he had been dreaming and struggled to force himself into consciousness. 'Awake! Awake!' he shrieked in pain. He groaned and rolled over, then opened his eyes. His bedroom was dark but he sensed the not inconsiderable bulk of his wife beside him and heard the faint whistle of her breath.

He had never had nightmares before the trip to Pakistan. No matter the risks, no matter the calumny of the conspiracy he was involved in, no matter the money to be gained or lost, he had always slept soundly. Now hardly a night went past without a visit from the Sheikh.

The message was always the same. The Sheikh was going to wipe the slate clean. If there was more to his dreams than simple anxiety, it could mean only one thing. They really had concocted some kind of nuclear attack.

Jim was crunching a Rennie as he entered Fuch-Smith's office.

'Thanks for coming,' said his boss.

'No problem,' said Jim, casting an eye at the young woman sitting in front of Fuch-Smith's desk.

'This is Sarah Newman, a new intern,' said Fuch-Smith. 'She'll be with us for a couple of months.'

'Hello,' he said clumsily.

Sarah Newman was wearing a huge beaming grin. She jumped up eagerly and offered her hand, her blonde fringe flicking as they shook. She seemed to bob up and down like a badly animated computer character. 'Nice to meet you,' she said.

Jim looked at Fuch-Smith. 'Eh, well, I'll come back later when you're free.'

'No, no, you're meant to be here.'

Jim looked at him doubtfully.

'Sarah's going to be doing some shadowing. It's for her economics doctorate.'

'Right,' said Jim, even more doubtful now. 'Shadowing?'

'It'll be fascinating.' said Sarah, enthusiastically.

'Fascinating?' said Jim, fixing Fuch-Smith with a gimlet stare.

'Yes, I'm sure, and Sarah won't cause you any bother.'

'Bother?' He looked at the short, idiotically grinning blonde. 'I'm not being shadowed,' he said truculently.

The expression on Sarah's face switched from grinning enthusiasm to desperation.

'No, it's OK, Jim, there won't be any problems.' Fuch-Smith gave Jim a piercing look. 'You understand? There won't be any problems.'

Jim's shoulders slumped. 'Well, as long as you don't actually expect me to do my job, then I suppose it's fine. You know that if I'm not comfortable I don't trade. It's that simple. And if I can't see the team's charts clearly I'm not going to be drawing them any lines. It's that simple too.'

Sarah was smiling again, submissively this time.

'Look,' Jim said to her, 'it's nothing personal. It's just if I can't focus, I can't operate. It really doesn't take much to ripple the water, and having you next to me all day is liable to throw the whole thing right off.'

'Don't be a diva,' said Fuch-Smith.

When he wasn't Moby he was a diva. Jim hated that. 'Look, you're all constantly telling me I'm a diva, so you must be right and if I stop producing like a diva don't come moaning to me, OK?'

'Well, that's settled, then,' said Fuch-Smith. 'I won't moan if you stop producing.'

Jim sighed. He looked at Sarah, who was all puppy grins again. 'You're going to be a very expensive intern but, hey …'

When he returned to his desk with Sarah in tow a new chair was already in place. This didn't please him. She sat down. 'I really hope you don't mind me intruding on you like this,' she said, with an assumption of automatic forgiveness.

Jim had a vision of his old boss, Frank, exploding. Frank would have leapt from his seat and screamed into her face with a stream of spittle and obscenity. She would have learnt a whole new set of joined-up concepts, all of which amounted to her being very unwelcome indeed. She was, in the final analysis, the lowest form of life on the floor, an imposition, a spy, a worthless sack of irritation.

He breathed in. 'Well, actually, I do mind a bloody great deal. You probably don't understand so let me explain. See that?' He pointed to the screen, 'That is Vodafone, one of the big fuck-off shares in the FTSE. It could trade a billion shares today. Two hundred p times a billion is two billion quid. That's quite a lot of cash. See the offer there?' He pointed at the screen where a list of numbers flashed different colours as traders bought and sold. 'It's the right-hand side of the screen. That's about five million shares for sale at two quid – that's roughly ten million pounds. See this chart.' He pointed to the right of the screen. 'That says it's about to go up a fair bit, or it does to me. So I buy that ten million quid's worth of shares.' He made a couple of clicks and two million disappeared off the total on that column. 'Now I'm ten million quid long of Vodafone because I looked at the chart and decided it'll go up. Now the chart says it's going up so here you go.' He clicked. 'I put ten million pounds' worth of orders on the bid.' A two-million share order appeared on the left column waiting in a queue for someone to sell. 'So now I've got ten mil long and an order for another ten mil if someone wants to give it to me. I could be right, I could be wrong, but there it is.'

'You're not really ten million pounds long, are you?' she asked, blinking and grinning nervously.

'Absolutely. With you sat next to me I've gone ten mil, maybe shortly twenty mil long.' There was a ringing sound from the computer. 'There you go, now it's twenty.'

'Right,' she said quietly.

'Now, normally I'd do this all day long, and by about four p.m., give or take, I'll be knackered but up two hundred and fifty grand. Two hundred and fifty K, day in, day out, which was roughly fifty mil up last year, click-click-click. But now there's something different, namely you, sat there staring at me, and somehow I've got to carry on in my merry way unaffected.'

'Sorry,' she said.

'Well, sorry's cheap. You see, I can simply stop and sit on my hands or I can trade and lose money or I can trade and hope you're not putting me off. But that's three possibilities, of which two are bad. Let's say you sit here for a month. That's four million less profit I make if I just do nothing. That's four million the firm's worse off.'

'Gosh, that's a lot.'

'But that ain't all. Five to ten per cent of that is my bonus, so let's say a quarter of a mil off my pay cheque.'

She had turned bright red.

The chart ticked up and they both looked at it. Then the chart ticked up again – and again and again.

'Fuck,' he said, peering at the big letter A flashing red on the chart. A stood for Announcement. There was news on Vodafone. He opened the article. Vodafone had said things were looking great in Poland and Turkey. 'In this instance we're going to make a lot of money.' He scowled.

'Don't argue with Lady Luck.' Nipper handed him a packet of Zantac. He popped out a tiny pink trapezium.

Sarah looked at Nipper enquiringly.

'Don't worry about it,' he said. 'It's the antidote to the acid lifestyle.' He flashed the packet. 'If you're not on it, you're not in it.'

She nodded enthusiastically. Then, she turned to Jim. 'Am I OK now, then?' she said, in a matronly tone. 'Am I allowed to exist and breathe your air?'

'Time will tell,' he said, watching the chart stab upwards. He put orders to sell in a penny higher, saw the price march up to it and munch through his stock. There was a ping from his machine: the sound of closure signalling victory.

'How much did we make?' she said.

'I made,' he grumbled, 'about three hundred K.'

'Phew,' she said blowing her blonde fringe up. 'That's pretty amazing.'

Vodafone was pulling back from its spike upwards. 'It could be better, it could be worse,' he muttered, reminding himself of Dirk.

It was a very good trading session indeed. The market had decided to go up in not only a straight line but also in a big leap. The FTSE had jumped a full ninety points, a rare move in an hour, and one that had him banking his whole week's profit. He felt the market was taking the piss out of him. There he was feeling utterly hacked off to have an audience and the market was going his way as if it wanted to give him no excuse to get rid of her.

He was flat and watching the clock when it hit midday, and the moment the second-hand crossed into afternoon he got up to head for the lift and lunch. Sarah got up too.

'Does shadowing include going to lunch with me?' he asked grumpily.

'Yes, if you don't mind.'

He took a breath to speak but swallowed the words and looked at her mutely.

'Jolly good,' she said, swishing her fringe.

He traipsed to the cafeteria, a luxury affair by any standards. If you wanted Parma ham and figs it would probably be waiting. Jim picked bangers and mash with thin, tasty gravy on, and a Coke. Sarah selected Caesar salad and a bottle of San Pellegrino.

They sat down at a table in the corner, the huge windows affording a fabulous view of London. It was a clear day so they could survey all of London – from Crystal Palace to Alexandra Palace, Heathrow to Waltham Cross – from their eyrie.

'I'm sorry you don't like me around,' she said, as he gazed out at London, 'but it's something I want to do – something I have to do. I hope you understand.'

'What exactly is it you're studying?'

'I'm doing a doctorate in economics. It's on the causality of trading and the macro-economic cycle.'

'Aha,' he said.

'Where did you get your degree?' she asked.

'Tesco,' he replied. 'What university are you at?'

She hesitated for a minute. 'Cambridge,' she said. 'Jesus College.'

'So what are you doing here?'

'Well,' she said, getting all bouncy again, 'this is the real thing, isn't it? It's not some dry old prof talking about stuff he's never done. This is the actual thing in action.'

'I suppose, but you know ...' He trailed off.

She leant forwards. 'Go on.'

'Nothing,' he said.

'No – do say.'

'There's nothing much to see here. You buy, you sell, sometimes you win, sometimes you lose.'

'Tosh,' she said, laughing. 'That's not what I just saw. You just made four profits for every loss. Now that's kind of impressive, if you ask me, and just the sort of thing I want to know all about.'

'Luck,' he said, 'just luck. You know the story. It's all random. Sometimes you have a good streak, sometimes a bad. The FTSE went up ninety points in an hour – how are you meant to lose money?'

'It's all new to me,' she said, munching lettuce, 'and fantastic material.'

'Fine,' he said, 'so long as the tables don't turn, and you can stay quiet.'

'I'll try,' she said, smiling her bloody irritating smile. 'I really will.'

Humph, he thought.

Chapter 15

Oh, yes. Jim walked into the long lounge. This is the one. He turned to the estate agent. The simpering girl had been replaced by the senior agent, a bejewelled over-coiffured older woman with a hard eye and quivering lips. 'How much is this one again?'

'Twenty thousand a month, but I think if you were to make a quick offer we could get the owner down to eighteen.'

He stepped away from her and went to the window to look down on the river. Eighteen thousand a month was one hell of a lot of money but it was one hell of a view. He watched the river flow along at low tide. This was the stretch where pirates had been put into cages and drowned as the tide rose. It was where Judge Jeffreys had held his court: he had sent felons straight from the pub he presided over to the waiting convict ships.

Jim wandered aimlessly around the four bedrooms, the dining room, the flashy kitchen and the study – a bay window and another stunning view. There were two spaces for his non-existent cars in the garage, which had an automatic swing door and vault-like security. This truly was a palace.

And he could knock out a single cheque for a year's rent and not miss the money. It was a weird feeling and he longed to share it with someone. He remembered his nan when she was all there – how amazed, how proud she would have been of him now. She'd have been scared, too, that his success would suddenly vanish. This was the ache he carried in him, the ache that had formed as she struggled to keep it all together on nothing but poorly paid work and state handouts. He had felt it when she winced at prices and counted her pennies.

He walked over to the master-bedroom window. He loved the river, always had: it carried the shit to the sea.

'OK,' he said to the agent, who was waiting, arms folded, for the dithering customer to do the obvious thing and accept the offer. 'If it's eighteen K you're done.'

'There's bits and bats like three months in advance, deposits ...' She waved a hand dismissively. People paying eighteen thousand a month in rent didn't normally sweat the details. 'Just leave it to me.'

'Great.'

With Sarah observing at his right, he had felt even less desire than usual to be at his desk but he was being lucky and coining it as the market rallied and rallied. He knew she wanted to ask, as he scribbled on the stream of charts the team brought to his desk, what he was doing and why, but he didn't let her. The first time she tried he had snapped at her: 'No, I'm not going to explain. It's why I get paid millions a year and, no, I'm not going to teach you how.'

He could tell she got the picture, believing that only a fool would blurt out the secret of making a fortune in trading. The reality was that he had no idea how he did what he did. He looked at a chart, thought he saw what was going to happen next and scribbled it down. He didn't know if it turned out to be right or wrong. All he knew was that they came back for more. If he refused them because he didn't know, it was the low point of their week. He tried not to disappoint.

Having an intruder in his trading life, however, had inspired him to get his personal affairs in order. With her haunting his desk he had discovered the impetus to get out of the office and get himself sorted. The flat was going through – and now he was in the firm's wealth-management office, sitting in front of its boss's massive walnut desk.

Wealth Management was a completely different world from the firm's trading floor. The traders' environment was like the inside of a repair garage, with its men, machines and their smelly oils, but Wealth Management was like an exclusive Harley Street clinic. The rich had piles of cash and assets and it was the job of Wealth Management to relieve the stress of administration.

Jules St George made Jim a cup of tea, then placed himself on the other side of his desk. He surveyed the young trader benignly. He was an oversized man, six foot eight, fit and probably built of seasoned oak. He looked his fifty years but seemed solid enough to make his century. He peered from behind half-moon glasses.

'Well,' he said, 'we really only cater to the super-rich, which you understand means those with at least a nine-figure worth. But happily, as we're all in the same family and as you are a favoured member, we can make available to you our advice and services. We're not cheap, you understand, but then we are quite good.' He smiled.

'What I want to do,' said Jim, 'is have my bills looked after and have a way of getting my cash working. I'm a trader, you know, and I should be trading my own account, but right now I don't have any of that stuff set up.'

St George smiled understandingly. 'That shouldn't be a problem. We don't do so much bag-carrying these days, but we still do a fair amount. When some sultan or other shows up in London, we're known to fix matters. Everyone fetches and carries for the ultra-rich, of course, myself included. I shouldn't think administering your affairs will put us to too much trouble. Our masters seem quite happy to take as much weight off your shoulders as possible.' He paused. 'Did you really make us three billion during the tunnel outrage?'

Jim twitched. 'Something like that.'

'Oh, well done,' said St George, and gave a single clap. 'How remarkable. I don't think I've had the pleasure of meeting someone who's made even one billion in a single day. That must be some kind of record.' His face beamed in a kindly-uncle way. 'Now, look here, I'll have the whole thing sorted out by our best people. I'll put them on the scent myself. Simply bag up all the bits of paper you have, pop them in a box and we'll take it from there. Just hand us all the rubbish you have – tax letters, phone bills, bank statements, receipts, anything, and we'll sort out what's what.'

'OK, but it won't be much.'

'Jolly good,' said St George. 'Now, someone you should meet is about to drop in.' He held a finger in the air. 'Hold on one moment.' He pressed a button on his phone. The door behind Jim clicked and someone entered.

Jim looked round.

'Ah, Terence,' said St George, 'meet James Evans.'

The thin sandy-haired man looked at Jim like someone studying a horse on the gallops, evaluating his line and fettle for hints to his form.

'Terence, James – James, Terence Kitson.'

Jim stood up and shook Kitson's hand. 'Nice to meet you.'

Kitson was smiling, his eyes narrow slits. 'Delighted,' he said, his mouth barely moving, his voice strangled somewhere at the back of his throat.

'Terence is my favourite broker in the team. When you want to put a position on, he's your man. Of course, there's a lot more to him than that, but I expect you're a man of your own mind so you probably won't need his full repertoire.'

'I do a fair amount of digging,' said Kitson, his voice dry and wispy, 'and I'll be happy to bring up the occasional opportunities as they come my way.'

'Thanks,' said Jim. 'I think I'm just going to punt big caps, commodities and indices. That's my area and I'm happy to stick with what I know.'

'Very good,' said Kitson. 'Sounds a sensible plan.'

Jim sat down again and Kitson took the beautiful antique chair to the left of him.

St George said, 'Well, I suppose we'll put your risk profile down as high and get on with it.'

'So,' said Kitson, 'what do you think about equities in the next three months?'

'Up,' said Jim. 'After that, no idea.'

'Very good,' said Kitson, the top half of his face screwed up as if he was staring into the sun. He fished out a card from his top pocket. 'Just call me when you need to trade. Are you a time-critical sort of chap or will I have a bit of time to react?'

Jim thought for a second. 'I'm not planning any high-frequency stuff,' he said, 'so I guess there won't be much I'll need instant execution on.'

'Very good,' said Kitson. 'I'm not really one of those brokers, to tell you the truth.' He smiled sheepishly. 'I'm just as likely to be in a jungle somewhere checking out

121

some godforsaken mine as I am to be in the office.'

'That's OK,' said Jim, 'This'll be medium-term stuff, nothing too large – not by house standards anyway.'

'Good,' said St George. 'That's settled, then.'

Kitson leant forward. 'I'm terribly sorry, but I have to ask. Is it true?'

St George interjected, 'Yes, it is.'

Kitson sat back in his chair. 'Well, that's quite something – quite something indeed.'

'Thanks,' said Jim. 'We got lucky.'

'Hum,' said Kitson, smiling like a blind beggar. 'That's not what I hear.'

Jim was like the golden goose, Fuch-Smith mused. As a child he had been annoyed by the fable – surely no one would be stupid enough to kill the golden goose for half an egg. It wasn't a good story, his infant mind had concluded, and it needed to be fixed. The goose had to get away and not be killed, or maybe there needed to be a good master who would look after it and they would live happily ever after on the proceeds. Maybe there could be goslings in the story and everyone could be rich from the endless daily supply of golden eggs. Whoever the storyteller was, he was rotten.

It wasn't until he had grown up that he had seen the story come true.

In many ways the firm was pretty good at rewarding people but time after time he had seen bad management, envy or greed destroy a perfect set-up. Often it was hard to tell who the golden goose was until they were gone. A star performer might rely on a personal assistant for stability or a junior team member. Suddenly, without the invisible support, the goose stopped laying.

Often the loudest people were seen as the valuable

players rather than the quiet people doing all the work, and often it was the big egos rather than the big producers that got the corn, leaving the golden geese to starve.

But Sebastian Fuch-Smith had learnt his lessons well. He knew exactly who his golden goose was and he was going to make sure it got the nurturing necessary to keep dropping those golden eggs and feeding the golden goslings with the right predictions.

He believed that everyone came to one special time in their life when they could get everything they needed for the rest. It was a heavenly gift that all received once. He had seen it with his parents and he had seen it with others. This time came and went, like the moment when bright green leaves burst from hard buds. It was a short exultant passage, the apogee of anyone's life. Now it was his turn.

Everything in his life was aligned and in a few short months all his dreams would come true. If he could keep his golden goose and goslings together, protect them from the predators that were sure to come sniffing, this glorious window of perfection could stay open. He would do everything in his power to make it happen.

As the US market opened Fuch-Smith came to Jim's desk. 'It's all done,' he said, dropping an envelope next to his keyboard.

'Thanks,' said Jim, not looking up from his monitors as the charts began to move and trading started. Absently he opened the envelope. His eyes dropped from the screens and he stared at the key in his hand, with its bright red top and inscrutable shaft of holes, grooves and ridges. He had deleted his old life and was now about to embark on the new.

The firm was always shipping its execs across the world.

When Fuch-Smith had heard he was thinking of moving, he had contacted the department that handled relocations. A small HR team, they saw to it that the bank's top people could beam their lives around the globe at the touch of a button. In effect Jim had told them to put his old life into storage and have the necessary accoutrements of a new life waiting for him a mile down the road.

When he packed, the vital artefacts of his life didn't fill one box. He looked at the half-empty Heinz baked-beans carton and decided to leave that as well. He would start out completely anew. His old life would be parked in a warehouse. His school socks, his old teddy bear, Nan's mincer, the knitted Spanish-dancer toilet-roll cover, the plastic flowers, the soda-water siphon that never had gas in it, the Bush radio, all the bits and pieces that were a mosaic of himself, would be frozen in a cardboard mausoleum and forgotten.

It was like jumping naked into the deep end of a cold swimming-pool, shocking, dreadful yet exhilarating. He examined the key: it was like Alice's cake – it'd make him nine foot tall.

It would be like waking up in someone else's body.

Chapter 16

The buzz of the bedside clock woke him. He sat up and looked across the room to the windows. He hadn't pulled the curtains because he'd wanted to fall asleep in the dark with the view and the lights. Now he could see the dimly lit Thames. The tide was out and much of the foreshore exposed. This was a fine dream he was living.

He fumbled with some buttons at the bedside and the curtains swished together. Then he turned on the lights and jumped out of bed, naked. He walked over to his cupboards and opened them. The first contained three business suits, some sports jackets and slacks. On the floor there was a selection of shoes and hanging on the back of the door some silk ties. In the next cupboard he found shirts, and drawers containing underwear, jumpers, T-shirts, swimming gear, handkerchiefs, gloves, bow ties, cufflinks and various objects whose purpose wasn't immediately clear.

Pants, socks, shirt, suit, he thought, in sleepy summary.

The bathroom had a TV embedded in the wall, which switched on at a panel beside him. The shower he was used to flushed hot and cold, fizzing and sputtering, but this one covered him with a sheet of perfectly warm water. Soon he was catching up on that morning's action in Japan.

Thank you, God, he thought.

He quite enjoyed the morning ritual of scribbling on the team's charts. He felt like a pop star writing autographs.

Very little was said and that was how he preferred it. He either drew a line or shrugged and said he couldn't make anything out. They knew he didn't have to do it so no one gave him any grief. Fuch-Smith would come round occasionally with the odd obscure stock chart, which Jim obligingly drew on. He had the distinct impression that Fuch-Smith's enquiries related to his personal trading, but he didn't care. Whatever it was, it was a quirky trade.

The intern sat next to him all day and didn't say a word. She might make the odd note, or leave the desk now and again, but she made no interruption. Sometimes this felt very strange. At others he thought it an impressive demonstration of self-control, but soon enough he took it for granted and forgot she was there.

Perhaps, he thought, this was how gorillas felt when they were observed by biologists.

Then one afternoon he found himself lost in a large position with the markets suddenly unfathomable and moving against him. He started to close as fast as he could, in a panic that something nasty was about to happen. As he closed the last trade an impulse flashed into his head. It overwhelmed him.

He turned to Sarah. 'Fancy coming out for a drink after work?'

She rocked back in her chair as if he'd punched her. 'No,' she blurted.

'Oh,' he said. He was more confused that he had asked than that she had turned him down. He looked back at the screen.

'I mean,' said Sarah, 'I've got something on tonight.'

'That's OK,' he said, opening up a new chart and peering at it.

She touched his arm. 'Some other time, maybe.'

'Yes.' He wondered what the hell had got into him.

His desk phone rang, which was also unusual. He picked it up.

A polite, high-pitched male voice said, 'Hello, Kitson here. Is that Jim?'

'Yes,' said Jim.

'I have an opportunity for you to consider. Tantalum in Niger. Large prospect with a billion in resource. Second drilling programme under way. Fifty cents Canadian placing with a good chance of the share hitting five dollars Canadian in the next two years. What do you think?'

'Where's it listed?'

'Toronto, but with plans to come to London.'

'Ticker?'

'Ticker code is TNQ on the TSX.'

Jim punched up the chart. 'Fifty cents. Right, I'll take it but dump it at a dollar, OK?'

'OK,' said Kitson. 'Any reason?'

'It'll crash after that.'

There was a silence on the end of the line. Then: 'Well, quite possibly, but it could also go to five dollars.'

Jim was about to disagree but thought better of it. 'OK, but dump it at a dollar.'

'Right. How much should I put you in for?'

'Half a mil.'

'Right you are.'

Jim hung up, realizing he might have said goodbye. Traders hung up like that all the time. 'Goodbye' and 'thank you very much' had dropped from the lexicon. There wasn't time, necessity or energy for pleasantries.

He made a mental note to be polite next time.

Ali Muhammad glanced up from his desk and out of his

study window to Hyde Park. The sun was rising and the light was creeping into an already busy London. He hated the nightmares that plagued him. He hated them more than the implication that he had been told of a nuclear attack plan, whose details were still locked in his amnesiac brain. The possible reality of a nuclear holocaust didn't worry him one jot. It was simply a matter of being somewhere else when it happened. Humans were swarming around the planet like a host of maggots, consuming and defiling anything beautiful, so why should he care if a few million maggots were blotted out? What did it matter if, as in his dream, the world fell back into the Middle Ages? He would do all right. He had already put in place the means to get by. Soon he would move his family to his compound in Canada and there they could sit out anything, cut off and provisioned.

A personal valley with a decade's worth of food didn't cost much in terms of the money he had, and as he always planned ahead, he could disappear when he had to. He could vanish like the boy in the Indian Rope Trick. He had covered all eventualities.

Yet he had been a little lazy, he told himself, as he hadn't prepared to disappear for more than a few years. He hadn't laid down his wealth in a form that would withstand a true biblical apocalypse. A million dollars in gold under the floor, yes, but a significant amount of portable assets? No. The dream was telling him to get out for good and plan for the absolute worst. The prospect of being holed up with his fat, boring wife and spoilt brood appalled him. Greeting the flash and bang of a bomb with open arms might be preferable to incarceration in a wilderness with his family.

He determined to find another nook at the end of the earth. Canada was perfect, his Asian face was no big deal there, and the place was empty, cut off, low key and handy for all things American. It had the good features of the US without the bad, like guns and lawyers, and a determined man could get a long way away from wherever he was located and meet no impediment to his flight. But that wasn't where his mind was dwelling, this grey morning. Instead he was planning how to get his millions out of harm's way.

He had often toyed with the solution to a chronic problem: how to fit fifty million dollars into a briefcase. This might seem a strange thing to want to do, but a rich man on the run has to carry wealth with him – on or about his person. A million dollars in cash is not a manoeuvrable amount. A dollar bill weighs a gram so even a million dollars in hundred-dollar bills is ten kilos. In usable twenty-dollar bills, a million was fifty kilos. That was much more than an overweight, unfit multi-millionaire could carry, let alone run down the street with. Fifty million in twenty-dollar bills would weigh two and a half tonnes.

What was more, cash smelt. Even a kilo of unusable thousand-dollar bills would have sniffer dogs bounding about and barking ecstatically.

A man who had to move fast also had to be able to move lightly. His assets had to go through a metal detector without raising attention; they needed to pass inspection under X-ray. Their owner might indeed need to run down the street with them, which he couldn't if the bag weighed much more than five kilos.

Fifty million dollars weighing five kilos would be a simple matter if financial instruments didn't have a name on them, but share certificates and other such assets would have zero worth if, as a fugitive, you had to fetch up at a bank and declare your identity.

A hundred million dollars as five kilos of anonymous assets would be a big challenge and the problems didn't just stop at hitting the value: weight ratio. What use would a bag of diamonds be at a petrol station in the middle of the Mexican desert? Diamonds, of course, are good, but after you'd shown up more than once with nice ones, someone might be waiting for your return.

The answer was to spread the money. Diamonds were good, and so were rubies and sapphires, and the sizes could go from small to pebble-sized. What was more, they could all be thrown into a tube of children's make-believe jewellery and thus camouflaged.

Stamps were good too, between the leaves of some pulp novel or photo album, or simply in a little brown envelope in one's top jacket pocket, twenty or thirty, ranging in value from a thousand dollars to a million. The small denomination valuables were as precious as the big-value items – they gave easy liquidity. A thousand-dollar item could raise a bacon-saving couple of hundred dollars without raising an eyebrow.

Coins were another favourite. Really valuable ones could look like junk and go discreetly into a coat pocket. With the right choices you could squeeze a few million into what resembled a handful of dirty metal. He had liked the idea of paintings but he had been told that while a small picture didn't show up as interesting in an X-ray, it would call attention to him if he had to open his case for it to be examined.

He decided the risk would be worth taking. He'd roll it up in a plastic bag. And there were watches too. Five Patek Philippes took care of another five million: he could wear one, pop another in his pocket and secrete the others loose in the case. Like coins, old watches could look like rubbish.

They were pretty hard to sell for anything like their real value but antiques dealers were already in the grey zone of rookery, so deals could be done. Then there were practicalities like working phone Sim cards, credit and debit cards loaded with cash but still inscrutable. They all had his name on them but how many Ali Muhammads were there in the world? As far as computers were concerned, there were millions and, if only they knew it, thirty were him. But bank accounts could not be operated, only drawn on, and then in places where you were unlikely to return. There was no telling what would be compromised or when, so such accounts were just caches that risked discovery.

Lastly there was eight thousand dollars in cash, a small enough sum to carry in his coat and below the declarable limit.

Then the briefcase would be filled with the usual businessman's crap of papers, phone, cables, aftershave, a pen and toothbrush. No one would be the wiser that the man travelling light with his wheelie-bag and briefcase was half walking museum and half safe-deposit box. Thus he would make his escape. But not yet … These things would take time to put together.

Chapter 17

Jim felt he had had a hard day. The markets had been brutal and he had narrowly escaped a serious mauling. His vision was as clear as it was on most days, so it was no surprise to him that he felt that there was something particularly bleak about the walk home that evening. The sky was its usual overcast grey, and it was damp, cold and windy.

At the first sight of the river on the Canary Wharf round-about he felt a presence join him. He winced. He was plain Jim walking home: no one would follow him because no one cared who he was.

He winced again: he was Moby, the billion-dollar whale. Everyone cared about him.

He looked around as he turned to go down the slip road to the road below. No one was there except a solitary office worker, like him, stumbling towards home.

The other guy was thin and bald. He walked head down, tired and slouched, wrapped in a heavy coat and scarf.

His image was somehow engraved on the back of Jim's retinas. As he walked, braced against the wind, he could still see the lone figure trudging on behind him. Was the man following him?

He rationalized.

Thousands of men were making their way home at that instant, bowed but determined to reach their own private sanctuary of family and hearth. He, like them, just wanted to get home and slump in front of the TV.

A hundred yards ahead a sharp right turn would take him along the straight route home to his wondrous new flat. He walked round the corner and stopped. He pulled out his mobile and pretended to make a call. He waited.

The man turned the corner and looked up at him as he passed. He had blue eyes that glinted and the hint of a grin. Jim blanked him.

As soon as thirty yards separated them, Jim started to walk again. The man was just like every other person going about his business. Yet as Jim walked he felt a continued unease. On Narrow Street the man went into a pub and Jim walked on.

Jim shook himself. The pressure of work was turning him into a nutcase. Or maybe the miserable winter weather was bringing him down. He imagined how good it would be when spring came and he could walk to work in the soft morning light and stroll home in daylight. Now he had a garage he could buy himself a car and do the test. The idea of driving seemed appealing but with less than a mile to travel to the office it was a faintly ridiculous idea. On the other hand there were weekends: rather than sit at home and surf the net, he could be out and about with a car.

On the other hand by the time Friday came he was ready to put his feet up and slob about.

If only he was one of those always-on types, who packed every minute with activity. They'd jet off to a party, be up late carousing every night. They seemed to have endless energy to burn. Jim couldn't see how they sustained it: by the time the night or weekend came round, he was ready to roll himself into a ball and sleep. How could anyone be boozed up in a nightclub at three a.m. and at work at seven, bright-eyed and alert?

Those hyperactive people must be on drugs, he thought,

but he knew that some were just made that way. They could stare at a screen for hours, but he couldn't do that. They could play all night and work all day, and he couldn't do that either. They could pack their weekends while he was happy to sleep and do his laundry.

It had started to rain in a harassing, irritating way. He tried to pull his coat tighter and walked a little faster. The sooner this shit day was over the better.

The trading floor was quiet at ten p.m. All the US traders were gone and the Japanese hadn't yet shown up. A skeleton crew of dealers that dealt the twenty-four-hour currency or commodity markets were the only figures dotted about. Yet still the lights blazed.

The janitors pushed their carts around the aisles and emptied the baskets of the day's detritus. Newspapers folded at the jobs page or the racing form, fruit peel, polystyrene cups, credit-card statements, bills, junk mail, reams of charts and data; whatever went in the bin during the day was gone by midnight.

The cleaners wore pale blue overalls. It was ordinary protective clothing but so cheap and tawdry that its principal purpose was clearly to define the wearer as barely human. Cleaning this Valhalla was an easy but boring task, not one to exult in: the cleaner was clearly marked as a pair of necessary hands animated by an inexpensive body.

At Jim's station the cleaner bent down and crawled under the desk, as he had a hundred times, to retrieve rogue litter. Hidden in the darkness, he located the keyboard cable of the computer above and quickly removed the small plastic dongle. The thin blue plastic gloves he had to wear served a different purpose as he fumbled around to reconnect the cable. There would be no fingerprints. His heart was racing a little, as it did whenever he was performing the operational part of his job. He felt flushed as he clambered up and started to push his cart again. However many times he executed his little piece of covert labour he always expected someone to be waiting for him when he crawled out. As yet nobody had been, so the game went on.

Jim was not expecting Sarah to be at his desk when he got in but there she was. It was seven o'clock, about half an hour before he would normally roll up. He wasn't going to say anything except good morning, but before he could speak she had fixed him with a sky blue stare. 'Fuch-Smith needs to see you right away.'

Jim blinked at her. 'OK.' He dropped his kit-bag onto his chair and set off. He noticed Sarah was in tow. 'You coming too?'

'Yes,' she said.

He squinted at her, then set off again without a word.

Fuch-Smith sat sullenly at his desk, poking his mouse at his email in-tray. He looked up as Jim came in and let Jim plonk himself down, flanked by Sarah, before he spoke. 'Last night someone tampered with that computer again.'

Jim grimaced. 'So what?'

'On one level, I agree, but on another this is a disaster.'

'It's just some other trader trying to bug me and, frankly, good luck to them.'

'No,' said Sarah, 'it's not that.'

'What's this got to do with her?'

'She's from the customer.'

Jim sat back. 'Oh, the customer … I remember the customer.' He scratched his head. 'What's the customer got to do with it?'

Sarah was looking very senior all of a sudden. 'I'm here to observe the situation,' she said

Jim peered at her. 'And what is the situation?'

'Someone's bugging this floor and we need to find out who and why.'

'And why isn't it just Nipper or Flipper or Dirk trying to log my trades for their private analysis?'

Sarah was gazing at him earnestly. 'Because we have a video of a cleaner under your desk taking the dongle away.'

'A video?' He looked at Fuch-Smith and back at Sarah. 'You've been videoing under my desk?'

'Yes.'

'So there you are,' said Fuch-Smith. 'All very worrying.'

'Let me get this straight. The cleaners are bugging my old machine and the intern is a spy who's videoing my crotch. Did I get that right?'

'Yep,' said Fuch-Smith.

'Anything else?' He directed this at Sarah.

'No,' interjected Fuch-Smith. The two blonds communicated silently.

'So, what's next?' asked Jim, irritated by the telepathic dialogue.

'We wait,' said Sarah, filled with a sudden enthusiasm that set her head bobbing.

'What for?'

Sarah smiled. 'For not very long, I hope.'

'I meant, wait for what?'

'We'll see,' she said, eyes sparkling.

Fuch-Smith seemed not to share her enthusiasm. 'Just pretend nothing's happening, can you, old chap? It'll all blow over, I'm sure.'

Jim peered closely at Fuch-Smith, then smiled. His boss had called him 'old chap'. That was how he addressed his blue-blood friends. It felt like an honour.

'OK,' said Jim, placated. 'Whatever.'

That day, running on the treadmill was hard. His legs felt loaded down and his chest heavy. He had sat for the bulk of his trading period staring at an unfathomable chart, wishing to trade but knowing he had no idea of the moves to come. His co-traders came and were sent away. Nothing seemed to make sense. Then suddenly everything clarified. With ten minutes to go it was clear the market was going to move in a narrow range for a few hours.

'Range bound till one,' he shouted, for anyone who cared to hear. Range bound was no use to him: no moves meant no profit.

He opened his browser and caught up with the news. The Four Horsemen of the Apocalypse were out and about, as they always were, and the famine, war and pestilence made no difference to the markets. Behind every index tick, the whole of the world's endeavours were rolled up into a single number. That number was equivalent to the weight of the earth and it took a big event or a sudden shock to move it by much. When it did move, it moved feverishly, like the shaky hand of an old man trying to feed himself. It was this shake that gave traders an opportunity to profit from second to second movements in the indices but normally so much cash chased the erratic jiggle that it became utterly unpredictable.

Yet when he looked at the chart of the market he saw a predictable transit across the future hours. Stock charts didn't look random to his eye or, for that matter, to anyone else's, so how could they be random, as the textbooks insisted? You could see they had unpredictable elements, but nothing like the kind of movement your mind would recognize as noise.

The white-dot splashes on a signal-free TV looked random – they held no pattern. They could be busy or faint but always featureless. So while he paid lip service to the belief that markets were random, he traded as if they were as regular and predictable as the rise and fall of the tides outside his window.

Whatever the truth of the matter, while the market might not be random, life made up for it with a good impression of randomness. So, whatever was going on under his desk, he'd live with it. For the money he was being paid, they could stick the bugs up his arse.

As he walked home, huddled in his coat, he watched the Mercs, Astons and Porsches of the rich bankers growl by. It was another cold, blustery evening. The high buildings of Canary Wharf funnelled any breeze from a zephyr into a raging Arctic blast that howled for a hundred yards until he dropped down onto Narrow Street into the world of old low-rise buildings. The first part of the walk was familiar: it was his old route home, the way to the life he had left behind.

He always looked at the old tenement building as if expecting to see himself on the walkway going back to his nan. Tonight he felt lonely.

That girl in the estate agents was nice, he thought. He should have said something. What an idiot he was. What about Sarah? She was out of his class, he concluded. And, anyway, who'd want to date a policewoman?

There was no shortage of women at the bank – in fact there were thousands of them – but they were all so high-stepping and thoroughbred. They exuded a professional spiky air, which would fizzle out to be replaced by exag-gerated cooing if they knew who he was. Dating that kind of girl would be more like a dentist's appointment than a night out. What was worse, somewhere in the employee handbook that no one read for fear of finding they were already fired, there was a whole set of rules discouraging fraternization between employees. Even the biggest guns could find themselves out on their ear if they made a pass at the wrong person. Dating was impossible.

As he rounded a corner, his senses prickled. Something was up. Ahead on the other side of the road a blurred bundle of humanity was remonstrating. He focused. An old man was being menaced by a younger, taller one, who'd got him by the collar and was shouting something at him. The old man was wheeling back and forth, his right arm out as if to balance himself or perhaps to launch a feeble punch.

Jim clenched his teeth and set off across the road. 'Hey! Hey!' he called, waving at the pair.

The young guy looked round. He had deep-set eyes in a gaunt, pockmarked, junkie-style face.

Jim was close now. 'What's going on?'

'Get your hands off me!' The old man was trying to yank himself free. 'Let me go.'

Jim walked right up to the attacker, avoiding his direct glare, and spoke to the old man. 'Are you …' he began, his back half turned to the other. He sensed the thug reacting, felt he was about to grab or punch him. He stamped his heel on the assailant's foot. Its owner's leg folded up like a straw.

Jim knew where his right elbow was going, but he was wrong. Rather than connect with the man's jaw, it met the left side of his neck. He spun round with the blow and saw the body fall. Then he turned back to the old man. 'Let's go.'

The old man snapped to attention and began to waddle

down the road with him. Fifty metres and they'd be round the corner out of sight. Jim snatched glances over his shoulder, but no one was coming their way. He'd have to stop to see more and he wasn't about to do that. Around the corner, out of sight of the scene of the fight, there was a pub.

'In here,' gasped his companion. Jim followed.

The old man stopped in the entrance, took a deep breath and stiffened. He pasted on a smile, then pushed through the door calmly. Jim followed. The old man led him around the bar and into a quiet corner. He slumped down and let out a huge sigh. Jim took his coat off and dumped it on the bench beside him. 'You all right?' he asked.

'Sure,' said the old man. 'Thanks to you.' He had an East European accent. 'Thank you so much for your help. I thought I was going to die.'

'No problem,' said Jim, as a sudden wave of shaking crossed his body.

'I am Max,' said the old man, 'and you are?'

'Moby,' said Jim. 'I mean Jim.' He laughed. 'It's Jim. Moby's just a stupid nickname.'

'Very nice and most fortunate to meet you, Jim,' said Max, holding out a quaking hand.

Jim shook it. 'Nice to meet you too. Who was that guy?'

Max looked sour. 'Some filthy Nazi thug. The world is full of them, even today.'

'Was he mugging you?'

'Yes,' said Max bristling.

Jim felt relieved: the faint possibility that he had misread the situation had crept into his mind. 'That's what I thought.'

'It is hard being old,' said Max. 'When I was young I would have torn his head off. Now,' he shrugged, 'I am little more than a lamb to the slaughter.'

'Get you a drink?'

'No, I get you this.'

'No,' said Jim, 'you sit there and I'll get them in.'

Max fished in his pocket and pulled out a note. 'At least let me pay. I will have a cognac.' He handed Jim a fifty-pound note.

'Wow, a big one,' said Jim, taking it.

'I am sorry, but it is all I have.'

'No problem.'

Jim came back with the glasses and dumped the change awkwardly on the table. 'They don't like ponies,' he said, sitting down.

'Ponies?'

'Fifties. Too many printed by private enterprise around here.' He grinned.

'I see,' said Max. 'Anyway,' he raised his double brandy, 'here is to my rescuer. May the gods of justice repay you tenfold.'

'Thanks,' said Jim, unsure whether or not to toast himself. Eventually he waved his pint glass and said, 'Here's to the downfall of all Nazi thugs.'

'Absolutely,' concurred Max.

'I'm starting to worry now,' said Jim. 'What if I really injured that guy? You know you can die if you get knocked out.'

'Phah,' said Max. 'The world would be a better place.'

'Maybe,' said Jim, 'but I don't want to go to prison – and for that matter I don't want to kill anyone either.'

Max smiled apologetically. 'You see, now I am angry, I want to kill that man with my own hands. Forgive me – I am not a bad person.'

'No,' said Jim, 'of course not. I understand. I'm as shook

141

up as you.' He held out his hand, which was quivering. He laughed. 'How lame is that?'

Max's were shaking slowly, his fingers flicking up and down, like a pianist's. 'I thought I should never be in a situation like that again. I thought I had had my share of violence and terror. But, no, there is no end to it, nothing bounded about man's ability to prey on another.' He beamed. 'But you, young man, are special. Not only was your kind intervention courageous but your execution majestic. Are you a fighter, a soldier? A doorman, perhaps.'

Jim blushed and laughed. 'No, not me. I just, well, learnt how to handle myself when I was little. It just fitted together. You stamp on someone's foot hard enough and they can't stand up or run after you.' He grinned guiltily. 'I did spar a bit once but it got harder the bigger I grew. The older you are, the better the other guy gets at bashing your head in. That kind of spoiled the picture.'

Max nodded.

'What's more, when you start sparring no one bullies you anymore, so it loses its original purpose. But, hey, it finally came in handy.'

Max shifted out of his coat. 'At my age you cannot afford a bad knock. As soon as you are off your feet it is all over. You lie in bed and fill up with water. First it starts at your feet and then your legs swell, your stomach, your lungs and you drown. That's the way we old ones go, drowning in our own water.'

Jim shuddered. 'I didn't know that.'

'That is why you must get up and be moving around. The moment you lie down the process starts. We are all just a sack of water and when we are old we cannot keep it evenly distributed. Gravity and motion is all that keeps us going.' He regarded Jim soulfully. 'When you are seventy-five, you have only so much stuffing left, so little wax to keep the candle burning. But,' he said, lightening up, 'thanks to you I shall go on my way unharmed.' He sipped. 'So, what about you? Clearly you are a fit and able young man, how do you make your way in the world?'

'I work in a bank, down at Canary Wharf.'

'A bank clerk. A good solid profession.'

'No,' said Jim, 'not a retail bank, an investment bank in one of the big towers. I'm a trader there.'

'Oh ... oh,' said Max, 'a merchant bank. I see ... I see. A trader no less.' He squinted. 'And what does a trader do?'

Jim took a sip of his beer. 'I buy and sell shares in companies for my bank and try to make a profit out of it.'

'Really?' said Max. 'That is impressive. Is that commission business? You buy and sell for other people and they pay you?'

'No,' said Jim. 'I buy and sell what I think is good and if I'm right I make the firm money. If I'm wrong I lose it.'

'That sounds hard, but also like a good living. Even I know they pay a prince's ransom to young men in places like that.'

'You're right both times, but I'm lucky and because I'm lucky it's easy. When I stop being lucky it won't just be hard it'll be impossible.'

'Don't you worry, my son. A good boy like you will always have luck. Let me get you another drink.'

The mixture of adrenalin and alcohol had gone straight to Jim's head but he felt great. The old man, his fragile ward, was charming and he was comfortable in the out-of-the-way snug corner.

Max came back with two cognacs and another pint of

bitter for Jim. 'A brandy with that will make it taste all the better.'

Jim looked at the small balloon glass with trepidation. Mixing drinks was the sort of trick that could set you on a path to losing your dinner on a pavement. Well, why not the once? This moment would never come again – at least, he hoped the run-up to it wouldn't.

'So,' said Max, 'you were saying without luck your job would be impossible. How can that be?'

'It's like betting on horses. The odds aren't in your favour,' said Jim. 'You can only win if you're lucky. There's no element of real skill, just an illusion.'

'So then you must lose money for your employer. Is that the case?'

'Not me,' he said, grinning. 'I'm a lucky sod and every horse I pick romps home in first place waving its tail at the crowd.' He laughed. 'It's a joke. You know, people have won Nobel prizes for stating that what I do is just a statistical anomaly, and they're absolutely right.'

'If your horses win, it is because you know horses better than the other man. It happens all the time. Never bet against a gypsy on a horse, my friend, or you will know how skill affects a horserace. So how do you trade? Do you haggle like in a market, or get tips like at the races?'

'No,' said Jim. 'I just look at the chart and it tells me what's going to happen.'

'Chart?' queried Max. 'Is that like horse form?'

'No,' said Jim. 'It's like a graph of the past prices. You must have seen them on TV when they're talking about the markets on the news.'

'You mean the mountainous pictures they show when they talk about how the dollar has done this and that?'

'Right,' agreed Jim. 'They represent how the price has

gone up and down in the days before. I look at those and say where it's going next.'

'And that is hard?'

'Well, apparently so, but not for me.'

'That is good for you. And this pays well?'

'Incredibly well.' Jim laughed. 'Obscenely well. I make more in a year than most people in their whole life. It's stupid but it's real. What can I say?'

'Say, "Thank you, God."'

'Thank you, God,' said Jim, raising his glass skyward. 'I really mean that,' he added, as much for the benefit of a potentially listening deity as for Max's appreciation. 'I must be the luckiest bloke in the world.'

'And today,' said Max quietly, 'I'm perhaps back to even in the fortune stakes. But then perhaps I was really lucky when I was very young. I will probably never know.' He pulled up his sleeve and looked at a long fat blue-black smudge that might have been an old tattoo.

'What's that?' said Jim.

Max pulled his sleeve down, reached over and ruffled Jim's hair. 'You young people, you know nothing about anything, do you?' He smiled, his eyelids dropping. 'It is just a wound from another world.'

'Oh,' said Jim, 'must have been nasty.'

'Yes,' said Max, 'it was.'

Chapter 18

Jim woke when his new alarm clock chirped harshly. He didn't want to move. He felt sick and knew exactly why. He had talked his head off to the old man the night before, and by the time the pub closed he'd been so off his face that he'd hardly managed to get home in one piece. His brains felt like they'd been taken out and refitted badly, squeezed into places where they weren't meant to be. He was still dressed in yesterday's clothes. He struggled up and made it to the bathroom. He knew he should drink several glasses of water but even the first didn't want to go down. He drank another and ran the shower, awkwardly getting undressed. He could tell he was still rather drunk.

'What an idiot!' he scolded himself. No amount of fun was worth this kind of awful after-effect. How the other traders coped with their constant drinking was beyond him. He stepped into the shower and let it boil him. He could call in sick, but that wasn't an option. No one took time off for sickness, not unless they were carried out on a stretcher. Throwing a sicky was like blasphemy and, what was more, they'd be waiting for him and his black marker pen, dependent on his scrawling to make their trading day. The thought perked him up a bit. How cool was that?

Wolfsberg liked to stand up when he took this kind of call. It made him more thoughtful, which made him more comfortable. He liked to look out of the window onto the cityscape and watch the tiny people move about below. However important the conversation, he would focus on the fact that the caller was an ant like those below, and while the mightiest of them might do battle with him, they were both just tiny insects fighting over nothing more than grains of sand.

He picked up the handset and, with its long cord dangling behind him, stepped the few paces to the great plate-glass windows.

'Good morning, Mr Davas. To what do I owe this honour?'

'Call me Nick.'

'Thank you, Nick. How can I help you?'

'I want to pay you a visit – just a courtesy call, you understand.'

'I'll be honoured, but may I ask the purpose?'

'Sure.'

Wolfsberg hesitated awaiting a reply that, it quickly became clear, wasn't coming. 'OK, Nick, what is the purpose of your visit?'

'Just to see, you know, how you're doing. You're important to me. You're one of my prime brokers. I want to see how you're doing your thing for me. I want to see what I'm buying for the billions I pay you in commission.'

'Absolutely, Nick, it would be our pleasure at any time.' Andrea, his senior PA, was standing behind him, and Wolfsberg turned to her, the mouthpiece covered. 'Find out how much Davas deals through us right away.' He returned to his client. 'When would you like to come in?'

'Some time this morning.'

Wolfsberg winced. 'Fine. Roughly what time?'

'About eleven, depending on air traffic.'

'Fine.'

'Goodbye.'

Wolfsberg hung up, then called through his door, 'And, Andrea, cancel all my appointments till further notice.'

'OK.' A minute later she was back in his office. 'He doesn't deal anything through us,' she said. 'It's all out of New York, three billion in commission.'

'Christ,' said Wolfsberg, 'Bond arbitrage, right?'

'Mainly, but lots of other stuff all over the map. He's HQ's customer number one.'

Wolfsberg scowled. 'Even the *Wall Street Journal* knows that, so why the fuck is he coming here?' He thought for a moment. 'Let's try not to piss off New York – that would be terminal. Get them out of bed and ask for guidance. We can't afford to screw the pooch on this one.'

Davas looked around yet another trading floor and turned to Wolfsberg, smiling. 'So, Alan, while I love to see brokers buying and selling, selling and buying, I have an over-arching desire to see the good stuff.'

'Good stuff?'

'Not the factory, the prop desk. Now that would keep an old man's attention.'

'We don't have a prop desk anymore. All that stuff's long gone.'

'Really?' said Davas. 'Then maybe Bill Rock led me astray.' His eyes drilled into Wolfsberg.

Bastard, thought Wolfsberg, smiling although his teeth were clenched. 'Maybe he's thinking of the R and D lab.'

'That might be it. I'm sure it would fit the bill.'

Andrea turned to them, her left hand elegantly poised in her suit pocket. It's a good job you pay me like the genius I am, she thought, typing into her upside-down BlackBerry.

'Gentlemen,' she said, 'I think that's the thirty-seventh floor.'

'Of course,' said Wolfsberg. 'Someone has to stress-test the models and there's nothing like a bunch of coneheads to make sure the system's clean.'

'Quite so,' said Davas. 'Where would we be without coneheads?'

'Shit!' Fuch-Smith jumped out of his chair. He reread the BlackBerry message: 'Hostile approaching prop floor. Hide Moby at all costs. Three mins to do.'

He dashed out of his office. Moby was headed for the door with his gym bag. 'Moby!' he screamed, like a man possessed. 'Jim – James!'

Moby stopped dead in his tracks and stared dimly at him.

'Meeting room, old chap,' panted Fuch-Smith, running up to him.

'Why? What's up?'

'Nothing. Just come into the meeting room, will you?'

Suddenly the lift pinged and Fuch-Smith flung open the coat-cupboard door and waited a split second to see who would come out. 'Fuck.' He bundled Moby and himself into the cupboard.

'What the fu—'

'Shut the fuck up! Just *shut the fuck up*!'

'Jesus, what's going on?'

'Please, please – shut up.'

Moby pulled an extremely pissed-off face at his boss but followed instructions.

Suddenly the cupboard door opened and Wolfsberg, his PA and a face Fuch-Smith didn't recognize were peering in at them.

'Do you keep many traders in your cupboards?' they heard an East European voice enquire.

'Oh, yes,' said Wolfsberg. 'You never know when you might need a spare.' He laughed. 'Coneheads,' he added, 'all mad as frogs in a box. That's why we don't do real prop trading any more. Let me show you some more.'

'Ribbit,' muttered Jim.

'Ribbit farkin' ribbit,' replied Fuch-Smith.

'You really are weird,' said Nipper.

Jim scowled.

'You just missed a visit by Nicolas Davas.'

'So?' said Jim acidly.

'Nicolas Davas – *the* Nicolas Davas, the fucking God almighty of Trader Land. The superman, the beginning and end of modern hedge funds. The one and only big Kahuna.'

'I've never heard of him.'

Nipper laughed. 'That's because you're a muppet. Do you know what he said?'

'No idea. I was in the cupboard shagging Fuch-Smith.'

'Wolfsberg goes, "Of course there's no money to be had here. It's all the bell curve, the normal rules. The kurtosis is all traded away." And Davas goes, "It depends in which dimensions your bell curves are embedded," and I chirp, "We tried that but we just got walloped," and Davas goes, "That would probably be me." Fuck, he's just waiting there in the nth dimension eating us up.'

'Good for him,' said Jim. 'Maybe he could buy us all a drink.'

He was half expecting something to be waiting for him on his walk home and, sure enough, there it was: a yellow Lamborghini parked outside the flat's front door.

The passenger-seat window buzzed down as he passed it

and he saw Max, or Nick Davas, looking at him. 'Come for a ride, Jim?'

'My nan told me never to take lifts from strangers.'

'And a wise lady she was too, but come for a ride with me – we have a lot to talk through.'

'Like what?'

'Oh, how me and you are just the same, how we should combine forces, how together we could rule the world. You know how the story goes.' He leant across and pushed something. The door popped open and swung up. 'Come, I have a bag of sweets and you can have as many as you like.'

'OK,' said Jim, 'so long as you've got the lemon ones.'

'Plenty of lemon ones.'

Jim lowered himself in and the door closed automatically. He belted himself up.

'This car,' said Davas, 'is my staff's idea of a joke.' He started the ignition to the sound of turbines. 'How you are meant to drive it safely on a legal road I do not know. Fortunately we haven't far to go, just the airport.'

'The airport?'

'Yes, we are going to my home. I have much to discuss with you.'

'Outside the UK?'

'Yes, but not far.'

'That's no-go. I've got work tomorrow and no passport.'

Davas laughed and flipped him a maroon booklet. 'I had one made for you this morning, but you are unlikely to need it.'

Jim flicked through it. 'Work?' he proffered half-heartedly, trying to ascertain whether the document was real or a forgery. On the page at the back was his name and the face of a kid aged about sixteen. It might have been him.

'When they know where you have been, they will beg you to stay.'

'Nan was right,' he observed.

Davas laughed.

'Is this real?' Jim asked, flapping the passport as Davas jerked away from the kerb in a roar.

'Of course.'

'I knew you were going to say that.' He inspected the sports car's garish fittings. 'You're a scary guy.'

'And so are you, Jim, if only you knew it.'

That's not a corporate jet, thought Jim. That's a fucking airliner.

Davas was right. Jim didn't need a passport, at least not to leave the UK.

'I must admit I like to be airborne,' said Davas, as they walked up the stairway to the door. 'The good thing about a big plane like this is I can fly half way around the world in it without stopping. It's an extravagance but then again I have no real excuse not to splash out.'

Jim nodded. He wondered how much cash the God of Trading might have. Ten billion, a hundred? The news reports said he paid up to five billion dollars in commission every year, so even if he was going fifty-fifty with his brokers, which was the average ratio for a good trader, he was still pulling down five billion dollars a year, which meant a cool twenty million a day. He wondered whether the Royal Mint could actually print that much in cash in twenty-four hours. It'd be a mountain of cash. He was dreaming a bit as they entered the 757. 'Neat,' he said, absently.

'Where are you?' asked Davas.

'Thinking,' said Jim.

'Thinking what?'

A butler took Jim's coat.

'Thinking I'm not too far behind you, old man.'

Davas stopped and looked at him impishly from old tired eyes. 'You know? You are absolutely right and that is why you are here. Would you like something to eat?' He waved at the salon's leather seats. 'Make yourself at home.' He turned to the butler. 'Jeffries, I'll have my usual and please ask my young friend what he would like.'

The butler addressed Jim: 'I'm afraid our selection tonight is a little limited, but we should be able to cater for most of your wishes.'

'Could I have a hamburger?'

'Certainly, sir. How would you like that done?'

'Medium.'

'Would you like Chicago, Cincinnati, New York, Wafu or perhaps McDonald's style?'

'Eh.' Jim thought for a second. 'McDonald's.' At the front of the plane he heard the door close.

'Cheese on top?'

'Yes, please.'

'Cheddar, Leicester, Jack, Mozzarella, Cantal or processed?'

'Processed.'

Jeffries raised his left eyebrow a smidgen. 'Chips?'

'Yes, please.'

'Potatoes or processed starch?' Jeffries coughed, 'I beg your pardon. Potatoes or fries.'

'Potato chips, please.'

'King Edward, Jersey Royal, Maris Piper, Duke of York or Congo?'

'King Edward.'

'A milkshake with that?'

'Yes, please.'

'Guernsey, Jersey, milking shorthorn or Swiss?'

'Strawberry, please.'

'Israeli or Mexican?'

'I'm easy.'

'Salad?'

'No, I'm fine, thanks.'

Jeffries gave a little bow. 'Dinner will be served as soon as we level out.'

The plane started to move with the muffled sound of whistling engines.

Davas had sat down opposite him. 'I am sorry to sweep you up like this but we have important work to do. I shall have you back at your desk as soon as possible and then this will all seem like some strange dream.' He smiled. 'So enjoy these rough material pleasures.'

Jim ran his fingers across the plush leather of the seat. 'Feels pretty smooth to me,' he said. 'Where are we going?'

'My home,' said Davas. 'Venice.'

The burger didn't taste anything like a McDonald's, neither was it anything special, but that didn't bother him. It proved tricky to eat without covering himself with meat juices, so he concentrated for a while on not plastering grease all over his white shirt. When he finished Davas took him to his study at the back of the plane. Jim expected it to be all screens and technology, but instead it was panelled and looked more like an ancient room in some big old house.

'No computers?'

'There is one in the desk, but I seldom use it. I prefer to read and think here. Too much clutter in the mind of an old man may cause problems.' He went to a cabinet and opened it to reveal a small bar. 'Cognac?'

'No,' said Jim.

'It's from Napoleon's cellar. It might be one of just a handful of bottles left.'

Jim was still doubtful.

'I shall ration you to a single glass – I would rather not lead you astray.'

'OK,' said Jim, smiling. 'I've only just got rid of the headache from last night.'

'And why not? After all, you deserved to celebrate a famous victory. Unlike my bodyguard who was rather surprised to say the least. He was expecting just to run away convincingly, not find himself seeing stars. But myself, I appreciate the power of the unexpected, the certainty of the long shot, the ever-present potential of the freak occurrence.'

'So what exactly was last night all about?' said Jim, taking the large balloon glass that was offered to him.

'Just a little game to find out who you are inside. Would you turn back, would you walk on by, would you just shout and scream, would you come to an old man's rescue, or would you look away?'

'Can't say I'm chuffed it was a set-up,' said Jim. 'It doesn't mean anything now.'

Davas sat down in a fat leather chair in front of the Louis XV writing desk. 'It's important to me. Sit down, let me talk to you.'

Jim took the facing chair.

'Let me tell you,' began Davas, 'I live in a harsh world. Everyone who meets me is my friend. Everyone says what a clever fellow I am and how they so enjoy my company and my brilliant wit. I attract the most charming, the most flattering, the most competent sycophants on earth, drawn to me like blowflies to a carcass, and because of that it is hard to trust anybody. So when I need to I play my games to try to get the real grasp of the person I want to know.'

'What did you find out about me?'

'That you are a violent, reckless young man with a drink problem.' Davas stared at him, then smiled and his eyes twinkled.

'Thanks,' said Jim. 'Nice to know someone's got me taped.'

'It's taken me months to track you down,' continued Davas. 'I knew you were out there. I could feel you in the market. You have bent my models and I see you when you bend them. I just had to find the how, where, when and who. Where and when were easy – if I take a bath, lose money, it's from London the trouble originates – so that left how and who.'

'How can you see me bending your models?'

Davas smiled. 'Imagine a lawn, but imagine a fourteen-dimensional lawn – no, let's just keep it like a standard lawn. The grass is my profit, and when I mow it, I collect it up by a series of trades. I go up and down with my mower, or wait for it to grow back. That's all I do. The lawn is a certain size and I take a certain amount of time to optimally cut it. Sometimes the grass grows fast, sometimes it grows slowly, but I'm the only one on the lawn because no one else can see it like I do, in fourteen dimensions. They might see a tuft of grass and clip it, they might accidentally munch a few blades through luck, but generally my lawn is untouched. Except, of course, when you plough through it in your higgledy-piggledy way. You and me, we're the only ones on the lawn and I see your path.'

'So you can actually see me trade?'

'No. I can see the trail of your trading. I can't see what you're doing, but I can see its effect. The grass is just a field of inefficiencies and I can see you chopping away at them.'

'That's pretty amazing.'

'Likewise, my boy, somehow you get into fourteen dimensions and, from our conversations last night, you're no theoretician. Which in a way is good, because if you knew where you were and what you're doing, you could do what I do, and sweep it all away.'

'I just look at the chart and make predictions, most of which look pretty simple to me, no fourteen dimensions in my book, just up, down and across.'

'That's one point five dimensions,' said Davas. 'Up and down is one and the half is forward. Sadly we can't go back in time so that makes the time dimension effectively half.'

'Right,' said Jim. 'I hadn't thought of it like that.'

'But the market itself is made up of thousands of participants all of whom you can think of as a dimension. In effect each market is an infinitely dimensional space. But you can clump these dimensions and build a model. If you have that model right you have a map, of sorts, of the future.'

'I think some lads at the office are keen to work on that kind of thing, but apparently you keep stopping them.'

'Perhaps,' said Davas, 'but these models need a little more computing than a few desktops. I have five hundred engineers who do nothing but run my simulations. Perhaps twice more than I need for security reasons but, even so, it is a non-trivial set-up. If it could be reproduced with any ease I wouldn't speak so freely.'

'So why are you taking me to Venice? You could offer me a job back in London.'

'Don't you think that would be a little lacking in charm?' asked Davas.

Jim shrugged. 'Maybe, I don't know. I've never been in this kind of situation before. I'm flattered, though – and, well, a bit confused. Fourteen dimensions is enough to do anyone's head in, right?'

Chapter 19

By the time Jim had drunk the ancient brandy the plane was descending. There was no announcement in three languages, no fasten-your-seatbelt sign, nothing but a slow descent and a gentle landing. After a short taxi the plane stopped and they were getting out. A black Mercedes was waiting, and as soon as they were inside, it drove across the airport to a checkpoint at which they were waved on. Then it was a short distance to a dock where a powerboat bobbed, its engine rumbling in readiness.

They stepped aboard and sat outside the small, luxurious cabin.

'I love this ride,' said Davas, as Jim gazed out into the inky night at distant yellow lights shimmering on the horizon.

A crewman cast off the ropes and jumped aboard next to the pilot, who pushed the twin engines' accelerators. There was a great roar as the nose of the boat rose and the craft surged forwards.

'About twenty minutes,' said Davas.

Jim stood up and held on to a brass rail that ran along the top of the cabin roof. Huge wooden staves driven into the lagoon seemed to mark the way, and as they tore headlong, other boats careered past them towards the airport.

The eerie shape of Venice soon began to resolve, the dark sky punctuated with occasional thunderless lightning forks. It was truly another world from London, a floating, alien place. The boat carved its exhilarating course like a water-borne motorbike, hugging curves and accelerating out of them with sweeping geometry.

Then they were passing down a great watery thorough-fare. The powerboat slowed, its prow dropping back to the water. The great canal was lined with huge palaces, brightly lit yet still cloaked in mysterious shadow. The boat turned into a side canal, and as it did so a building at the end lit up, and on it something moved; to the left a black hole was appearing in the solid edifice. The boat drove in, there was a clank and a whine, and the missing wall reappeared slowly from the canal.

'That's really cool,' said Jim, grinning at Davas. 'By the way, is it Max or Nick or Mr Davas?'

Davas smiled. 'Max is fine.'

As they climbed out of the boat a door opened and eight servants lined up in front of them. Davas nodded approvingly as he passed, the women curtsying and the men bowing. He greeted them all by their first names and smiled paternally.

'Angelina,' he said, to the last woman, clearly the senior of the group, 'it's nice to be home. It's been so long.'

'Two months, sir,' she said. 'We've missed you.'

'How kind,' he said, and crossed the threshold.

Jim followed, trying not to look surprised or awed.

They walked up a short flight of stairs and entered a grand hall.

'Wow!' said Jim. 'This really is a palace.'

'Yes,' said Davas, 'a fifteenth-century palace, and the foundations may as well be pure gold for what it costs to stop it falling into the lagoon. But at some point cost becomes simply a curiosity.'

A huge fire burnt in a great hearth and the walls were

hung with tapestries and small old master paintings. The ancient wood, brick and tile floor was covered with exquisite Persian rugs and every piece of furniture seemed irreplaceably fragile.

A burst of girlish laughter floated down from the gallery above and they heard the patter of running feet.

'Come with me,' said Davas. 'I have one thing to show you tonight and then I must retire. We will talk in the morning.'

He set off across the hall to a great flight of dark wooden stairs. Jim followed, and was stopped in his tracks by the sight of three staggeringly lovely women.

'Ah, my beautiful stars,' cooed Davas, who had also paused. 'Thank you for coming to meet me, but this evening I am busy and have neither the time nor the energy to give you my attention.' They seemed downcast and exclaimed sadly in a mixture of languages. 'I am sorry,' said Max. 'I will spend time with you all before I leave again. Now you must go away and leave me to my work.'

'Now I understand,' said Jim. 'That was nine dimensions right there.'

'A great deal more, I assure you,' said Max. He stopped at a door, opened it and went into a large, plain, windowless room. A table stood in the middle with various indeterminate objects on it. Davas walked over to it and picked up a wire-covered gauntlet, which he switched on. He gestured with it and lights flickered on. 'Why can nothing be instant in this light-speed world?' he muttered.

Faint but recognizable images appeared on the walls. 'Right,' said Davas, and at a flick of his finger, the room went dark and all around them were charts. 'I take it you recognize these?'

'Dow, FTSE, S and P, Nikkei, dollar, gold, oil.'

'So let's have a look at the last fifty years.' Davas swung his arm and the charts loaded, drawing back to 1960.

'That's really cool,' said Jim. 'I've never taken it back that far. A few months maybe. I do intraday, intraweek stuff, but rarely long term.'

Davas flicked a thumb and squashed each chart into half the space of its frame. 'Does that say anything to you?'

Jim whirled round. Something was wrong but he didn't know what. 'Can you give me, like, the last ten years?'

'Certainly.'

With another gesture the charts drew inside their wall-sized frames.

Jim spun on his heels. 'Oh, shit! That's really ugly! I mean, they're all really fucking monstrously ugly. That can't be right.'

'What can't be right?'

Jim's mouth was hanging open. He closed it hastily and collected himself. 'That's saying down, but not like crash. It's saying down and out – but that can't be right.'

'Are you sure?'

'Sure of what? That it's wrong?' Jim swung around and around. 'Jesus Christ, why didn't I see this already?' He did a double-take on the Nikkei. 'That's weird. The Nikkei's different but still just as bad. Christ, Max, what am I seeing? What are you showing me?'

'Look at these.' He pulled up sugar, cocoa, the euro, carbon credit, UK interest rates.

Jim shook his head. 'There's got to be something wrong with your charts. I'm seeing things.'

'Are you seeing this?' He clenched his fist and made a pull-down motion. The screens flashed and a green dialog popped up in the corner of each screen. 'Simulation.' The charts started to draw ahead, much as Jim would have filled in the blank space with his marker pen. Across went the trend, through winter, spring and summer, then crashed. Not a normal crash, not ten per cent, not twenty, but a vertical slump all the way to zero, and not in a year or a month, but in a day.

Jim's head spun. That was right – the sims were spot on. This was what he could see: the end of the markets, one after another crashing to nothing. It was all over. Everything was about to come to a single shuddering finish.

'Fuck,' he cursed. 'It can't be – it just can't.'

Suddenly the main lights were on. 'That is what I wanted you to see, but stop now, think about it tonight, dream about it, and we shall look at it again tomorrow. That is what I am seeing in fourteen dimensions but tomorrow, together, we can try to see it in fifteen. In fifteen everything may be different.'

The door opened and Jeffries entered. 'Mr Evans, please allow me to show you to your room.'

Davas held out his gauntlet, indicating to Jim that he should follow the butler. 'I need this reality embedded in your mind, Jim, before we can take it further.'

'Goodnight then, Max,' said Jim. 'I doubt I'll get much sleep, though.'

Jeffries showed him to his room. 'If you'd care to place your clothes in a pile outside your door I'll ensure they're waiting for you, laundered, in the morning.'

'Thanks,' said Jim.

'If that is all, sir, I'll leave you now.'

'Thanks,' said Jim again, looking around the dark lavishly decorated room. There was a selection of small ancient portraits in intricate frames on the walls. He walked around the large room and studied them. They looked like real people, not the flat caricatures he expected of old paintings. The subjects must have been rich and powerful, but they also seemed very young. Not a shallow modern youthfulness underlined by trainers and jeans, but the structural youthfulness that only young faces possess. He guessed the princesses and rich merchants had been in their twenties or early thirties. Forty was old then, he thought, so those men were in their prime in their mid-twenties, the movers and shakers of their time.

Now you had to be fifty to rule the world, but then twenty-five was old enough. Not because twenty-five was a particularly good age, simply that older people had, like children, dropped dead, leaving plenty of room for the young and fit. It had been a smaller world, a comparative handful of people scraping a living in the filth that constituted civilization.

He was standing, Jim mused, in a palace, the dominant building of its time, yet it was tiny compared with the gigantic structure that housed his bank. In its time this could well have been the headquarters of a fifteenth-century global economic powerhouse.

Jim lived in a world swollen beyond recognition. Now a shopping centre could be bigger than the Vatican, a once-great Roman road only as wide as a modern alley.

People didn't die at forty anymore, unless they were very unlucky. They hung on till they were twice that age and consumed more material goods than the characters in the palace's portraits could have imagined, even from their pampered outlook. Those mighty people had lived like paupers in comparison to modern folk, with no electricity, clean water, entertainment on demand, refrigeration or healthcare.

His mind flitted back to the charts. Was the whole thing

really about to end? Was some huge meteor about to slam into Earth and wipe out humanity with a giant hammer blow? Would humanity go the way of the dinosaur in a matter of months? Could such a gigantic enterprise as the modern world simply stop?

There was a pair of blue and gold pyjamas on the bed in his size. He looked around for a television but there was none so he went into the bathroom and got undressed. The marble was snow white Carrara, and the fittings appeared to be solid gold. The shaving mirror lit up automatically when he looked into it and showed every bristle and blocked pore on his face with its distended lens. Hurriedly he turned away and went into the shower, a glass cubicle in the corner of the room big enough to fit several people. There was a daunting control unit on the wall with at least a dozen buttons, and a screen that mentioned sauna, steam and foot massage. He glanced at the built-in phone and wondered if it would connect him to some kind of shower-customer support.

He pushed a button that said 'music' and, as he had expected, music began to play. It was something classical and soothing, so he left it on. He looked at all the different nozzles and hit a button, prepared to leap out if he was bombarded with either scalding or freezing water but, to his surprise, it was the perfect temperature. He sat down beneath the cascade on the warmed marble bench.

Under the waterfall he tried to visualize the charts one by one in his mind. But the detail wasn't there. It can't happen, he thought. Something like that simply can't be in a chart – at least, not that far ahead.

How could an asteroid be in a stock chart? Nobody knows it's coming, and if it was known, the markets would be collapsing as the news spread. What else could cause such a move? The Second World War hadn't had such an effect on them – and even mass devastation would leave some kind of trading behind. Venice belonged to a past world with a few million in it yet it still had some kind of market trading. Not necessarily the same thing, he thought. There could be no Dow but there would still be markets. But no dollar price, no traded gold. How could that be? If there were people, there would be gold trading. Then again the exchanges might disappear, but if they did the price wouldn't reset to zero.

What had the end of those charts looked like? Again, he struggled to recall and failed.

But it had been a simulation, nothing more; it might have looked bad to him but that wasn't to say Davas's sim hadn't been utterly bolloxed. There was no connection between him thinking that the chart over the last ten years meant the future trend was sick and what Davas had drawn up. Why should he believe it anyway? There was no point in being the richest dead shorter on Planet Earth.

As the hot water continued to flow over him, his face was contorted in concentration. In his mind Davas's predictions ran across the wall. They looked so right – they felt true, he thought. He recalled appreciating their progress, agreeing silently with the ticks as they spanned the year. He remembered the horror as he had grasped what was about to happen next. Like a rider on a rollercoaster about to tip over the crest of a gigantic drop, he had anticipated the gut-wrenching collapse.

He turned off the water. Each day played itself out in a second, a skinny bar representing the developing price. A little pixel to the left showed the open for the day and another to the right showed the progress of the price and eventually turned into the close price. Did the terminal crash on the last day cover the whole trading period or was it cut short? A whole day? Did the Nikkei trade on further the next day? Surely for the Nikkei to crash it would have to be the next calendar day because Japan was asleep when the West traded. He moaned. He was going to have to wait till morning for the close look he needed.

He stepped out of the shower and dried himself. He bundled up his clothes and walked out into the bedroom. Something caught his eye in the wardrobe mirror. The smiling face of a ghostly girl.

'Blimey,' he exclaimed. But the ghost was gone. He grabbed the pyjamas from the bed and put them on, awkwardly stepping into a pair of slippers that lay to one side. He went back to the wardrobe and opened it. It was empty save for a couple of silk dressing gowns with the same blue and gold motif as his nightwear.

He examined the back of the door. It seemed solid enough. He pressed on the door panel behind the mirror. It moved slightly as if it wasn't firmly attached. He knelt down and examined the bottom of the panel. Sure enough there was a little gutter, a groove just wide enough for a panel to slip along it. There was a movement and his heart was instantly jumping in his chest. He sprang to his feet. The back of the wardrobe was open and the girl was there.

'Come with me,' she said, in a foreign yet American-tinged accent. 'I want to show you something.'

'You gave me a fright,' said Jim, a bit fazed.

'Sorry,' she said. 'Please come.'

Jim stepped into the wardrobe and through it to a narrow passageway beyond. 'Where are we going?'

'Please don't talk,' she said. 'At some points the walls are very thin.'

'OK.' Any minute now I'm going to wake up in my own bed with a hangover.

The passage was cold and dry and by the light of the girl's small torch he saw that the floor was brick. It led a winding course, constantly turning left or right, rising up or dropping down in short staircases. It was truly a labyrinth and while Jim tried to memorize his way back, he was soon utterly lost.

This passage must go all over the house, he thought. He imagined scheming Venetians, listening in on the plotting of others, popping out to poison someone's drink, or secretly visiting a lover. His heart was pounding in his chest and sweat had appeared on his top lip. The old aromas of ancient wood and dust filled him with strange emotions. On they went, up and up, then down and down as the secret passage took its tortured path to wherever he was being led.

She touched his arm and they stopped on a corner. She shone her torch at the edge of the turn, then fiddled with something and extinguished the light. She pulled away a piece of wood and the light from the room beyond shone in. She touched at his arm and motioned to him to look through the gap. It was the viewing room.

Davas stood in the middle with what looked like two gauntlets and a headset on. The walls around him were covered with multicoloured swirling patterns that he appeared to conduct. Dates and times swung across the wall screens and reports saying, 'Rendering, Simulating, Halted, Data out of range,' flashed on and off as Davas twisted and turned.

'This is too slow,' he cried in exasperation. 'Give the renders more computer processing power! We must have more!'

A face appeared on the far wall projection. 'We're

running CPU at full. Even the new clusters are at a hundred per cent.'

'We must get more!' cried Davas. 'There is so little time.'

'Yes,' said the face, and disappeared.

Davas whirled towards Jim and the girl, his huge transparent visor flashing like a kaleidoscope. He held out his hand towards Jim, who jerked back as a blast of colour flashed through the gap, and images cascaded onto the walls in front of them.

'Now give me the oil majors,' cried Davas. 'Seventy to eighty-two.' A sea of swirling extravagant amoebas sprang into life, weird flower-like forms that rolled and twisted and re-formed as Davas conducted.

'It's got to be here. Take the dimensions up.'

The face reappeared. 'We can't go to twenty-three – the core might fragment. The dataspace could shred and we'll be down for days.'

'You promised me this!' he cried. 'You promised me this by last week! No ifs, no buts.'

'Sir, we haven't tested it enough. We didn't want a down.'

'Give me just the indices and oil. Just the sixteen and Nymex. If we shred, we shred.'

'Yes, sir.'

'10' flashed up, then '9, 8, 7, 6, 5, 4 ...'

'3' seemed to hold the screen for several seconds, then the count went to '4' and '5'.

'Come on!' shouted Davas. 'Give me the model.'

The moments hung in the air like dust in sunlight and then the numbers ticked down to '1'.

The room went dark.

Jim took a deep breath.

'Well?' cried Davas.

There was a crash and a wild flash and the room was filled with a shower of sparks. The walls erupted in a blaze of reds, oranges and yellows, splashing like flames around the space.

'Yes!' cried Davas, flailing his arms like a dwarf fighting a giant. '*Yeeees!*'

Exploding galaxies roiled around the room, blinding supernovas erupted and boiled away, collapsing into more cataclysmic detonations.

Another blinding flash sent Jim reeling back. It was followed by darkness. He leant forward to the crack and tried to see in.

A small face appeared on the far wall.

'We're shredded, sir. The dataspace cascaded and swamped. We're down.'

The main lights came on. Davas stood, head bowed. 'Get me more,' he said quietly. 'We must go deeper. Soon it will be too late.'

The girl leant forward and replaced the cover to the slit.

'Follow me,' she said, and turned on her little torch. She squeezed past him and they began to retrace their steps. Jim was lost in thought. What was Davas doing? What were all those crazy, amazing graphics? Did he say twenty-three dimensions? More than four sounded outlandish, but twenty-three was double the number that even the mysterious string theory dealt with.

How did you manipulate twenty-three dimensions? All he did was look at a screen or a printout and scribble. What use could he be to someone who worked in all those dimensions when he worked in apparently just one and a half?

Suddenly he realized he was following the girl along a

different route. He wondered where she was taking him now. Up they climbed, twisting round in a spiral that he guessed flanked a staircase somewhere in the palace. The way grew thinner and so low that he was shuffling along, head bowed. People must have been much smaller when this place was built. Suddenly the girl stopped and, with a quick movement, slid open the wall.

'Through here,' she said, stepping into the area beyond. Jim found himself in a well-lit room with heavy drapes across a large window and a wood fire burning in the grate. The two other women he had seen at the top of the stairs sat waiting on a large embroidered sofa.

'Sit down,' said the girl pointing to another wide seat. 'We want to ask you some questions.' She joined the other women and waited for Jim to take his appointed chair.

The light now revealed that the girl who had led him here had golden-blonde hair pulled up in a bun at the back, a button nose and large, oval eyes. Her lips were so red and large that they might have swollen with some allergy. Next to her sat an Indian woman, black-haired, tall and graceful. She looked at her lap, batting long lashes when she occasionally sneaked a glance at him.

He became acutely aware of his attire and smiled nervously. The third girl was staring at him intently. Her hair was a chestnut brown that glowed with a glossy sheen. It fell in waves down her neck and onto her shoulders. An American-style cheesecake smile was glued to her face as she cocked her head from one side to the other.

'What is happening?' said his blonde guide. 'What is wrong with Pappy?'

'What do you mean?' asked Jim.

'We want to know if Pappy is sick,' said the brunette. 'Whenever we see him,' she said, in what was almost but not quite a Dutch accent, 'he is tired and worried. He frets, he is exhausted. He wants nothing else but to play with his pictures.'

'We are worried for him,' said the Indian girl. 'He is not looking after himself.'

'He's got his concerns,' said Jim, 'but I don't think he's sick. He's predicting a big crash.'

The women looked at each other, then back at him.

'Go on,' said the Dutch girl.

'That's it. He's worried about a big crash coming and he's trying to understand it, so he can ride it out, I suppose.' He saw the charts in his mind's eye. 'Or something.'

'It must be bad,' said the blonde.

Jim nodded. 'Oh, yes, that's for sure, but if anyone can take advantage of it, it's your pappy.'

The girls looked at each other again and the blonde jumped up. 'Let me guide you back. You must be exhausted.'

'I'm OK,' said Jim. 'There's more than enough excitement to keep me on my toes.'

'Follow me.'

They went back into the twists and turns of the dark passageways and soon Jim was lost again. He wondered how far he was actually walking. When you were creeping along in the dark, ten metres could feel like a hundred. It was a thrilling journey, a secret way taken by princes and rascals carving their histories into the ether. Eventually he climbed out of the wardrobe and turned to the blonde girl. 'Before you go, can I ask you your name?'

'Cygna,' she said, 'but you may call me Cy.'

'Where are you from?' he asked.

'Fiji.' She leant forward. 'Look after Pappy for us,' she said, and kissed his forehead. Then she disappeared into the darkness beyond.

'I'll do what I can,' he said, as the back of the cupboard slid silently into place. But that won't be much if we get whacked by a fucking comet, he thought.

He turned and noted his clothes were gone from the bed. That's not good news.

Chapter 20

His eyes flicked open to a knock at his door. He sat up. 'Come in.'

It was six thirty. Jeffries entered with a tray, followed by a maid carrying a basket. 'Breakfast and your laundry, sir,' said the butler, setting the tray on his lap. 'I trust you slept well.'

'Like a baby,' said Jim. 'I've been waking up every three hours crying.'

'I'm sorry to hear that. I hope you'll find your laundry satisfactory, though I fear there might be a little too much starch in your shirt. The master tends to a heavier cloth and this may have led to over-enthusiasm on the part of the laundry-maid.'

'I'm sure it'll be fine,' he said, regarding his English breakfast with enthusiasm.

'I will return at seven forty-five sharp as the master wishes you to join him for the market open.'

'OK,' said Jim. 'I'll be ready.'

As soon as Jeffries and the maid had left he tucked into his breakfast. He didn't usually have breakfast, but the hamburger of the previous night was long gone and he was ravenous. Not many hearty breakfasts to go before the big day. A whole planet on Death Row? he thought. How crazy was that? It was all rubbish. All the books said the future was random, and given the choice between his rightness and death or being wrong and living, he'd take the latter anytime. So what if two billion to one market-predicting monkeys had met and agreed that the sky was going to fall? It didn't make it fated to happen. For every four or five he got right he got one wrong, and this would be it, especially as it was so far out in time. Predicting the end of the world eight months away was a muppet's game. He stuffed a forkful of egg, bacon and toast into his mouth. As he munched he was determined to deny what he had seen. He would conquer Davas's prediction with reason. It was just a nonsense result cooked up by an old guy who knew too much and a young one who knew jack-shit.

'Hurry up seven forty-five,' he muttered. He just had to see those charts again.

Davas handed him a gauntlet. 'Give this a try. Just put it on like a normal glove, and you can manipulate any screen as if you had a mouse in your hand. It will try to interpret your moves, or you can talk and, with luck, it will do as you wish. Of course it won't know you as it knows me but, even so, it should pick up on your basic needs.' Davas put on his own glove. 'Reset glove two, new user Jim.'

A blue slab appeared on the wall in front of them and flashed 'Learning'.

'Off you go,' said Davas.

'Dow chart, daily five years,' said Jim tentatively. The chart lit up the wall. He reeled in surprise. 'That's amazing! Project Dow chart to December 2011.' The line moved itself forwards. 'Right wall, five-year Nikkei,' he called, 'project to December 2011.' The right wall flashed up and began to draw. 'Amazing!' he gasped. 'How can you have this? It can't be real.'

'It's real enough,' said Davas, 'but it's not generally available, just like a B-2 bomber.'

'Give me dollar yen on the right wall and project it twenty years.'

Jim watched it draw, wincing in anticipation as the daily bars crawled along. 'Yes,' he exclaimed, as it crashed but drew on for days and weeks above the zero line.

'What?' said Davas.

'There *is* a world past the crash. OK, so the yen is eight to one with the dollar by Christmas but there is an exchange rate. That means there isn't a fucking great asteroid on its way.'

'That appears to be so, maybe, but look. Top hundred markets, 2015, daily.' The walls lit up in a flash and, one after another, they were tiled with blank charts. 'Forget the odd after flicker. Within a few months everyone is dead – I mean everything is gone. Currency, commodity, companies, indexes, futures, options, warrants, all gone.'

'Maybe Jesus comes back and takes us all to heaven.'

'Wouldn't that be nice?' said Davas. 'And maybe that's near enough the truth.'

'Come on, Max, you've just got a bug in your crazy software.'

'Aha,' said Davas. 'Why do you think you are here? You could see it before I drew in the future. That is why I brought you. You have the eye of the natural. I showed you the long-term chart and you could see it was all wrong. You said it looked "sick", remember. Now you want my software to be bugged. Well, so do I.

'Do you think I wish to book a front seat for Armageddon? I saw it when I was little, and I have no wish to revisit the Apocalypse again, my young friend. This is surely not to be an act of God. We are seeing the acts of men, and if we can only peel back the layers of time and space, we may discover the forces acting before it is too late. This is why we are here, to turn back a tide. Look,' he said, raising his arm. 'This is a basic probability grid.' A grey area appeared. 'Zoom in on level one.' The grey area resolved into a checkerboard of black and white squares.

'Luck is either black or white, heads or tails. You are right or you are wrong. This grid is a two-dimensional grid of heads or tails, rights or wrongs. Land on a white square and you are heads and right, on a black and you are tails. This is a simplification of all we know about chance. But the world is not a single coin. It is an infinity of coins nested like a Russian doll, coins embedded in coins embedded in coins, and so on. See!'

He gestured and the checkerboard expanded to reveal a simple white square containing another grid of black and white tiles.

'In a lower dimension the white square is made up of a balance of black and white squares. It is white because there are more whites than blacks. Landing on the black square sends you not to heads but to tails. But that black square is made up of yet more black and white tiles and – see – they are irregularly distributed. Substitute a white square within the black square within the white square and the outcome of the whole model might change entirely.'

He waved his hands like a conductor ordering the music to rise.

'S and P 500.'

A huge braided tangle of sweeping curves flashed onto the screen, pulsating like some deep-sea jellyfish. 'Market open,' flashed a sign, which flew round the room in orbit. 'Excellent,' he said. 'FTSE 100.' Another jellyfish flashed up, writhing and twisting, colours shimmering through its translucent body.

'This is the dataspace of a hundred shares, a dozen

dimensions of each rolled up into curves and densities. It is a visualization of the market as it trades.'

Davas pushed his hand forwards and the image expanded towards them, as if they were falling into the giant creature. The multicoloured intertwined cords grew, revealing that each was made up of others woven in a smaller, tighter mesh. 'You see how the market is actually a being. It moves about like a primitive animal. As traders we seldom influence it, just as when we look at a star we cannot touch it.

'This monster lives in dimensions we can only touch indirectly. Billions of people moving around the world are its cells, but their influence is too tiny to affect its behaviour. We, on the other hand, push this thing around every day. Because I can see it, I can clip its tentacles and catch the detritus falling from its body. This is where real power lies, in a secret universe with a hidden entrance.' He clicked his fingers and the FTSE creature disappeared. 'And soon this and all of us will be gone, wiped out by some terrible disaster, one that even I cannot pinpoint and which most probably I will be unable to avert.'

'FTSE chart, September 2011 daily,' called Jim.

The chart drew.

'Intraday, ninth to the thirteenth.' The chart slowly redrew.

'Zoom in on the tenth, eleventh and twelfth.'

It was instant. 'OK,' said Jim. 'So it all goes tits up on the afternoon of the eleventh and there's circuit breakers firing off until the market is closed early fifty per cent down. Then nothing the next day, so in effect there's no market from then.' Jim stared at the chart. How was he supposed to understand such a fucked-up picture?

He stared and stared at it and began to pace. He rummaged instinctively in his pocket.

Thank God, he thought, on finding his stomach settlers. He broke one out and popped it into his mouth. 'Give me the week up to the eleventh, intraday.'

The chart readjusted itself. 'There's a sag in the market leading into this that looks a bit odd,' he said. 'In the last few trading days the market just faints off. Maybe it's me shorting the arse off it.' He snorted. 'Hold on,' he said, 'give me ten a.m. to three p.m. on the eleventh, one-minute bars.'

He punched the air in excitement. 'Erase the bar at ten-o-five p.m. and replace it with a twenty point up tick. Then recalculate the chart.'

The room suddenly went dark and the lights came on.

'Damn,' said Davas. 'Bloody computers! Why are they always breaking down when you need them most? You know it–'

The light dipped again and the chart flashed up.

'No!' exclaimed Davas.

'There's your bug,' said Jim. 'Just that little data glitch was all it took to tip your mighty stealth bomber out of the sky. Just a single bleeding data point error.'

'No,' said Davas. 'Five FTSE chart, right wall.' Up it flew still with a huge market crash chewed out of it for the next year. 'Does that still look sick to you?'

'OK, yes, it looks very sick – but not dead.'

Davas flapped his hand. 'Project the next ten years with Jim's data edit.'

The chart began to draw slowly and, sure enough, there was still a market trading. Some kind of normality had returned.

'Give me a Monte Carlo space for the ten minutes around Jim's edit.' A frame flew onto the wall in front and a bar moved slowly across the screen.

'Rendering,' it flashed.

'This will take time,' said Davas, who was smiling now, his eyes glistening. 'We are going to see what are the chances of your edit actually happening. Come on, computers, give me my probabilities.'

The bar disappeared to show a blank black screen. 'What are we looking for?' asked Jim.

'White pixels. Each one would represent a possibility.' He waved a hand around to no apparent effect. 'Not many to be seen. Coloured pixel count,' he ordered.

'93, topical,' flashed the screen.

'Oh, really,' said Davas. 'Show me.'

A split second later a planet of pixels was turning on the wall.

'What's that?'

'That's the chance of your data correction occurring. Hold on. Total pixel count?' he called.

'88212323678512374590467,' flashed the wall.

'Ninety-three chances in eighty-eight bazillion?' asked Jim, deflated.

'Yes,' said Davas. 'If we just sit here, yes. But if we can find out what makes the ninety-three chances, maybe we can improve on that. The chances of you being born were no less, but luckily your mother and father were in exactly the right place at exactly the right time to overcome the odds.'

'Excellent,' said Jim. 'I knew we had nothing to worry about.'

'My son,' Davas clapped his hands, 'you are a marvel. I have spent millions trying to move that result and you did it by eye. How you see what you see is beyond my intelligence.'

'It's cockney clusters. You just can't beat 'em.'

Davas pulled off his glove. 'That's for sure. I'm going to

need to play with this result some more and the full system will be down for days.' He sighed, then his tired face brightened. 'But now there is hope.'

'So what are you going to do?'

'Try to trace back the thread to its root, then follow it through space and time till I can find out what causes the result. If I can pin that down to a concept or area, other friends can take it into the physical dimension and perhaps change the direction of outcomes.'

'But what do the ninety-three planets mean?'

'That something pretty drastic is to happen on the morning of the eleventh of September.'

Jim's face dropped. How could he have missed the significance of the date?

'Oh, yes,' said Davas, heavily. 'Not the date for a meteorite to land on Earth.' He turned to the screen. 'Call the boss when available.'

'Connecting,' said the screen, to Davas's obvious surprise.

'Max,' said the American President, 'what have you got?'

'Susan,' said Davas, 'I had not expected you to be up and about.'

'Don't you read the papers? I'm in Jakarta.'

Davas laughed. 'I've got great news. It can be turned around. It isn't a destiny, it looks like a single action. Maybe we can find it. Whatever it is, it's obscure.'

'That's good news. Praise the Lord.'

'I'll keep you posted.'

'Whatever you need.'

'Thank you, Susan. I will get back to you on that.'

'Any time.' The screen went blank.

Jim was stunned. He stood frozen, staring at the blank space where the US President had been talking only ten seconds earlier.

'She has found religion,' said Davas. 'This mess is scaring the pants off all of us.'

'How come?' said Jim, not articulating well.

'Jim, when you get to a certain size the game changes.' He motioned around him. 'When you are this big you had better be working for the house or you don't get to play at all … and, my son, it is all a game in the end, win or lose, live or die. It is just a matter of what you play for.'

Davas led Jim out of the room into a library. A desk in the centre of the room was ringed with a wall of monitors. 'What do you know?' said Davas. 'We actually made the right amount of money in London this morning. No Jim mowing my lawn for me.' He laughed and pressed a small button.

There was a whiz of servos and the screens rose, then fell, packing themselves away in the ceiling and desk.

'Nice toys you've got,' said Jim, smiling weakly.

'None of them can see what you can,' he said, tapping his head. 'I must thank you for that insight. It is a blessing. I've been like a blind man building a house of cards.' He shook his head.

Jim was staring over Davas's shoulder, his faced glazed and passive. He was turning the ball of pixels around in his mind. Ninety-three chances in eighty-eight bazillion. What did it all mean? Ninety-three probabilities in an infinite skein of possibilities. Even if it was true, what did it mean? And how could it help? It was just a massively complicated log table of results that could change and mutate at the flap of the proverbial butterfly in the desert. Perhaps not. What did he know? He was no maths genius. He only saw what went up or down, not what twisted and turned and knotted and curved and tangled and spun in a warp of infinities.

He jumped up, 'Wait! I've got an idea. It's either brilliant or stupid.' He was grinning at Max like a maniac. 'Show me the ninety-three pixels again. Take me back into the screen room.'

'Sure,' said Max.

Max handed Jim a gauntlet and slid on his own. 'Retrieve Jim's probability plane.'

'No,' said Jim, 'simulate it again.'

'Correct that instruction, re-render.'

There was a flash and darkness. Then, unexpectedly, an engineer was on the screen. 'What's up? I mean, what's happening, sir? The clusters are going ape. Whatever you're doing is draining core resources like a vampire.'

'Just rendering,' snapped Davas.

'Sorry, that's weird, sir. I might have to pull the plug if it looks like we're going to shred.'

'You do that,' said Davas, exasperated.

'Oh,' said the engineer, 'normality returns, over and out.'

With a little flash the screen with the probability plane-toid filled the wall.

'Pixel count?'

'103,' flashed on the screen.

'Yes!' exclaimed Jim. 'Rerun sim every fifteen seconds.'

The engineer was back. 'What are you people doing? It's gone crazy again.'

'Just try to keep us live,' said Davas. 'How many dimensions are we at?'

'Fourteen.'

'Just try to keep us alive at that. Over and out.' He flourished and the engineer vanished.

The picture reappeared and the report said 103 again. 'What's your conjecture, Jim?'

'Just wait a minute.'

'104,' said the next screen.

'Yes,' spat Jim.

'What is happening?'

'No – wait. Just a little longer.'

'112,' said the next screen.

'230,' said the next.

'389,' said the next iteration.

Then there was a bright flash and all was darkness.

The lights came up and Jim was smiling. 'You need more cockney clusters, Max, that's all.'

'So what are you telling me? What is happening?'

'Chances are improving. You told the most powerful person in the world the news, the information started to move and our chances got better.'

'Someone must have traded.'

'Who knows?' said Jim. 'But the information has shifted your blob thing and now the odds of a happy ending are four hundred to a bazillion rather than ninety-three. You can win this thing. Clearly the market thinks it's in human hands, or whatever that blob thing of yours really represents.'

'Jim,' said Max, patting him on the back, 'I'm going to have to requisition you.'

Jim pulled away. 'What do you mean?'

'I mean I must take you away from your bank. The world cannot afford to be without your mind.'

'How's that going to work?'

'I shall sort it out with your bank and, what is more, put twenty-five million into your account, another twenty-five million if we're having a drink on the twelfth of September.'

'Right,' said Jim, 'you sort it with the bank and I'm all

yours. It's a jazzillion to one on that we're all dead so what's either of us got to lose?'

'My son, you're done.'

'Only if we're talking millions of pounds.'

'The dollar is still the currency of trading, is it not?'

'OK. Dollars it is.'

Max smiled. 'The trick, as always, is to keep your winnings.'

'A piece of cake,' said Jim. 'How hard can it be to save the world?'

Max smiled, 'How I miss the confidence of youth.'

'Don't worry, Uncle,' said Jim. 'I've got plenty to spare.'

Chapter 21

The clouds over the lagoon were an iron grey and the wind blew icy spray into Jim's face. There was something forlorn about going back to London alone, even if it was via personal powerboat and private Boeing. He took his mobile phone from his pocket and realized it was switched off. He switched it on. There was a flood of SMS and he was bitterly pleased that even a few hours without his presence was enough to have them panicking. Perhaps they knew he was leaving and were freaking out. If they actually had any idea as to what was going on it would put all sorts of things into a different perspective – no point sweating for a bonus to pay off a million-pound mortgage when in a few short months the house would be a heap of rubble.

But what exactly did the charts predict? What could switch the world economy off like a light? Perhaps he was missing something important, something trivial but key. He wondered about the pixel score. Was it still going up? How far had it risen since he had left Davas? Twelve hundred pixels felt like progress, but in reality it was just one plankton of hope floating in an ocean of fatal destiny. But there were eight months or so to find the needle in the haystack and that might be enough …

It had to be enough.

He drew the chart of his life with his fingertip and it didn't end on 11 September 2011: it went on and up long after that date. He felt in his gut that it would all turn out OK.

But, then, he might be one of the few left behind, king of a devastated planet.

If there were two people left alive, there would be trading and there would be a market. Back in the Middle Ages there had been plenty of trading but no recognizable records for traders. Perhaps the world would be set back a few hundred years but not wiped out. That wasn't a comforting thought – not oblivion, then, just the Dark Ages. But perhaps something fantastic would happen, some amazing development that would deliver Utopia where materials were so plentiful they became free, like air. Yet in reality even air was traded: carbon offset meant it was no longer free.

He set his face against the cold wet wind and tried to see the airport through the gloom.

Anyway, nothing good happened that fast, he thought. More chance of aliens coming to turn us into hamburgers than something appearing out of thin air and taking the world's mammoth economy to a higher level in a few short weeks.

The plane was basically a flying house for Davas and Jim sat alone in it, thinking random thoughts as it taxied for takeoff. His phone had kept ringing so he'd turned it off. There was no point in going to the office today. Tomorrow morning would do. He reclined the leather seat. Fuch-Smith would go ape and so would the other traders. They depended on him. They wouldn't make a trade unless he'd blessed their chart. They weren't even traders anymore, just trend followers, order-executing puppets of his freakish trading mind.

His thoughts turned to his nan. What would she have made of all this? Not much, he thought. It would be nonsense to her. The decimal points were in the wrong places and, in a way, they were for him too. Had Max really agreed to pay him fifty million dollars?

In trading terms it wasn't that much. He shovelled it around all day long, like a porter pushing sausages around Smithfield. But this money was going to be his. It was hard cash not the notional currency he traded in, which was a lot less real than it seemed at first glance …

He sat up in his chair. 'Hello,' he called forward. 'Hello there?'

The steward appeared, 'Can I help?'

'Can I get Mr Davas on the line?'

'I'll bring a phone right away.'

When the man returned, Jim punched a few buttons. 'Max, when did your charts go tits up?'

'October.'

'OK. Then it's already happened.'

'What do you mean?'

'Something happened in October that went into the market information to culminate in the crash. What are the chances of a certainty in this world?'

'Fifty-fifty.'

'No, I mean in our kind – your model.'

'Well, the odds are absolute. It's the number of one type of point divided by the other.'

'So the disaster is like a gazillion-to-one on favourite.'

'Almost as much of a certainty as you can get.'

'So …'

'But let me finish,' continued Davas. 'These probabilities are very fragile. It is like standing on a balcony. The chances of you ending up lying on the ground below dead are billions to one, but the moment you jump over the rail the odds go right up to a near certainty. Thank God this whole thing is chaotic. As such we can still turn it around.'

'That's good, that's really good, but whatever's going to happen was set on its way in October. So something has been dispatched, like the fucking comet that killed the dinosaurs. The rock left a certain orbit in October and is heading this way with little between it and us to stop it.'

'I see,' said Davas. 'That's an interesting thought but it could also mean there is simply no further information out there to change the prognosis. Currently all available information available to the hive mind creates a picture of certainty. But it doesn't have to be that. It might just be cosmic synchronicity.'

'Uh?'

'I don't know,' said Davas. 'Who knows? It could be *deus ex machina*.'

'Right,' said Jim. 'That's a few too many long words for me.'

'Very well,' said Davas. 'It is not supernatural, it is information flow. Every action is like throwing a stone in the sea of information. The ripples go out and the configuration of the world is changed. It is not an instantaneous process, just rippling information moving across an ocean of data. We spoke to the President and she spoke to people and the info flowed around. Consequently the information was absorbed into the collective consciousness, our chances of survival improved, that collective knowledge percolated into the market and tweaked our little planet of hope.'

'That's how I think it works,' said Jim, 'but we have to imagine there's this thing set on its way and we have to find it somehow and push it off course.'

'We are at twelve thousand now, by the way. At that growth rate we could get to a slim chance by September.'

'Keep me SMSed on the score,' said Jim, 'and I'll keep pestering you with ideas. I think it's sat somewhere waiting to happen. It's some kind of ticking time bomb.'

'I'm now sure,' said Davas, 'that this is a dealt blow and if we can find the arm that holds the sword we can bind it and, by Zeus, chop it off.'

'I'll keep thinking,' said Jim. 'Let's keep that planet growing.'

Chapter 22

When the car from the airport drove him to his door he saw an intern from the bank loitering about outside looking tired and glum. He got out and watched the familiar figure walk smartly over to him.

'Hello,' said the nameless junior. 'They're worried about you back at base. They want you to check in.'

'Tell them I'm not dead and I'll come in tomorrow morning.'

'You couldn't call your boss, could you?' the intern begged. 'If I report that back it isn't going to win me any Brownie points.'

'OK.' Jim took out his phone and switched it on. There was a rush of bleeping, then the number was ringing.

'Oh!' squawked Fuch-Smith's PA. 'Is that you, Jim? I've been calling your phone all day.'

'What's the problem?'

'I'll put you straight though to Seb–' The phone didn't go on hold but sounded as if it was snatched out of her hand.

'Moby, what the fuck's going on?' panted Fuch-Smith. 'Jesus, I can't believe you just vanished like that.'

'I'll be there in the morning, fill you in then.'

'How about now?'

'It won't make any difference.'

'I'm doing my nut here, mate. I've got to know what you've done. Whatever the offer, we'll double it. Whatever you need, you've got it.'

'Stop.' Jim looked at the intern. 'Whatever you think it is, however bad you think it might be, don't worry, it's so much worse. But tonight won't change a thing. I'll tell you about it tomorrow, because right now I don't have the bandwidth to come in and puke it out, OK? But tomorrow I'll be up for it.'

'Where are you?'

'Just got home.'

'I'm coming over right away.'

'Don't do that.'

'I'm coming over *right now* and if you don't let me in I'm going to break your fucking door down. This just can't happen.'

Jim emitted what sounded like a cruel laugh. 'Oh, yes, it can.' He hung up. He looked at the intern, who was listening intently. 'Job done,' he said. 'You can get back and collect your Brownie points.'

'You quitting, then?'

'If only it was that simple,' he said, fishing out his keys.

Jim opened the door to Fuch-Smith, who was looking embarrassed and flustered on the threshold. 'Sorry, old chap, but I had to come. I'm in shock. I got a call from Wolfsberg this morning, saying something about you being out of here and seconded. I can't take it all on board.'

'Come in,' said Jim.

'Oh, nice pad,' said Fuch-Smith, walking into the lounge. 'Great view – rather like ours if I might say so.' He admired the accidentally minimalist layout of a twelve-foot square TV and an expensive white leather sofa. There was a pile of magazines on the floor and a stereo to the right of the picture window that looked as if it might have fallen off the ISS space station. There didn't seem to be any CDs to play on it, though.

'I like it. Yours is maybe a bit nicer.'

They gazed at each other for an awkward moment.

'You can't go,' said Fuch-Smith, smiling as if it was some kind of certainty that Jim would stay. 'Tell the fucking Americans to stick their offer. We'll better it here.'

'Sit down,' said Jim.

'It's not that fucking Davas?' said Fuch-Smith, slumping onto the sofa, which squeaked.

'In a way.'

'Fuck, fuck, fuck,' spat Fuch-Smith. 'You can't work for that bastard. He's a hundred per cent evil, Satan's own. You can't go over to scum like that.'

'He's not scum,' said Jim, indignantly.

'How much is he offering you?'

'Fifty mil, this year.'

Fuch-Smith was clearly aghast. 'Oh, fuck! That's a lot. But it's not real, right? You'll never see it.'

'Upfront,' said Jim. 'Well, half up front.'

'Upfront? Twenty-five mil?'

'Dollars, mind you.'

Fuch-Smith gaped at him. 'Oh, fuck, I'm screwed.'

'It's much worse than Davas pissing in your punchbowl. I saw something yesterday that changes everything. It's the end of the world, Seb, as we know it. The charts just die in September. They all fall off the map in a couple of days. That's it for all of us – curtains, over, finished.'

'But you know the charts – you know that's impossible.'

'I think I do, and it's all there in black and white. End, over, finished. That's why I'm working with Davas – to figure it out and maybe help stop it.'

'OK.' Fuch-Smith collapsed back in the sofa. 'Now we've got the good stuff out of the way, tell me the bad news.'

*

There was a collective gasp from the small audience.

'That's bullshit,' exclaimed Flipper.

'Bullshit,' agreed Nipper. 'Total bullshit.'

'Maybe,' said Jim. 'God, I fucking hope so.'

'Why is it bullshit?' said Dirk. 'Why *exactly* is it bullshit? I'd like to know because I've been trading options for months that price the world like it's warming up for a going-out-of-business extravaganza. What's more, I'm up big-time.'

The room looked away from Jim to Dirk, who squinted through his glasses, bald dome shining with sweat. 'You fucking plebs know nothing. You think the sun comes up every morning and smiles its smile on your happy little life like nothing can go wrong. You have no fucking history, none at all. Disaster and catastrophe, that's the fucking history of the world. Here, London, right under your stupid noses, was the centre of a vibrant, flourishing Britain for nearly half a millennium. For four or five centuries this was the metropolis of a million people. The Square Mile is London. It's the Roman city, a high point of civilization, the epitome of human progress in its time. Then, a few years later, everything was gone. London lay desolate for three centuries, lost to a world so ignorant, so lost, that the depraved dregs that remained thought the walls of the city were so huge, giants had built them. One minute it was fucking toga-filled streets, the next, nothing, just treasure buried in the ground and coins strewn on empty pave-ments.' Dirk flung himself back in his chair.

'Oh, fuck you,' said Nipper. 'Go on, cheer me up.'

'You oik!' snapped Dirk, bolt upright now. 'The whole world's fucking hanging by a thread – can't you see that? It's like one of those tossy watches Wolfsberg wears, so delicate even a tiny knock stops the bloody thing working. The world's economic system is like a set of dominoes lined up for one of those bloody record attempts. Kick one and the whole lot comes down.

'There's seven billion people on this planet and they're fed and watered "just in time", like cars getting made in a Jap factory. Fucking planes and ships and cars and trains shuttling about at full pelt keeping the big global mouth filled. Pull on the right thread and the whole patchwork comes unpicked. Then it's a global rout, a rolling massacre of famine, war, disease and death.'

There was silence.

'Well, there's a fucking good short, then,' said Flipper.

'Look,' said Jim, 'I don't agree with Dirk. This thing, whatever it is, can be turned and I've been asked to help. You should see the electronic stuff they work with – it's amazing. Makes our kit look like cavemen's tools.'

Fat Joe was about to stuff another doughnut into his mouth when he paused. 'Look,' he said, 'just send me my chart in the morning. Then you can go piss up a tree for all I care.'

They all looked at Jim, a hungry gleam in their eyes.

'What do you reckon?' he asked his boss.

Fuch-Smith's despondent face exploded into a wide grin and his floppy quiff practically stood on end. 'I say fuck this doomsday nonsense. We can work together like that.'

'And I say,' added Fat Joe, through the doughnut, 'that Jim just shuts the fuck up and gets his marker pen out.' He got up. 'I'm going back to work.'

The team trotted out after him.

Jim looked at Fuch-Smith. 'Should work,' he said.

'How hard can faxing you a few sheets of paper be?'

*

'Fifty mil,' said Wolfsberg.

'Pounds or dollars?' asked Jim.

'Pounds.'

Jim hesitated, his mind fogged. What did these numbers mean? Where had reality gone? 'If Davas agrees, it's yes, if he says no, it's no.'

'You do what's right, of course,' said Wolfsberg. 'I believe every word you say. Bill Rock was filling his shorts on the phone. He'd got one hell of a call from someone. Don't think they told him what you just told me, but he'd clearly experienced a moment of extreme dilation.' He opened his drawer and pulled out three Havanas. 'The big red one, huh?' He offered them to Fuch-Smith and Jim, who declined politely, then lit his own. On the other side of the frosted partition his assistant looked on in horror. Smoking in the bank? It was like pissing on the doormat at Buckingham Palace.

'Well, we've all got one coming, but everyone getting it at the same time will be a sight to see.'

Jim's phone rang.

'Something's happened in the last hour,' Davas said. 'Our little planet's gone to a million units. Heavens knows why.'

'Great,' said Jim. 'That must be because …' He trailed off.

'Must be because?'

His face had gone a little wan. 'Eh … must be … well … perhaps something I've said.'

'You said what to whom?'

'Well, you know … I'm at the office.'

'Ah … and you told your buddies?'

'I'm afraid so.'

There was a long silence. 'Jim, you're a fool … but a brilliant one. That big flapping tongue of yours has just given us another million chances to watch the sun come up on the twelfth. What's more, it means something important. It seems we've got to get information flowing – perhaps it's the secrecy that keeps this thing hidden.' And with that he hung up.

Jim stuffed his phone back into his pocket, smiling.

'What happened?' asked Fuch-Smith.

'Our conversation seems to have improved the odds quite a bit.'

'What are they?'

'Infinitesimal but getting better.'

'And I thought we had problems with that key logger,' said Fuch-Smith, clutching his forehead. 'Hell's teeth, what a mess.'

Something buzzed through Jim's brain as if a hot thin wire had been shot into it from above. It was a high-pitched fizzing sound that travelled sideways from left to right 'What did you say?'

'What?'

'What did you just say?'

'I said, what a mess.'

'No, before that.'

'Before that?'

'Yes.'

'What – before I said it was a mess?'

'Yes.'

'He said,' Wolfsberg interjected, 'he thought he'd had problems with the key logger.'

There was a burning sensation in Jim's stomach and he tried his pocket for an antacid. 'Fucking key logger.' He found the pack with his fingertips, broke one out and put it into his mouth. 'I want the fifty mil up front.'

'At Christmas,' counter-offered Wolfsberg.

'Up front, in escrow with Wealth Management but under my control.'

'Done,' said Wolfsberg.

'You already owe it to me, right?'

'Yes and no,' said Wolfsberg, exhaling a plume of smoke. 'I hope we live to see you spend it.'

Jim smiled. 'Got to go,' he said. 'Got some running to do.'

He was running like a madman. Why hadn't he remembered the key logger? It was obvious – perfect, devastating, easy. If you key logged the trading computers of an investment bank you could get the passwords of the machine, then plant Trojan software on it to take control of them.

The machines wielded massive financial firepower. In seconds they could trade billions of pounds, long or short on anything, anywhere, any time. If all the traders on the floor let loose at the same time in the same direction, they could crash any stock, trash any bond, flatten any currency in seconds. It would cost the bank a fortune to unwind the resulting position but the short-term effects would be devastating.

Every now and again some fat finger would press the wrong button and crash a stock or bond by accident. But that was an outcome of one smallish blow-up. What if a few hundred trading computers went berserk at the same time? What if whole trading floors or groups of banks suddenly ran out of control, training the full firepower of the world's traders on the unprepared markets all in one co-ordinated moment?

It would blow them to pieces.

The global capital system was woven together into one fantastically convoluted network and if it could be hijacked and its trading turned in on itself the damage could put the markets out of action for weeks or months.

And what returned would be different. The arena of Davas's models would be dead, but while the world economy might suffer horrendously, it wouldn't end. The same old markets would come out of the ashes – but under new management and in new guises.

That was the answer. Someone had planted a bomb by hacking into trading platforms to make a concerted attack on the financial system timed for the tenth anniversary of 2001's 9/11 atrocity. It was not global Armageddon, after all, just a huge technical hiccup.

The treadmill was winding down and he jumped off. The shower was bitterly cold but it didn't shake him from his conviction. He was on the scent.

'That's astounding,' said Max, 'beyond impressive, except for one thing.'

Jim's heart sank. 'What?'

'You haven't even sent me your bank details and already you've saved the world.'

'Ah.'

'Ah,' echoed Max.

'But you're a man of your word, right?' said Jim, lamely, suddenly feeling sick.

'For fifty million dollars?' Max laughed. 'What do you think?'

'I've got to say yes.'

'Naturally,' said Max, 'and, Jim, send me your bank details before you tempt me too much.'

'Right away.'

'Anyway,' said Max, 'the chance of you saving the world in your lunch break is approximately nil, as the model says.

But you could be right. It'll take a couple of weeks to find out and you never know. Maybe you are *deus ex machina*.'

'One more thing,' said Jim. 'While I'm with you I'm going to keep working with the bank by sending them my charts. With luck, I'll be able to buy a Russian rocket for August and be in orbit on the big day.'

'That's fine,' said Davas, 'we've got two million pixels telling me they're on the side of good, and you can come on the Space Shuttle with me if you like.'

'Really?'

'No,' said Max, 'not really.'

'Pity,' said Jim.

'But you can work with your group, so long as I have your undivided attention when I need it.'

'OK.'

'But don't stop thinking because until those charts start pointing up higher than nil we're still standing on the edge of the abyss.'

'Keep the pixel scores coming.'

Chapter 23

A loud banging shocked Ravi awake. There was a bright light in his face and he raised his hands to cover his eyes. Someone was shouting, but before he could register what had been said, something went over his head and all was black again. A blow knocked the wind out of him. His hands were tied together, then he was flying through the air, thrown.

He hit the ground, hands grabbed him and began to drag him brutally along. He was wetting himself.

Wide awake now, he was pleading and squealing, his voice muffled by the bag over his head, but he was man-handled down a flight of stairs. He knew he was about to die. The cold night air hit and the ambience of the outside world filled him.

'Where are you taking me? I've done nothing! I'm no one, nobody at all!'

He was lifted, dropped onto a metal floor and dragged a bit further. Then there was a sharp clang as a metal door closed.

'What's going on?' he whimpered.

Someone lifted him onto a bench. 'It's OK,' said a male voice. The powerful hands moved him again.

Ravi heard the sound of metal clicking and could feel movement around his body. There was a zipping noise and he felt belts holding him upright.

'Just try to relax,' said the man's voice. 'It's all over now.

No more excitement for a bit. Take a few deep breaths and try to think nice thoughts. It might be uncomfortable but you're safe.'

'Where am I?' he quavered.

'Shut up,' said another voice, further away.

'Please,' he begged.

He felt a big hand on his chest. It pressed firmly on his sternum, the fingers curling and digging slightly into him. 'Shut ... up ... '

'OK,' he said, and began to cry.

The hand moved away and the room he was in started into motion. He was being taken somewhere.

Ravi had no idea how much time had elapsed. The hood made the passing of time impossible to gauge. Apart from a tiny bit of light coming in from the neck of the bag, all was darkness. Nothing was said to him, but the sirens around him told him he was the centre of official attention.

Oh, Jesus, what had he done? He had known that what he was doing might get him into trouble, but the money was good and he needed it. A thousand a month on the black to keep himself afloat. How much harm could it do, placing little plastic bungs on the backs of computers? It wasn't like hurting someone or taking their money. It was just like overhearing a private conversation. What he did was no worse than riding through a red light on his pushbike or dropping litter. There was no victim. So why was he being treated like a murderer?

When the bag came off his head, he was in a small, feature-less room with a chair in the middle bolted to the floor. His arms and legs were cuffed to it and he noticed, with horror, that the chair was not only a commode but also incorporated sockets and manifolds that suggested things could be slotted in or bolted on for an assortment of sinister purposes.

He seemed to sit there alone for an interminable time.

He would tell them everything he knew – his whole life story in minute detail. Jesus, they were going to torture him! He was about to live through, and probably die in, his darkest nightmare.

It didn't matter what he said, they would torture him anyway, just to make sure he was telling the truth. It was the same the world over. All the freedoms and laws of the West were a charade and a lie. When they needed to they would act like the evil dictators they so publicly vilified. There was no difference between any of them. He was crying again.

The door opened. A man and a woman entered.

'Hi there, Ravi,' said the woman, in an American accent. 'We're going to ask you a few questions.'

'I'll tell you everything,' he blurted, his voice thick with sticky saliva, 'everything. Anything you want to know.'

'Sure,' she said.

The man walked behind him, then suddenly grasped his shoulder. 'This isn't going to hurt,' he said. It was a British voice.

Ravi whimpered as the needle went in. Then he felt a sudden rush of clean air in his head and a wave of well-being swept over him. He smiled. These guys, the Yank girl and the British chappie, might be OK, after all.

They were probably his only friends in the world.

Suddenly his bowels moved. What a clever idea the commode was – and the orange smock was a lovely colour, iridescent and shimmering.

Chairs had appeared magically in front of him, with a

small folding table. His friends looked strikingly impressive behind it. He was smiling at them and they were smiling back.

'So, Ravi,' said the woman, 'what have you been up to at work in those banks?' She was so beautiful – too beautiful to be human. She must be a goddess, an incarnation of Shakti.

'Will you forgive your humble servant for what he's done?' He could feel her love for him and knew he'd be OK.

'Sure. As long as you tell me all you can remember. You must tell me every little detail.'

'I will,' he said.

'Who pays you to plant those little plugs?'

'Mr Tony gives them to me and he pays me, gives me new ones and takes the old ones back.'

'How much does he pay you?

'A thousand pounds a month in cash. We meet for a drink at the Horse in Streatham and I give him a bag of the things with some notes about where I put them. You know, where and what machine I got the things back from, just like he told me to do.'

'Do you do anything else for him?'

'Sometimes he gives me a CD and I have to put that into a drive of a particular machine and then I switch the machine off and on. I leave the machine to get going again and come back later and get the disk. He gives me five hundred quid for one of those.'

The man was smiling at him. He had a really slick tape-recorder. He was handsome, a great guy to have on your side.

'Did that happen often?' said the beautiful lady.

He wondered what her name could be.

'Did that happen often?' she repeated.

He smiled and nodded. He was drooling. He laughed. 'Every now and then,' he said. 'It was good when it happened. Five hundred is a lot of money.'

'Are you OK?' said the handsome guy.

'Yes,' he said. 'I'm fine.'

'What do you know about Mr Tony?'

'He's a lovely fellow,' said Ravi, his head rolling around on his shoulders. 'He's my friend.' He rattled his shackles and began to cry uncontrollably, his mouth gaping, his bottom lip hanging loose. 'He's my mate, he is, my best mate ...'

'Can you describe him to me?'

Two villainous thugs came through the saloon bar door and clocked the room. Marco didn't like the look of them and watched them in the bar mirror. They were walking towards him – definitely coming his way. He got up and headed for the door leading to the toilets and the lounge bar; it was the other way out. They were coming towards him pretty fast but he wasn't going to make eye contact, just keep heading for the door and hope they weren't anything to do with him. He was going to make it, he knew; he always did. His heart was thudding. The thugs were just there for a drink. A few more steps and he'd be out of there.

There was movement directly behind him and he bolted. Too late. Two sets of hands were on his shoulders and held him fast. He stopped. 'Hey,' he said, turning, 'let me go. What is this about?'

'Police,' said the tallest. 'You're under arrest.'

Cuffs snapped on his wrists.

'Hey! What is this?' protested Marco. 'You're not police.'

The other man was flashing his warrant card at the pub's customers and bar staff.

'OK, so you are police. What d'you want?'

'All in good time,' said the officer.

For Jim the weeks passed in a surreal transit. Some days he was at the office like any other day, others he would be shuttled to Davas's palace to pore over charts and models. It was early March, and as they worked, they watched the models move and develop.

A new planet of hope had appeared in the void of doom. Jim thought it was something to do with his dongle idea, but he was disappointed that it was still only a few hundred thousand elements while the main planet of hope had grown to a respectable ten million graphical atoms. Even so, their scale was almost non-existent in comparison with the size of the doomsday void.

They had their successes but the picture just wasn't making sense. When Flipper had asked Jim what would happen to the Zimbabwe maize market on the Day of Judgment he had laughed. But the idea had stuck in his head so he'd tried to look up the market. To no avail: the information wasn't directly available. It rather shocked him that some world markets were still so-called 'open outcry' and not in the global electronic marketplace. A market had to be minute, practically non-existent, if it didn't warrant the investment to turn it electronic. Open outcry was the old way of doing business, where men sat around a table and pushed orders at each other on slips of paper. In the developed world it was gone. Yet along the margin of global trading there were many micro-markets.

The Kathmandu stock exchange actually existed, as did the Mongolian futures milk contract, but they weren't covered by the bank's dealing screens. Who knew how much they dealt – if, in fact, they dealt at all? As far as mainstream traders were concerned, they, their cities and countries might as well not exist if they weren't on the screen.

Jim queried Davas about them and a few hours later Davas told him the plane was on its way to pick him up.

'What is it?' Jim demanded. 'Tell me what you're seeing.'

'The models are pretty rough and it's all preliminary, but there's an afterlife in some of these open-outcry exchanges. It's early days but you should come right away so we can look at them together.'

'Make sure you've got plenty of fax paper,' said Flipper, as Jim turned for the door.

The data visualization room was in darkness but the walls were lit as brightly as movie screens. It was like standing in a cinema, Jim thought.

Davas had been busy and the walls were filled with images. His hair was tousled and, in slacks and an open-necked shirt, he looked like an eccentric professor delivering a lecture. 'Look,' he said, waving at the charts. 'They all show life after death.'

'They look pretty screwed up to me,' said Jim.

'Yes,' said Davas, flicking his wire-smothered gauntlet from side to side, 'but they are trading. There might be just a smattering of activity but it is something – and, what is more, some keep going and going. They don't fizzle out like others. It is hope for humanity at least, if not for many of us.'

Jim studied the charts as Davas popped them up.

Ugandan sorghum, Nepali peanut oil, Laotian rice. 'None of this is European or US.'

'But, as we know, there is no open outcry in the West any more.'

'Do all open-outcry markets survive?'

'I'm looking into that.' He pulled up a map of the world and a few tiny red areas lit up against a sea of white. 'It doesn't seem so. The ones that do are in obscure places. I've got Research hunting down more and Coding is trying to optimize the results. It's all very rough and sketchy. Maybe when we've got all the data in they'll be dead like the rest, but I think we're on to something.'

It seemed rather forlorn to Jim. 'At least there's some-where to be on the tenth,' he suggested. He took off his suit jacket and hung it over a chair back.

'I'm buying up property in these markets now. Do you want some?'

Jim's trading reflex kicked in. 'I'll send you fifteen million. Put half in property and half in whatever you think will work as money.'

'Next door to me?'

'You bet,' said Jim. He imagined a large, creeper-covered bungalow in some impenetrable jungle hinterland, himself, glass in hand, sitting on his veranda in a rocking-chair at sunset, bats swooping past–

'It's funny,' said Davas, interrupting his brief reverie, 'I feel like a little boy again, dancing on the edge of the void.' He smiled sadly in the gloom. 'Maybe I should get up that morning, take a deck-chair up on the roof and watch it all unfold. What's a few years more to me?'

'You're full of shit,' said Jim, prosaically.

'Please,' said Davas, 'let an old man wallow for a moment. Look.' He picked up a big red arrow and flipped it round the map. 'Here,' he said, 'there's nothing. Nothing.'

'There's nothing pretty much everywhere.'

'I know,' said Davas, 'but nothing on the whole of the Atlantic rim. How can that be if there is still life in the world?'

Jim looked at the map. 'Why not? The Pac rim's pretty much dead too.'

'But not quite as dead.'

'Insufficient data for me. I do charts not maps.' He grinned.

'Well,' said Davas, 'I do neither. I do dimensions. But that blank space looks blanker than the other blank spaces to me.'

Jim laughed ironically, 'I'll try to keep that in the back of my mind. How are our planets doing?'

'Good news there,' said Davas. 'Major growth on Planet Two. It's about to catch Planet Hope.'

'I told you my bugging theory had legs.'

'Yes,' said Davas, 'but apparently still only tiny ones.'

The large unsightly scrapyard had once been a Second World War bombsite. But between the *Luftwaffe*'s levelling of the area and someone claiming title to it, A. N. Other had filled it with tonnes of twisted, rusting metal. It had long since become the hub of all kinds of nefarious business and the ownership of the ground had passed into new hands. Exactly who owned it and its contents now wasn't clear, but the man with the keys was Charlie Wilde, a fifty-six-year-old occasionally jovial villain.

Charlie was a bit of a local hero, who used to show up in the local papers handing out money to projects like the youth boxing club or the local kids' football team. He was a charmer, and someone you could always do a deal with for whatever it was you had, just so long as it didn't involve drugs or guns.

So it was a surprise to Charlie when, with an almighty crash, a police van rammed through the scrapyard gate. A stream of unmarked cars, with temporary blue flashing lights magnetically held to their roofs, tore in and dozens of armed police in black armour poured out of them. A team of four made directly for his grey Portakabin as he watched, horrified, through the mirrored window. Before he had time to open the door they burst into the small office building, aiming their submachine-guns at him and the other occupants.

Dumbfounded, they threw their hands into the air.

'Hello, Charlie.' A man of about Charlie's age, wearing a white raincoat, came into the crowded cabin. 'You've got yourself some grown-up trouble this time.'

Charlie wanted to say something, but he was showing deference to the men with guns.

'Go on,' said the policeman. 'Say whatever it is you want to say.'

'Phil, where's your fucking warrant?'

'Sorry, Charlie, you're out of luck. You've got twenty-four hours to spill your guts or you're on a plane to Cuba.'

'Cuba?'

'Yeah, mate, you know, the US bit of it.'

It was then that Charlie noticed the outlines of a man and a woman standing in the doorway. They looked like bad luck.

He laughed in an accommodating way. 'No problems, Phil,' he said, 'no problems at all. You know me, I'm just a good honest criminal. I'll give you what you need. Can't think what could be so serious but I'm sure you'll give me a steer.' He looked at the armed policemen with their machine-guns and smiled nervously.

'Come on,' said the inspector. 'Let's get a move on, then.'

Chapter 24

As Jim got into the boat, the door to the dock opened and Jeffries appeared. 'Excuse me, sir, but would you please return? Mr Davas requests your attendance.'

Jim stepped out of the launch and the engine cut.

'Look at this,' enthused Davas. Planet Two had doubled in size and was fluffing out at every fifteen-second refreshing of the simulation. 'Now I am growing more interested in your madcap idea.'

'What's causing it?'

'Our friends must be catching rats.' The planet ballooned again. 'This is looking good. I expect they're turning London upside down because of your theory, making progress along the lines of enquiry. Or maybe this is absolutely unconnected, caused by something else entirely. Yet it only appeared after we shared your notions with the ether.' The old man had developed a bounce in his slow gait. 'We'll crack this yet.'

'Six months is a long time,' Jim reminded him.

The bounce diminished. 'Not really.'

But the planet was swelling – a few hours of that and it'd represent real hope – at least in that collection of dimensions.

They were transfixed as they waited for each fifteen-second snapshot. Perhaps the growth would accelerate – or stop suddenly.

*

Craig's briefcase was a portable vault of legal papers and they were always heavier than he could carry comfortably. Whenever anyone asked him what was in it, he felt like saying, 'About fifteen years in prison,' but he never did. He just said, 'Work, lots of it.'

He hated lugging it through the interminable corridors of Heathrow. At one time they'd allowed him a little folding trolley to carry it on, but now the rules were so tight that it was a wheel-free bag or nothing. Even then they tried to tell him it was too big, but he flashed his frequent-flyer card and said it was impossible to check in his case, that he'd never heard such nonsense and, if it was true, then as a partner in his huge accounting firm he would instruct them to fly with another airline. It was a bluff but it had worked whenever he needed it to.

His obesity made it even harder to walk with his heavy load and it seemed miles to and from security to his seat on the plane. His flights always seemed to be parked at the far end of the terminal configuration – probably to spite him.

As an international corporate tax adviser, he practically lived on a plane and the grind was getting the better of him. He would often note a blue tinge on his lips when he arrived at a destination. It was a subtle but ugly warning that all was not well inside his shambling bulk. He snorted with a degree of relief when he noted that the Immigration check line wasn't too long and readied his passport. Just another quarter of a mile to walk and he'd be in his car on the way home.

He handed his passport to the official, an Asian woman in a headscarf, who swiped it through the reader. She read the screen. 'Where have you just come from?'

'Monaco.'

'How long were you there for?' she asked, scanning the screen absent-mindedly.

'Just two days,' he said, smiling harmlessly, 'out yesterday, back today.'

'What kind of business?'

'Accountancy,' he said, still smiling.

There was an awkward silence.

'I'm sorry,' said the official, 'but my computer is glitching. You'll have to wait a minute.'

'Well, you can see it's me, can't you?' he said. The smile was now a rictus. 'Can I go?'

The official sighed. 'I wish,' she said sadly. Suddenly two men were flanking her. She looked up at him through heavy-lidded eyes. 'Can you follow my two colleagues?'

'Yes,' he said, with a start, 'yes, of course.' The queue behind him was staring. 'Is anything wrong?'

'Please follow my colleagues. They will help you.'

Jim's mobile rang an SMS alert: 'We're at a 2% probability,' the message read. He jumped up from his seat. 'Yes,' he shouted, punching the air. The floor looked over at him. 'We're at a two per cent probability of reversal.'

There was the sound of half-hearted clapping.

'Whoopee,' said Dirk, laconically, turning back to his screen. 'Better close out some of those wacky options.'

For Sir Ken, the Club was the only place in London where he could have a smoke. It was against the law, but the law didn't apply to the Club. It applied to the others, those who needed to be ruled for their own sake. Smoking should have killed him a decade ago, but somehow that law didn't apply to him either.

He was very happy to sit alone in the coffee room, as it

was euphemistically called, and scan the *Financial Times* or the *Telegraph* at his solitary leisure. He wasn't allowed working papers in the Club or a phone and he was happy about that, but he had a little PDA strapped inside his wallet and now and again he would check stocks in his portfolio on the web to see if they'd moved by much.

When he was young, share trading had been life, but now stocks were like pet goldfish to him, swimming around in his tank, sending more money into his bulging accounts. Occasionally one would roll over and be found floating dead on the surface but on the whole they were racing certainties, tip-offs from his immense private network of contacts eager to indebt him.

His hair was black, greasy and combed across his scalp in a poor show of taste but a high display of social class. For important Americans it was necessary to have perfectly coiffured hair but for a British man of breeding it was important to show an aesthetic lack of care for looks and especially matters of hairdressing. A proper barber was old and barely capable of movement; his eyes should be dim and his metal comb worn by years of usage to blade-like sharpness. The barber's role was to shorten hair, not to turn it into some ridiculous soufflé.

No City gentleman sported good hair. Plenty of hair was fine, but delivery in a modern, stylish mode established its owner as a spiv, an interloper, a barrow boy. He gazed out at the quiet room, his watery eye wandering over the scant clientele.

Bertie Whatsisname was coming over to him. He took a puff of his cigarette, his long bony fingers covering his mouth for an instant.

'What ho,' said Whatsisname, sitting down next to him.

'Good day,' he said, regarding him with mild disdain.

215

The preposterous man had an ostentatiously large gold safety pin sticking his tie to his shirt. 'So, dear Bertie, to what do I owe this visitation?'

'Well, old chap,' said Bertie, 'it's a curious situation. I think you may know, or perhaps you don't, but a long time ago – and we are talking a long time – I used to work for some wallahs in Whitehall.'

'Really? What kind of wallahs? Treasury?'

'No, I'm afraid not, nothing so cosy. No, the chaps now in the ghastly green building over the river.'

'Oh,' he said, 'MI6. How very interesting.'

'Well,' said Bertie, 'they've asked me to get you to come along with me to pay them a visit.'

The cigarette fell onto the table. 'Really?'

'Really, old chap,' said Bertie, picking up the cigarette and placing it in the ashtray.

'When?'

'Well, now, actually.'

Sir Ken knew that something was very seriously awry. 'Of course.'

'That's very decent of you.'

'Did they say why?' he asked, his voice a couple of tones higher than usual.

'I'm afraid I'm just the runner, dear boy.'

'Yes,' he said. 'Of course. Just let me finish my smoke.'

'Most certainly,' said Bertie, smiling.

'Five per cent,' said Jim to Fuch-Smith, raising his beer glass.

'Cheers,' said Fuch-Smith, clinking his bottle. 'Doesn't sound like great odds, but I'll drink to it anyway.'

'Fucking hell, Seb,' exclaimed Jim, 'it was like one chance in a quadrillion billion a few weeks ago. Now it's one in twenty and we're practically on the beach. What's more, we've established it's not the whole world going up in smoke.'

Fuch-Smith said 'mate' like it meant something. His finely polished voice gave the common currency of a working-class greeting the special ring that only a six-figure education could produce. 'Mate, I hope this is all some awful mistake. I promise if it is I'll go to church every Sunday.'

'Look,' said Jim, 'I've actually spoken with the President of the United States. I've heard her sigh with relief. I've seen the look on her face that I see on yours when we talk about this situation. I've seen the stuff Davas works on. He's the Wizard of Oz. If anyone can crack it, it's him. It's no wonder prop desks lose money, it's no wonder they say the market's random – it's because he's out there sweeping the tables bare under our noses. We're operating in one and a half dimensions and he's in fourteen, fifteen – fuck knows how many.' He gulped his beer. 'That's why we're going to sort this out before it's too late. Davas has got his global simulation supercomputers.'

'And he's got you.'

Jim smiled. 'Well, I've got the cash to prove he thinks I'm useful. Anyway, we're going to sort it and then we can all get back to drawing charts and swearing at each other.'

'You won't be back,' said Fuch-Smith.

'He doesn't need me, not for what he does, I'm just a kid with a strimmer who zips over his multidimensional lawn and leaves a little trail. He could shift up a dimension and move the whole surface somewhere else and I'd be left trading noise like the rest of you. With a bit of luck he won't be arsed and we can get on with our lives.'

'Here's to the other ninety-five per cent,' said Fuch-

Smith, 'and another fat Christmas bonus.'

Jim's had already been paid and was sitting in a vast, embarrassing pile in his account. The bank had panicked and called him when Davas's payment had come in. Davas had to have his staff make all kinds of calls to establish the payment as legal and proper. Jim had spent about an hour online just looking at the balance – an unbelievably large chunk of cash to be all his. Finally he had sent it to Wealth Management.

'Did I tell you?' said Fuch-Smith. 'I bought back forty acres of the old family land last week. I thought, to hell with it, borrowed the money in-house and just wrote the cheque. I showed the deed to my mother and the old girl shed. And so did I – blubbed like a baby. Only a few more windows and the stable block to go, then on to clawing back more acres. It's all so nearly done that there has to be another Christmas.'

'There will be,' said Jim. 'We're going to make it.'

Jim stood next to Max. He was rather hot in the heads-up display visor.

'OK, take it to twenty dimensions,' instructed Davas.

The kaleidoscopic creature folded and twisted into a new flailing beast and Max rolled its life backwards and forwards in time.

'Stop,' said Jim. 'Step it forward. More … more … there. Let me take it.' He plunged his hands into the heart of the creature and zoomed into the innards. 'Surely it shouldn't be hollow.'

'I don't know,' said Davas. 'It suggests there is a lot of deep fate in the time period while superficially it looks volatile.'

'False volatility?'

'Again, I don't know,' said Davas. 'These models are not to be read like runes, they're intended as ways of turning millions of chaotic curves into predictable trends. We're using them for purposes they're not designed for. It's all conjecture, speculation and guesswork.'

'Thanks,' said Jim. 'Thanks for telling me.'

'The thing is, Jim, you're the master here. None of the progress we're making comes from my mind. You're the one seeing all these connections, putting all the pieces together. I'm just a burnt-out old man. Where you see patterns I hear noise, where you see the trail I just see a wilderness. I'm done.'

Jim waved his arms in his favourite gesture. 'Six per cent, Max! Six per cent! We're nearly there.'

'I know, my son,' said Max, 'but my weary bones have just about had it.'

'Control,' called Jim. The engineer appeared. 'How many dimensions can you give me full blast?'

'Twenty-nine. But no more.'

'Give me thirty.'

'No,' said the engineer. 'We're not tested to thirty. We might shred.'

'Give him thirty,' said Davas. 'Give him all he wants.'

'Give me the key probability map with a thirty D render.'

'OooooKaaaaay,' said the engineer, 'yes, sirree.'

The room went dark and suddenly the black of darkness was replaced by the black of projected darkness.

'Thirty D,' exclaimed Davas. 'I amaze myself.'

'Thirty D of black,' marvelled Jim. 'Awesome. Let's hope we have our planets in here.'

'But,' said Davas, 'we're outside the space. Let's see if she holds when we're actually on the inside.' He flexed his fingers and a little white smudge flew towards them. It was their six per cent probability space.

'Hold on,' said Jim. 'Wonder if I can do this? Normalize all positive regions.'

The lights went out in a bright yellow and red flash.

'Hell!'

'Sorry, guys,' came the voice of the engineer, 'we're up, but video feed just crashed. Hold on.'

There was another flash and the screen was back.

'Oh, my God,' said Max, 'or, as you would say, Jim, fuck me.'

Jim stared at the cube of spheres, all floating in space. 'That must be fifty different chances. Fifty different ways to stop this thing.'

'Information is flowing and it is on our side. That surely means God, too, is with us, for surely He is truth and truth is information. Let us start pulling these lovely planets apart. Maybe together they hold the key to the remaining ninety-four per cent.'

Chapter 25

A helicopter was flying over. What an ugly sound it made, Ali Muhammad mused. But his office was so close to the Saudi Arabian and US embassies and, for that matter, the Palace that he had half got used to the thundering drone of fly-bys.

He stopped what he was doing and listened. The aircraft didn't seem to be going anywhere. Instead the drone seemed to be circling at a distance. He brought up the surveillance cameras while he listened. Curzon Street was quiet and so was the entrance to Berkeley Square. In fact, it was a bit too quiet. Curzon Street was clear of traffic. He flicked through the other channels. 'Oh,' he said aloud, 'that won't do.'

The police were stopping the traffic in Berkeley Square and, from the lack of vehicles coming down Curzon Street, that route also. The helicopter was still circling.

Don't panic, he thought. It doesn't mean that this is it.

He scanned the roof and the back alleys. Nothing.

He pulled out a little gadget from his desk and switched it on. He went quickly to the window and looked out with it. It was practically his favourite gizmo of all time. It shone an infrared beam and lit up camera lenses wherever they gazed. It was magical. In effect it gave red eye to video cameras. Whenever he thought there might be a hidden camera, he brought it along. There were cameras every-where – the world seemed to be on a surveillance trip.

There were two red flashes as he scanned.

Oh dear, he thought, backing away from the window. They could be webcams shooting London vistas. He jumped back to his screen.

Four identical black cars were racing down the street. Were they coming to his door? If they were, they'd be there in moments. The lights went out as the power died in the office but his UPS kept his computer on. 'OK, let's go,' he said.

He popped a memory chip out of the front of his computer. Its hundred gigabytes stored all his information. Nothing concerning his operations existed outside the chip. He kept nothing physical: everything was shredded and powdered. Even utility bills, once paid, were atomised. He ran a clean machine.

Men were jumping out of the cars.

He pulled a large brown envelope out of his drawer and tore off the top. He was giggling excitedly. This was it, the beginning of the new life he'd longed for. If he pulled it off, he'd have complete and utter freedom.

Greed had bound him to his old unhappy life and now events were forcing him into the one he craved. He dashed across the room to the coat cupboard, clouds of dust billowing from the envelope. He poured some over his head and shoulders.

It was one of his best ideas and now he was using it. He had bought a job lot of second-hand socks headed for recycling in China and collected a little dust from each pair. The envelope contained the DNA of a thousand people. That was a saleable product, he had thought. What a perfect way to mask your own genetic fingerprint. He opened the cupboard and grabbed the cardboard box on its floor. Part of the wall came with it. It was a hatch into the next building, a flat he owned. He bent down and pushed it open on the other side less than an arm's length away.

Don't forget the case, you fool. He reached up to the shelf above and took down a large flowery shopping bag. You haven't got long. He threw the bag into the hatchway and climbed after it, turned and closed the cupboard door with a handle at the bottom of the frame. He took the hatch cover and reversed into the other building, pulling it back into place.

He had flown builders in from Pakistan and they had done a fine quick job. No time to waste, he thought, as he ran through the flat and out of the door onto the landing. He tore down four flights of stairs and then, fumbling in a pocket on the front of the bag, fished out some keys, which he used to open the door of yet another flat. He closed it behind him and made for the window. Below, there was a small courtyard, no more than ten feet square. He opened the window and climbed onto the small black fire escape and trotted down it, panting.

This was the weak point of his route: it was just possible that someone might see him from above. He walked smartly to another door, unlocked it and went inside. He closed the door and began to get undressed. He pulled out some clothes from the bag and put them on, then covered himself with a black *chador*. He stuffed his suit into the bag with his shoes and slipped on a pair of sandals. He checked his new femininity in the mirror. He was a very modest woman indeed. Under the robe no one would know what a desirable catch he was. He chuckled manically, moving across the dingy bed-sit to its front door. He walked sedately down the stairs, practising what he imagined would look like a woman's gait, until he reached a metal door on the ground floor that opened into an underground car park. It was shared with the surrounding offices, apartments and a hotel around the corner.

He wondered what was happening back at the office, and had an almost irresistible urge to turn back and find out. But it was self-destructive and he suppressed it.

He walked up into the hotel's reception area and out onto Berkeley Street. A crowd had assembled by the police cordon, and many officers were wandering comfortingly around. He turned away and set off towards Piccadilly. Soon enough a cab with its yellow light on was in his sights. He flagged it down.

'Eurostar, St Pancras,' he said, in a high-pitched tone. It would be tricky if the handicapped toilets were out of action, but merely a delay. In a few hours he would be in Brussels, then Germany, Moscow and Toronto.

Chapter 25

Davas and Jim watched in horror as the planets that filled the screen suddenly shook, shuddered and began to shrink. The chances of redemption had risen exponentially to hit a fifty per cent chance while the indices were starting to bend and flex, sometimes seeming ready to pop back from oblivion to normality. They sat hypnotized as the chance of salvation seemed to collapse before their eyes. The morning's miraculous growth was falling away at a terrifying rate.

Clearly something in the world outside was happening – and happening fast. Information was flowing and it was bad news. Something had gone wrong.

Jim reckoned it was still all about the dongle. Since they had passed on that information, a single small hope had expanded to form their ephemeral near salvation. It had to be connected with that. Whatever had been going right had suddenly gone into reverse.

Davas wasn't so sure: it was probably connected but he was a firm believer in the law of unexpected consequences and was not prepared to rely on such a simple theory.

The little planetoids of hope had also mainly evaporated. They were in effect almost back to square one.

'We've got to get some more brains in,' said Jim. 'We need more help.'

Davas snorted. 'The world is not brimming with minds like ours.'

'We're traders, not detectives,' said Jim. Through the

gloom of the viewing gallery he could see Davas hated the idea.

'Very well,' said Davas. 'I shall ask for the two most brilliant investigators our friends have got and then we will see if the model grows. If it does, fine, but if not, we will cancel the plan.'

Jim woke up. Something was out there. He sat up in bed and switched on the light. The bed was a large four-poster, with an elaborately embroidered canopy and, in the left corner, Cygna was kneeling upright, rather like a cat, watching him.

'Oh,' he said, dazed. 'What are you doing here?'

'Nothing,' she said.

He rubbed his eyes. 'You been here long?'

'No.'

He looked at the open wardrobe door. 'Did you come from Narnia?'

'Where is Narnia?'

'Don't worry,' he said. 'It was a joke.' He smiled. 'What do you want?'

'Nothing,' she said. 'I was bored.' She pulled a sad face.

He was now wide awake and his mind was being overrun by emotion. She was just an arm's length away, her beauty a few centimetres from him. She hadn't come into his room for a simple look.

She was clearly Davas's woman and pretty much a paid hand from what he could judge. Powerful men and harems were nothing new. Neither was the punishment for interloping.

Yet there she was, quietly looking at him, in just a white silk dressing-gown. All he had to do was lean forward and she could be his, at least for the night. The idea was becoming increasingly irresistible.

They looked at each other in silence.

It was some kind of Davas test, he thought, of course it was. But he didn't care. This was a test worth failing. A gorgeous angel was waiting for him to act and this might be one of his few chances to enjoy a woman before it was all over. He had to take advantage of it.

There was a creak and he turned to the wardrobe. It was the other two women. They floated over to Cygna and took her arm silently. She tried gently to throw them off but they were insistent. She looked sadly at him, then slid off the bed and followed them back to the wardrobe.

'Goodnight,' he said.

They said nothing, disappearing back to Narnia.

If he had started to make love to Cygna, their arrival would have been pretty embarrassing ... then again, perhaps not.

There were papers with his breakfast tray and as he drank his orange juice he flipped through them. He took his black marker pen and drew the continuation of this morning's charts. There were no mysteries today, just a series of choppy actions. No one at the office had complained about his remote predictions. There were no comments at all, which he took to mean that they were all working out fine.

Occasionally Davas had glanced at his charts. 'Astrology,' he had said. 'I wouldn't use these even if I needed to. It's so far from how I operate it would drive me mad. We take all the factors we can find and build a gigantic model. Then we create a theoretic framework, which we use to highlight all the anomalies and inefficiencies, wherever they may be, and trade away those inefficiencies. We build deadly fighter jets, while you just flap your arms.' He smiled. 'I can see how you make reasonable money with these, but one day you'll do so well you'll bend your charts and they won't make sense to you anymore.'

Two CVs lay under the charts. One was for an MI16 officer, the other a DIA operative. Jim hadn't heard of MI16 or the DIA.

The CVs made fearsome reading. The man and woman seemed to be inhuman super-people. Not only had they various doctorates but the CVs alluded to things that made his blood run cold. Were they killers? It certainly sounded like it. If they were, they were killers with the minds of physics professors and the bodies of world-class athletes. What the fuck would he and Davas be letting themselves in for if they got involved with them? The thought of world disaster was somehow less fearsome than the prospect of meeting these monsters. His appetite was gone.

He got up and dressed, then went to Davas's study. 'I'm really not so sure about my idea after all,' he said, laying down his papers.

'I agree,' said Davas, 'but the model doesn't. There's a new planet in the sky and it's a whole quarter of one per cent.'

Jim slumped into his seat, 'Well, that's good, I suppose.' He slipped further down in the chair and threw the CVs onto the desk. 'These scare the shit out of me.'

'Me too,' said Davas, 'but, you know, you are like me, worth a thousand of such people.'

'Not according to the model.'

'Right, not according to the model, not right now perhaps, but on the other hand, they are just expendable soldiers. We are not dispensable. If we solve this conundrum I'll be back keeping the US economy afloat and you'll be the star at your bank. You might not realize it, but what you do keeps thousands of people from starving.'

Maybe,' said Jim, 'but that won't save me if I climb into a den of lions.' He drew his life chart with his finger. It was still there – that was a relief. 'OK, let's get them in.'

Ali Muhammad looked at the map on the car seat next to him. It was at least a day's drive to the compound. He'd push on as far as he could, jet-lag permitting. He was tired and aching. He wasn't used to travelling cattle class. Sitting with the common people had been nasty and his thoughts had turned increasingly to arrest.

He had really fucked up, he was starting to think. The whole on-the-run thing had seemed like a romantic dream that would never come true. He was smart enough to stay undercover so that they would never catch him – the proof of that was the years of successful operations he had pulled off, each one firewalled from the last. There was no reason it couldn't have lasted for ever – but something had gone wrong. Somehow they had found him and now he was a non-person. The reality of that was sinking in. How long would he have to go into hibernation for? Five years perhaps, but now it was reality, it seemed like a hell of a long time. Wandering around the arse of Canada for five years felt like a prison sentence.

He thought about the three beautiful children he would miss. He hadn't realized how much he loved them, how much he wanted to hear them shouting and screaming as they smashed the place up, how much he had enjoyed sitting with them at dinner as they stuffed food into their pudgy faces. What was happening to them now? Were they in police cells with his pig of a wife or were they still at home, relatively unmolested? That was another life, he told himself. Now he had to focus on a clean slate. He had more than enough money to build a new life and identity.

It would be a perfect new life, too. No falling for a demure young girl destined to become a fat, ignorant, neurotic woman. No falling into a high-pressure job, however exciting. No danger, no schemes, no scams, just a quiet life, carefully travelling the world and enjoying what was on offer.

He'd go to Mardi Gras, see the World Cup, run the bulls at Pamplona.

He hesitated. If it was all still there, that was. Dusk was falling and the road ahead led on to a grey point in the distance.

Of course it would still be there. Whatever was planned was only a pinprick, a few tens of thousands of lives lost and a trillion or two dollars gone up in smoke.

In the end, it was all showboating. Even if they got their hands on a few nuclear weapons and took out a few cities, it wouldn't be much more than a psychological blow to the developed world. When Kobe had been flattened by an earthquake, as surely any nuke could have achieved, what had that done to the world economy?

Nothing.

And what had been the real cost of 9/11, apart from the self-inflicted wound of governments clamping down on freedoms?

That was the beauty of the brothers' strategy: it got the enemy to hurt itself, confused by a series of provocations. How witty and clever was that?

He rubbed his eyes. There was a funny sensation inside his brain, as if a bubble had burst and set something free. He saw the face of al-Karee, smiling at him. At last he was remembering his meeting all that time ago.

Another bubble burst. 'We're going to take the world back to what they call the Middle Ages, when it had the purity to host us. We will wash away this filth in a great flood, just as in the time of Noah.'

The Sheikh was smiling benignly at him.

Nuclear bombs, he remembered. Three.

Something was wrong, very wrong. His world was unbalanced. He was having a nightmare. He had to wake up.

He cried out as he woke to a great shaking. The car was careering up an icy embankment. 'Oh, God!' he cried, slamming on the brakes in a vain attempt to stop its wild trajectory. But the car leapt over the brow of the hill and took off. He caught a glimpse of what looked like a frozen river to his right before the vehicle smashed into the jagged wall of the valley, rolled over, and tumbled down …

It was some time before Ali Muhammad came round, and when he did he was barely conscious. The car was nose down on the frozen riverbed, the rear suspended on the rocks above. His seatbelt held him at an angle looking down on the whiteness of the ice. He felt numb and stunned. Moments passed and he recalled his mobile. With immense difficulty he extracted it from his jacket pocket. His arms were heavy and his hands seemed swollen and clumsy. He couldn't feel his legs but sensed the warmth of blood on his face and across his body.

I'm in big trouble, he thought vaguely.

He tried to focus and switched on the phone – his old day-to-day phone: how stupid was that? At last there was a signal and he called home – why? It was ringing and he realized he was sobbing. The answerphone picked up.

'Oh, God,' he said, and disconnected. He was going to die here – he could feel himself draining away.

No, he thought. Live. He dialled 911. He had to survive.

It was impossible that he could die now after all his careful planning …

It was a beautiful day, he thought. The sun was so hot and bright. He dropped the heavy load of his briefcase and wandered across the fragrant meadow. He sat on a little rise in the ground. It was very comfortable so he lay down in the long grass. He closed his eyes. He'd have a nap before he went on …

From the phone in the footwell of his smashed car a voice said, 'Hello? Can you hear me? If you can't speak, bang the phone or make any kind of noise.' There was silence, 'Hello?'

Ali Muhammad couldn't hear because he was dead.

Chapter 27

'You must be John and Jane.' Davas greeted the agents as they got off the boat. 'I'm Nicolas.'

'Hello,' said John Smith. He had an open friendly smile but it struck Jim somehow as threatening – it would remain quite comfortably on his lips as he slit your throat. He looked genial but profoundly dangerous.

'Hi,' said Jane Brown, shaking his hand with a firm grip that suggested she could have snapped his fingers like straws, had she been so inclined.

'I've got to ask,' said Jim. 'Are they your real names or are they, like, code names?'

Jane laughed then shook Davas's hand. 'No, they're real enough. Kind of funny though, huh?'

'Your name is pretty generic too,' pointed out John, slightly sarcastically.

'True,' said Jim.

'We have much to do,' said Davas. 'Please follow me.'

Jane waved at a screen. 'This, I think, is all us. The dates, everything, fits with the Trojan investigation Jim kicked off. The day before yesterday we were at the door of Target One and he'd flown the coop. That's when your probability field collapses – just a few minutes after we'd broken his door down. Obviously we tried to close all routes but clearly he's gone to ground so now he's lost to us and so is the linkage to other leads.'

Jim forwarded the model through time. 'Hold on –
something's happened. It shrinks right down – it's practically gone when your target gets away.' He zoomed in. 'It
goes to nothing, pops up big again, shrinks and now pops
up.'

Smith's clamshell phone rang. 'Yes … Yes, it is. Go
ahead.' He listened intently, throwing looks at Jane to
signify he was hearing something interesting. 'OK … OK.
Got that. Will revert.' He disconnected. 'Ali Muhammad
phoned home last night. He sounded in a bad way. The call
was from a mobile in Canada at around five p.m. EST.'

Now Jane took out her phone. 'Gregor, we're going to
need all info for Canadian 911 calls from five p.m. EST
yesterday onwards and any connected incidents involving
an Asian. Get all the data and scan it for Ali.'

'Impressive,' said John. 'Very impressive indeed – if, of
course, it's not a simple coincidence – not that we're
allowed to believe in coincidences.'

Jane awarded him an old-fashioned look. 'That,
gentlemen, is a little joke of ours, but another time. I'll be
surprised if the second change of probability is a 911 call.
That would be impressive, not to say a little awesome.'

'I wouldn't go that far,' said John. 'A tool like this must
be beset with weaknesses, however clever it seems.'

'It's a vast experiment,' agreed Davas, 'but so far it seems
to be working out.'

The model suddenly kicked into life.

'Well, looky here,' said Jane. 'Something stirs.'

'What happens if you ask it questions?' enquired John.

'Questions?' queried Davas. 'What do you mean?'

'Well, you know, questions. Short sentences that require
an answer.'

'It's like a magic eight ball, right?' added Jane.

'Well, not really,' said Davas. 'It's just a predictor.'

'No, it's not,' said John. 'If you put information out into the world it tells you how the outcome is affected. That's the same as asking a question.'

'Shit!' exclaimed Jim. 'You're right.'

Davas was shaking his head. 'I don't see it.'

'Look,' said Jim, 'we've done it already. When we accepted these guys onto our team we looked for the effect of requesting them, and when it was positive, we let it ride. That's the same as asking a question.'

'OK,' said Davas. 'Perhaps.'

'That half per cent in the background is you two,' Jim elaborated.

John and Jane looked at each other.

'She's most of it,' said John. 'She's the brains.'

'I'd go along with that,' she said, twitching her nose and glancing at Jim.

'So,' said John, 'let's ask it some questions.'

'OK, but what and how?'

'Let's get some US Navy SEALs and start them heading across country looking out for the bad guys,' Jane suggested.

'At random?' said John.

'No,' interjected Jim, 'quarter up the world, then move them around it and see if we get a new growing probability field.'

'That's not going to work, is it? They won't throw anything up if they're just wandering around aimlessly.'

'Unless,' said Davas, 'they're in a big, loud tank, with "US Terrorist Hunters" written on it.'

'Right,' said Jane, 'and newspapers trailing them, reporters embedded. Hell, that would certainly prompt a few questions.'

'You've lost me,' said John.

'Yes,' said Jim. 'Yes! Brilliant.'

'Oh,' said John, catching on, 'actually that's a fantastic idea. Spread the information that we're tracking terrorists and see its effect on the models. It's like Blind Man's Buff. We go left a bit, right a bit and the model tells us if we're getting warmer.'

Ali Muhammad's planet suddenly exploded back to two per cent.

'Your phone should ring shortly, I think,' said John to Jane, as it began to purr.

She answered it and paused. 'I can't talk now, Mother. I'll call you back tonight.' She smiled thinly at John and put it back into her pocket. But the phone call eventually came through. Someone fitting Ali Muhammad's general description had been found 120 miles west of Toronto, dead in a wrecked car. His briefcase had contained lots of interesting valuables and five passports. John and Jane had headed straight to the airport: a military jet would take them from Venice to Toronto. The trail was hot again.

The police interview room was painted a pale turquoise, the grey linoleum worn and chipped through long use. The table was bolted to the floor, its plain steel frame topped with laminated chipboard. Jane and John sat on tubular chairs backed with fraying canvas to pick through the treasure trove before them.

'Quite the collector,' said John, picking up a Patek Philippe triple calendar, minute repeating wristwatch. 'I wonder if it has a tourbillon.'

'That's a couple of million dollars right there,' said Jane.

'And the rest,' said John, trying it on. 'I shall have to take it into custody.'

'Bingo,' said Jane. 'Wonder what's on here?' She held up a chip she had just extracted from Ali Muhammad's top jacket pocket. 'You keep looking, I'm going to get this sent right along.' She lifted her case on to the table top and took out a small laptop. She plugged in the chip. 'It's protected, naturally.' She clicked on the touchpad. 'That wasn't too hard.' She copied it and started the send. 'Let's see what we have.' She stared intently at the screen. 'Ah, sixty-four K encryption. Nasty. They should have nailed that coder to a tree.'

'How much you got there?'

'About eight gig.'

'How long's that going to take to crack?'

'Forever. Unless it's got a back door.'

'It's sure to.'

She pursed her lips. 'I hope so.'

'Send my team a copy,' said John. 'If your lot hasn't one maybe my lot does.'

She nodded. 'OK. I'd send it to the Russians but we'll probably just get an enormous bill … Oh, what the heck? Let's get quotes from Moscow and Beijing.'

He opened an envelope. 'More goodies,' he said, taking out a ruby the size of a gaming chip. He poured a pile into his palm. 'How much is this little lot worth?' he mused.

'It won't be cracked till the third of September?' said Davas, appalled.

'Or maybe not at all,' said Jane. 'You know how encryption works, Professor?'

'Of course, Jane, but are you telling me that, these days, your people can't crack a few gigs of data within hours?'

'That's right.'

'You mean no one has found a way of factorizing big numbers?'

'That's right.'

'So, after decades of sucking all the best mathematical minds into your secret research institutes, you still haven't cracked the basic problem over splitting numbers into their divisors?'

'That's right,' she said, for the third time.

'Hah,' he grumbled. 'That is truly pathetic.'

'But factorizing is just long division, right?' said Jim, who was looking confused.

Davas waved him quiet. 'Yes, but sadly it's not quite that simple.'

'We'll have all the CPU available on the project. They'll be working on it on the grid. Anything that's not vital is coming off and this is about all that'll be run.'

'It had better not come near my grid,' Davas said sharply.

'Yours isn't on the program.'

'When I'm down, you can use it,' said Davas, disgruntled. 'I shall have my team connected to the program.'

'Thanks,' said Jane. 'I'll pass that on.'

Davas turned to Jim. 'That gives us about a week's grace with new information if we don't crack the question before then.'

'Let's hope the other idea works out better.'

'Morning,' said Nipper, as he walked to his desk. 'Are we going to live or die?'

'Die,' said Jim, baldly.

'That's OK, then,' said Nipper, 'because I'm short.'

'Good,' said Jim.

'The question is,' said Nipper, 'why isn't this a proper rumour by now and why isn't it hitting prices?'

'No one really believes it, and if they did, what are they meant to do? Sell their assets and have an orgy?'

'Why not?' said Nipper.

'What are you doing here, then?'

'My girlfriend wouldn't let me go on an orgy.'

'You're clearly not the only one.'

'You don't actually believe it, though, do you, Jim? You don't really think it's likely we're all for it?'

'It's a strong possibility,' said Jim.

'Well, I'll take it on faith that it's going to be all right. I don't know how a car moves, I don't know how a mobile phone can speak to someone on the other side of the world, I have no idea how the TV hanging on my wall can show me a football game playing a hundred miles away or, for that matter, how the match can be recorded on a shiny little disk. It's all magic, it's all invisible, and I believe in it.

'Billions of people in the world, so they say. I don't know if there are. The Queen's in her palace, but I've never seen her. The sun in the sky is a fiery nuclear reaction hanging in the vacuum of space. If you say so. I take it all in good faith and I believe I'm not going to die this September, but I am going to be stood next to a Zimbabwe maize trader on the eleventh and I'm going to be buying all his contracts.'

Jim laughed.

Chapter 28

Spring was in the air and Jim admired the new green growth breaking out on the trees in the squares of Canary Wharf. Proceedings seemed to have ground to a halt. The models were pretty static, only the occasional flare-up adding fractions to the positive-outcome score. For some reason the SEAL team idea was taking a lot longer to get together than they had expected.

Weeks passed, Smith and Brown calling in occasionally to update them with little but excuses.

Finally Davas phoned the big guy. 'Sorry to trouble you, Susan, but our request for a group of SEALs to go on a noisy terrorist hunt seems to have run into the sand.'

'I've been watching that,' she said. 'They don't know why they're being sent on an apparently ridiculous mission so there's passivity.'

'Can you …'

'Sure.' She paused. 'Can you explain the reason to me so it makes sense?'

'Yes,' said Davas. 'It is a highly visible display. This information flow will get into lots of nooks and crannies and when it does it will affect behaviours, which will show up in our model affecting the markets. Then we shall know if we are getting physically closer to whatever is the enemy. It is an attempt to flush them out.'

'OK, I follow that. That's how you got to that top lieutenant, right?'

'Exactly,' said Davas. 'The closer we got to him, the more that information fed back into our models, changing the market and our projections. It's a giant feedback loop. It works in the same way as a sweep for listening devices. They call that "howl-back". It's a novel approach but we've proved it works.'

'OK,' said the President. 'I'm a believer, but this stuff is treasury technology, not military. If they saw the books they'd be believers, too, but they only hear about the cheques that go out.'

'But we mustn't pollute the signal by giving out the reason behind the actions.' Davas was pacing back and forth. 'It must be done double-blind. Otherwise the signal we get back will be horribly confused. No one but ourselves can know the trick or it will be ruined. If people know what we are doing the hotter/colder signal will not reach us. We will get all sorts of interference.'

The President screwed up her nose, a sign, Davas knew, that meant she had a problem needing resolution. She clicked her fingers. 'Screw the military. You know what? I'll send some old White House Secret Service guys to do it. They'll love it.' She smiled. 'I'll haul them into the Oval Office, tell them if they're prepared to go on a suicide mission they need to go straight to Andrews Airforce base and that God will be with them. We'll cut out the passive aggressives at the Pentagon. I'll make some calls.'

'Great!' bellowed Davas.

'Give me a couple of days, Max.'

'Thanks,' he said, 'and kill the military expedition or we'll be getting two signals.'

'Will do. *Adios*, Max.' The screen blanked.

'This had better work,' said Davas to Jim. 'Time is flying by and we are stuck at seven per cent.'

'What do we do if we suddenly get growth?'

'Zero in, flood the area and try to catch our quarry.'

Jim sighed, 'Max, we need more. This is long-shot thinking.'

'Suggestions gratefully received,' replied Davas, grumpily.

'How's the property in Kathmandu coming?' asked Jim, by way of protest.

'My son, if we fail, we shall be big in Kathmandu.'

'What's the food like there?'

'As I recall,' said Davas, mournfully, 'pretty poor.'

Davas had asked him to have breakfast with him in the morning. That sounded rather ominous to Jim. A change of routine was seldom a good sign. It was like being called to the principal's office when you had done something bad and could guess it was connected.

It seemed a strange scene to Jim, the huge dining room with just two people perched at each end of a long table. The windows that gave onto Venice were stained glass and effectively blocked out the view. The heraldic devices that adorned the walls and ceiling were painted in gold and red, offset by the dark brown of the beams and panels. There was no fire in the grate: outside it was a warm Italian spring morning.

'I shall have to make some investigations,' said Davas, as they moved into the final lap of breakfast. Cereal, fruit, tea and toast had been rounded out with kippers. Jim had noticed that his skinny bachelor body was filling out on his regime of regular eating. Likewise his ever-extending breaks from the office meant his visits to the gym were less and less frequent. Davas was not the keep-fit type, and while his palace was crammed with antiques, it was without one item of exercise equipment.

'I'm going to have to disappear for a bit – a month, maybe more,' said Davas.

This was it, thought Jim. The bad news he'd somehow been expecting. 'What's the plan?'

'I must speak to some people and find out what this thing is.' He sipped his coffee. 'I keep thinking that it makes no sense. Nothing is so big that it can turn out the lights of the whole world. Nothing short of being hit by a planetoid could do that. I can't imagine anything so large that a few men could engineer almost the total extinction of human life. We are missing something, and if we can work out what it is, we shall be close to finding the answer. I can no longer just sit here and hope our fine ideas in our hermetically sealed bubble will pay off. I must take action.'

'Can I join you?'

'No,' said Davas. 'The people I shall talk to would refuse to see me if anyone unknown to them is with me. I am a trusted broker of long standing. I can meet people quickly on my own and get the information I need. Without security, I may not reappear, but that is a risk I shall have to take.'

'What do you want me to do?'

'Stay here and watch the screens. Our other little bets may come off and someone has to drive the system.'

Jim nodded.

'It must be nuclear,' said Davas. 'It just has to be an instantaneous event, but for such an instant cessation of activity it would have to be some kind of enormous first strike and that simply cannot happen.'

'What makes you say that?'

'I have asked them both and they tell me it cannot happen. I believe them. They don't aim these missiles for mutual assured destruction now – even the military have adapted to that reality.'

'We've established it's human and terrorist, but what about biological? Is there really nothing that can transmit fast enough?'

'No, the bug would need to be a pandemic now – perhaps even from last year. Even with modern travel, the most virulent disease would take months, even years, to deal such a blow. And even then, if it took hold, it would be controlled to some extent by natural forces and the mathematics of epidemiology. However bad, the process would be too slow.'

'You can't poison the world overnight,' said Jim.

'There's no known technology outside nuclear destruction that could do what we're projecting. We've gone over and over it, and even with a nuclear strike, it's unclear how it could possibly happen.'

'How about the Second Coming?' said Jim, almost meaning it.

'I will call in at the Vatican on my way and ask if they have a view.' Davas took another sip of coffee. 'I shall move all my staff to safety as well, except Jeffries, who will stay on to look after you. I'm having a 777 turned into a seaplane and if it's ready in time, you can stay here right up to the last day. Otherwise I suggest you get yourself to Kathmandu a week or so in advance.'

'You mean just pack it in and let it happen?'

'Well, that's up to you. You can go to London and wait for the flash. What else can you do on the last day in history?'

'Try trading it?'

'We're building like crazy in Nepal so you should be able to trade from there, and if it doesn't happen, you'll have had an expensive break and ended up with some pretty inter-esting property in some remote and immaculate parts of the developing world.'

'When are you off?'

'About midday – first to Jerusalem and then wherever it takes me. I'll keep you posted but nothing to pollute the datastream. You have to sit it out in case I stir something up or something else kicks off – to use another of your expres-sions, Jim. I'm leaving the future of the world in your hands.'

'It'll suck just sitting here and waiting.'

'I know, my son,' said Davas, 'I know exactly. That is why I must drag my poor ancient rear around the world's ugliest fleapits in the hope of finding a clue. This is the point in my life when I was meant to be buying my way into the history books, not earning my way there by working miracles.'

Jim drew his personal chart. 'My life chart suggests all your flashy simulations are wrong. You see,' he said, drawing it in thin air again, 'it goes on and it goes up.'

'Jim,' said Davas, smiling, 'you are going to be the king of Kathmandu.'

'No,' said Jim. 'I'm going to draw a few more charts with my felt-tip pen and push your sims off your money lawn so you'll have to retire.'

'From your mouth to God's ear,' said Davas. 'That's a trade I'll gladly make.'

Jim felt like a ghost, hanging around the Venetian palace. It was like living in a museum, beautiful but cold. Davas had made an exquisite collection of artefacts.

Paintings lined the walls, in ornate gold frames. He hadn't heard of Rubens or Titian before and didn't think much of the fat, semi-naked men and women prancing around in their work, but he knew instinctively that each one was worth a fortune. Everything that Davas owned was. There was a profusion of old tapestries and carpets, too, all depicting scenes from what Jim deduced must be ancient myth or stylized hunting.

Armour from around the world and across time stood to empty attention in corners and by doorways like a troop of fossilized bodyguards. There were ceramics, too, fine Oriental vases in one room, crude medieval ones in another, fancy European porcelain from the eighteenth century elsewhere. Then there were the clocks, hewn from solid bronze or encased in exquisite cabinets, the ancient wood twisted by time like the palace itself. Every item seemed to Jim a frozen moment from another universe.

There was only so much marvelling he could do. If the world was going to end, these treasures were just a load of rubbish doomed soon to lie at the bottom of the lagoon. Some day a future generation of humans might excavate Venice in search of booty and come across the remains of the palace buried in the sticky grey mud. Some of the treasures might survive – the non-ferrous metal pieces, the glass, the pottery might come through intact, pathetic curios of an extinct civilization.

Could the earth be swept clean? Or were the scars inflicted by Jim's generation of humanity too deep to be completely erased?

Such were the depressing thoughts he was having now that Davas was gone. Smith and Brown were spinning in their void, two stagnant planets revolving on their stationary axis. He searched for Davas among the dust of probabilities that now stretched out through the dataspace like cosmic nebula. He was kind of proud of the dust: he put it down to information that was filtering out. It created the possibility of new chances of survival, which were spreading slowly in the digital vacuum. But dust was not enough and he couldn't find Davas among it.

At approximately ten to one, as he liked to consider the ratio of dust to vacuum, things could turn out in their favour in any case. A ten-to-one outsider could win – it happened every day. Ten to one, however, were not odds that many people were happy to play against when life was at stake. It meant long runs of losses with few consecutive wins. Accepting a one-in-ten chance was a desperate measure and Jim saw it as almost a guarantee of damnation.

Fifty-fifty, though, was another matter. Fifty-fifty was a friend. He felt he could rely on enough luck to be on the right side of those odds. It was nonsense of course. Fifty-fifty was Russian roulette with half the barrels filled – not the sort of game to be playing when the penalty for losing was oblivion.

He took to wandering the secret passages of the palace, entering through the wardrobe. He explored the twisting ways that spread right across the building, inching along with an LED penlight. After his second expedition, Jeffries had left a map on his bedside table, with a large yellow high-beam torch. That cancelled out the excitement, but as he studied it, he realized it would be just as much fun if he knew where he was going. There were small rooms and quirky features scattered through the passages – gates with gimmick latches, trapdoors, secret viewing points, sliding doors with clever mechanisms, hidden rooms and covert entrances to the palace itself. The building was like an elaborate toy, a mysterious, historic fairground attraction.

There was a secret study at the top of the building, a room that seemed like a wormhole to the sixteenth century. The floorboards were thin, gnarled and uneven. The walls were white stucco, yellowed, like old cheese rind, with age. The black beams still showed the cuts and chips made long ago by craftsmen as they fitted them into place.

He liked the warm aromatic space. Light from a rosette of mullioned glass illuminated the tiny area with a subtle yellow light. Hiding there was like being transported back in time. He would sit for hours on an old rough chair, letting his mind wander. If only he could come up with another breakthrough.

He was starting to imagine that the scenario wasn't a nuclear event after all. It was technological, but software. A catastrophic worldwide computer failure would do the job. If all the computers in the world crashed at the same time it would be an apocalypse of a different kind. Wouldn't that be a bullet in the head for the world?

For a start, all the computerized markets would cease. Planes would fall from the sky, ships would be uncontrollable, cars would grind to a halt, phones wouldn't ring, lifts wouldn't rise, water wouldn't flow and there would be no electricity. The money supply would fail and the whole modern world would cave in. The impact of a total computer shut-down would create such a cascade of disruption the system might collapse under its own weight.

Wasn't it a technical attack that the terrorist hedge-fund manager was planning? Weren't his sell bots trying to crash part of the financial system? Might there not be a wider conspiracy, a distributed attack set for the eleventh, an attack so huge that it would bring down the global network and its computers with it?

Everything was connected. Even his training shoes were linked to the internet. That meant they could run his bath for him, or switch the TV on. His MP3 player could read how many steps he took from his shoes and email him a good track to play while he was running. Absolutely cool, but likewise a virus in his shoe could drill into next door's wi-fi max network, hijack it and from there hijack the building's network, the road's network, the district's, the city's. It was only the notional firewalls between his training shoes and his microwave, his flat and his neighbour's, his building and the world that stopped anyone doing anything they liked to any computer on the planet. They were ultimately physically or electro-magnetically connected in a digital nervous system. If you could break down those walls, step around or through them, you could trash the whole system and with it the human world.

That had to be it.

He talked with John and Jane, who made enquiries.

Nothing changed on the model. He didn't believe the result. He watched and waited but nothing developed. Perhaps it was such a secret that no one knew except a tiny group of isolated people, waiting for the day when they would click a little icon and send the whole of modern society into the rubbish bin.

Meanwhile the overt terrorist-hunting group had landed in France, to a media uproar, and a shiny new planet was born.

Hotter, thought Jim.

The sight of gnarly old Secret Service men wearing T-shirts that read 'Terrorist Busters' jumping in and out of their gleaming black Hummers on the Champs-Élysées made him want to laugh. But the ludicrous spectacle was achieving its stealthy purpose.

'We're here to find the bad guys,' said the French translation of Colonel X's muffled reply on TF1's evening news. 'We know they're close by and we're tracking them down.'

'And how, Colonel, do you hope to achieve this by driving around France?'

The colonel smiled enigmatically, landscapes in motion on his leather face. 'We're deploying some pretty awesome technology here. So it's not about the how, it's about the who, the where and the when. Those terror-monkeys are in line for payback time.'

The TF1 anchor didn't look very amused as he made some apparently dry comment before the segue into the next story, but tears of mirth were rolling down Jim's cheeks.

As the team moved from Paris to Lyon, the planet changed and fluctuated. They moved noisily back north to Alsace, holding press conferences and not-so-secret secret meetings at high-profile security establishments, and as they went, the planet grew and shrank. It was going to take time to quarter the world at this rate and Jim had no idea what he was expecting to happen.

But, whatever it was, France didn't generate too much feedback.

When the group arrived in India the planet dwindled, and no matter where they roamed, nothing stirred their planetoid pebble of good fortune.

Spring was nearly summer and time was fast running out.

Chapter 29

Jim was out of ideas. He worked on the models. He ran and reran them, flew about them so that they became, in their huge complexity, a forest he knew as well as his own face in the mirror.

What made it worse was Davas's silence. Jim had expected at least the odd message saying he was OK, or that things were interesting, or at least a ping. But there was no traffic. There was just under four months to go and if Davas was dead there wasn't much he could do about that. If he was alive, he had his reasons for staying dark.

The only hope lay in the contents of Muhammad's chip when it had been decrypted, and the random long shots represented by the gathering dust.

He went back and forth to London just to keep himself from getting too lonely. He dropped into the office, but working there seemed pointless and tame. He hung around his flat, which soon became even more dull than watching data clouds spinning on their axes. He actually tried to go shopping, but there was nothing he couldn't afford and nothing he wanted to own.

It was turning out to be a beautiful summer and, like a child during the school holidays, as each day passed the next became more precious to him.

Eventually, rather than go to London, he sat in the dark pulling the models to pieces, trying to understand how the data fitted together and what the patterns could mean. What did a spinning strand of a planet represent? Was it an idea, an interaction, a person even? He couldn't make much sense of it, but as it moved and changed he could feel that, somewhere beneath all the complexity, there was meaning.

The days dragged on.

One day he flew into City airport to pay his respects to the traders and shake some of the palace dust from his mind. The floor was subdued and, after a few cursory greetings, he ended up in Fuch-Smith's office.

'The house will all be finished by the big day,' said Fuch-Smith. 'I was thinking about where I should be on that morning.'

'Nepal,' said Jim, 'Harare or Ulan Bator.'

'Right. Any particular reason?'

'Their markets don't die. I'm not suggesting they're the only places left, but operating markets do suggest some kind of stability and social cohesion. Anywhere else is just a guess.'

'So I should go to Africa or Asia?'

'Well, it's a pretty small subset, really.'

'Nothing in the Americas? I've folks in Argentina.'

'Pass,' said Jim.

'The family doesn't believe me, of course. They think I've gone bonkers.'

'Take them to the Himalayas for a holiday, but make sure you book it early and you've a way to get back out again. It's going to be a popular destination for those in the know and that'll be an increasing group.'

'Hell,' said Fuch-Smith. 'It feels so foolish even to consider the end of the world. I mean, what are we supposed to do? Walk around with one of those sandwich boards saying, "The End Is Nigh. Repent"? What will be the point of surviving anyway? I'm starting to think it would be better to go out with it than live a few sorry months up a mountain.'

He felt very sorry for Fuch-Smith. His erstwhile boss believed him entirely but was trapped. 'You can come and stay with me,' said Jim, 'just you and Jemima, mind. Tell her it's a holiday.'

'I can't leave my family behind – or hers for that matter.'

'But they aren't prepared to go anywhere, are they?'

'No,' he said.

'Then do the next best thing.'

'That's very kind,' he said, 'but no thanks. It's not going to happen, is it? Even the Roman empire didn't fall overnight. Germany survived the war. It's just a huge cock-up – these things always are. It'll be a typical IT disaster only written a bit larger. We'll burn candles for a couple of days and then it'll be back to normal.'

'Who knows?' said Jim. 'It's a pleasant dream.'

'Well, on the day I shall be riding my grounds on my new mare. Did I tell you?' he said, smiling. 'We're up to three hundred acres now.'

'You won't. If you're not in Kathmandu, you'll be at your desk ready to trade the arse off the big event. If there is a September the twelfth you'll need to hold on to that fat bonus to pay off your shiny new debt mountain.' He grinned.

'You've got a point, old chap,' said Fuch-Smith. 'And where will you be? In your monastery in Kathmandu?'

'Probably, but certainly not at the top of a high building in a trading centre.' He smiled grimly. 'Anyway, how's our trading going?'

'Solid as a rock,' said Fuch-Smith. 'We're going to have a monster year if we see the whole of it. The risk department is totally flummoxed. They keep telling me there has to be something bent about our performance, some magic account with losses hidden away in a secret drawer. But I tell them to go on and find it and, of course, they can't. The world's become a perverse place. I should be as happy as a dog with two dicks, but the bad news looks like it's going to come all at once.'

Jim looked out of his lounge window onto the Thames. The river was flowing fast as the tide went out. He hadn't had much opportunity to enjoy his new home. He'd spent most of his time in Venice and even then he'd hardly seen the city up close. He blew on the window, then drew the chart of his life on the condensation.

Either one of the charts was wrong or something would happen fast.

At five thirty he woke to the sound of his mobile bleeping. It was an alert from the main computing grid: the model had cleared fifteen per cent. He jumped out of bed and started to dress, punching in Jeffries's number as he did.

As always, the butler sounded completely awake and with it.

'I need to get back from London.'

'Certainly, sir,' said Jeffries. 'The small plane is at City airport. I'll scramble it for you.'

Jim wondered if Davas was in the 777 somewhere, and if he was, where he was and what he was up to. Perhaps he was already hiding in a bunker somewhere, waiting for the end. Maybe this was all an elaborate joke and he had been away making some trading killing out of the building chaos. There was always hope. He'd prefer to be a live rich fool than a dead rich genius. But enough of wild fancies: something good was happening. He had to find out what it was and do something.

'Is there a car coming for me?'

'I'll organize that as soon as you disconnect.'

'No, I can handle it.'

He punched in another number and waited as the phone rang. Don't go to voicemail, he begged silently.

'Hello,' said a sleepy voice.

'Seb, you want to come to Venice and see how it all happens? Something's going down.'

'Venice? Now?'

'Yes.'

'Abso-bloody-lutely.'

'Come round my flat soon as you can and we're gone.'

'Right-ho.'

Jim sat in the back of a black cab waiting impatiently for Fuch-Smith to appear. He kept looking at his watch, expecting it to have moved a lot further than it had.

It wasn't such a bright idea, he thought. A mixture of excitement and sleepiness had made him call Fuch-Smith, a moment of confused thinking. He could always just tell the driver to go, but he didn't.

Suddenly Fuch-Smith was getting in. He looked as if he'd run the three-quarters of a mile from his apartment to Jim's. 'Sorry,' he said, 'you must have the last cab on the road in London.'

'All right, guv? City airport?'

'Yes,' said Jim, and added to Fuch-Smith, 'glad you made it.'

Fuch-Smith seemed impressed as they were shown straight to the plane. The Gulfstream V was nothing on the Boeing, but it cut a dash. Jim had been backwards and forwards so often in it by now that he was inured to the grandness of it all.

'This is the life,' said Fuch-Smith, buckling himself into one of the plush seats in the passenger compartment. 'It's like a flying drawing room. Very nice indeed. I think Bill Rock has one of these – or, at least, the firm does.' The plane began to taxi. 'That's quick,' he remarked. 'No hanging around, then.'

'No,' said Jim. 'It won't be long before we're there – couple of hours max.'

'It's like a time machine,' said Fuch-Smith. 'You don't realize how much time you waste messing around at the airport till you experience this sort of thing. Two hours doesn't even get you on the plane at Heathrow or Gatwick.'

The aircraft was turning on the runway.

The captain's voice came over the intercom: 'Gentlemen, we'll be on our way in just a moment. We're expecting a smooth, uneventful flight.'

Jim smiled. 'Fucking hell. Seb. The odds are down to six to one. That starts to sound survivable.'

'Do you think I should stop buying land? Might be tricky to pay for anymore if things go well.'

'Going short money is a no-win trade,' said Jim.

'You're going to have to sub me if they boot me out the door on the twelfth.'

'No problems,' said Jim. 'I'm minted, as you know.'

'Minted and then some, thanks to yourself and Davas.'

'The carnival's in Germany, that's why,' said Jim.

Fuch-Smith was gawping at the screen as Jim pulled and pushed the models around. 'I have no idea what you're saying or doing,' he said.

'There's something in Germany and it doesn't like our little provocation.'

'Right,' said Fuch-Smith. 'Who, what, where, when, how and why?'

'Don't worry just now. See those big patches of white that make up that kind of cloud? They represent the combined positive possibilities of an event occurring that reverses the collapse that the overall model predicts. It totalizes one chance in six for a positive outcome, or one-sixth of the necessary score to make the positive outcome a certainty.'

'So why has it just grown?'

'Because we caused an event that created information of a certain kind that creates information that feeds back into the markets that then feed into the models that predict the outcome.'

'That's simple enough,' said Fuch-Smith, 'so why is the cloud spinning?'

'Spinning?'

'Yes, spinning. Well, that's what it looks like to me. It looks like it's tumbling. Rolling on the spot, so to speak.'

'What are you talking about?'

'Well, look at it, mate – can't you see it?'

Jim stared hard at the cloud. It shimmied a bit but that was just the projection. He stared at it harder. 'Give me another dimension of the cells,' he said, 'and gradient them from red to white.'

The room fell dark, then came alive with a burst of colour.

'Oh, fucking hell!' exclaimed Jim, transfixed by the throbbing, rotating cloud, which billowed with red and pink shadings. 'You're right.'

'Don't need to be bloody Einstein to see it moving.'

'Apparently not,' said Jim.

'What's it mean?'

'I ain't got a clue,' muttered Jim.

'Can't you ask the computer?'

Jim shrugged. 'Why does the probability field rotate?'

An engineer appeared in the video window. 'Some of the embedded dimensions are interlinked and fluctuating. It can cause a rotation in higher dimensions.'

'Can you tell us which they are?'

'Hold, please.' There was a pause. 'It'll take about two hours. We have to analyse the streams backwards. Is that OK?'

'Does the sim stay up?'

'We have to take it down and after diagnosis run it back up to speed.'

Jim took a deep breath. 'OK, do it.'

He lifted off his headset, then eased off the gauntlets. 'We're done for lunch,' he said.

The lights came up.

'Well, Jim,' Fuch-Smith began, 'I'm utterly awestruck. From what alien species does this stuff come? The next time I see one of our IT boys I'm going to punch him. Useless bozos. It's hard to believe my own eyes – it's like a scene out of some science-fiction movie. I'm humbled.'

'Davas is the man,' said Jim. 'That's for sure.'

'So what's happening?'

'Well,' said Jim, 'you've spotted something that's potentially incredibly important. Something inside the clouds is moving, which means that something in some dimension or other is changing, causing more changes in multiple dimensions, and whatever it is is tied together with the whole mess.'

'Sorry, old chap, but my brain stops at the four dimensions.'

'Any measurement that doesn't cross over another is a dimension if you want it to be. Strawberry flavour can be a dimension. You move up and down the strawberry value in the strawberry dimension depending on how strong the strawberry flavour is. However powerful it is, it won't cross over and affect the size of the strawberry ice cream you're eating. Size is another three dimensions.'

'OK.'

'Time might slow down when you taste the ultimate strawberry ice cream or you might travel ten miles to get it, but there is no strawberry minutes past five or five and a half strawberry kilometres home.'

'I'll take your word for it.'

'Anyway, you've spotted something that means probabilities are moving around because they seem to be attached to certain dimensions that are moving in tandem. Basically, the boffins'll examine what's going on and find out what's making the cloud move. That might give us a clue. So, you see, you're a genius among peers.'

'Not me, mate,' said Fuch-Smith. 'Even my old mum would have spotted that.'

'Let's get out of here for a couple of hours,' said Jim, 'or I'll go crazy sitting around waiting.'

'Coffee, St Mark's Square,' said Fuch-Smith.

'Done,' agreed Jim.

Jim was enjoying his coffee. In all the months in Venice, he'd had so much to do with and for Davas that he'd had neither the time nor the inclination to leave the cocoon of the palace. Jeffries had piloted the launch to the dock at St Mark's and they had walked on duckboards to get to the cafés that circled the square. It was hot for the two Englishmen but Fuch-Smith was buoyant and stylishly at ease. He was quickly at home anywhere, wafting through the environment as if everyone was smiling and waving at him. Jim admired that and envied his poise, which he knew he could never emulate. Fuch-Smith had imbibed his confidence with his mother's milk. It was all about an upbringing that enabled the old upper class to cling precariously to the top of the pile.

While privilege was gone, a certain graciousness still gave the old boys a better chance of a crack at success. But he didn't mind: for every silver spoon there were ten East End barrow boys on the trading floor. For every Old Etonian there were twenty grammar-school kids clambering up the slippery pole. At the top they found not dukes or earls, but Americans.

He looked at his watch as the pigeons fretted and fussed around their table. Two hundred and thirty minutes had elapsed so they should make tracks. He'd seen the blue sky, and now he had to see the data.

Chapter 30

Back in the sim room Jim called up the engineer. 'Have you got the results?'

'Yes.'

'What's moving the cloud?'

'The time and space dimensions.'

'Time and space?'

'Yes.'

Jim looked at Fuch-Smith, then turned back to the screen. 'So it's the influence of time and space that's moving the cells?'

'The cells aren't moving. It's their values that are fluctuating. It just gives the impression of movement. The changes are caused by fluctuations in time and space factors which make the cells appear to animate. It's a kind of optical illusion.'

'OK,' said Jim, 'but the animation is caused by the three space dimensions and the time dimension.'

'There are three time dimensions.'

'Three?'

'Well, six, but Professor Davas uses only half of each, three forward looking and three backward looking.'

'Thanks, and that's enough,' said Jim, grimacing, 'I get the idea.'

The screen vanished.

'You do?' said Fuch-Smith.

'Enough to be going on with for now.' He waved his arms

in a gesture that blew the model up large. 'Focus on the agent planets, and give me a colour gradient red to green on cell values.' The two planets were coloured in a gradient between red and green. 'Run them from creation to now.' The planets started to spin and pulse. 'This is the effect of the two coppers working with us,' he said, 'See how they're spinning? That's got to be them moving around.'

'Amazing,' said Fuch-Smith, 'but how can you tell they're moving? I mean, how can this thing know somebody's moving? It's a flipping Bollinger band, for God's sake.'

'As they move around they generate fields of information that percolate into the market and feed into the model. This is just a small slice of that tapestry but that's where they fit into it and that's where their impact sits. They're like tiny cogs in a huge watch and now we can see them spinning.' Jim held his arms up. 'Give me twenty-five dimensions.' The room went dark, then exploded into a shower of sparks. He pushed his hands forward and the planets grew larger on the wall. He held them in his virtual hands and pulled them closely together. The planets whirled and tumbled in a kaleidoscope of primary colours, which mixed together in cascades of electric pink, russet and mauve. Splashes and sparkles grew, and shrank, twisting and glittering like clusters of gemstones rolling across a black velvet cloth.

'Look,' said Jim. 'Jane's planet's been stationary for the last three days. According to our theory, she's not moving about much, but Smith is on the move. Let's test the theory. Call Jane Brown,' he said.

She picked up immediately. 'Agent Brown.'

'Hello, Jane, this is Jim. Got to know something. Have you been in the same place for the last three days?'

'Yes,' she said. 'I'm back at home base, doing some digging.'

'And has John been out and about for three days?'

'Yes – Malaysia.'

'Thanks, that's all I needed to know.'

'Progress?'

'Maybe … and you?'

'Zip.'

'I'll keep you posted. Over and out.' He lowered his hand as if he was hanging up an invisible phone and the call terminated. 'Yes!' he exclaimed.

Fuch-Smith watched the planets spinning. 'Do you think this can tell when you eat and sleep? Stuff like that?'

'I have no idea. These models are just an infinite collection of answers all rolled up into a giant ball. The trouble is, they don't give out the questions.'

'Pity, that.'

'Show the clown group.'

The huge complex cloud was billowing and turning, like a giant red and green hurricane. Something was going down in Germany and the cowboys were worrying the hell out of it. Perhaps they'd flush something into view.

'Call Brown.'

'Agent Brown.'

'It's me again.'

'Two calls in two minutes. What's up?'

'The terrorist hunters are whipping up a storm in Germany. I reckon something or somebody's there.'

'So are we going to quarter it up or try for a missile detect on it?'

'What do you think?'

'Missile detect would be quicker.'

'Explain that to me.'

'Well, if you get more signal going left, you go more left until you get less, then you go right. That way you vector in on the shortest route possible, depending on your manoeuvrability.'

'Sounds like a plan.'

'You direct them and I'll feed back.'

'OK. I'll be right back.'

'Got anymore bright ideas, Seb?' asked Jim, smiling.

'How about some chairs in here? Looks like this could be a long one.'

The anti-terrorist cowboys were in Berlin, making their spectacular way around the city.

The media couldn't get enough of trailing them around the world. Here was a procession so fascinating that no one could resist watching and speculating about what was going on. The secret agents weren't secret: their CVs were suddenly out in the public domain. They were heroes, every one of them, decorated and illustrious. They were like the Rolling Stones of the intelligence industry out on a James Bond world tour. The media couldn't believe its luck. When they had appeared in Berlin, the probability planet immediately swelled like popcorn in boiling oil. It was decided to send them to Munich by road in a huge cavalcade, flanked by a military convoy of light tanks and armoured personnel carriers. The cloud grew and twisted faster. Rather than roll, it began to shear into two counter-turning halves. Fuch-Smith thought it meant two things closely linked were moving in opposite directions, but Jim couldn't see that as anything more than a guess.

The road to Munich seemed to be progressing well. The stormcloud was growing steadily, reaching twenty-three per cent halfway along the route.

Jane Brown swung into high gear. A one-in-four chance

suggested that something was near, very near. If the reading got much hotter they would have to seal off a large area and go from house to house. The German authorities knew something major was afoot but they had no idea what.

She made the call. Dialling into the hotline, she would be connected to an anonymous senior intelligence officer in Germany. There were no introductions or pleasantries, just a message to be relayed and a confirmation to be received.

'*Ja,*' said the voice, 'listening.'

'A nuclear weapon has been captured by terrorists and has been hidden somewhere in a German city. Our agents in convoy are using our newest detection devices to trail the route the bomb has been shipped along. While we have not discovered the location we are making progress in finding it. Please mobilize your forces as emergency action may need to be taken. Message over.'

'Received,' said the crisp German voice.

Jane smiled. What she had told them was almost true.

The German authorities freaked out. They mobilized their armed forces and sent every policeman to stand out on the streets. All emergency services were at their posts on high alert and deferring to Washington.

As the group passed Nuremberg the planet shrank. Jim and Fuch-Smith studied the map, wondering if they should detour the group. It was getting late. The instruction went out that the convoy should head for Heidelberg and consider holing up there for the night. Within thirty minutes the stormcloud was growing, rotating faster and faster. Now it was a mauve blur, flashing with purple lightning as the two opposing poles spun counter-cyclically, churning the tempest into a swirling globe.

They decided to push on and head the group for

Mannheim. While the cloud was growing so quickly, they couldn't stop. If the enemy knew they were coming they would move fast. They had to go on until the prey was captured and destroyed.

The planet was still growing but progress had slowed.

'It's Frankfurt,' said Jim in the end. 'Get them to Frankfurt.'

The convoy turned north and headed for the city. Within minutes the cloud was turning a deeper shade of red and suddenly the counter-clockwise rotation changed. Now the mass of coloured pixels was rotating round a central axis, like the depression of a Caribbean storm. Streaks of red and green twisted together, feeding into the eye to reappear on the outer rim of the cloud. From there they were sucked back into the eye. Jane was now in an operations room on an open squawk to Jim and Fuch-Smith.

'We've got half of Germany heading for Frankfurt,' she said.

'Good,' said Jim. 'We're clearing fifty-fifty. How far are we from town?'

'Twenty klicks.'

'It's looking good. In twenty minutes we'll be into the eighty per cent range.'

'The Germans are all set up for a dragnet.'

The S&P chart projection was starting to come to life, prices on 11 September flicking up and down from zero as the virtual tempest roiled ever greater.

'The odds are in our favour,' said Jim. 'Remember, it knows we're coming. This isn't going to be a surprise attack.' He was elated. Everything was coming together. They were going to pull it off. Davas's tool was going to solve the riddle. The answer lay somewhere in Frankfurt and in a few short minutes they would have it.

Seventy-five per cent: that was a three to one on racing certainty. Those were the odds on the favourite in a two-horse race. Salvation was nearly in the bag.

Chapter 31

Five men jumped out of a minicab and ran towards the Frankfurt railway-station entrance. With rucksacks on their backs they darted forwards, stubby machine-guns at the ready. As they ran into the station they opened fire on anybody unlucky enough to be ambling across their path. There was screaming and panic as travellers scattered in all directions. One of the men put his rucksack against a pillar at the main entrance, then ran back to the main group. They dashed across the main concourse and up onto the platforms. There was a loud roar and a demolition charge erupted, bringing a large part of the station frontage crashing down.

Across the city there were more explosions as a group of armed men stormed the deserted Judengasse museum and began to fire from the first-floor windows at any passers-by.

The group at the station boarded a train and began to walk down the carriages, shooting anyone who couldn't flee fast enough.

In Sachsenhausen Strasse, two figures entered a dimly lit back-street from a dour apartment block. They had already donned their crash helmets and headed for the Enduro bike parked by the kerb. The tall man sat pillion and tapped the rider on the shoulder. The bike drove away, onto the main road heading south.

'All hell's breaking loose in Frankfurt,' said Jane, 'early

reports. Sounds like war's broken out. What's the model saying?'

'Nothing. We're on seventy-eight per cent. What's going on?'

'Don't know. Wait … wait. This has got to be some kind of diversion. Damn. Going dark.'

Jim groaned. 'We're fucked, I can feel it. This is the same thing all over again. Any minute now our chances are going to evaporate.'

The German police were heading for the station and the Judengasse museum while the real target was heading south on a trial bike. The diversion was working perfectly.

The score dropped to seventy-one per cent. Jim and Sebastian groaned. Sixty-nine, sixty-eight …

'It's all over,' said Jim. 'That's a person and he's on his way. Jane?'

'Yes?'

'We've lost him, the score's cratering. We're in the sixties and falling fast.'

'That was al-Karee, I bet you,' she said. 'He's the only one capable of putting on that kind of show at short notice. No time now. Later.'

They sat and watched their hurricane wane to a storm, then to a pink cloud that shrank to a small revolving planet.

Meanwhile CNN ran on the far wall. Frankfurt was burning. An unknown number of men were holed up in two locations, the station and the Jewish museum, in a brutal siege with German police. Up to five hundred, including women and children, were dead in the station alone, said the reports.

Jim was slumped in his seat. Fuch-Smith stood up and laid a hand on his shoulder. 'Don't worry, you'll nail those bastards, old chap. We're going to make it – I know it in my bones.'

Just four hours' sleep wasn't the only reason it was hard for Jim to get out of bed. He felt as low as he could get, and just wanted to curl into a ball and forget about everything.

But Jeffries was having none of it. Jim's breakfast was on his lap and the curtains were thrown open to let in the inviting morning light.

'A successful evening, I hear,' said Jeffries.

'No. Crap,' he said. 'Complete crap.'

'I'm sorry to hear that, sir. I'm sure today will be better.'

Grudgingly Jim took his coffee. 'Jeffries,' he called.

The butler turned. 'Yes, sir?'

'Do you know what's going on?'

'Of course, sir. The master always keeps me informed.'

'About the eleventh?'

'Yes indeed, sir.'

'So what do you think?'

'Oooh,' said Jeffries, 'it'll all come out in the wash. These things generally do. I believe in God.' Jim was mystified by this and it must have shown because the butler went on, 'Divine intervention will do the trick.'

'We could have used some divine intervention last night.'

'I'm sure things will work out in the end.'

'Any word from Max?'

'Still none to report,' said Jeffries. 'Will that be all?'

'Yes, thank you, Jeffries.'

Jeffries gave a little smile and a bow, and as he left, Fuch-Smith poked his head round the door, then glided into the room. He was wearing a blue and gold dressing-gown, his floppy quiff giving him a rakish air.

'Dying to get going, old chap. Dying to see the map.'

'Let me get this coffee down my neck and I'll be straight there.'

'Good show. See you in five.'

Jim gulped his coffee, then put the tray aside.

Jeffries was right: his personal chart showed God was going to step in. God didn't talk to the markets but He was meant to connect with people. He sighed. He was clearly preparing to die – why else would he be getting religious?

God might be in heaven and looking after his nan, but Jim hadn't any desire to join her – and, of course, his mum and dad – just yet. He liked life, always had, however un-satisfactory some of it had been.

He especially liked being a success. And he wasn't just any old success: he was a Chelsea-Football-Club-winning-the-double kind of success. Now would be a bloody infuri-ating time to die. He'd be parked on a cloud with a harp, telling all the other angels how he'd made it big and then, *boom*, before he'd had time to enjoy it, it had been snatched away.

He slid out of bed. Where the fuck was Davas?

'Good God,' spluttered Fuch-Smith. 'Is something buggered?' He went to take a closer look at the screens.

The sim was all fogged up.

'Thirty-five per cent.' Jim's eyes were wide with horror. 'What the fuck is this fog? Call Jane Brown!'

'Morning, guys, have you no drugs to keep you awake?'

'No,' said Fuch-Smith as Jim barked, 'can you send some?'

'Sure, we'll dispatch a selection. We've been kind of missing you all.'

'Sorry,' said Jim, still rooted to the spot, 'but we just had to crash.'

'Well done, you two,' said Jane. 'That was a huge coup.'

'Really,' said Jim, sceptically, collapsing into a chair. 'Well, there's something weird at this end. The model's gone foggy.'

'We busted them wide open.'

'Yes, but we haven't stopped them,' said Jim, fidgeting now.

'No, but they're on the run. That's a huge step forward. It's harder to run than hide, much harder.'

'All I can see is a bloody pea-soup fog on my screen. That doesn't look like progress to me.'

'I know – I've got a feed coming in. I wish I could move the frigging thing but it's just a video.'

Jim stood up to relieve the tension. 'What do you make of it?'

'I reckon that's probabilistic noise,' said Jane. 'It's like saying anything could happen, outcomes are evenly distributed. What we had before were tight zones of possibility clumped up, rather like lightning bolts looking to strike a small target. Now a billion things could turn the tide and grow into the big one.'

'Sounds a bit wishful to me,' said Jim.

'So does the whole damn system, but here we are, having flushed the biggest turd in history into the river. That's got to be a win.'

'So you think we've got them badly disrupted?' He was feeling a little better now and sat down again.

'You bet.'

'Have you got any lead on al-Karee?'

'Not yet. There's still the disasters going on at the station and museum keeping the Germans busy, but things will kick off today you can be sure of it. I think we've got al-Karee in our sights here and he's running like a rabbit. He's heading this thing up, for sure. We found his hidey-hole at last and he's skipped out the back. The shit on the ground is just a diversion. The question is, where has he gone?'

'What's the plan?'

'We're sending the cowboys to Paris and we'll play hotter and colder as we go. Gonna need you wide awake.'

'OK, but there's limits.'

'I know. I'm heading out in two hours – I'm coming on over. You can teach me to fly your computer and then go off to bed.'

'OK, sounds like a plan.'

'Me too,' said Fuch-Smith. 'I'll give it a go – we can take shifts.'

'Sure,' said Jim. 'Going to have to go 24/7 if we're going to catch this bastard.'

He put on a gauntlet and the helmet. 'Got to fly this soup and see if there's anything interesting in there.'

'Can I come?'

Jim laughed. 'We're not going anywhere,' he said, 'but put that glove on anyway.'

A moment later, Fuch-Smith was kitted up. 'It's like flying,' he said, as he squinted into the visor's screens and gazed through space to the planets and stars below. 'Blimey, I feel really dizzy.'

'If you get disoriented, look out of the bottom of the glasses. That'll give you a fix.'

'Right,' said Fuch-Smith, spellbound.

'Now imagine you're Superman. Hold out your arms and fly.'

He wheeled, and barrel-rolled the galaxies of data rotating round him 'Oh, cripes, that's amazing ...' A wave of nausea assailed him. 'Oh, I'm going to vom.'

'Just look out the bottom of your glasses.'

'Ugh, this is harsh.' He was breathing quickly, trying to regain his balance. He stared out over the abyss to the pulsating nebula ahead – he was flying towards it at an amazing speed.

'Look over to your right. See that arrow? That's me. Give avatar my face.'

'Oh.' He spotted Jim's face, a planet in orbit a million miles away, 'Got you.'

'OK. Try to follow me.' Jim's planetoid head streaked towards him and pulled up. 'Flying to the right now.' He veered off.

Fuch-Smith rolled his arms and followed. 'I think I'm getting the knack.'

'Filter out the bottom half scoring cells,' said Jim. The fog cleared. 'See those planets? Each one represents something that's a major chance in our favour. This one,' he said, as they flew past a small green and red planet, 'is the data that's getting decrypted. That fluffy mauve planet is what's left of last night's screw-up. Those two,' he said, swooping down, 'are Smith and Brown. The others, fuck knows because I don't. One could be Davas, one could be me or you, or it could be a disease, an assassin, a known flaw in their master plan. They're all positive chances of escape for us that are factored into the price of various markets. It's like looking at a slice of your brain in a CAT scanner. That fog's probably a remnant of last night's storm. He's leaving a trail and this is how it looks when you slice through the model in these dimensions on this axis.'

'This is so exhilarating,' said Fuch-Smith, realizing he hadn't registered what Jim had just said. 'Totally mind-bending.'

'You want mind-bending, watch this. Full model FTSE 100 live twenty-five dimensions.'

An ocean of throbbing colour reared up before them, enveloping them in a blast of tumbling electric forms.

'I'm lost!' Fuch-Smith cried. 'Where are you?'

'Bind user two.'

Fuch-Smith was catapulted through the chromatic ether and locked to Jim's side.

'This is the London market in action, a billion factors all interacting in time and space.'

'Amazing.' Now he was staring, mesmerized, at the multifaceted plasma that shook and quivered around him. 'But this can't be stocks and shares – they're too ugly, too dirty to be like this.'

'It's just people, ain't it?' said Jim. 'Just big numbers playing games together. Everything's numbers – we're just a long string of numbers held on a big wet computer. We're all just a bag of water and a sprinkle of data. This is what you see when you strip away all the shit. It's a giant creature and we're a cell in its body. In fact, we're not even a cell. We're like impulses along its nervous system, little photons on the back of its eyeballs.'

'Maybe it's just a video, just a pretty spreadsheet.'

'Maybe. Or maybe it's just good TV.'

'Well, guys, what have we got?' said Jane.

'Progress,' said Jim. 'The cowboy cloud's starting to condense, nothing special but it's building. I think we should send it south and see what happens. He has to be heading for Spain or Italy, don't you think? If I was him I'd run as far as I could from where I'd started.'

'Spain,' said Jane, 'is where I'd be going right now. It's got plenty of scope for hiding and plenty of coastline to hop off.'

'I'd go to Amsterdam,' said Fuch-Smith.

'Well, we'll turn south from Paris and if we get shrinkage we'll head for Amsterdam.'

'I'd go back to Frankfurt,' interjected Jeffries, taking Jane's kitbag.

'Good thought,' said Jane. 'Let's see where the model leads us.'

As the cowboys headed west, Fuch-Smith and Jane took turns to practise with the models under Jim's guidance, and gradually the computer grasped what their imprecise gestures and comments meant. When things were going well, they felt as if they were conducting an orchestra but otherwise it was like trying to play the piano with a mallet. Frequently they found themselves lost in obscure quadrants of data, whose meaning was lost in its complexity, and would withdraw to the parts of the model they felt they understood.

A fog drifted in the dataspace – data drifting around the models like dust in a draught. Many factors were in play, lots of tiny chances brewing in their favour, like microscopic drops of moisture: if only they would condense into a single pool …

The cowboy cloud looked pretty stable as it headed for Paris.

'You know,' said Jim, 'he's on the run so perhaps no one knows where he is and, as such, there's no information flow. They could drive right past him and the model would never know because no one else would know.'

'Someone must have a pretty good idea of where he's headed – it can't be a total secret.'

'Maybe there are several possible locations,' suggested Fuch-Smith. 'Maybe it's several people going different ways.'

'Maybe we're just not getting any warmer. When we hit Paris again, we go south.'

'It'll be about nine p.m.,' said Jane. 'I'll take the night shift so you guys can get some shuteye. Unless he's near Paris, which looks unlikely, nothing much can happen before tomorrow and I only need a couple of hours' sleep, tops.'

There was a huge police presence in Paris as the cowboys approached. After the Frankfurt outrage, the French authorities were worried they would suffer the same kind of eruption. The Germans had told them about the missing nukes and they were terrified that the weapons could be somewhere in their city. A few years ago the media would have been blaming the Americans for the flare-up in Frankfurt, but times had moved on: the terrorists had succeeded in their primary goal of driving a wedge between East and West and set an agenda of harsh battle-lines in which old friends became secret enemies and old enemies became overt allies.

The city braced itself for a sudden outburst of violence, but none came. The cowboy convoy drove down the rue de Rivoli, the Champs-Élysées, then on to La Défense. It turned south, and about an hour later the planet was shrinking.

'Amsterdam?' said Jim.

'Amsterdam,' agreed Fuch-Smith.

'Let's turn them around,' said Jane.

'Why not take them through Brussels on the way?' suggested Jim.

'Sure. That's a six-to-seven-hour route,' Jane mused.

She passed the order, and within a few minutes the convoy was heading for Brussels.

'Amazing,' said Fuch-Smith as, seconds later, the planet was rotating differently, cells popping up on the outer shell. 'It's like magic.'

'It's the power of the media,' said Jim. 'They're like a swarm of transmitters on the cowboys' tail broadcasting every little move.' He pulled up the TV news screens. 'Look, they're all showing the convoy taking a detour. The cowboys are no joke now, not after Frankfurt. That U-turn sent the message that there's a new hunt on.' He laughed. 'This could actually be fun,' he said.

'I wonder what the old boys think is going on,' said Fuch-Smith. 'It must be freaky for them to be pushed around by some invisible hand.'

'Right, bed-time,' said Jim, stumbling to his feet. 'Call me if it starts getting really hot. Anything over sixty per cent or weird.'

Chapter 32

Jim could sleep anywhere, anytime. He just closed his eyes and was gone. While the great drama was playing out around him, he lay snoring, his head buried deep in his pillows.

As he slept, the convoy trundled north, every kilometre adding to their chances. Jane sat alone, watching the planet grow. On the one hand it was a marvel, but on the other a menace, she thought. It was like witnessing the invention of a deadly weapon. It would change everything. There was clearly so much going on that they didn't comprehend. The swirls and patterns all meant something unique and they were only grasping a tiny part of the picture. Here was a new Rosetta stone, a key piece for a whole new science, a device with ramifications far beyond her imagination. In a sense it was a kind of time machine, a true fortune-teller, a genuine oracle. Radar had been magical seventy years ago: it saw through space like no eye could, used invisible beams and abstract concepts to reveal a picture that had given the Allies in the 1940s a key edge in defeating a terrible enemy.

Was this new tool any less astounding than radio waves had been only a handful of years before? The electromagnetic spectrum had been unknown to mankind for 99.9 per cent of human existence and the genius of science and philosophy had missed it for thousands of years.

While humans had preened and posed, fighting to prove they knew all the answers, they hadn't even scratched the surface of what was going on, any wisdom they had over-shadowed by their stupendous arrogance. Even now it must be the same story, she thought, as she watched the models slowly morph.

In the final analysis, it was human arrogance she fought, a force of utterly astonishing proportions. Mindless belief was the root of all evil, not money. Warped faith, ingrained insanity, random acts to support untenable ideas – these were the sustenance her enemies fed on. She was part of an unending battle between the smart and the stupid. Land no longer held the key. Ideas were the field of combat – to be fought over with the forces of Reason. Sadly that wasn't how people were wired: when their primitive models failed, they resorted to violence. Win an argument and you earned a kick in the head. That was why she did what she did: someone had to kick back for Reason.

The cowboy planet was growing nicely but it didn't look as though it would terminate in Brussels. Amsterdam seemed the logical next stop. The media was reporting every twitch and turn of the convoy as if it was some kind of sporting event. They were trailing about a hundred metres behind it, marshalled by a separate troop of local police, as it ploughed on relentlessly into the night, lights flashing and sirens blaring.

What a gas, she thought. The media didn't care that in a traditional operation their coverage would destroy a mission before it had even begun. They had no interest in the stakes: they would do anything to get their story and to hell with the consequences. Well, it was great for once to make them stooges, to be the user rather than the used.

At sunrise the procession would reach Amsterdam and things looked promising.

Chapter 33

Jim, Fuch-Smith and Jane stood glued to the model. The cowboys were in Amsterdam and the score was at eighty per cent. He was there – he must be. Al-Karee was surrounded. The convoy circled the city and the score stayed constant.

'He's playing dead,' said Fuch-Smith. 'He's lying in someone's basement and waiting.'

'We'll try to quarter him down a bit more over the next few hours, then the Dutch'll go house to house.'

'Just twenty per cent and we're done,' said Jim. 'I think I'm going to bust a blood vessel if I have to sit here and stress out for another two hours.'

'Relax,' said Jane. 'There's nothing we can do now except sit and wait. We know he's there. We've just got to let the folks on the ground do their thing.'

They turned as the sim-room door opened, expecting to see Jeffries carrying in a tray of coffee and refreshment. Instead it was Davas.

Jim jumped up from his chair. 'Max! You've come just in time. We've got al-Karee pinned down in Amsterdam. It looks like he's behind the whole thing.'

'Excellent,' said Davas. 'Better than I had hoped.'

'I'm Sebastian,' said Fuch-Smith, holding out his hand.

'Good to meet you,' said Davas. 'Ms Brown, I am glad to see you too.'

'Likewise, Professor.'

'I bring my own news, which is serious and also mysterious in it own way. But first let me at the model.' Davas took off his old leather jacket and pulled on a gauntlet. 'How many dimensions can you give me?'

'Forty-three,' came the reply.

'Oh, very good. I'll have them all.' He raised his arms and began to perform.

Davas moulded the clouds of data like a potter throwing clay on a wheel. He twisted the moving images, tore and folded them as he drilled into the models to filter out the information that interested him. He spliced the market for corn with the movements of the dollar against the yen, then stripped from it hybrid data to inject into the slithering psychedelic mass that represented the Dow Jones index.

Abruptly the hypnotic light-show stopped.

'Confusing,' he said, pulling off his visor. 'Most confusing. We're very close but there are so many factors it is just a horrible tangle of things, any of which could clear the whole space or for that matter fill it up.' He reinstated the basic model. 'This is what I have brought you from my travels. It is less complicated than worrying.'

He sat down in the chair, suddenly becoming the shrunken, tired old man he was. 'There are three nuclear bombs on the loose. It's a classic tale of well-meaning idiots making life harder rather than easier, and more security meaning less safety.' He sighed.

'Our friends the Israelis sold some bad people three dummy nuclear weapons for five hundred million dollars on the basis that their organization would be badly hurt by spending that much money on a lot of scrap metal. All they figured they needed to do was replace the cores with false nuclear charges and it would be a perfect scam.

'Five hundred million in black money for them and three

useless weapons for the bad guys. They thought no one would check the plutonium – if anyone tried to do that they would wreck the bomb and be killed by radiation. So as long as the bombs showed the right sort of weights and measures and clicked a Geiger counter in the right sort of way, they should pass muster. Well, you can probably guess the rest.'

'The bad guys managed to arm them?' said Jane.

'Yes. The thing is, it's hard to steal a nuclear bomb chassis because it's big. But the core is small – heavy but small. So it's easier to obtain a core and move it about than steal and get away with a huge lump of iron the size of the nose cone of an ICBM rocket. So the pinch point was the chassis, not the charge, and once they had the chassis it was just a matter of fitting the nuclear cores they already had.'

'That can't be easy,' said Jim.

'Not easy but possible. They have even refitted the tritium – another Mossad so-called precaution out of the window.'

'But three bombs mean three cities,' said Fuch-Smith. 'London, New York, Washington. That doesn't close down all the markets in the world.'

'I would agree,' said Davas, 'but that's not what the model says. It says Armageddon.'

'Maybe there's more than three,' said Jane.

'Hold on a minute,' said Jim. 'Our percentage is down.'

'Damn,' said Fuch-Smith.

All eyes turned to the model. 'It's only a tiny bit off,' said Jim. The hurricane was spinning slowly, its red and green bands spiralling into the eye only to reappear at the edge.

'Computer, is the spin faster than one hour ago?' called Jim.

'Yes,' flashed the screen in big red capitals.

283

'Thanks.'

The confirmation disappeared.

'Max, we've discovered rotation of the probability object means it's moving in time and space, and it looks like our man is moving, but slowly.'

'On foot?' said Fuch-Smith, perplexed. 'Surely not.'

'Push bike?' said Jim. 'No way. He won't show his world-famous face with half the world's media in Amsterdam and the cowboys strutting about.'

'Maybe his face is different now,' suggested Jane.

'Boat,' said Davas. 'He's on a boat.'

Jim hauled on his gauntlets and pulled up a satellite image.

Davas stood up, apparently rejuvenated. 'Let's see if we can pin this gentleman down. Computer, if the delta on the main screen probability object represents a relative movement of object B from object A, object A being the US military convoy, where is object B?'

'Gathering data,' said the screen.

'You never showed me that!' protested Jim.

'It wasn't applicable,' said Davas, dismissively. 'Anyway, there's no reason it will parse.'

A big red flag flew across the screen and flickered over the Amstel river.

'Zoom,' said Jim. 'Zoom into object A.'

The river expanded as the flag skipped back and forth between two travelling boats, one coming inland, the other heading to the sea.

'That one,' said Jim, zooming in on the outward-bound vessel with a clenching gesture. The flag was hopping about less.

'Hold the cowboys in one spot,' Jane was saying into the squawk box. 'Tell them to wait.'

They watched the boat intently, zooming in so that every detail was as clear as if they were floating ten feet above it. The wheelhouse appeared to have aerials on its roof and a small white dome.

'Canal boats don't usually have radar,' commented Jane.

An inflatable dinghy was strapped to its olive-green roof, and window-boxes filled with gaudy flowers decorated the forward length. Two orange buoys lay on a jumble of ropes in the prow, and aft, in the well, there were two garden chairs.

'So are the bombs on board?'

'The boat's too small,' said Jane.

'Note our score,' said Davas, 'still eighty per cent. Wait a moment.' He pulled up the charts.

'No one knows that we know where he is,' said Jim.

'We are missing something. This is only eighty per cent of the picture. We are one per cent closer to capturing him but still twenty per cent away from success,' said Davas. 'If we grab him now, we cannot guarantee to turn the tables.'

'We've got to pass the information on,' said Jane. 'We can't just sit on it.'

'Call the President on the highest priority.'

A well-dressed young man appeared on a screen. 'Will a five-minute delay be all right, Professor Davas?'

'Yes, thank you.'

The five minutes seemed to drag on for an eternity, and as Jim stared at the fluorescent hands of his watch, time seemed to be stuck in its forward half-dimension, as if a heavy load was dragging it back.

'Max,' said the President, sleepily, 'is this a sweet dream or a nightmare?'

'We have pinpointed al-Karee. He is holed up on a barge off Amsterdam and heading out to sea.'

The President was suddenly entirely alert. 'That's outstanding. When do we grab him?'

'I think we should contain him for the moment and just follow.'

She looked disappointed. 'Really?'

'I think three nuclear devices are already in place and that capturing al-Karee may ensure that they are detonated. You should inform a small group of your most trusted lieutenants and in a day or so we will know if it is safe to pull him in. The moment the model says, 'Go,' we should jump, but right now we cannot be sure that this is the answer. It is looking strong but not certain. We will keep the boat under surveillance and if it appears to be going to land or to meet another ship, we will step in. Do you agree?'

The President raised her eyebrows. 'What can I say, Max? Your crazy trading software can find this needle in a haystack while the whole of the Virginia complex hasn't had a clue in a decade.' She was trying not to yawn. 'Whatever you say goes. Now I'd better get off. I have a lot to do. *Adios*, Max. *Adios*, team.'

Jane was watching the boat on the screen. 'Good news. I think the boat's sea-going. It's hard to tell from this angle but it looks like it to me. It's a bit more than a river or canal boat. The prow looks pretty high, but if it's a river boat we'd expect it to head for the shore or make a rendezvous near the river mouth.'

'Tell the cowboys to split up,' said Jim, 'and head slowly along the north and south side of the river.'

'You took the tactic right off my lips,' said Jane.

But the boat didn't dock: it headed out to sea, then turned south along the coast. They sat transfixed in the darkened room watching it motor placidly through calm waters oblivious to their gaze.

Davas sat up. 'When do we get the decrypted files?'

'Tomorrow,' said Jane, 'or not at all.'

'I'd forgotten all about them,' said Jim. 'It's such a long time since we sent off that chip.'

'Any progress reports on it?'

'No,' said Jane, 'only that it's meant to be tomorrow.'

'Can't possibly work,' said Davas. 'Right first time?' He huffed. 'There is no probability of that happening.'

'Well, we've got the cat in the bag,' said Jim, 'so we probably won't need it.'

There was a knock on Jim's bedroom door. His head had just touched the cool centre of the plump linen pillow. He sighed. What on earth could Jeffries want now?

'Come in,' he said, and sat up in bed.

It wasn't Jeffries. It was Jane, in the house blue and gold dressing-gown, holding two glasses and a bottle. 'Can I come in?' she asked, already closing the door behind her.

'Sure,' said Jim, with a fair element of surprise in his voice. Words temporarily failed him.

'I thought,' said Jane, sitting on the bed beside him, 'with just over a week to the end of the world, it might be a good moment for a nice nightcap and a little fornication.'

'Really?' said Jim. He tried to imagine himself as his suave blond friend. What the hell would Seb say now? He'd have a smooth response lined up for sure. 'That sounds like a good idea,' he said. How lame was that? 'What have you got there?' he followed on, to fill the silence.

'A little pillage from Max's drinks cabinet.'

Now Jim recognized it. 'But that's his brandy from Napoleon's personal cellar!'

'Really?' she said. 'Ha, the stylish old goat. Hold these,' she said, passing him the glasses. She pulled out the cork.

'Don't want to waste any,' she said. 'We can always apolo-gize on the twelfth.' She poured out two large measures.

The Fuch-Smith spirit suddenly swept over Jim. He moved to one side and pulled a pillow into the gap. 'Jump in, then,' he said. 'Let's get cosy.'

She put her glass on the bedside table and slipped out of the dressing-gown, revealing her slender, toned body briefly as she slid between the sheets. He felt the electric presence of her smooth skin next to his. They clinked glasses.

Any minute now, thought Jim, Davas is going to come bursting through that door with some news.

But he didn't.

Jim woke to the light of morning and the door opening as Jeffries entered with a trolley.

Jane sat up in bed, the sheets discreetly around her.

'I've brought you breakfast,' said Jeffries, clearly speaking in the plural from the evidence of two trays.

'Thanks,' said Jim.

'That's great,' said Jane.

'Mr Fuch-Smith is looking to hand over to you in about forty minutes, if that would be convenient?'

'Sure,' said Jane. 'No problem.'

'Very good.' He laid the trays on their laps, then went across the room to draw back the curtains. 'Another beauti-ful Venetian day,' he announced.

Jane sipped her orange juice and smirked at Jim, who grinned back.

'If that will be all?' said Jeffries, heading for the door.

'Thanks,' said Jim again, for both of them.

The door closed.

'Davas has probably got all these rooms wired,' said Jane.

'You reckon?' said Jim, feeling a little embarrassed.

'Wouldn't you?'

'Eh, no,' said Jim, picking up the sheaf of charts Jeffries had brought with the breakfast, 'it'd be a bit pervy, don't you think?'

'It's called security.'

'But still pervy.' He drew a continuation line on the top chart.

'Maybe a little.'

'Well, I don't think he has.' He was staring at the next chart.

'I'll give it a sweep tonight.'

Chapter 34

Fuch-Smith looked half dead. 'Absolutely nothing, old chap. The blasted tug's just chugging down the coast with the cowboys drifting slowly along so they can pounce if anyone comes ashore. The probability model is solid around eighty per cent, give or take the odd flicker, so we've got a kind of siege on our hands.'

'Has Davas crashed?'

'He went at about six this morning – he's been doing a bit of to-ing and fro-ing, making sure we can see even if we get thick cloud cover. Stuff like getting a bigger feed into your ops, Jane, all that clever techie stuff. I've just been sitting about, keeping the old man company, chatting, that kind of thing. Feeling a bit like a spare you-know-what.'

'You're a diamond geezer,' said Jim. 'We'd still be staring at a blank wall if it wasn't for you.'

Fuch-Smith smiled wearily. 'Going to get some much-needed kip. Wake me if those files come through.'

'Late afternoon if we're lucky,' said Jane, 'so don't let it keep you awake.'

The time dragged interminably as they watched the boat crawl imperceptibly across the map and the morning slipped past.

'Hello,' said Jane, stiffening, 'what's this?'

'What?'

'There's a ship heading towards our boat.' She zoomed in on it. 'Now that's a nice piece of equipment,' she said, zeroing on it. 'It'll move a bit quicker than that old tub he's on.' It was a hybrid ship, half sailboat, half power yacht. 'It's certainly looking like it's on some kind of intercept … Squawk on. Guys, are you watching this yacht?'

'Yes, we are,' said a man's voice. 'It's a charter out of Poole, England. We're tracking down more details.'

'What's the plan?'

'We've got instructions to wait and see. So long as we don't lose contact with any parties we're holding back. The moment there's any risk of losing our contact we'll strike all parties.'

'What kind of strike?' asked Jane.

'Air-to-sea missile.'

'So we're going for a kill not an apprehend?'

'Roger on that.'

'Is Davas up to speed on this?' chimed in Jim.

'All parties.'

'Over and out, squawk off,' called Jane. 'Al-Karee obviously wants to get somewhere faster.'

'And at quite a risk,' said Jim.

'The cowboys must be keeping him offshore as hoped,' said Jane.

Jim stared intently at the yacht. 'But he must want to go south or he'd just head over to the UK and jump off there.'

'If the yacht's going to pick him up,' said Jane, 'you've got to think he's chosen a serious ocean-going craft. That means he could go anywhere on the planet. In fact it's about the perfect vehicle for travel in the case of an Armageddon event – engines for speed, sails when you run out of fuel and no one likely to bug you.'

'So where would you go if you were him?'

'North Africa,' said Jane, 'or the long way around the

Cape to the Middle East. I might try the Suez canal – I don't think they're sticklers for checking crew when you pass through it, and it would save a lot of time.'

'I'd go to New Zealand, if I didn't know better,' said Jim.

'And where will you be heading on the tenth?'

'Doesn't look like I'll be heading anywhere at this rate – can hardly run away now, though I'll hope to hitch a ride with Max if and when he beats a retreat.'

'Eighty per cent says we're going to pull this off,' said Jane.

Jim winced. 'We're still short twenty. Got to get to a hundred per cent to really shift the picture. One per cent short could be enough to fail. It's like being an inch past the edge of a cliff – close ain't enough.'

'I know,' said Jane, 'but I reckon we've got it taped. Whatever happens we're going to bag al-Karee. That's got to be the missing twenty per cent.' She shook her head. 'But if it was, the plan to grab him, should have pitched the score near to a hundred per cent, as news of the plan inevitably leaked out.'

Jim sighed. 'The answer's going to come – it's got to.'

'That yacht's looking like a winner to me. It's going right for the target, maybe thirty to forty-five minutes off.' It was racing towards the barge, dashing south to catch up with it. It was much faster even without its sails up, cutting through the calm seas at about twenty knots, closing the distance with powerful grace.

And now the barge was slowing, still moving in the water but dawdling. When the yacht was a couple of hundred yards away it lowered a small speedboat with two crew.

'This is the moment of truth,' said Jane.

'Come on, you bastard,' muttered Jim. 'Let's be seeing you.'

As the launch pulled alongside, two figures appeared from the cabin. They wore hats and one was significantly larger than the other. On the screen they appeared blurred and indistinct, magnified but not clear, enlarged but not highly detailed. It was like watching wildlife through slightly out-of-focus binoculars.

'Are you getting this?' Jane called across the link.

'Yes,' came the voice.

'Hell,' said Jim. 'Could be anyone.'

'The tall guy is the right height for al-Karee,' said the voice from the squawk box

The apparently taller figure climbed down into the speed-boat.

Jim's eyes were burning as he stared unblinking at the picture on the wall.

The figure sat down and, as he did so, looked up.

'Did you see that?' exclaimed Jim. 'Do it again, you fucker, show us your face.'

'Did you get it?' called Jane.

'Enhancing now.' There were distant cries of joy from the team on the other end of the squawkbox. 'It's a match, a no-beard match. It's the man himself.'

'Hooya,' said Jane.

Jim was grinning. 'Now let's see where this new boat goes.'

'That ship can be anywhere in a three-thousand-mile radius from here by the eleventh – that's most of the way to a lot of places.'

'He'll go into the Med, then head for Lebanon or Libya is my guess,' said Jim. 'He'll have a whole series of links there to get him under cover again.'

'And we'll be on his tail every second of the way.'

Davas bounded into the viewing room. 'Good afternoon,

boys and girls,' he said, and bounced over to them, 'you will never believe this but we are about to receive a transmission of the decrypted data we have been waiting for.'

'When?' asked Jim, jumping out of his seat in anticipation of getting his visor on.

'Any moment now,' said Davas, starting to put on his gauntlets. Jim followed his lead.

'It's got to be just a lot of crap,' said Jim, challenging fate to deliver the opposite.

'That would be a shame,' said Davas, 'considering the hundreds of millions it has cost to unscramble it. We should doff our hats, if we were wearing any, to those who did the work. It really was a huge job. One day encryption will surely kill us all.'

'Ever thought of tackling the subject again, Max?' asked Jane.

'No,' he said emphatically. 'The main problem cannot be solved. It is why we exist. If things could be decoded quickly, complex arrangements such as ourselves would simply disintegrate. All order is enciphered energy. If it could be broken down, the energy of the universe would be drained away to the lowest levels of entropy and nothing would exist except the coldest of matter laid uniformly across eternity.'

'OK,' said Jane, shrugging, 'just wondered.'

'Some complicated things are unpicked by a single insight while apparently simple things can be underpinned by the most complicated foundations. This is one of those cases … Anyway, it's probably a discussion best left for a dinner in happier times.'

'Here we go,' said Jim. 'Oh, lots of stuff – lots and lots of papers.'

'Contracts,' said Davas, waving his hands in the air. 'Investment contracts. Dozens of different kinds.'

'Mountains of derivatives – this guy was trading big. Ouch, that one had to hurt. Currencies, commodities, interest-rate swaps. There's billions sloshing around here or the same few hundred million going round pretty fast.'

'Here's a collection of property,' said Davas, 'again a pretty fast transaction cycle. Money passing through one place to another. We shall have a full index in about three minutes.'

'He was a busy fellow.'

'Unless he's got a partner, there's a whole load of dead funds lying around somewhere,' said Jim. 'This looks like a huge money laundry.'

'Which of course it would be,' said Davas.

'Yes, but it's not a simple system. There's all sorts of messing around. See if we can map it.'

'Indexing coming up now.'

'Let's try and get it all linked up.' All the documents were suddenly floating in front of them like a confetti storm, linked by hundreds of metres of twine forming a crazy cobweb.

'Oh dear,' said Davas. 'Such disorder.'

'Let's see it by date.' The model lined up the papers in serried ranks. 'That's not much better,' said Jim.

'Let me try something.' Davas started to wave and jab his hands as if he was punching some invisible opponent whose head was about chest high. 'How about that?'

'OK,' said Jim. 'It's pretty, but what is it?'

'I've sequenced the documents by time, association and amount. This is a model in three semantic dimensions.'

'Interesting, but what does it mean?'

'That our dead friend was making losses in one place to make profits in another.'

'Like going short and long on a stock so the net position

is zero while you have a profit in one account and a loss in another?'

'Got it,' said Davas, still shadow-boxing. 'There! He opens two accounts in two places, makes two equivalent trades, then takes the profits from the winning one and moves it.'

'What else have we got?'

'Lots of investments in fine-sounding companies in unlikely places. We shall look some of them up.'

'Not getting many records on these names,' said Jim.

'What a surprise,' observed Davas.

'Lots of company name changes going on.'

'Big profits from those transactions – someone's paying a lot for these companies.'

'And there goes the profit out of one trading account into a mirror account in the name of another company.'

'Let's find where it's ending up – there must be a final home for all this.'

'There's about a net five billion dollars,' said Davas, bent over to study something in the phantom world of his visor. 'Oh, there's the five hundred million for the bomb chassis and another five hundred million out a few months before – probably the cores and tritium. Ha! That is cheap when you think of the cost of building your own.'

'That leaves four billion buried somewhere.'

'Not much to run a war on, really,' said Davas. 'Luckily for them they haven't much of an overhead.'

'OK, I've got a list of properties.' Jim pulled back. 'Ah – this looks like where it's at.'

'It's a good interest-bearing resting place. Plot the locations.'

A map in their visors filled with flags. 'Pretty much all over the world, then.'

'That fellow was a real star,' said Davas, 'running the whole show from a chip in his top pocket. He should have worked for me instead of those Nazis.'

'Hold on a minute, I'm going to try something. Let's get all the addresses in a list and add "plus doomsday", then run them through a search. Here we go.'

'Good grief!' exclaimed Davas.

'No!' muttered Jim.

'Put the view up on the goddamn wall,' shouted Jane.

'Sorry,' said Jim, and flicked his wrist.

'Tenerife?' queried Jane. 'That's, like, nowhere.'

'Just one moment,' said Davas. He raised his hand and a satellite image of the islands flooded into view. They were just brown dots in the cobalt ocean off Africa, seven irregular lumps that resolved into a short chain.

'Take a look at Isla de la Palma.' They zoomed in.

'It's a giant volcano,' said Jim, 'with a bloody big hole missing in the middle.' From space it resembled a green canine tooth, with a large chunk chipped from the centre.

'And the whole island's cracked down the middle,' said Davas. Jim zoomed in. 'And this is the address on the paperwork.'

'That's not an address, that's a mine,' said Jim, overlaying it on the satellite image.

'Geothermal research,' said Davas, 'is what my translation says. Site for excavation for the purposes of geothermal-energy exploitation. It's in the volcano itself.'

'Computer,' said Jane, 'pull up everything you've got on the volcano Isla de la Palma. Give me the details in order of relevance to threats against human life.'

'The top could fall into the sea,' said Jim. 'That's what I'm reading here. It could happen any time, producing general devastation around the Atlantic rim. A two-hundred-foot-high tsunami moving at a thousand miles an hour.'

'Jim, you are out of date. This model says the whole island could split into three and drop into the ocean. There is no continental shelf, so it falls into ten thousand feet of water in one giant splash. The island is like a wigwam made of three huge slabs of rock with a volcano in the middle and a huge wedge cut out of it by the last eruption. You are talking about a six-hundred to two-thousand-foot wave.'

'But tsunamis are only an inch high till they hit the shore.'

'Yes,' said Davas, 'but those ones are made by the ocean floor sinking or rising a couple of inches over an area of many miles. This is a mountain falling into the sea. A six-thousand-foot mountain spread over two hundred square miles. That will send a most massive wave around the world. It will be like the impact of the meteor that destroyed T. Rex.'

'I don't buy it,' said Jim. 'What about Asia? It's protected by the Capes.'

If Jim could have seen him, Davas was shaking his head. 'It's not just losing half of Europe and the east coast of America and South America, it's the shipping. Half the world's shipping lost in a single moment. The whole human food chain breaks down. There are not enough ships to carry the food and produce that the world needs to exist'

'OK, but why don't the Asian exchanges reopen?'

'Because China invades Russia, or India, or both,' said Davas. 'As soon as the wave strikes, everyone has to make a grab for land or their people will starve. Without the ability to ship food, it's a fight to the death for four billion souls.'

'Then someone starts throwing nukes and it's all over,' said Jane.

'That is what this says to me,' said Davas.

Jim zoomed into the entrance of what looked like a shaft into the base of the volcano core indicated by the white line of a concrete portal at the end of a track, There, the road entered the mouth of a tunnel. 'So that's where your three bombs are. Underneath a fucking volcano. How mad is that?'

'And you know something? We're all as safe as gold in Fort Knox,' said Jane, unexpectedly.

'Why?' said Jim, lifting his visor.

'Because that fucker is on a boat at sea, the very same sea he plans to send a tidal wave across. And you know something else? These guys are quite happy to send everyone else to meet their God – everyone except themselves. While he's on the sea, there won't be any loud bangs.'

'Well,' said Jim, 'I've got a plan. Let's see if we can get him to pay his troops a final pre-event visit. That way we can grab them together. It's a fair chance that while they're meeting their beloved leader we can arrange to screw up the party.'

'I reckon that's where he's going anyway,' said Jane. 'His course is pointing straight there. Computer, draw the course of subject ship.'

'Bugger me,' said Jim. 'You're right. ETA?'

'Computer? ETA of subject ship's arrival at Isla de la Palma, September the ninth.'

The door opened and Fuch-Smith walked in, yawning. 'Have I missed anything?' He gazed blearily at the walls of graphics.

'Yes,' said Jim. 'We've got it figured.'

'Bloody hooray.' Clearly he was disappointed not to have been in on the action. 'About time if you ask me.'

'It would seem that September the tenth is going to be a big day.'

'What's the model showing?'

Jim pulled it up. 'Ninety per cent.'

Davas pulled off his headset. 'Computer, close all open lines and report.'

'Auxiliary squawk terminated,' said the screen on the main wall.

'Careless but informative,' said Davas. He waved his hand in a gesture that Jim had repeated a thousand times. The world indices were on the wall and their future over the next few weeks was flickering and flashing as the chart trails thrashed like whips from the extremes of normal levels and zero.

Davas took a deep breath and stretched his arms wide. 'Gentlemen and, of course, lady, we stand on the very tipping point of history, unsure of which way the heavy load of humanity will be sent. In one direction oblivion lies, and in the other a mundane normality in which children cry for ice-cream and adults bemoan their tiny difficulties. We have come so far from certain disaster to this moment of near salvation that if we can throw a little more weight onto the right side, we will be safe.' He sighed. 'We are so close.'

'It's just good preparation from here on in,' said Jane, 'so relax, Max, we'll get you the last ten per cent.'

Jim was watching the charts writhe in uncertainty. He wanted to draw them himself, but he couldn't see their trajectory. 'This can still go pear-shaped,' he said. 'We've seen these probabilities collapse before, but this time it's our last shot.'

'You wait,' said Jane. 'Tomorrow that'll be ninety-two per cent and the day after ninety-five, and on the big day it'll be one hundred per cent.'

*

Jane was standing by his bed in the blue and gold dressing-gown.

'Is that a gun in your pocket or are you pleased to see me?' asked Jim.

'It's a gun.'

'Of course. That old chestnut doesn't work if you're talking to a woman. Have you come to shoot me?' he wondered light-heartedly.

'Yes,' she said, drawing the pistol. She took quick but precise aim and fired.

Jim felt the harsh blow on his chest and sat upright, eyes bulging. Oh, Christ, he thought. Only a dream, thank God. He lay back and looked at her sleeping form.

What was he doing sleeping with her? She was a killer. She could probably swat him like a fly and would if she was told to. How could he have let his balls override his brain like that – and not once but twice? That was exactly what he wouldn't do trading. Letting your emotions rule was a short-cut to disaster – and there he was, letting an assassin into his bed. It was convenient to think of her as some kind of glorified policeman, but her body told him more. It was lean and scarred, young but twisted. Long beautiful legs ended in calloused feet with bent toes. Slender fingers gripped like vices, arms and legs crushed. Her lips bruised, sharp bones dug, her movements snatched and jerked. If there was sweetness it was well hidden; if there was lust it was well controlled; and if there was passion it was expertly portrayed.

Yet on the other hand …

Chapter 35

'Morning,' said Fuch-Smith. Jim was wearing his suit trousers and a formal shirt, but Fuch-Smith was in casual garb. His chinos, brown loafers, rugby shirt and light jumper appeared at once informal and kinetic. He looked as if he was going somewhere.

Jim noticed the suitcase by his side. 'You off?'

'Yes. Nothing left for me to do.'

'Back to work?'

'Off on that holiday with Jem and the family.'

'That holiday?'

'Just in case. I'm taking as much of the clan to Australia as will come.'

'Oh,' said Jim. 'Is that a vote of no confidence?'

'Just an out-of-the-money put option. You know, insurance.'

Jim grunted. 'Right, that's smart.'

'Bought it some time back and now it looks like I might actually enjoy the break.'

'You're right to go,' said Jim. 'No use sitting here a spectator.'

'I'd love to, but I'd prefer to read about it in the papers on the twelfth.' Fuch-Smith offered his hand and Jim shook it. 'What are you going to do?'

'Don't know,' said Jim. 'I'll ask Davas. I guess I might be needed if it goes tits up.'

'Let's hope not, eh?' He sounded determined.

'Yeah, right.'

*

Davas was in the computer room, flicking through charts. He searched like a man turning the pages of a book intent on finding a single sentence. Jim sat down next to him. 'Anything interesting?'

'It is all interesting but not what I need.'

'What's that?' said Jim, his eyes on the charts.

'A little more certainty.'

'We need another five per cent.'

'That would do nicely,' said Davas.

'So it's looking like it's all down to the final day.'

'Yes,' said Davas. 'Now it is all up to a group of people with small brains and big guns running up the hill. Was it not always so?'

'So are we done?'

'Possibly – either that or done for.'

'Are you staying?'

'Absolutely,' said Davas. 'For one thing I have huge positions to watch.' He laughed. 'And for another, I would not miss this for anything. This is a ringside seat on the biggest event in history.' He smiled kindly at Jim. 'But you can go if you wish.'

'Fuck that,' said Jim. 'Anyway, this could go chaotic. So, you'll be too busy trading.'

'Good point,' said Davas. 'You can save the world while I trade it. That could be a powerful combination.'

'I want half the profit,' said Jim.

'Twenty-five per cent.'

Jim didn't hesitate. 'Done.'

'What about from the twelfth onwards?'

Jim sat down. 'That's a good question, Max. I'm a bit confused to tell you the truth. I've kind of got cut off from reality. The bank's weird enough, but this is a whole new level of weirdness. I'm just an East End boy with no roots. All this *Alice in Wonderland* stuff's getting to me. I might take a bit of time to find out where the real world is.'

'This is the real world,' said Davas. 'Everything else is just a comfortable illusion.' He threw up an image of a revolving data universe representing all the stock markets trading, their activity ebbing and flowing. 'This is the reality that puts bread in the mouths of the billions. The invisible energy that makes humanity what it is.'

'But, Max, it's a cold world, one I'd swap happily just to spend a single moment with my Nan.'

'Yes,' said Davas, and sighed. 'It is a cold world, but it has a great purpose.' Live footage from major cities – TV newsfeeds and CCTV – began to flash across the wall. 'Think of all the people on the very edge of starvation who cannot afford an extra cent's worth of rice. Think of all the people hanging by a thread, only able to survive because the market drives the hardest bargain. Thousands live or die on the smallest tick in the price of grain and the engine that drives it is made efficient by what we and all the other traders do. It is a benign activity, and as for all the money you make, well, you can always give it back. Although, I may add, not as efficiently as the markets can.'

Jim watched the cities fly by as broadcasters from Beijing, Mumbai, New York and Tokyo delivered their muted news in front of their local landmarks. Behind the animated American anchor Times Square was a blaze of advertising. The pretty Chinese reporter was standing in an apparently empty Tiananmen Square. The images fluttered by, digital pages turned by Davas's gloved gestures. 'It's all a bit insane.'

'It is,' said Davas, 'but there you have it. Life is a series of games and this is the biggest one in town.'

Jim drew his life chart with his finger. It was looking good.

'Let us get past the eleventh and take it from there. Better not to get ahead of ourselves,' said Davas. 'The enemy has still a one-in-twenty chance of throwing the world back to the stone age, so perhaps plans are a little presumptuous.' He flicked up the satellite image of the yacht sailing peacefully through calm waters towards its destination. He motioned and the seas scrolled by, zooming back to a bigger picture. From across the world warships were heading for Isla de la Palma. From space they were nothing but tiny dots sprinkled across the ocean, converging slowly on a distant destination. Yet up close they were the most powerful war machines ever created, steaming straight for the modern mountain of Armageddon.

Jane burst in. 'I can't believe he left!'

They turned in their chairs. 'You mean Seb?' said Jim.

'Who else?' she spat.

'I said he could,' Davas told her.

'I don't care,' said Jane. 'What sort of a creep would bail out now?'

Jim smiled. 'There was no point in him staying. It was the smart trade.'

'I don't care,' said Jane. 'You never leave the team till it's over. Never, whatever.'

'We are here, and that is all that is needed. Look, ninety-five per cent,' said Davas.

'Only five per cent short of the end of the world. Great. Let's all go home.'

'Come on, Jane,' said Jim. 'That five per cent's out of our hands.'

'The hell it is.'

'There's nothing more to be done.'

'Nothing?' She shot a look at Davas.

Now Jim noticed a certain silence coming from him. 'Nothing,' he said adamantly. He felt a wave of Davas's silence sweep over him again. He turned to him. 'Nothing, right?'

Davas looked at him blankly.

'Yeah, nothing,' said Jane.

'What?' said Jim, staring at the old man, who had suddenly curled up in his chair. 'What's she talking about?'

'Nothing.'

'Nothing?'

'Really nothing.'

'Really nothing?'

'Really, really nothing.'

'Fucking hell!' exclaimed Jim. 'What is it?'

Davas stiffened. 'It is really nothing … nothing for you, anyway.'

'Tell him, Davas.'

Davas didn't respond.

'Tell me, Max – you have to tell me.'

Davas stood up. 'This is unnecessary, stupid, dangerous thinking. It is inappropriate, wrong, and I cannot agree to it.'

'What are you talking about?'

Davas threw up his hands. 'Nothing! I am talking about nothing.' He spun around to Jim. 'Put your visor on, put your gauntlet on, stand up and see what she is talking about. Then you will understand what she is suggesting.'

Jim donned the equipment. Suddenly there was a flash of coloured light and he was in a city. Davas was standing next to him. There was a deafening crash.

'Christ!' Jim ducked. Armed black figures ran ahead and

there was a roar as streaks shot past him in the air. There was a cacophony of explosions, and helicopters flew in. 'Max? Is this a sim?'

'All right,' said Davas, 'You are going online.' There was a burst of gunfire as more black figures darted past them. 'Identify targets.'

A map of the scene appeared as an overlay on the cityscape, with points moving around it. Jim was in some kind of massive computer game with graphics so lifelike it was hard for him to tell whether the images were real or synthetic.

Davas gestured and zoomed into a figure with an RPG. A quick flick, and the point was marked hostile. The map morphed and Davas identified other points.

The friendly black figures swarmed about the map at Davas's bidding and fire rained down from the sky. The noise was overpowering. A tank crashed through a building to the right and suddenly Jim was running with the troops along alleys. They stopped at a corner as another explosion detonated, then dashed forwards into a hole in the wall. Bodies lay on the floor and blood trickled down the walls; detached limbs were tangled in the rubble.

Jim ripped off his visor. 'Jesus, Max, what are you showing me?'

'Nothing.' He slumped into his seat. 'Satisfied?'

Jim looked at Jane. 'And what?'

'Don't you understand?' Davas asked him.

'No,' said Jim, putting his visor on his seat. 'I don't.'

'She wants you under the volcano, using this.'

'What?' exclaimed Jim. 'Me? You're joking, right?'

'No one's ever used this technology. I wouldn't even have had it made if it wasn't for all this mess. It might not even work,' said Davas.

'It doesn't matter, because it's an overlay on what's going to be used anyway,' said Jane. 'Another system in addition to what we plan to use.'

'Wait,' said Jim. 'What are we talking about?'

'When we go in, the guys will be wired and directed. This system will be another level of intel that can be piped to the ops room.'

'But you would have to be in there,' said Davas. 'You would be running with the soldiers, like a human camera, a one-man mobile control centre. You would be like this room on legs.'

'Our forces wear a little tag and it talks to your equipment everything talks to you. We synthesize it all, then relay it back and forth between us, with you and the troopers in a seamless kill-net.'

'Kill-net?' said Jim

'It's hopeless, pointless, dangerous and stupid,' said Davas.

'It's not,' said Jane. 'It's not even dangerous. He'll be at the back.'

'Come on,' said Jim, 'you're not telling me you can't train your own people?'

Davas laughed, a crazy, high-pitched giggle. 'They're flying the test rig to the main aircraft carrier right now. It's the base station. This is the only operating post and the team there will be needed to operate the control centre.' He rubbed his eyes. 'So there would be no time, you see. I don't think they'll get it working anyway.'

'It's built to be moved,' said Jane.

'Well, that will be all right, then,' said Davas, suddenly sober. He looked at Jim. 'Maybe you should go on holiday too.'

'Is four days enough time?' said Jim.

'Yes,' said Jane, 'but it's three – we've got to get on station for the event.'

'Don't be stupid,' exclaimed Davas. 'He's not a soldier. What difference can a piece of buggy software make in the hands of a novice in the middle of a pitched battle?'

'Well, there's an easy way to find out,' said Jim. 'Patch into your HQ and tell them I'm up for it if I can get to grips with the software. Then we'll see what the model does.'

'That will only tell us what they think, not the reality,' said Davas.

'OK,' said Jane. 'Let's see what the model has to say. It's been right so far.'

Davas stood up. 'I can see you are both insane. While you make the call, Jane, I shall take Jim to be fitted out – or should I say fitted up? We must move quickly if we are to embark on this madness.'

As the door closed behind them, he said to Jim, 'You shouldn't do this. You said you were afraid of madness, and this is truly it.'

A few minutes later Jeffries struggled into Davas's study with two stainless-steel boxes, one large and oblong with a smaller square one on top. He set them down by the desk and unfastened the catches, heaved out a large rucksack and held it by the harness. 'If you'd step this way, sir,' he said to Jim.

'How heavy is it?' he asked, feeling a significant weight on his back. Fine living at the palace had put pounds on his previously spare frame and taken the edge off his fitness.

'Sixteen kilograms.' Jeffries was adjusting the straps. 'I'll leave a little room for extra clothes but if you pull these it'll tighten.' He clipped the cross belts together. 'How does that feel?'

'Fine,' said Jim, wondering how far he'd manage on the

treadmill with such a load on his back.

Jeffries lifted a visor helmet from its box. It was a green armoured dome with twin cameras mounted like eyes in front of the visor screens. He lowered it onto Jim's head, then took out some device Jim didn't recognize and set about moulding the helmet to his head. 'Tell me if it's too tight.'

'It's fine.'

Next came the gauntlet, which was, like the helmet, apparently free of wires.

'Shall I switch on?' said Davas, unhappily.

The screens came on and Jim could see the room they were in and Davas standing in front of him. 'Wow,' he said, 'cool.'

Davas was wearing a gauntlet and was sitting in front of his monitor.

'Can you kill the sound?' said Jim. 'It was deafening last time.'

'I'll turn it down but not off. You might need to be used to the sound of explosions on the day.'

'Let's get started, then,' said Jim.

Jane was standing in the doorway, a smug look on her face.

Jim's heart jumped. 'Ninety-eight per cent! But it's only been a couple of hours!'

'What is their problem?' shouted Davas. 'How could their confidence in themselves be so low? How can our chances be so much higher because of this crazy scheme?'

'Reputation,' said Jim, smiling like a cartoon character. 'They think you work miracles.'

'Well, I don't,' snapped Davas.

'Let's eat,' said Jane. 'Eat, train, sleep, eat, train, sleep, repeat.'

*

The system was a giant computer game controlled in much the same way as the market simulation, but focused on overlapping maps of what was going on around them. Rather than the markets interacting in multiple dimensions, the headset displayed information on the resources of a raging battle. Friend and foe swarmed around an ever-revealing map layered with values and conditions. Jim was soon flying around it as he had done with the fluctuations of currencies or capital entering a bond market.

But here the real world was the ultimate layer and lives, not money, were at stake. The simulation was stark, realistic and bloody to the extent that he often felt he could smell smoke and charred flesh. Jane was in there too, trying to learn the system, acting with a kind of military decisiveness that seemed at once awesome and horrifying. But his months of experience, and the system's understanding of his moves, dwarfed her ability to react and execute complex moves.

The soldiers might be just computer droids but to him they were humans directed into a world of horror and carnage.

As they traversed a battle they were protected by a squad of five guard droids, protecting their generals. Weighed down by his equipment, Jim was ponderous and helpless, and as he and Jane ran at the rear of the simulated conflict, the guards protected them.

This wasn't going to be a safe game.

'Shit,' muttered Jane. 'I'm hit.'

'You're reset,' said Davas.

The 'hit' error came up often, and Jim had long since realized that while the three per cent he had added to their chances of survival in the doomsday model had been a painless contribution, things were about to get very real.

Eventually they lifted off their visors.

'Well,' said Jane, 'now we're proficient in clearing out a Middle East township, it's a shame we don't have any caves to practise on.'

'Tonight,' said Davas, 'you will have all the tunnels your heart desires.'

'Great,' said Jim. His ears were ringing with the clamour of battle. 'How's all this going to work underground?'

'It uses magnetic instead of radio waves,' said Jane. 'That way walls, caves, whatever, won't block the signal.'

'Right,' said Jim. He was starting to feel envious of Fuch-Smith's holiday. 'We seem to be getting killed a lot.'

'You noticed,' said Davas.

'It won't be like that on the day,' said Jane, comfortingly. 'We'll be way back. Anyway, the body armour will take care of it.'

'Cool,' said Jim. Body armour sounded good.

'It should be all over before we get far in.'

Jim thought about the three per cent positive outcome he had added by volunteering. Three per cent of seven billion people was two hundred and ten million souls. In theory that was how many lives his gesture was worth.

He unbuckled his pack and slid it off. He tried to trace his life chart but his finger wouldn't do it.

'Oh, blimey,' he laughed nervously, 'this is going to be interesting.' The colour had drained from his face.

'It's OK to be scared,' said Jane. 'I am too. It's natural.'

'I'm not scared,' said Jim. 'I'm terrified.'

Chapter 36

Jim lay awake, his mind stubbornly refusing to switch off. Jane slept beside him, curled up on the far side of the bed. There had been no wild lovemaking that night. It had been the last thing on his mind and she had seemed to want only a little human warmth close by.

He had no one to write a note of farewell to. All that money brewing up interest in the bank had no beneficiary except himself. No distant relative would get a windfall if he ended up face down in a tunnel. That seemed particularly desolate. A few days ago the whole world had been on the brink and it had seemed just a simple puzzle that had had to be solved against the clock. Now everything had changed. He was about to throw himself into a vicious world of shrapnel and bullets in which his death might mean nothing to anyone.

He had to do it, that was for sure, but there was only one outcome that had anything positive about it: survival. And nothing could guarantee that. His only reassurance was that he couldn't draw his chart. It wasn't that it had crashed – that would have panicked him – it just couldn't be drawn ahead because he couldn't know the outcome. There was simply nothing for his mind to work on.

He turned over and tried to get comfortable. It wasn't like him to lose sleep. Two hundred and ten million people would be behind him, and if there were any links in those massively multidimensional fields from them to him, they would carry him through.

*

The cave maps grew in their visors, as the troops poured down the caverns. The soldiers' sensors fed back information: temperatures, sound levels, magnetic anomalies, air pressure, vibration, chemical changes and countless other data. Sensors were dropped along the way that fed back yet more data so the tunnels lit up like a motorway on a busy night. It was a much simpler picture than the chaos and mayhem of the townscape – no fancy graphics, no aerial fire, no bad guys popping up on rooftops. It seemed much more controlled and safe, but Jim knew that that was probably because the sim had been lashed together quickly.

The sim ran smoothly, the troops sweeping through the smoothly rendered mock caverns of chocolaty computer graphics an unstoppable wave of killer robots. The two mobile generals choreographed the battle with perfect precision, opening up the hidden recesses of the complex in a few action-packed minutes.

'Too easy,' said Jim, pulling his helmet off. 'No defensive pinch points, no booby-traps, no hidden sections.'

'Later,' said Davas. 'They have promised another level by this evening.'

'Go again,' said Jane.

Jim pushed his helmet on again. 'Ready.'

They ate dinner in silence, each lost in their own thoughts.

Jeffries entered. 'I found this in the cellar. Lafitte 1799. The level of the wine is to the bottle's shoulder, which is exceptional.'

'Good choice,' said Davas. 'It's the last ...' he hesitated '... in the world.'

Jim glanced up at Jeffries, then at the dusty bottle. He swallowed his mouthful. 'A lot's happened since that

314

bottle was made.'

Davas smiled. 'It's been waiting all this time for the right moment.'

Jeffries performed a series of operations with a small collection of tools to tease the ancient cork from its home of two centuries. It didn't go without a fight, breaking into small pieces that he picked out with a pair of prong tweezers. He poured a little and sniffed it. 'Delightful,' he said admiringly, then poured their glasses.

Davas asked him to join them, then got to his feet. 'Dear friends,' he said, 'here is to success and a safe conclusion to this monstrous task. May we deny the plans of the evil-doers. May our gods be with us.'

They clinked glasses.

Jim tasted the wine. Its dusty but sharp taste filled his mouth. Memories rose and swirled in his mind like dust punched from a cushion. This was history in a glass, a condensed essence of time. Generations had come and gone, wars and disasters had blown past, like dead leaves, as the bottle had lain in its dark cellar. Great men, both evil and good, had been born and passed away; their influence had risen and fallen to little result. Families had raised children and flourished or withered, their children repeating the process. Hopes and fears had been realized or lost. Nothing on the active surface of the living world had stayed the same: the passing of time had seen things change beyond recognition.

'So here we are,' said Jim, 'standing on a tiny pixel in a huge sim, sat on the exact axis the future is spinning around, and it's up to us to shift it just a bit so the whole thing doesn't go belly up.' He smiled. 'Well, why not?'

'To history,' said Davas.

They clinked glasses again.

*

Jim's head was sore when he woke up and he had a little difficulty in opening his eyes. He remembered having had a bit too much of the Napoleon brandy from the imperial cellar and could recall thinking so at the time.

Jane was up and the shower was running.

In his semi-consciousness he could just about imagine that he was dreaming everything. When he opened his eyes he would be staring up at a picture of Mario holding his plunger, stuck onto the old *Toy Story* wallpaper, at home in his little single bed and maybe his Nan would come in with a cup of tea.

The alternative possibility of resetting the clock faded in and out of his head as he slipped between sleep and waking. However, harsh reality soon overwhelmed fantasy. He was where he had to be, a 'here and now' that shouldn't really exist. Probabilities, however remote, could happen. He was lying on linen sheets in a Venetian palace with a beautiful assassin in his shower and he was about to go off to save the world. Waking up in a council flat in Wapping with a cup of tea from his Nan seemed not only a much more likely outcome but altogether preferable.

He opened his eyes and sat up. 'Good morning, Apocalypse,' he cried.

'Morning,' said Jane, padding into the bedroom wrapped in a towel.

The jumpsuit was awkward and hot. It was a complicated garment, with all sorts of things going on inside it whose purpose was a mystery.

'Exciting, huh?' said Jane. 'I love military aircraft. This will be my first time in a fighter. OK, it's not really a fighter, it's a submarine buster, but still pretty cool.'

Jim waddled after her.

'Meant to have been taken out of service two years ago, but you know how it is. Anyway, safest plane in the sky, perfect for a carrier landing.'

'Carrier landing,' said Jim, waddling faster to catch up.

'Yeah,' she said. 'Now, that is going to be a blast, right?'

'Right,' said Jim. 'Do these things carry sick bags?'

'An S3B?' She grinned at him evilly. 'I don't think so.'

'This plane normally has a crew of four of whom two can't be with us today because of space constraints. Please sit back and relax,' continued the pilot. 'Our flight time is going to be approximately four and a half hours during which you should touch absolutely nothing, especially if it has a flashing light next to it.' The engines started with the sound of a giant vacuum cleaner. 'We are fitted with four ejector seats, but sadly, as you have received no training, you will wave me and my co-pilot goodbye should we need to leave in a hurry. But, relax, that isn't going to happen, as this grey wolf is the nearest thing to a sky truck you'll come across.'

'Punch it, Chewie,' said Jane, over the intercom.

'Yes, sir,' came the reply.

Not good, thought Jim.

Thankfully, the S3B didn't perform a spectacular takeoff but rolled around the airport and joined the queue with the commercial aircraft. It took sedately to the skies as if the pilots had heard Jim's silent prayers for a smooth ride. At 20,000 feet the sea below was a hazy white azure, the sky a tranquil turquoise blanket. He closed his eyes and tried to nod off. He failed. What was wrong with him? This never happened.

His life chart was broken, and now cold fingers of fear

317

crept over him. Tomorrow, the tenth, would be the day he died. Why else couldn't he draw his chart forward? It would stop. A simple flick of his finger would usually cover months, perhaps years, so now there wouldn't be a next year for him. On the other hand how could there be any certainty of any kind? There might not be a world at all after tomorrow, not just for him but for all humanity.

Sleep would be a release, but the oxygen pumping into his mask was keeping him alert. He felt Jane touch his shoulder and turned. Was she smiling under the mask? She gave him a thumbs-up and he responded likewise.

He might as well look brave.

More than four hours in an ill-fitting flight suit, harnessed into a plane seat, seemed like an eternity. Yet, like all extended unpleasantness, it began to draw slowly to an end. It was hard to see where they were aiming for as their seats were behind the pilot's and forward visibility was limited. Then, as the jet's nose dipped, a tiny dot in the ocean stood out, and as the plane descended, it grew. It looked as if they were planning to land on a grey straw floating on an enormous pond, a kind of impossible target that not even the best shot could hit. But the grey dot soon became a matchbox, then a grey book floating in a deep blue angry sea. They seemed to be falling like a brick, the plane pitching and rolling in the side winds that buffeted it.

They do this every day, he thought, as the aircraft carrier loomed below. White breakers on the churning sea rushed by and it seemed all too likely that the plane could come down too fast and smash into the rear but suddenly the nose was up and the landing strip was out of view. The plane shook as it hit the deck and there was a jarring wrench as it jerked to a standstill.

Jim heard himself grunting.

'OK, folks, hang on there for a moment. Welcome to the USS *Ronald Reagan.*'

Jane was lifting her visor, so he followed suit and took off his mask. 'Nice one,' he said, forcing a smile.

Something was going on under the plane and in a few moments it was moving along the carrier's runway. The skies were leaden and it was raining. It was quite a contrast to the sunny Mediterranean. The plane halted near the aft of the ship and the engines cut.

'We're going down the elevator,' said Jane.

There was a judder and the platform the plane was on began to descend into the cavernous bowels of the aircraft carrier.

Jim nodded to Jane in silence. Fuck it, he thought. If he was going to go, this was the way to do it. Half the world was facing their end without knowing it. Old men asleep in their beds, kids bored at their school desks, women walking their dogs – all were stalked by sudden death, oblivious to the danger hanging over them. And perhaps they would never know anything about it, if things went to plan in this little corner of the world.

Everything might turn on a single decision, on a moment of good or bad luck, and he would be inside that singularity, one of a few moving parts that would decide the fate of the world. Suddenly the chilly fingers of fear were drawn back. The charts had said the world was doomed but now, because of what Davas and he had achieved, there was no certain future, either good or bad. Like the cat in Schrödinger's experiment, he was alive and dead at the same time; only tomorrow would decide his actual state.

The plane moved again as it was towed off the elevator and pre-parked so they could get out. The side door opened, he struggled out of his harness and clambered down to the floor of the vast hangar.

He shook the pilot's hand. 'Nice one,' he said, smiling. 'Thanks for the trip.'

The pilot smiled back and the co-pilot nodded.

Three men were running across the floor. Jim recognized John Smith.

'Well, well,' said Smith, 'here we all are again.' He smiled. 'Jim, Jane, this is Bill and Will. Bill is ops and Will is tactical. We'll be going into action with Will, and Bill is co-ordinating the big picture.'

'Right,' said Jim.

'Let's get you two briefed.'

It seemed practically antediluvian to be looking at pieces of paper rolled out on a table top, and Jim's heart sank.

'So,' said Will, 'at four a.m., Unit One is going to freefall behind this ridge and secure the mine mouth, which we believe is unguarded. But we can't be totally sure, so this is a crucial first stage. Then four choppers will land a hundred men, the first wave to storm the mine, followed by the immediate deployment of another two hundred in two further waves. It's touch down, out and dust off. At the same time a force will land here and move *en masse* up the road to the mountain and swamp the area. As long as the first wave gets off properly it should be over in minutes.'

'We're in the first chopper wave?' said Jane.

'Yup, you and Smith are going to run shotgun for Jim and you'll be in the fourth chopper coming up at the rear.'

'Am I going to have all hundred soldiers on my heads-up?' asked Jim.

'Yes.'

'We've been modelling sixty-four, but I suppose that'll be OK.'

'You'll have sixty-four up front and the rest behind. The thirty-six will act as reserves.'

'That's a relief. A hundred guys crammed together on my screen could get a little busy.'

'It's bound to be messy, though,' said Will. 'We have no real idea of the topology down there or how many people are inside.'

'We do know there's a bomb around,' said Smith. 'There's low-level radiation all over the island. It's almost impossible to avoid leaving a trail with these things, especially when they're in kit form.'

'So, it's a nice simple plan. Drop on the target, find the bombs, secure them,' said Jane.

Bill looked around the group. 'Any other business?'

'Do we get any practice before the off?' asked Jim.

'That's next,' said Will. 'All the kit's laid out in Hangar Three, we're set to have a run-through in forty-five minutes.'

'Well,' said Jim, 'I'd like to get going on that as soon as possible. A simple plan with complicated untried tech isn't a simple plan.'

Will nodded. 'Amen.'

Hangar Three was a grey metal cavern that smelt of oil. On its own it would have been an impressive architectural space where, in an awesome way, quantity had that special quality all of its own. Yet what took the eye was a grid of sixty-five glowing white plastic balls, nine foot high and cradled in a black socket like an oversized mood lamp. Sixty-four balls were in an eight-by-eight grid with one to the side. A harness of wires from each machine snaked across the floor to a central control room at the back of the building. A black cube sat across the face of the balls. This was the projector that shone the view of the sim onto the inside of the ball.

'This looks too clever to work,' remarked Jim.

'Yup,' said Bill, 'it sure does, but my guys had it working just eight hours from getting the crates on deck.' He grinned proudly. 'Now all you've got to do is show us what it can do.'

There was a whistle in the distance behind them, followed by the sound of dozens of feet running in time. It was a thunderous drumming that made Jim's heart pick up to the rhythm. From the hangar beyond, a troop of black-clad men entered at a jog. They halted and came to attention in front of them.

'Gentlemen,' said Will, 'this will be our final session before the mission ahead. This is the moment all the pieces come together. As well as innovation and our brothers in arms, we have God to help us win the day. Hooya.'

'Hooya,' they chorused.

Jane helped Jim kit up and, to his despair, the whole troop had to wait at least five minutes for him. The ball had a curved door in it that unlocked and swung inwards. It was on rollers, and once he was inside, it rolled with him as he walked about to keep him centrally placed.

His vision was confused: the projection on the white ball collided with the sim overlay. He turned off the camera and relied on the internal projection in his visor. He started to move forwards and backwards to orient himself, expecting to fall over. But the system worked perfectly, allowing him to move around as if he was running in the real world.

'OK, I'm good,' he called to Control.

'Roger,' replied Bill.

'Roger,' checked Will.

Up came the tunnel mouth and around him the troops – this time real men feeding back into a live system – charged forward.

There were two main tunnels ahead. They both looked much bigger than the previous passageways in the older models. Jim grabbed the forces behind him and sent them down the second branch. Suddenly both tunnels branched into myriad offshoots.

'Anyone got signs of life?'

The silent negatives flashed on his heads-up display.

'Don't go down anything that's too small for a truck,' he broadcast. 'If you hit a passage too small to get a big load down, back out and find one that can.'

He patched between the troops' cameras. There was nothing to see, except featureless passageways. He moved deeper into the mountain aware that if he went too far he risked losing contact with some, particularly those at the front most likely to engage the enemy. A group was flashing him. He switched to it and saw a door.

He shifted, collected up another dozen soldiers and sent them comms: 'New focus, door located. Proceed.'

The soldiers kicked it down and threw in stun grenades, then backed away as far as they could. On detonation, they charged into the room. There were targets everywhere, none stunned. Jim's hands flailed in the air as he pulled down the locations and targeted the soldiers' fire. They were out-numbered at least four to one for now, maybe a hundred enemy troops alert and fighting back from behind defences of piled rock. He could see the three bombs set to one side and his troops pouring through the door or running down the shining red trail he had laid for them.

The cavern was a bloodbath, his men hitting hard and

being hit hard back. But the defenders were gradually being overwhelmed. The directed attacks crushed their positions one by one in a wave of focused and brutal aggression. While a defender might suffer a moment of confused hesitation, the attackers knew exactly where they had to fire and where to go next through the smoke, dark and noise. As the battle progressed, his men's attacks focused on the few that survived until in a final climax the last nest of resistance was blasted into oblivion.

'Secure the room and search for concealments.'

Suddenly hundreds more friendly troops were swarming into the tunnels, a shower of tiny lights in his heads-up display. He sent them along the other passageways: search and destroy.

He searched the room, hopping from one heads-up to another. What a mess. Thirty-five of his own men were down, perhaps a hundred enemy bodies.

He looked away from the footage to a strange corridor opening up to a small group of soldiers. It was a wide offshoot where others were narrow. He put a magnet on one squad and sent them ahead while other units gravitated towards them. The squad stopped and he could see through their cameras a large opening onto a dark space beyond, lit sketchily by the white light of their infrared torches.

'Hold,' he instructed. 'Reinforce, then attack.' Seconds passed, then forty men were in the tunnel, drawn like ants to their destination by a red trail in their visors.

'Go.'

There was a crash of grenades and the troops rushed into the space. They met with three nests of defence and he brought fire raining down on all three as the soldiers rushed the positions without pause.

'Clear,' came back the report.

'Search room high and low.'

Suddenly his world shook and he almost lost his balance. There was a white flash and the screen died.

'Sim over,' came a voice in his headset.

'Got more?' he requested.

'Nope.'

'Can you mod this one?'

'Not much. Numbers, lethality and fire rate, but that's about it.'

'OK, turn them right up and let's go again,' said Jim.

'Roger, give me five.'

'Take a breather for five, guys,' broadcast Jim to the men. 'Then we go again.'

Jim was shown to his quarters, a small cupboard of a room with a smaller-than-a-cupboard toilet. This, he guessed, was a luxury apartment for visiting dignitaries. On the bed lay a set of military clothes. 'Major Evans' had been embroidered across the top pocket.

'Major Evans,' he marvelled. Was that for real or a joke? He showered and put on his new clothes. Unlike the jump-suit they fitted him well. He looked at himself in the full-length mirror on the back of the door. He laughed, feeling proud but at the same time bordering on insane. Maybe a few hand gestures and the world would change once again. Suddenly there would be a bright white light, the world would stop turning and a flashing sign would call an end to a sim that had got so far out of control that it needed to be reset.

There was a rattle, then a wall shook and creaked. He jumped back in shock.

It was Jane, dressed in fresh agency black. 'Ready for dinner with the admiral?' She laughed. 'Major?'

He scowled. 'After tomorrow I'm expecting a promotion to Saviour.'

'Well, let's hope not,' she said. 'That rank doesn't have great long-term prospects. Come on, haul that ass, soldier.'

Chapter 37

There was something distinctly dreamlike about the morning. Climbing into the helicopter in the cold grey windy night, loaded with his equipment, couldn't have been more alienating. Nobody was talking, and even if they'd tried, the thunder of the rotors would have drowned their words. Everyone seemed lost in their own thoughts, sitting on the uncomfortable floor of the Sikorski as it sliced through the dawn. He was a babe among hardened veterans, and he wondered whether the confusion and terror he felt in his stomach was obvious on his face.

So this is unexpected, he thought, in the internal dialogue that juddered through his mind like the engine vibrations through the metal floor. What a strange set of unlikely events had landed him here. It wasn't that long since he'd been a little kid running around the car park chasing pigeons. Fear gripped him like the onset of flu, creeping through his veins to pool nauseatingly in his guts. In a few short minutes it would all be over one way or the other.

Smith had a slender torch in his mouth and was doing a Sudoku while Jane was writing a letter or drawing – he couldn't see which in the low light. In thirty-five minutes they would be setting down just before full daylight. Ten minutes after that they would have either secured the world or witnessed for a millisecond the detonation of three nuclear weapons.

If it went wrong they'd probably never know it. A nuclear

blast would vaporize them all in an instant. At one second they'd be alive and then they'd cease to exist. He started to feel quite good about that: dying would be like going to sleep – at one moment he'd be conscious, then everything would be forgotten. There would be no realization of doom, no pain, no agonizing last seconds, no feeling of hopelessness, just an unknowable point of extinction. Billions of people left behind would face a lingering death, one of starvation and war.

Would he wake up in heaven he mused? What were the chances of that?

The fanatics could do with a dose of atheism. And what if they were right and God awaited them? How utterly cursed would they be?

The minutes were dragging past. When he was trading the hours raced by.

Jane handed him the paper she was writing on. In the dim light he realized it was a picture of him sitting on the floor, his head set on his knees. It was an accomplished drawing and he looked quite the soldier.

She held up five fingers, then two, and pointed at her feet. 'Five to boot,' she mouthed.

He nodded. Just five minutes to boot up. He pointed at the picture and gave her a thumbs-up. He watched the glowing hands of the Bell and Ross wristwatch bound to his arm. Three hundred seconds would take what seemed like an hour to pass.

What were the odds of there being a God? Pascal had thought they were better than zero on his way to inventing the science that drove the mathematics behind trading. There was almost an infinite number of things in the universe so a trillion to one event wasn't that hard to come by. With that in mind, the probability of God seemed quite strong. In fact, as the seconds ticked on, Jim's belief in Him was swelling rapidly to conviction.

If I get through this, I'll give all my money to charity, he thought. Well, at least five million. Or maybe I'll start with a million and see how it goes. A million's a lot of money after all.

He felt a nudge in the leg. It was time.

He pulled on the visor and felt Jane tighten it. The control cable was snapped on and he saw a flash as the system started to boot. His head began to sweat.

The workspace came on and the subsidiary programs were booting too.

'This is Control, are you reading me?' said a voice.

'Yes – can you hear me?'

'Affirmative. Levels are good.'

'I've got locations on everyone in the helicopters,' said Jim. 'Four packs of red dots all lit up nicely.' He had a sudden rush of excitement.

'Roger that. Six minutes to touch down.'

Jim had a thought and began waving his hands around. 'Great,' he said, 'bloody marvellous. We've got radiation sensors.'

'Wait – confirming that,' said Bill over the link.

'Well, that's what I'm getting here.'

'Roger that, but undocumented.'

'No problems. I'm just going to put it on an overlay. It could lead us right there.' This better not crash it, he thought, pulling the two maps together. 'Looking good.'

Jim turned off his heads-up cameras and flicked through each camera on the whole group, sixteen at a time. He 'smileyed' everyone and the smiles flooded back.

'Everything's working perfectly,' said Jim. 'Something's got to go wrong.'

'Roger,' said Will's voice. 'It's saving it for when it really counts.'

The helicopter was falling fast and everyone was rising. Their forms were clear in infrared, twenty-five wicked cyborgs hanging from their straps, ready to go into the final battle.

Jim felt elated, his heart racing, his whole body fizzing with a kind of effervescence, as if his blood was filled with champagne bubbles. This was it.

There was a hard bump and the doors flew open. Four packets of red dots fanned out from their containers and began to charge towards the mine entrance. The helicopters lifted off immediately.

Jim, Jane and Smith were the last out and, rather than run, they walked as Jim concentrated on the picture ahead.

There was indeed a trail of radiation and he sent the whole party along it. Unlike the models, the shaft was a clean, straight, wide path. There were no obvious forks, just a clear road leading into the volcano.

Jim started to jog. 'This thing is going in a long way,' he said. 'We've got to keep up.' He was waving his arms around as he jogged, cursing as he went. Trying to negotiate the rough slope and keep his eyes on the running troops at the same time was harder than he had anticipated.

He made some calculations on the incline. 'A mile and a half to get right into the middle of the mountain. It'll take time.'

The bore of the tunnel was about twenty feet wide and a dozen high, a roughly circular cut filled with uneven rubble to make the roadway. The surface made the going awkward but the men were making tight progress at about four m.p.h. – around one m.p.h. faster than Jim.

What would they find at the end of the tunnel? He looked

through the lead soldier's camera. It was just a straight tube going into the heart of the mountain, with a grey shape in the far distance.

'Got something,' a voice from Control said in his head-phones.

'I see it.'

'Door,' came the report from the unit.

'This could be it,' said Jim, 'or not.'

Seconds passed and soon cameras were examining the barrier.

The wall was of corrugated iron with a metal-plated door, snug-fitting with no lock, just a single handle. No light seeped from beneath it.

The order came: 'Open the door.' It was Bill's voice.

The first soldier turned the handle and pushed it wide open.

'It's clear,' reported Jim. 'Got that?'

'Roger,' said Control.

There was another door of the same construction a hundred yards ahead.

'Go again,' came Will's command.

As soon as the soldier turned the handle, the shriek of a siren rent the air. He pulled the door open to reveal another tunnel.

Shit! thought Jim, stopping in his tracks. Here we go.

The soldiers were surging down the tunnel along the glowing radiation trail. 'It's heating up,' he said to Control. 'We must be getting close.'

I'm still alive, he thought. So far so good.

'Door,' came the report.

Jim braced himself. This was it. They were nearly two miles into the mountain. Any further and they'd be in a lava chamber or out in the caldera.

He watched through the lead soldiers' camera as they broke down the door and piled into a lit cavern. There were three large crates, and two young men in front of a console, one kneeling to work inside it, the other standing, facing them, hammering at a button. Jim called the targets but his men were already spraying bullets, cutting the two figures down. There were now eight soldiers in the cavern and a dozen targets, some roused naked from where they slept, some half dressed, dozens of men with guns ready to fight to the death in the hot, airless cave. He was targeting them as the marines erupted into the cavern, gunning down the defenders in a hail of fire. There was a huge explosion and the cameras went dead. A shock wave of compression knocked Jim backwards, expelling the air from his lungs.

He stumbled forward trying to catch his breath and bring up images from the cavern, but there was nothing to see except smoke and dust. 'What you got?' he called to the nearest figure he could see.

'Cave-in, sir. Concussion down here. Way blocked.'

Jim waved his hands wildly. On an overlay the tunnel was lighting up with a flooding green glow. 'Pull back,' he shouted. 'Extreme radiation.' He dispatched silent orders, pulling the soldiers up the mine shaft as fast as possible. He turned and began to run too. 'You getting all this?' he called, puffing with exertion as he ran up the steep hill.

'Affirmative. Evac immediately.'

Soldiers were streaming past him now.

'You got something to wash this kind of shit off?' he called to Will.

'Affirmative.'

'Thank God for that.' Two million quid to good causes if I'm not irradiated.

He looked for Smith and Jane and saw them fifty metres ahead. 'Screw this equipment,' he muttered to himself, and slipped off anything that wasn't practically bolted on. It had been like running with someone on his back.

He watched the soldiers' radiation meters as they scaled the slope. He was twenty men down, and some of those coming out of the mine were hot with radiation.

He forwarded the information. It took the tiniest grain of plutonium in your lungs to kill, and only a few atoms to cut your life in half.

He concentrated on his running. Plutonium was heavier than gold, and wouldn't travel far in a conventional explosion. It should fall straight to the ground and not carry. That was what he told himself as he ran, scanning ahead for the mine entrance.

So, the nukes had failed to go off and instead the enemy had blown themselves up in a conventional explosion. He rewound the film as he stumbled ahead. In the replay the man punching the button on the console was staring at them with terror in his eyes. What was he scared about? Dying, having failed to take the whole world with him?

The few months without working out much had taken their toll: he was fighting for breath and the white light of the tunnel entrance seemed incredibly far away. At last he emerged into daylight and switched into normal light mode. The soldiers were being hosed down by a soldier standing on the cab of a tanker. They'd got that in place fast, Jim thought. They must have been moving it into position the moment he and his men had hit the tunnel.

'Keep walking past,' he heard someone shout through a bullhorn.

He ran forward and was hit by a spray, then a jet of water. A line of tankers waited beyond.

There was a flash of white light and a crackle as his headset went dark.

'Shit.'

He threw off his gauntlets and started to feel around the helmet for the screws that fixed it to his head, only to be hit by another blast of water, so hard this time that it toppled him. His helmet filled with water. He couldn't breathe – he was choking as he wriggled on the floor like a crab marooned on its back. He twisted onto his hands and knees and the water poured out. He caught his breath and tried to pull off his helmet with both hands. His temples were hurting like crazy but the helmet was lifting slightly. Another dousing submerged him again. He shook his head and tried to breathe. The pain was excruciating but he had to get the visor off.

Something grasped his head in an armlock and he heard a creak as the helmet flew off, crashed to the rocky ground and bounced away.

It was Jane. 'Move your ass,' she said.

'Yes, ma'am,' he spluttered.

The sunlight was blinding but he could see the soldiers stripping off as they were hosed down.

'Move down the line,' a voice ordered through the bullhorn.

Naked, they walked on, the second tanker spraying each person with detergent. A third repeated the process with water. By the end Jim was freezing, and happy to climb into a jumpsuit.

'Well, we're still here,' said Smith, as he smoothed down the Velcro fastenings on his own.

'Yes,' said Jim, 'but what a fuck-up.'

'I think we won, though,' said Smith, flattening his hair. 'The question is, did we get the bombs?'

'There were three crates against the back wall and plenty of radiation after the explosion.'

Smith's concern was written on his face. 'Radiation, eh? Nasty.'

'Let's hope the Fairy Liquid worked.'

Jim slept fitfully on his allotted bunk. It had been a long, scary day and he wasn't clear what exactly had happened. As an outsider in the military reality that had enveloped him he'd felt like a spare part. Without access to the world's markets and Davas's multi-dimensional world, he felt obsolete. A lengthy series of medical treatments and tests had followed the action. Until then he'd had no idea there were so many things that doctors could stick into your body.

Finally Jane came into his tiny cabin.

'Well,' he said, 'what's the news?'

She shrugged. 'Digging into a radioactive volcano is going to take time, but Davas is happy enough.'

Jim clenched his fists. 'And that's all that matters. As long as the models say it's over, it's over.' He fell flat on the narrow bunk. 'When are we getting out of this place? The enforced radio silence is killing me.'

'This morning,' said Jane, 'after we've had yet another decontam check. What's up?'

'That bastard got away, I'm sure of it.'

'Al-Karee? What makes you say so? How could anyone get out of a cavern a mile underground?'

'He might not have been there, or there could be another way out. Who knows? I'm just aggy, that's all.'

'Pretty unlikely, don't you think?' She smiled. 'Don't you worry, they'll drag his rotten corpse out of the rubble in due course.'

'Well, I hope so. That'll be a happy day.'

'A few more tests and we will be out of here.'

'As far as more tests go I think I'd prefer not to know,' said Jim.

'Really?'

'I've had enough. My chart says ...' He tried to draw his life chart in the air. 'Well, never mind. I'm not glowing in the dark. I'll get my groove back.'

Chapter 38

'Out in first class, back in economy,' said Smith, and climbed into the helicopter.

Jim and Jane followed him.

'I think I prefer it,' said Jim, thinking about the commercial flight they were to take to Madrid before a connection to Venice. A night in a nice hotel before they flew onwards sounded like a good way to decompress. Davas had wanted to send one of his jets but the islands were in a state of subtle lockdown after the sudden arrival of a large part of the US fleet and the consternation that had ensued.

The Spanish authorities didn't know whether to be angry or grateful. One man's averted apocalypse was another's violation of sovereignty. However, the enormity of what had almost happened quickly sank in and demands to visit the scene soon turned from a pressing necessity to a regretfully declined invitation.

This uproar was opaque to Jim. It merely meant he had to queue with tourists heading home, oblivious that they owed their lives to the three figures standing among them.

For Jim 11 9 11 – or, as Jane would term it, 9 11 11 – was a kind of weird anticlimax. Nothing had really happened, or so it felt. He had jogged down a dark tunnel, watching a surreal movie. Then he had run back up the dark tunnel, been given a cold shower, had his orifices violated and been sent on a series of rollercoaster helicopter rides. It all felt like an unresolved dream, a memory of a computer game that had leaked from his fantasy world into reality.

Davas had been happy on the phone. The charts were all fixed; the global economy could be charted into the next decade; nothing stood between the world and another generation of progress. Armageddon had been averted, humanity saved, a Herculean battle fought and won.

Jim looked at Jane. 'I feel shit.'

'Sick or blue?'

'Down.'

'That's normal.'

'You'd be wise to see a shrink,' said Smith, grinning toothily. 'I always do after a big one. Costs a fortune, but it's worth it.'

'Really?'

'What do you think?' laughed Smith, looking intently into his eyes.

'Really!' said Jane. 'I wish I'd had counselling the first time I went through something like that.'

'You probably shot a few insurgents instead,' said Smith.

Jane threw him a sharp look.

'I'll cheer up once I'm trading again,' said Jim, smiling a little.

'Shock, denial, anger, bargaining, loneliness, despair, acceptance,' stated Smith. 'Don't let it bother you. We all get it.'

'I tell you what is bothering me,' said Jim. 'It's my chart. I can't draw it. It's like all the market charts before we fixed them. It just stops.' He drew it. 'There.' He stabbed at the final point. 'That's about now.'

'Maybe I shouldn't be flying with you,' sniggered Smith.

'Maybe we should get you more tests as soon as we get to Italy,' suggested Jane.

'You've just got to the despair bit faster than us,' said

Smith. 'You can read the markets, but don't think you're Nostradamus. Stock charts is one thing, but tea leaves are quite another.'

'OK,' said Jim, 'I'll go along with that. After all, who's most likely to kill me in the next few days? Probably one of you.' He grimaced.

'Great,' said Smith. 'Acceptance already.'

'Let's get drunk,' said Jane.

'Before or after we get to Madrid?' wondered Smith.

'Before,' said Jim.

As Jim took his mobile out of the plastic crate that had passed through the metal detector he noticed an unread SMS. It was from Jane. 'I wouldn't, whatever,' it said.

'I would,' said Smith, looking over his shoulder, 'but I'd give you a head start.' He laughed.

'No, you wouldn't, you fucker,' said Jim.

'I'll recommend you to my shrink. He'll sort you out.' He put an arm around Jim's shoulder. 'Look, you saved my family. You saved Jane's. We love you. Just in a professional heterosexual kind of way, you understand. You're going to be fucked up for a couple of months and then you'll be your old self. Don't worry – your crystal balls are only good for the stock market. Try to relax.'

He wanted to vomit but felt unable to move. His head was thudding so agonizingly that he wanted to fall straight back to sleep. He groaned. What had they done?

He remembered climbing onto a fountain, fortunately not filled with water. Surely not. Had Smith picked a fight with four Spaniards bothering a drunken girl of questionable profession? Had Jane decked three of them? What time was it?

'Oh, shit,' he sat bolt upright, 'the flight.'

It was midday so the plane had long gone.

Jane was splayed across the bed, out cold. He shook her.

'What?' she said, not moving.

'We missed the flight.'

'So?'

'It's midday.'

There was a pause. 'And?'

'We need to get to Venice.'

'Aha.'

'Remember?'

'Give me an hour.'

Jim lay down. 'OK.'

At two thirty he woke again.

Jane was drinking something red. 'Want one?' she said, when she noticed he was awake.

'Probably.'

'I wonder if Smith got out of jail.'

'*What?*'

'They let him go. He's got diplomatic immunity up the wazoo.'

'I don't remember.'

Jane chuckled. 'I can't say my recollection's too clear either. But I must say I'm impressed by your left-right combination.'

Jim held his still-throbbing head. 'I don't want to know.'

'Davas has a jet parked at the airport for us.' She started to prepare him a sharpener.

'How's the Spanish prison system?' Jane asked Smith as they checked out.

'Bracing,' he replied, peering at her through black sunglasses. He looked more dangerous than usual, a thick stubble having appeared on his face overnight. 'Almost as invigorating as the look on the consul's face when he sprang me. He was obviously unaware that his ability to still inhale through his long nose was purely a side effect of our existence on this earth.'

'Sorry we pegged it like that,' said Jim.

'No,' said Smith. 'I was acting in a diversionary capacity. You needed to escape.'

'You're a good egg,' said Jane. She looked at Jim. 'That's right, isn't it? A good egg?'

'Roughly,' said Jim.

Jane lifted Smith's dark glasses. His right eye was black. 'Nice,' she said.

'Apparently the local constabulary was uninformed of my superior status,' he said, letting Jane drop the glasses back into place. 'They were all apologies later, of course.'

Jim signed the bill.

A giant Rolls-Royce was parked outside with two ceremonially attired guards at attention beside it. They saluted as the three approached.

'Someone got a status update,' said Jim.

Hands slapped machine pistols as the chauffeur opened the door.

Smith grinned. 'Remember, brothers, we are but mortal.'

'That much I know for sure,' said Jim.

There was something corrupting about the Gulfstream. It was hard to sit on the soft leather seats without feeling you deserved to. Yet ten dollars was the price of a human life in Africa, the price of the medicine needed to save it. Yet the jet cost half a million African lives a year to run. Jim would trade for half a million dollars in a single move. That was equivalent to the difference between life and

341

death for fifty thousand human souls.

People needed to be slathered in luxury to get out of bed once they had reached a certain level of comfort. Maslow's hierarchy meant that to keep the wheels of economics turning, the talented resource generators needed greater and greater extravagances to drive them on. Benign Communism had died on the cross in the reign of Tiberius. Progress was predicated on human greed and encapsulated in the pigskin they sat on as they flew to Venice.

Yet a multitude of charitable ten-dollar bills had not saved the world; instead billions of dollars of wasteful bureaucratic spending had built the technology that had turned the world away back from extinction. Such was the absurdity of the random walk.

Suspended ten miles above the ground, separated from the freezing air by millimetres of frail metal, Jim pondered these thoughts and finally ordered another drink from the steward.

The landing at Venice was heavy and unexpected, yet another reminder to Jim of his apparent mortality. The sun was rising on a beautiful Italian morning.

Chapter 39

Jane and Smith were waiting for him in the hospital's reception area. Jim was trying to adjust his shirt as he walked in to meet them.

'Clear?' asked Jane.

'Apparently,' said Jim.

'Well, that's good,' added Smith.

'They've taken gallons of blood for further tests.' Jim fished for his mobile.

'It's not often they get to see it glowing in the dark,' Smith pointed out.

Jim ignored him as he dialled Davas.

Jeffries answered.

'It's Jim. Is Max there?'

'Oh, hello, mate. Yes, he's in, but he's busy, see?'

Jim started, 'Oh,' he said. 'Mate' had sounded all wrong. 'How's it going?'

'Mustn't grumble, Jimbo, you know how it is.'

'When do you think he'll be free?' Jim looked at Jane and Smith anxiously and pointed at the phone.

'Don't know. He's up to his ears right now.' Jeffries's voice seemed distant, as if he wasn't speaking directly into the phone. 'I'll get him to call ya.'

'I haven't got my stuff back yet. Did it get sent off OK?'

There was a slight pause. 'Yeah, went a couple of weeks ago – you should have had it by now. If you don't get it in a couple of days call me again.'

'OK, see you.'

'*Ciao.*'

Jim hung up. 'Something's wrong. Jeffries was talking to me like a East End geezer. The line wasn't clear, like someone else was listening in.'

'We'd better get over there,' said Jane.

'Then what?' said Jim.

'Find a way in,' said Smith. 'While you were being prodded around we've got retooled.'

'I know a way in,' said Jim.

'Good,' said Jane. 'The place is a fortress.'

'Well, then, let's get going,' said Smith. 'We'll give Davas a surprise party.'

The brown wooden speedboat cut through the opaque Venetian water with dynamic urgency. Smith was at the wheel, standing up.

'Slow down,' said Jane. 'We don't want to be busted for speeding.'

Smith pulled back on the throttle. 'Quite right,' he said, and sat down.

The ornate palaces of weathered stone rose up from the waters like floating churches. The modern era had been good to the ancient structures as European funds had paid for the reversal of their ruinous decline and their tasteful restoration. The slowly churning waters of the Grand Canal slapped against the boat as it wallowed along the wide, watery thoroughfare. There was little to break the illusion that they had been transported back centuries, except for the persistent chugging of the marine engines propelling boats on their way.

'What a dramatic view,' said Smith, revving the engine a little higher as they passed under the Rialto bridge. The smell of the water was primitive and pungent but strangely familiar.

'You want this?' said Jane, offering a small pistol to Jim, as Smith accelerated a little more. 'I always carry a spare.'

'Yes,' said Jim, taking it. He looked at it a little doubt-fully.

'Be careful with it. Try not to shoot anyone friendly.' She pointed to a small lever over the trigger. 'That's the safety. Red point means safe. Slide it and it's live. It has six shots. If you need to use it, run up to the target, press it into their chest and pull the trigger. That way you can't miss.'

Jim stuffed it into his jacket pocket.

The boat pulled into a side canal. Smith turned back to Jim. 'Pull down the right side of the building?'

'Yes,' said Jim. 'At the T about a hundred yards along here, go left. Follow the canal round, and in front on the other side of the next canal you'll see the palace. You'll need to go right across the front of it, then turn down the canal on your left, which is the one on the right side of the front of the building. Halfway down there's an alcove with a statue. We pull over there.'

The palace was as inscrutable as ever. The dark mullioned windows revealed nothing of what was going on inside. The cracked plasterwork and faded colours blended with the dark waters that splashed against the grimy green-black brickwork at the water line. They cruised by, then turned into the side canal. Tall, window-less walls covered them with cool shade and there was no sound except those of the gurgling engine and the churning of the propeller.

Smith slowed the engine to a minimum and, seeing the alcove, cut it, then quietly coasted in. He jumped out and tied the boat to the statue as Jim and Jane scrambled out.

Jim walked behind the statue and shifted the lion plaque to the right. The panel in the right of the alcove moved a little and, with a firm push, he swung open the door.

Jane said nothing but looked at him with approval.

'Follow me,' mouthed Jim.

They pulled out the cheap torches they had bought in a tobacconist's and entered the dark passage.

Jim pushed the iron gate open, relieved that it had not been locked in the interim. He had forgotten about it and wondered whether they shouldn't have come better prepared. Hopefully they would find Davas engrossed in some simulation or other and they could sneak out without him ever knowing they had been there.

The passage felt claustrophobic with three people in it. On his own it had seemed wide enough but now it felt like a cramped rat-run, barely big enough to take them.

He could hear his heart beating and the blood rushing in his ears.

Coming to the viewing point over the sim room, he realized that there was no light on. They would have to go down the wall, across and up again before descending another tight staircase to see into Davas's study.

The faint yellow beams of their torches made the climb look precipitous and forbidding, lighting the wood and brick, and the centuries of grimy patina. Yet someone must clean these passages, he thought, or they'd be choked with cobwebs. They were clearly a cherished period feature.

At last they were at Davas's study and standing by the hidden door. Jim slid open the viewing slot.

He raised his hand in alarm. Davas was sitting slumped and despondent in his desk chair, his hands and feet taped together. There were three others in the room. Two were seated and held what looked like small machine-guns while the third was moving around. Horrified, he recognized the famous face of al-Karee.

He took Jane's shoulder and pulled her to the viewing slot. Then Smith took his turn.

A faint glow from the study lit their faces.

Jane pointed to herself and Smith, then into the room. Smith nodded.

Jim blinked and gave a thumbs-up. He stood back a little to indicate how the door would slide open. He put his hand over the door release and watched them take out their pistols.

Jane counted down on three outstretched fingers. Three, two, one …

Jim pulled on the latch and the door swung open with a wooden rumble. Jane and Smith jumped out and Jim followed, fumbling for the tiny pistol, which slipped out of his pocket and jumped into his hand as if it knew exactly what to do. Staring at the safety he flipped it off as there was suddenly a burst of shooting. He looked up to see al-Karee turning in surprise and horror. Jim held out his hand automatically and fired and fired.

There was a small splash from al-Karee's forehead and a startled look, instantaneously followed by eruptions from his chest as Jane and Smith's bullets hit him.

'In my left drawer!' howled Davas. 'There's a box cutter in my top left drawer.'

Jim lunged for it as Jane and Smith spread across the room taking aim at the door. He yanked it open, shuffled through the flotsam and located a slim scalpel. He dropped the pistol onto the desk and, crouching, cut the black tape from Davas's ankles. 'Pull your hands apart as much as you can,' he shouted, and severed the bond. They jumped up.

Jim grabbed his gun. Jane and Smith were retreating to

the open panel, training their weapons on the door.

'Let's go,' cried Jane.

'What about Jeffries?'

'Go, go, go!' cried Smith.

'I'm here,' said a voice behind him in the passage.

Smith grabbed Davas and bundled him through the hidden door, pushing Jeffries ahead. The study door swung open as, off balance, Jane yanked Jim into the passage too. A flash and a bang followed.

Jim slammed against the wall and fell. He felt a crushing pressure, then a shooting pain down his side as nausea swept through him. He groaned. He was lifted into the air and suddenly he was moving, bouncing along as though he was flying.

His body was on fire, molten lava carrying him along on an incandescent wave. He was riding a flaming horse through burning fields.

Jane flung Jim to Jeffries and Davas and jumped into the boat. Smith slammed on the throttle and they sped down the canal, then slowed into another. There was a huge explosion from the palace and the sound of a boat behind them.

'Get down!' shouted Jane, her face dripping with Jim's blood.

Jeffries rolled him into the footwell, pulled Davas into his lap then bent over him, flattening himself as far as he could. There was a burst of machine-gun fire as the other boat rounded the corner and Smith swung into the next canal, bouncing heavily off the far wall. He pressed down on the throttle as if it had more to give and the boat careered off the shallow waters and shot towards the main canal.

Their pursuers sped after them, the boat's prow high in the air, blocking their chance to fire on it. They flew under a bridge, barely missing its low arch, then bounced up and down on the shallow water. The big boat slowed and Jane opened up with three shots. A figure in the back of the other boat fell across the stern and slid off into the wake as the boat sped on.

Smith turned into the main canal, narrowly missing the rear of a gondola that was being paddled out of the way, the gondolier panicked by the sound of gunfire. Now two police boats were racing headlong towards them.

The second boat was now in the main canal and there was the crackle of machine-pistol fire over the noise of the engine and the thud of the boat's hull against the water.

The police boats swung round to block the canal and shouting came from a loudspeaker above the wail of sirens.

There was no way Smith was stopping now. He aimed between the prows of the police boats and braced himself on the wheel. Jane spun around and rolled into a ball in the front seat.

The boat smashed through the gap, its prow ramping up over the lower bows of the police launches. The tail of the outboard crashed into the hull of one boat and split from its mounting.

The police boats surged in the water, trying to get back into position, their ruptured hulls colliding.

The pursuers were firing now and the police fired back as the boat sped towards them. Moments later it struck the police launches at full speed and exploded.

Smith was screaming with pain, his left side punctured with fragments of debris and the boat was sinking.

A crowd poured out onto the quay and were immediately pulling people out of the water. There were more sirens and the sound of a helicopter above. Further down the canal a black cloud from the burning palace spread across the sky ...

*

'Pretty,' said a voice.

He nodded, or thought he did.

'Yes, you're pretty banged up.'

He opened his eyes. Jane was in a white gown looking down on him. The left side of her face seemed odd. Eventually he realized, after a struggle, that it was swollen and green-black. 'The others?' he asked, with great difficulty.

'They'll make it. Nothing too broken.'

'What 'appened?'

'Well, you've had your innards remodelled, Smith's peppered pretty bad up one side, Davas nearly drowned, Jeffries cracked some ribs and I've got a few more scars to add to the collection.'

Jim was trying to sit up, but failing to move. Something or someone was pinning his shoulders. He gave up the effort and looked at the male nurse restraining him.

'Just relax,' said Jane, pulling up a chair. 'It's all working out just fine.'

Jim held up his right hand and pointed a finger at her. He began to draw the chart of his life. It went upwards.

'That's good,' she said.

'Yeah,' he whispered.